REALMS

Grey Lady

THE VALE

Fellsmarch

FROZEN SEA

Invaders Bay

NORTHERN ISLANDS

Wizard Head

Marisa Pines Camp

Firehole R.

Chalk Cliffs

Marisa Pines Pass

Way Camp

Hunters Camp

Queen Court

Fortress Rock

Alyssa Plateau

The Harlot

Spiritgate

Delphi

North Rd.

KINGDOM of ARDEN

Temple Church

Heartfang Mtns.

Middle Sea

Ardenswater

Heartfang Mtns.

Bittersweet Keep

THE INDIO OCEAN

Ardenscourt

East Rd.

Bastons Bay

Ardenswater

Heartfang R.

Bright Stone Keep

Bitter Springs R.

Watergate

Gryphon Pt.

The Claw

The Wastes

WE'ENHAVEN

Hidden Bay

THE
DEMON
KING

THE
DEMON
KING

A SEVEN REALMS NOVEL

CINDA WILLIAMS CHIMA

Disney • HYPERION BOOKS
NEW YORK

I feel blessed to be surrounded by patient people—in particular, my family: Rod, Eric, and Keith, who are most tolerant when I go into crazy-author-woman mode:

Friend or relative: *When does Cinda write?*

Long-suffering spouse: *All the time.*

Thanks to my local writing workshops, Hudson Writers and Twinsburg YA Writers, and my online and sometimes in-person YAckers critique group, especially Kate Tuthill, Debby Garfinkle, Martha Peaslee Levine, Jody Feldman, and Mary Beth Miller. Goddesses, I'm totally up for another retreat.

Thanks to my early full-manuscript readers, including Marsha McGregor, Jim Robinson, Eric, Rod, and Keith. Your feedback kept me going; your suggestions made the book better.

And, finally, of course, thanks to my editor, Arianne Lewin, and agent, Christopher Schelling. Nothing happens in this business until somebody believes in a book.

Printed in the United States of America

First Edition

10 9 8 7 6 5 4 3 2 1

ILS No.   V567-9638-5

247 2009

Library of Congress Cataloging-in-Publication Data on file.

Designed by Elizabeth H. Clark

ISBN 978-1-4231-1823-7

Reinforced binding

Visit www.hyperionbooksforchildren.com

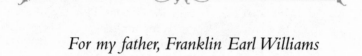

For my father, Franklin Earl Williams

CHAPTER ONE

THE HUNT

Han Alister squatted next to the steaming mud spring, praying that the thermal crust would hold his weight. He'd tied a bandana over his mouth and nose, but his eyes still stung and teared from the sulfur fumes that boiled upward from the bubbling ooze. He extended his digging stick toward a patch of plants with bilious green flowers at the edge of the spring. Sliding the tip under the clump, he pried it from the mud and lifted it free, dropping it into the deerskin bag that hung from his shoulder. Then, placing his feet carefully, he stood and retreated to solid ground.

He was nearly there when one foot broke through the fragile surface, sending him calf-deep into the gray, sticky, superheated mud.

"Hanalea's bloody bones!" he yelped, flinging himself backward and hoping he didn't land flat on his back in another mudpot. Or worse, in one of the blue water springs that would boil the flesh from his bones in minutes.

Fortunately, he landed on solid earth amid the lodgepole pines, the breath exploding from his body. Han heard Fire Dancer scrambling down the slope behind him, stifling laughter. Dancer gripped Han's wrists and hauled him to safer ground, leaning back for leverage.

"We'll change your name, Hunts Alone," Dancer said, squatting next to Han. Dancer's tawny face was solemn, the startling blue eyes widely innocent, but the corners of his mouth twitched. "How about 'Wades in the Mudpot'? 'Mudpot' for short?"

Han was not amused. Swearing, he grabbed up a handful of leaves to wipe his boot with. He should have worn his beat-up old moccasins. His knee-high footwear had saved him a bad burn, but the right boot was caked with stinking mud, and he knew he'd hear about it when he got home.

"Those boots were *clan made*," his mother would say. "Do you know what they *cost*?"

It didn't matter that she hadn't paid for them in the first place. Dancer's mother, Willo, had traded them to Han for the rare deathmaster mushroom he'd found the previous spring. Mam hadn't been happy when he'd brought them home.

"*Boots?*" Mam had stared at him in disbelief. "Fancy *boots*? How long will it take you to grow out of those? You couldn't have asked for money? Grain to fill our bellies? Or firewood or warm blankets for our beds?" She'd advanced on him with the switch she always seemed to have close to hand. Han backed away from her, knowing from experience that a lifetime of hard work had given his mother a powerful arm.

She'd raised welts on his back and shoulders. But he kept the boots.

They were worth far more than what he'd given in trade, and he knew it. Willo had always been generous to Han and Mam and Mari, his sister, because there was no man in the house. Unless you counted Han, and most people didn't. Even though he was already sixteen and nearly grown.

Dancer brought water from Firehole Spring and sloshed it over Han's slimed boot. "Why is it that only nasty plants growing in nasty places are valuable?" Dancer said.

"If they'd grow in a garden, who'd pay good money for them?" Han growled, wiping his hands on his leggings. The silver cuffs around his wrists were caked with mud as well, deeply embedded in the delicate engraving. He'd better take a brush to them before he got home, or he'd hear about that too.

It was a fitting end to a frustrating day. They'd been out since dawn, and all he had to show for it were three sulfur lilies, a large bag of cinnamon bark, some razorleaf, and a handful of common snagwort that he could pass off as maidenweed at the Flatlander Market. His mother's empty purse had sent him foraging in the mountains too early in the season.

"This is a waste of time," Han said, though it had been his idea in the first place. He snatched up a rock and flung it into the mudpot, where it disappeared with a viscous plop. "Let's do something else."

Dancer cocked his head, his beaded braids swinging. "What would you . . . ?"

"Let's go hunting," Han said, touching the bow slung across his back.

Dancer frowned, thinking. "We could try Burnt Tree Meadow. The fellsdeer are moving up from the flatlands. Bird saw them there day before yesterday."

"Let's go, then." Han didn't have to think long about it. It was the hunger moon. The crocks of beans and cabbage and dried fish his mother had laid up for the long winter had evaporated. Even if he'd fancied sitting down to another meal of beans and cabbage, lately there'd been nothing but porridge and more porridge, with the odd bit of salt meat for flavor. Meat for the table would more than make up for today's meager gleanings.

They set off east, leaving the smoking springs behind. Dancer set a relentless, ground-eating pace down the valley of the Dyrnnewater. Han's bad mood began to wear away with the friction of physical exertion.

It was hard to stay angry on such a day. Signs of spring bloomed all around them. Skunk cabbages and maiden's kiss and May apples covered the ground, and Han breathed in the scent of warm earth freed from its winter covering. The Dyrnnewater frothed over stones and roared over waterfalls, fed by melting snow on the upper slopes. The day warmed as they descended, and soon Han removed his deerskin jacket and pushed his sleeves past his elbows.

Burnt Tree Meadow was the site of a recent fire. In a few short years it would be reclaimed by forest, but for now it was a sea of tall grasses and wildflowers, studded with the standing trunks of charred lodgepole pines. Other trunks lay scattered like a giant's game of pitchsticks. Knee-high pine trees furred the ground, and blackberry and bramble basked in sunlight where there had once been deep pine-forest shade.

A dozen fellsdeer stood, heads down, grazing on the tender spring grasses. Their large ears flicked away insects, and their red hides shone like spots of paint against the browns and greens of the meadow.

Han's pulse accelerated. Dancer was the better archer, more patient in choosing his shots, but Han saw no reason why they shouldn't each take a deer. His always-empty stomach growled at the thought of fresh meat.

Han and Dancer circled the meadow to the downwind side, downslope from the herd. Crouching behind a large rock, Han slid his bow free and tightened the slack bowstring, trying it with his callused thumb. The bow was new, made to match his recent growth. It was clan made, like everything in his life that married beauty and function.

Han eased to his feet and drew the bowstring back to his ear. Then he paused, sniffing the air. The breeze carried the distinct scent of wood smoke. His gaze traveled up the mountain and found a thin line of smoke cutting across the slope. He looked at Dancer and raised his eyebrows in inquiry. Dancer shrugged. The ground was soaked and the spring foliage green and lush. Nothing should burn in this season.

The deer in the meadow caught the scent too. They raised their heads, snorting and stamping their feet nervously, the whites showing in their liquid brown eyes. Han looked up the mountain again. Now he could see orange, purple, and green flames at the base of the fire line, and the wind blowing downslope grew hot and thick with smoke.

Purple and green? Han thought. Were there plants that burned with colors like those?

The herd milled anxiously for a moment, as if not sure which way to go, then turned as one and charged straight toward them.

Han hastily raised his bow and managed to get off a shot as the deer bounded past. He missed completely. Dancer's luck was no better.

Han sprinted after the herd, leaping over obstacles, hoping to try again, but it was no use. He caught a tantalizing glimpse of the white flags of their tails before the deer vanished into the pines. Muttering to himself, he trudged back to where Dancer stood, staring up the mountain. The line of garish flame rolled toward them, picking up speed, leaving a charred and desolate landscape in its wake.

"What is going on?" Dancer shook his head. "There's no burns this time of year."

As they watched, the fire gathered momentum, leaping small ravines. Glittering embers landed on all sides, driven by the downslope wind. The heat seared the skin on Han's exposed face and hands. He shook ash from his hair and slapped sparks off his coat, beginning to realize their danger. "Come on. We'd better get out of the way!"

They ran across the ridge, slipping and sliding on the shale and wet leaves, knowing a fall could mean disaster. They took refuge behind a rocky prominence that pierced the thin vegetative skin of the mountain. Rabbits, foxes, and other small animals galloped past, just ahead of the flames. The fire line swept by, hissing and snapping, greedily consuming everything in its path.

And after came three riders, like shepherds driving the flames before them.

Han stared, mesmerized. They were boys no older than Han and Dancer, but they wore fine cloaks of silk and summer wool that grazed their stirrups, and long stoles glittering with exotic emblems. The horses they rode were not compact, shaggy mountain ponies, but flatlander horses, with long delicate legs and proudly arched necks, their saddles and bridles embellished with silver fittings. Han knew horseflesh, and these horses would cost a year's pay for a common person.

A lifetime's earnings for him.

The boys rode with a loose and easy arrogance, as if oblivious to the breathtaking landscape around them.

Dancer went still, his bronze face hardening and his blue eyes going flat and opaque. "Charmcasters," he breathed, using the clan term for wizards. "I should have known."

Charmcasters, Han thought, fear and excitement thrilling through him. He'd never seen one up close. Wizards did not consort with people like him. They lived in the elaborate palaces surrounding Fellsmarch Castle, and attended the queen at court. Many served as ambassadors to foreign countries—purposefully so. Rumors of their powers of sorcery kept foreign invaders away.

The most powerful among them was named the High Wizard, adviser and magical enforcer of the queen of the Fells.

"Stay away from wizards," Mam always said. "You don't want to be noticed by such as them. Get too close, and you might get burnt alive or turned into something foul and unholy. Common folk are like dirt under their feet."

Like anything forbidden, wizards fascinated Han, but this was one rule he'd never had a chance to break. Charmcasters weren't allowed in the Spirit Mountains, except to their council house on Gray Lady, overlooking the Vale. Nor would they venture into Ragmarket, the gritty Fellsmarch neighborhood Han called home. If they needed something from the markets, they sent servants to purchase it.

In this way, the three peoples of the Fells achieved a tenuous peace: the wizards of the Northern Isles, the Valefolk of the valley, and upland clan.

As the riders drew closer to their hiding place, Han studied them avidly. The charmcaster in the lead had straight black hair that swept back from a widow's peak and hung to his shoulders. He wore multiple rings on his long fingers, and an intricately carved pendant hung from a heavy chain around his neck. No doubt it was some kind of powerful amulet.

His stoles were emblazoned with silver falcons, claws extended in attack. Silver falcons, Han thought. That must be the emblem of his wizard house.

The other two were ginger-haired, with identical broad flat noses and snarling fellscats on their stoles. Han assumed they were brothers or cousins. They rode a little behind the black-haired wizard, and seemed to defer to him. They wore no amulets that Han could see.

Han would have been content to remain hidden and watch them ride by, but Dancer had other ideas. He erupted from the shadow of the rocks, practically under the hooves of the horses, spooking them so the three riders had to fight to keep their seats.

"I am Fire Dancer," Dancer proclaimed loudly in the Common speech, "of Marisa Pines Camp." He skipped right over the ritual welcome of the traveler and cut into the meat. "This camp demands to know who you are and what wizards are doing on Hanalea, as is forbidden by the Naéming." Dancer stood tall, his hands fisted at his sides, but he seemed small next to the three strangers on their horses.

What's come over Dancer? Han wondered, reluctantly emerging from his hiding place to stand beside his friend. He didn't like that the charmcasters were trespassing on their hunting ground either, but he was savvy enough not to go up against hex magic.

The black-haired boy glared down at Dancer, then flinched, his black eyes widening in surprise before he resumed his cool disdainful expression.

Does he know Dancer? Han looked from one to the other. Dancer didn't seem to know him.

Even though Han was taller than Dancer, the wizards' gazes seemed to flow over him like water over a rock, and then back to his friend. Han looked down at his mud-stained deerskin leggings and Ragmarket shirt, envying the strangers' finery. He felt invisible. Insignificant.

Dancer wasn't cowed by charmcasters. "I asked your names," he said. He gestured toward the retreating flames. "That looks like wizard flame to me."

How does Dancer know what wizard flame looks like? Han wondered. Or is he just bluffing?

The boy with the falcon signet glanced at the others, as if debating whether to respond. Getting no help from his friends, he turned back to Dancer. "I'm Micah Bayar, of Aerie House," he said, as if his very name would put them on their knees. "We're here on the queen's orders. Queen Marianna and the Princesses Raisa and Mellony are hunting in the Vale below. We're driving the deer down to meet them."

"The queen *ordered* you to set fire to the mountain so she could have a good day's hunting?" Dancer shook his head in disbelief.

"I said so, didn't I?" Something in the wizard's expression told Han he wasn't being exactly truthful.

"The deer don't belong to the queen," Han said. "We've as much right to hunt them as she does."

"Anyway, you're underage," Dancer said. "You're not *allowed* to use magic. Nor carry an amulet." He pointed to the jewel at Bayar's neck.

How does Dancer know that? Han thought. He himself knew nothing of wizards' rules.

Dancer must've struck a nerve, because Bayar glared at him. "That's *wizard* business," the charmcaster said. "And no concern of yours."

"Well, *Micah Jinxflinger*," Dancer said, now resorting to the clan insult for wizards, "if Queen Marianna wants to hunt deer in summer, she can come up into the high country after them. As she always has."

Bayar raised black eyebrows. "Where she can sleep on a dirt floor shoulder to shoulder with a dozen filthy *kinsmen* and go a week without a hot bath and come home stinking of wood smoke and sweat with a case of the night itches?" He snorted with laughter, and his friends followed suit. "I don't blame her for preferring the accommodations in the Vale."

He doesn't know *anything*, Han thought, recalling the cozy lodges with their sleeping benches, the songs and stories told around the fire, the shared feasts from the common pot. So many nights he'd fallen asleep under furs and clan-made blankets with the thread of the old songs winding through his dreams. Han wasn't clan, but he often wished he was. It was the one place he'd ever felt at home. The one place he didn't feel like he was clinging on by his fingernails.

"Princess Raisa was fostered at Demonai Camp for three years," Dancer said, his chin thrust out stubbornly.

"The princess's clan-bred father has some archaic ideas," Bayar replied, and his companions laughed again. "Me, I wouldn't want to marry a girl who'd spent time in the camps. I'd be afraid she'd been ruined."

Suddenly Dancer's knife was in his hand. "Repeat that, jinxflinger?" Dancer said, his voice cold as the Dyrnnewater.

Bayar jerked hard on his reins, and his horse stepped back, putting more distance between Bayar and Dancer.

"I'd say women have more to fear from jinxflingers than from anyone in the camps," Dancer went on.

His heart accelerating, Han stepped up beside Dancer and put his hand on the hilt of his own knife, careful not to get in the way of Dancer's throwing arm. Dancer was quick on his feet and good with a blade. But a blade against magic? Even two blades?

"Relax, copperhead." Bayar licked his lips, his eyes fixed on Dancer's knife. "Here's the thing. My father says that girls who go to the camps come back proud and opinionated and difficult to manage. That's all." He smirked as if it were a joke they could all share.

Dancer did not smile. "Are you saying that the blooded heir to the throne of the Fells needs to be . . . *managed*?"

"*Dancer,*" Han said, but Dancer dismissed his warning with a shake of his head.

Han sized up the three wizards as he would his opponents in any street fight. All three carried heavy elaborate swords that hadn't seen much use. Get them down off their horses, there's the thing, he thought. A quick slash to the cinch strap would do the trick. Get in close where their swords wouldn't do much good. Take out Bayar, and the others will cut and run.

One of the ginger-haired wizards cleared his throat nervously, as if uncomfortable with the direction of the conversation. He was the elder of the two, and stocky, with plump, pale, freckled hands that gripped his reins tightly. "Micah," he said in the Vale dialect, nodding toward the valley below. "Come on. Let's go. We'll miss the hunt."

"Hold on, Miphis." Bayar stared down at Dancer, black eyes glittering in his pale face. "Aren't you called Hayden?" he inquired in Common, using Dancer's Vale name. "It's just . . . Hayden, isn't it? A mongrel name, since you have no father."

Dancer stiffened. "That is my Vale name," he said, lifting his chin defiantly. "My real name is Fire Dancer."

"Hayden is a wizard's name," Bayar said, fingering the amulet around his neck. "How dare you presume—"

"I *presume* nothing," Dancer said. "I didn't choose it. I am clan. Why would I choose a jinxflinger name?"

Good question, Han thought, looking from one to the other. Some among the clans used flatland names in the Vale. But why would a jinxflinger like Micah Bayar know Dancer's Vale name?

Bayar flushed red, and it took him a moment to muster a response. "So you claim, Hayden," Bayar drawled. "Maybe you fathered yourself. Which means you and your mother—"

Dancer's arm flashed up, but Han just managed to slam it aside as the knife left his hand, and it ended, quivering, in the trunk of a tree.

Come on, Dancer, Han thought, hunching his shoulders against his friend's furious glare. Killing a wizard friend of the queen would buy them a world of trouble.

The charmcaster Bayar sat frozen a moment, as if he couldn't believe what had just happened. Then his face went white with anger. He extended one imperious hand toward Dancer, took hold of his amulet with the other, and began muttering a charm in the language of magic, stumbling over the words a bit.

"*Micah,*" the more slender fellscat wizard said, nudging his horse up close. "No. It's not worth it. The fire was one thing. If they find out we—"

"Shut up, Arkeda," Bayar replied. "I'm going to teach this base-born copperhead respect." Looking put out that he was forced to start over, he began the charm again.

Try and be a peacemaker and see where it gets you, Han thought. He unslung his bow and nocked an arrow, aiming at Bayar's chest. "Hey, *Micah*," he said. "How about this? Shut it or I shoot."

Bayar squinted at Han, as if once again surprised to see him. Perhaps realizing he would, indeed, be dead before he could finish the hex, the wizard released his grip on the amulet and raised his hands.

At the sight of Han's bow, Miphis and Arkeda pawed at the hilts of their swords. But Dancer nocked his own arrow, and the boys let go and raised their hands as well.

"Smart move," Han said, nodding. "I'm guessing jinxes are slower than arrows."

"You tried to murder me," Bayar said to Dancer, as if amazed that such a thing could happen. "Do you realize who I *am*? My father is High Wizard, counselor to the queen. When he finds out what you did . . ."

"Why don't you run back to Gray Lady and tell him all about it?" Dancer said, jerking his head toward the downslope trail. "Go on. You don't belong here. Get off the mountain. Now."

Bayar didn't want to back off with his two friends as witnesses. "Just remember," he said softly, fingering his amulet, "it's a long way down the mountain. Anything can happen along the way."

Bones, Han thought. He'd been ambushed too many times in the streets and alleyways of Fellsmarch. He knew enough about bullies to recognize the trait in Bayar. This boy would hurt them if he could, and he wouldn't play fair doing it.

Keeping his bowstring tight, Han pointed his chin at the wizard. "You. Take off your jinxpiece," he ordered. "Throw it down on the ground."

"This?" Bayar touched the evil-looking jewel that hung around his neck. When Han nodded, the boy shook his head. "You can't be serious," he snarled, closing his fist around it. "Do you know what this is?"

"I have an idea," Han said. He gestured with the bow. "Take it off and throw it down."

Bayar sat frozen, his face going pale. "You can't *use* this, you know," he said, looking from Han to Dancer. "If you even touch it, you'll be incinerated."

"We'll take our chances," Dancer said, glancing over at Han.

The charmcaster's eyes narrowed. "You're nothing more than thieves, then," he sneered. "I should have known."

"Use your head," Han said. "What would I do with truck like that? I just don't want to have to be looking over my shoulder all the way home."

Arkeda leaned in toward Bayar and muttered in Valespeech, "Better give it to him. You *know* what they say about the copperheads. They'll cut your throat and drink your blood and feed you to their wolves so no one will ever find your bones."

Miphis nodded vigorously. "Or they'll use us in *rituals*. They'll burn us alive. Sacrifice us to their goddesses."

Han clenched his jaw, struggling to keep the surprise and amusement off his face. It seemed the jinxflingers had their own reasons to fear the clan.

"I *can't* give it to them, you idiot," Bayar hissed. "You *know* why. If my father finds out I took it, we'll all be punished."

"I told you not to take it," Arkeda muttered. "I told you it was a bad idea. Just because you want to impress Princess Raisa . . ."

"You know I wouldn't have taken it if we were allowed to have our own," Bayar said. "It was the only one I . . . What are *you* looking at?" he demanded, noticing Han and Dancer's interest in the conversation and maybe realizing for the first time that they understood the flatlander language.

"I'm looking at someone who's already in trouble and getting in deeper," Han said. "Now, drop the amulet."

Bayar glared at Han as if actually seeing him for the first time. "You're not even clan. Who are you?"

Han knew better than to hand his name to an enemy. "They call me Shiv," he said, fishing a name out of memory. "Streetlord of Southbridge."

"Shiv, you say." The wizard tried to stare him down, but his gaze kept sliding away. "It's strange. There's something . . . You seem . . ." His voice trailed off as if he'd lost track of the thought.

Han sighted down the shaft of his arrow, feeling sweat trickling down between his shoulder blades. If Bayar wouldn't give, he'd have to figure out what to do next. Just then, he had no clue. "I'll count to five," he said, hanging on to his street face. "Then I put an arrow through your neck. One."

With a quick, vicious movement, Bayar yanked the chain over his head and tossed the amulet onto the ground. It clanked softly as it landed.

"Just try to pick it up," the charmcaster said, leaning forward in his saddle. "I dare you."

Han looked from Bayar to the jinxpiece, unsure whether to believe him or not.

"Go on! Get out of here!" Dancer said. "I reckon you'd better think about how you're going to put that fire out. If you don't, I guarantee the queen *won't* be happy, whether she asked you to start it or not."

Bayar stared at him for a moment, lips twitching with unspoken words. Then he wrenched his mount's head around and drove his heels into the horse's sides. Horse and rider charged downslope as if they were, in fact, trying to catch the fire.

Arkeda stared after him, then turned to Dancer, shaking his head. "You fools! How is he supposed to put it out without the amulet?" He wheeled his horse, and the two wizards followed Bayar at a slightly less reckless pace.

"I hope he breaks his neck," Dancer muttered, staring after the three charmcasters.

Han let out his breath and released the tension on his bow, slinging it across his shoulder. "What was all that about your Vale name? Have you met Bayar before?"

Dancer jammed his arrow back in his quiver. "Where would I meet a jinxflinger?"

"Why did he say what he did about your father?" Han persisted. "How does he know that . . ."

"How should I know?" Dancer said, his face hard and furious. "Forget about it. Let's go."

Obviously Dancer didn't want to talk about it. Fine, Han thought. He had no room to complain. He had enough secrets of his own.

"What about this thing?" Han squatted and studied the jinxpiece warily, afraid to touch it. "Do you think he was bluffing?" He looked up at Dancer, who was watching from a safe distance. "I mean, do you think they need this thing to put the fire out?"

"Just leave it," Dancer said, shuddering. "Let's get out of here."

"That jinxflinger didn't want to give this thing up," Han mused. "Must be valuable." Han knew traders of magical pieces in Ragmarket. He'd dealt with them a time or two when he worked the street. A taking like this could pay the rent for a year.

You're not a thief. Not anymore. If he said it often enough, it just might stick.

But he couldn't let it lie. There was something malevolent yet fascinating about the amulet. Power emanated from it like heat from a stove on a cold day. It warmed his front, making the rest of him feel colder by comparison.

Using a stick, he lifted the amulet by its chain. It dangled, spinning hypnotically in the sunlight, a green translucent stone cunningly carved into a snarl of serpents with ruby eyes. The staff was topped with a brilliant round-cut diamond larger than he'd ever seen, and the snake's eyes were blood red rubies.

Han had dealt in jewelry from time to time, and he could tell the craftsmanship was exquisite and the stones were prime quality. But the lure of the piece went beyond the sum of its parts.

"What are you going to do with that?" Dancer asked behind him, his voice overgrown with disapproval.

Han shrugged, still watching the spinning jewel. "I don't know."

Dancer shook his head. "You should pitch it into the ravine. If Bayar took the thing without permission, let him explain what happened to it."

Han was unable to fathom pitching it away. It didn't seem like the kind of thing you'd want to leave lying around for somebody—maybe a child from the camps—to find.

Han fished a square of leather from his carry bag and spread it on the ground. Dropping the amulet in the center, he wrapped it carefully and tucked it in his bag. All the time wondering, How had it come to this? How had he and Dancer ended up in a standoff with wizards? What was the connection between them and Dancer? Maybe it was just the latest in a long line of bad luck. Han always seemed to find trouble, no matter how hard he tried to avoid it.

CHAPTER TWO

UNINTENDED CONSEQUENCES

Raisa shifted impatiently in her saddle and peered about, squinting against the sunlight that dappled the trail.

"Don't squint, Raisa," her mother snapped automatically. It was one of a collection of phrases that stood in for conversation with the queen, including, "Sit up straight," and "Where do you think you're going?" Along with the all-purpose "Raisa *ana*'Marianna!"

So Raisa shaded her eyes instead, searching the surrounding woods. "Let's *go*," she said. "They were supposed to meet us here a half hour ago. If they can't be on time, I say we leave them behind. The day is wasting."

Lord Gavan Bayar nudged his horse closer and put his hand on Switcher's bridle. "Please, Your Highness, I beg you, give them a few more minutes. Micah will be keenly disappointed if he misses the hunt. He's been looking forward to it all week." The handsome High Wizard smiled at her with the exaggerated charm adults use on children when there are other adults around.

Micah's been looking forward to the hunt? Raisa thought. Not nearly as much as *I* have. He's able to come and go as he pleases.

He's probably still angry about last night, she thought. That's why he's making us wait. He's not used to anyone saying no to him.

Raisa kneed Switcher, and the mare tossed her head, breaking the wizard's grip. Switcher snorted, shying at a leaf skidding along the ground. She was as eager to be gone as Raisa.

"*I'm* often late," Raisa's younger sister, Mellony, piped up, urging her pony forward. "Maybe we should try to be patient."

Raisa threw her a scathing look, and Mellony bit her lip and looked away.

"Micah likely lost track of time," Lord Bayar went on, trying to settle his own horse, a large-boned stallion. The breeze ruffled his mane of silver hair, streaked with wizard red. "You know how boys are."

"Perhaps you could give him a pocket watch on his next name day, then?" Raisa said acerbically, eliciting the "Raisa *ana'*Marianna!" response from her mother.

I don't care! she thought. It was bad enough she'd been cooped up in Fellsmarch Castle since solstice, closeted with tutors and overburdened with three years' worth of catch-up lessons on useless topics.

For instance: *A lady can converse with anyone, of any age or station. At table, a hostess is responsible for assuring that everyone participate in conversation. She should direct the conversation away from politics and other divisive subjects and be prepared with alternative topics should the need arise.*

If a *lady* should do this, Raisa wondered, should a man do the same? Is he required to?

Both Raisa and her mother had changed during the three years she'd been gone to Demonai Camp, and now it seemed they were constantly at odds. Her clan-born father, Averill, had been a buffer between them. Now he was always traveling, and Marianna persisted in treating Raisa like a child.

These days, Raisa couldn't help hearing the whispers that followed after the queen. Some said she paid too little attention to finances, policy, and affairs of state. Others said she paid too much attention to the High Wizard and the council on Gray Lady. Had it always been this way, or was Raisa just noticing it more because she was older?

Maybe it was her grandmother Elena's influence. The Matriarch of Demonai Camp was full of opinions about Vale politics and the growing influence of wizards, and she had never hesitated to express them during Raisa's three years with her father's family.

After the relative freedom of Demonai Camp, Raisa found it a misery to force her feet into the pinchy shoes and elaborate stockings favored at court, and to sweat and itch under the ruffled girlish dresses her mother chose for her. She was nearly sixteen, nearly grown, but most days Raisa resembled a tiered wedding cake on two legs.

Not today. Today she'd pulled on her tunic and leggings and clan-made boots, layering her hip-length riding coat over all. She'd slung her bow over her shoulder and slid a quiver of arrows into the boot attached to her saddle. When she'd led Switcher from the stables, Lord Bayar had run his eyes over her and glanced at the queen to assess her reaction.

Raisa's mother tightened her lips and let go a great sigh, but apparently decided it was too late to force her daughter back inside to change clothes. Mellony, of course, mirrored their mother in her tailored riding jacket and long, divided riding skirt, a froth of petticoats cascading over her boots.

Mellony was the image of their mother. She'd inherited Marianna's blond hair, her creamy pale complexion, and looked to grow as tall or taller. Raisa favored her father's side, with her dark hair, green eyes, and small frame.

So here they were, dressed and eager for the hunt on a fine sunny day, and it was being squandered waiting for the tardy Micah Bayar and his cousins.

Micah was a daring horseman and aggressive, competitive hunter. Though he was just sixteen, his dark, dangerous good looks had half the girls at court swooning over him.

Since her return to Fellsmarch, he'd courted her with a flattering intensity she found hard to resist. The fact that their romance was forbidden made it all the more appealing. Fellsmarch Castle was full of eyes and ears, but they still found places to meet unsupervised. Micah's kisses were intoxicating, and his embraces made her head swim.

It was more than that, though. He had a savage, cynical wit that picked apart the society that had birthed the two of them. He made her laugh, and little did these days.

Raisa knew that a flirtation with Micah Bayar was risky,

but it was a way of rebelling against her mother and the constraints of court life. Rebellion only went so far, though. She was not empty-headed Missy Hakkam, ready to trade her virtue for a bit of bad poetry and a kiss on the ear.

And patience was not Micah Bayar's long suit. Hence their dispute the previous night.

She'd looked forward to hunting with him, but she wasn't willing to wait forever. Time and opportunity were leaking away. The story of her life.

Captain Edon Byrne and a triple of soldiers were mounted up and ready too, conversing quietly among themselves. Byrne was the captain of the Queen's Guard, the latest of a long line of Byrnes in that position. He'd insisted on providing escort on the day's hunt, over Lord Bayar's objections.

Now Byrne called over to them. "Shall I send one of my men after the boys, Your Majesty?" he asked.

"You could all go, if it was up to me, Captain Byrne," Lord Bayar drawled. "Queen Marianna and the princesses will be perfectly safe. There is no need for you and your men to drag after us like the overlong tail of a kite. The clans may be savage and unpredictable, but they're unlikely to try anything with me along." He fingered the amulet that hung around his neck, in case Byrne had missed the point. The High Wizard always enunciated his words slowly and distinctly when he spoke to Captain Byrne, as if Byrne were a half-wit.

Byrne met the wizard's eyes unapologetically, his wind-burned face impassive. "That may be, but it's not the clans I'm worried about."

"Well, obviously." Bayar smiled thinly. "When you and

the royal consort have repeatedly delivered young Princess Raisa right into their hands." Distaste flickered over his face.

That was another thing that annoyed Raisa: Lord Bayar never used her father's name. He called Averill Lightfoot Demonai the royal consort, as if it were an appointed office that anyone could hold. Many in the Vale aristocracy despised Raisa's father because he was a clan trader who'd made a marriage many of them wanted for themselves.

But, in fact, the queen of the Fells had not married lightly. Averill had brought with him the support of the clans and counter-balanced the power of the Wizard Council. Which, naturally, the High Wizard did not like.

"Lord Bayar!" the queen said sharply. "You know very well that Princess Raisa is fostered with the clans as required by the Naéming."

The Naéming was the agreement between the clans and the Wizard Council that had ended the Breaking—the magical calamity that had nearly destroyed the world.

"But surely it is unnecessary for Princess Raisa to spend so much time away from court," Bayar said, smiling at the queen. "Poor thing. Think of all the dances and pageants and parties she's missed."

And stitchery and elocution classes, Raisa added to herself. A bloody shame.

Byrne studied Raisa as he might a horse he was thinking of buying, then said in his blunt fashion, "She doesn't look any the worse for wear to me. And she rides like a Demonai warrior."

That was high praise, coming from Byrne. Raisa sat up a little straighter.

Queen Marianna put her hand on Byrne's arm. "Do you really think it's so dangerous, Edon?" She was always eager to bring any argument to a close as quickly as possible, even if it meant throwing a bandage over a boil.

Byrne looked down at the queen's hand on his arm, then up into her face. His craggy features softened a fraction. "Your Majesty, I know how much you love the hunt. If it comes to following the herds into the mountains, Lord Bayar will be unable to accompany you. The borderlands are full of refugees. When a man's family is starving, he'll do whatever it takes to get them fed. There's armies of mercenaries traveling through, heading to and from the Ardenine Wars. The Queen of the Fells would be a valuable prize."

"Is that *all* you're worried about, Captain Byrne?" Bayar retorted, eyes narrowed.

Byrne didn't blink. "Is there something else I *should* be worried about, my lord? Something you'd like to tell me?"

"Perhaps we should go on," Queen Marianna said, decisively snapping her reins. "Micah and the others should have no difficulty catching us up."

Lord Bayar nodded stiffly. Micah's going to hear about this, Raisa thought. The High Wizard looked as though he could bite off someone's head and spit out the teeth. She urged Switcher forward, claiming the lead. Byrne maneuvered his great bay horse so that he rode beside her, with the rest following after.

Their trail climbed through lush upland meadows

sparkling with starflowers and buttercups. Red-winged black-birds clung impossibly to swaying seedheads left over from the previous year. Raisa drank in the details like a painter deprived of color.

Byrne looked about as well, but to a different purpose. He scanned the forest to either side, his back straight, reins held loosely in his hands. His men fanned out around them, riding three miles to their one, scouting the way ahead and monitoring their back trail.

"When does Amon come home?" Raisa asked, trying out her hard-learned conversational skills on the dour captain.

Byrne studied her face for a long moment before answering. "We expect him any time, Your Highness. Because of the fighting in Arden, he's had to take the long way around from Oden's Ford."

It had been more than three years since Raisa had seen Amon—Byrne's eldest son. After her three years at Demonai Camp, she'd returned to court at solstice to find that Amon was gone to Wien House, the military school at Oden's Ford. He meant to follow in his father's footsteps, and soldiers began their training early.

She and Amon had been fast friends since childhood, when despite their difference in station, a lack of other children at court had forced them together. Fellsmarch Castle had been lonely without him (not that she'd had much time to be lonely). When I'm queen, Raisa thought, I'm going to keep my friends close by. It was one more entry on a long list of good intentions.

Now Amon was on his way back to the Fells, traveling the hundreds of miles from Oden's Ford on his own. Raisa envied him. Even among the clans, she always traveled with some kind of guard. What would it be like, choosing her own way, sleeping when and where she liked, each day brilliant with possibility and risk?

The hunting party turned west, following a trail that stitched its way along the side of the valley. Though they were hundreds of feet above the Dyrnnewater, the roar of its cascades floated up to them.

They passed through a narrow canyon, and it grew noticeably cooler as the stone walls closed in on either side of them. Raisa shivered, feeling a twinge of worry, a vibration in her bones as if the rich web of life around her had been plucked by unseen fingers.

Switcher snorted and tossed her head, nearly ripping the reins from Raisa's hands. The gloom on either side of the trail seemed to coalesce into gray shadows loping alongside her, their bodies compressing and extending.

Gray wolves, the symbol of her house. Raisa caught a glimpse of narrow lupine heads and amber eyes, tongues lolling over razor-sharp teeth, and then they disappeared.

Wolves were said to appear to the blooded queens at turning points: times of danger and opportunity. They had never appeared to Raisa before, which wasn't surprising since she was not yet queen.

She glanced back at her mother, who was laughing at something Lord Bayar had said. The queen hadn't seemed to notice anything unusual.

Had Raisa been riding out from Demonai with her clan friends, they'd have taken her premonition as an omen, poking and prodding at it like a snake in the dirt, studying over its possible meaning. Being of the Gray Wolf lineage, Raisa was expected to have the second sight, and this skill was respected.

A voice broke into her thoughts. "Are you well, Your Highness?"

Startled, Raisa looked up into Byrne's worried eyes, gray as the ocean under a winter sky. He'd come up next to her and taken hold of Switcher's bridle, inclining his head so he could hear her answer.

"Well . . . um . . . I . . ." she stammered, for once at a loss for words. She thought of saying, *I have a peculiar feeling we're in danger, Captain Byrne*, or, *By chance did you see any wolves along the way?*

Even if the gruff captain took her seriously, what could he do?

"I'm fine, Captain," she said. "It's been a long time since breakfast is all."

"Would you like a biscuit?" he asked, digging into his saddlebag. "I've some in my—"

"That's all right," she said hastily. "We'll have lunch soon, right?"

The canyon opened into a pretty, upland meadow. The deer herd had been seen grazing there a week ago, but they were gone now. In this season they were likely heading to higher ground, and with the wizard Lord Bayar along, the hunting group couldn't follow. They were pushing at clan boundaries as it was.

They stopped for their midday in the meadow, just outside

the mouth of the narrow canyon. The meal was an elaborate affair, laid out on fancy cloths, with cheese and cold meats, fruit, and bottles of wine and cider. While the rest of them ate, two of Byrne's soldiers scouted ahead, looking for traces of the missing herd.

Raisa had little appetite. She sat, arms wrapped around her knees, still unable to shake the feeling of disquiet that pressed down upon her, pinning her to the ground. It was just noon, but the day seemed to darken, and the sunlight and shadow that dappled the ground dissolved away. Gray shapes prowled the gloom, returning each time she blinked them away.

She peered up through the leafy canopy overhead. Although the sky to the south was a clear blue, overhead it had gone milky gray, the sun a bright disk swimming in a gathering haze. Raisa sniffed the air. Her nose stung with the scent of burning leaves.

"Is something burning?" she asked nobody in particular. She'd spoken so quietly she didn't think anyone had heard, but Byrne rose from his seat at the edge of the woods and walked to the center of the meadow, scanning the slopes on all sides. Frowning, he gazed at the sky for a long moment, then looked over at the horses. They shifted, stamping their feet and straining at their tethers.

Raisa felt the growing conviction that something was terribly wrong. The air seemed to catch in her throat, and she coughed.

"Load up the horses," Captain Byrne ordered, setting his men to clearing the camp and packing up the picnic things.

"Oh, do let's stay longer, Edon." Queen Marianna raised a

glass of wine. "It's so pretty here. It doesn't matter if we don't take a deer."

Lord Bayar sprawled next to her. "I can't climb much farther without violating the Naéming and all that. But you go on, Captain Byrne, and find our princesses a deer. I will stay here and look after the queen."

Raisa stared at the scene before her—the blanket spread under the trees, the darkly handsome wizard with his boots crossed at the ankles, bejeweled hand resting on the blanket. Her pretty blond mother, a confection even in her riding clothes, cheeks flushed like a girl's.

It reminded Raisa of a painting in the galleries at home—a frozen moment that left you wondering about what had happened before, and would happen after.

"I'll stay with you, Mama," Raisa said, plunking herself down at the edge of the blanket and looking the High Wizard in the eye, knowing instinctively that they were enemies. Wishing her father didn't spend so much time away.

Byrne's soldiers had continued to load the increasingly restive horses, though it wasn't easy. Now the tall captain came and stood over them. "Your Grace, I think we'd best go back. There's a fire close by, and it's headed this way."

"A *fire*," Lord Bayar said. He scooped up a handful of damp leaves, crushed it in his gloved palm, and let the soggy mass drop. "How is that possible?"

"I don't know, Lord Bayar," Byrne said doggedly. "It doesn't make sense. But there is one, and it's upslope from us on Hanalea. I've seen them come down on people before they can get out of harm's way."

"But that's only in late summer," Queen Marianna said. "Not early spring."

"Exactly." Lord Bayar rolled his eyes. "You're an alarmist, Byrne."

Queen Marianna touched Bayar's arm, looking anxiously from him to Byrne. "I do smell smoke, Gavan. Perhaps we should listen to the captain."

While they talked a sullen dusk had fallen over the meadow. An odd wind sprang up, blowing upslope, carrying the smoke away from them, like some hidden beast inhaling. Raisa scrambled to her feet and walked out into the clearing, looking back toward Hanalea. As she watched, a dense, purplish cloud billowed skyward from the ridge above, under-lit by orange and green fire. A whorl of flame rose from the ground, a fire tornado sixty feet tall. She could hear it now, too, the pitch pines snapping in the heat, the throaty roar of the inferno.

It was like one of those dreams where you try to scream and it takes several tries to make a sound. "Captain Byrne!" Her voice seemed small against the howl of the fire. She pointed. "It *is* a fire. Look!"

Just then, a dozen deer exploded from the trees, bounded across the meadow, and raced into the canyon, oblivious to the would-be hunters in their path.

Immediately after, Raisa heard the pounding of hooves, and three riders burst into the meadow from the direction the deer had come. Their horses were lathered and wild-eyed, the riders only a little less so.

"It's coming! Right behind us! A wildfire! Run!" shouted

the rider in the lead, and it took Raisa a moment to recognize cool, sardonic Micah Bayar behind that soot-smudged face. It was the missing Micah and his cousins Arkeda and Miphis Mander.

By now, everyone was up, the picnic forgotten.

"Micah?" Lord Bayar blinked at his son. "How did you . . . ? What did you . . . ?" Raisa had never seen the High Wizard so inarticulate.

"We were on our way up to meet you and saw the fire," Micah gasped, his face pale under the dirt, his hair hanging in dank strands. There were deep cuts on his hands and what looked to be a nasty burn on his right arm. "We . . . we tried to fight it, but . . ."

Byrne led Queen Marianna's horse, Spirit, over to her side. "Your Majesty. Quickly now." Holding firmly to Spirit's bridle with one hand, he scooped the queen one-armed into the saddle. "Careful," he said. "Sit tight. She's spooked."

Raisa squirmed up onto Switcher's back, murmuring reassurances to the mare. Only a hundred yards away now, the forest canopy was alight. The fire bore down on them, flames leaping from tree to tree in a mad rush downhill, traveling much faster than seemed possible in this season. The air scorched Raisa's lungs, and she pressed her sleeve over her mouth and nose.

Lord Bayar stood frozen a moment, eyes narrowed, looking from Micah to Arkeda to Miphis, and up at the onrushing flames. Then he caught his own horse and swung up into the saddle. Angling his horse close to Micah's, he grabbed a fistful of Micah's coat and pulled his son close,

33

speaking to him with their faces inches apart. Micah nodded once, looking terrified. Lord Bayar abruptly released him and wrenched his horse away, digging his heels into the stallion's sides, leaving his son to follow or burn.

Raisa stared at them, bewildered. Did the High Wizard expect his son to have put the fire out on his own? Micah was powerful, but he didn't even have an amulet, and he'd not yet been to the academy.

"Your Highness! Hurry!" Byrne shouted.

They all rode hard for the mouth of the canyon.

If Raisa had hoped to find shelter in the canyon, she found it a mixed blessing. Embers were no longer falling on their heads, but a blisteringly hot wind roared between the walls, so thick with smoke she couldn't see the horse in front of her. It seemed to muffle sound, though she could hear people coughing and choking ahead of and behind her. The way was so narrow that at least they couldn't get lost, but she worried they'd asphyxiate before they emerged on the other side.

Byrne rode up next to her again. "Dismount and lead your horse, Your Highness," he said. "The air is fresher near the ground. Be sure to keep tight hold of the reins." He moved down the line, passing the word.

Raisa climbed down off Switcher, wound the leather reins around her hand, and stumbled down the rocky streambed. Byrne was right: the breathing was easier below. The skin on her face felt brittle and hot, like the skin on a roasted chicken. She was tempted to kneel down and bathe her face in the water, but Byrne harried them along relentlessly. The air grew even thicker as they neared the exit from the canyon, and Raisa's eyes stung, her vision blurred by tears.

When she blinked the tears away, she was again surrounded by wolves, the size of small ponies, their backs at shoulder height on her. They crowded in around her, snapping and growling, their wild scent competing with the stench of smoke, their stiff guard hairs brushing her skin, pressing against her legs as if to force her from the trail.

"Hanalea, have mercy," Raisa whispered. No one else seemed to notice. Was she hallucinating, or could they be real, forced to share the trail by the advance of the flame?

Raisa was so focused on the wolf pack that she nearly collided with Micah, who'd stopped abruptly in front of her. The wolves faded into smoke. Somewhere ahead, she heard Byrne swearing forcefully. Thrusting her reins into Micah's hand, she fought her way past the others to the front of the line.

"Stay back, Your Highness," Byrne said, pushing her behind him. She could see that the trail beyond the exit was awash in flame. The fire had split around the ridge, pouring down the slope on either side of the canyon. They were trapped.

"All right!" Byrne said, his voice ringing through the canyon. "I want all of you down in the stream. Lie flat and immerse yourself if you can."

Gavan Bayar forced his way to the front. "What's going on?" he demanded. "Why have we stopped?"

Byrne stepped aside, allowing Bayar a clear view. The wizard stared out at the inferno for a long moment. Then turned and called, "Micah! Arkeda and Miphis! Come here."

The three boys shuffled forward until they stood before the High Wizard. They were shaking, teeth chattering, and looked scared to death. Bayar yanked off his fine leather gloves and stowed them in his pocket. He drew a heavy silver chain from his pocket, fastened one end around his wrist and the other around Micah's.

"Arkeda and Miphis. Grip the chain here and here," Bayar said, pointing. They each took hold of the chain between Bayar and Micah as if it were a poisonous snake. "Don't let go or you'll regret it," the wizard said. "But not for long." He turned to face the fire, seized his amulet with his free hand, and began speaking a charm.

As he spoke, the three boys staggered and gasped and cried out as if they'd been struck a heavy blow. The two in the middle kept a desperate hold on the chain, while all three turned paler and paler as if they were being drained dry. Beads of sweat formed on Lord Bayar's face, then evaporated in the searing heat. The High Wizard's seductive voice wound over and through the roar of the fire, the crackle and hiss of exploding trees, and the boys' labored breathing.

Finally, grudgingly, the fire responded. The flames flickered and shriveled and rolled away from the mouth of the canyon like a retreating tide, leaving a desolate, smoking landscape behind. Bayar kept at it, beating back the fire with sorcerous words until the flames were entirely gone, though it still looked as dark as the end of the world. He slid the chain from his wrist and made one final gesture. The skies opened up and rain came pouring down, hissing as it struck the hot earth.

There followed a communal release of held breath, and a smattering of awed applause. Like marionettes cut loose by the puppeteer, Micah and his cousins collapsed to the ground and lay still.

Raisa knelt next to Micah and rested her palm on his clammy forehead. He opened his eyes and stared up at her as if he didn't recognize her. She looked up at Lord Bayar. "What's wrong with them? Are they going to be all right?"

Bayar gazed at them with a peculiar, cold expression on his face. "They'll recover; though I daresay it's a lesson they'll never forget."

Raisa tried to imagine her own father thrusting her into the middle of a spellcasting with no preparation or explanation. And couldn't.

But then, he wasn't a wizard.

Byrne had walked some distance out of the canyon and stood in the rain, kicking at the still-smoldering debris. "Strange," he said. "I've never seen a fire like this before, that burns in the wet."

"Lord Bayar," Queen Marianna said, gripping the wizard's hands, "that was truly remarkable. You saved all our lives. Thank you."

"I am glad to be of service, Your Majesty," Bayar said, forcing a smile, though he looked as though it might crack his face.

Raisa looked over at Byrne. The captain gazed at the queen and her High Wizard, rubbing his bristled jaw, a puzzled frown on his face.

CHAPTER THREE

AMBUSHED

All the way back to Marisa Pines Camp, Dancer strode along, slender shoulders hunched, his usually sunny face clouded, his body language discouraging conversation. After a couple of tries, Han gave up and was left to wrestle with his questions alone.

Han knew nothing of wizardry beyond his mother's dire warnings. Did it come on in childhood or not until much later? Did it require amulets like the one that seemed to weigh down his bag? Did wizards need schooling, or did charmcasters have an inborn knowledge of what to do?

Most of all, how was it fair that some people had the power to make others do their bidding, to create fires that couldn't be put out, or turn a cat into a hawk, if the stories could be believed.

To break the world nearly beyond repair.

The clans had magic too—of a different sort. Dancer's

mother, Willo, was Matriarch of Marisa Pines Camp, and a gifted healer. She could take a dry stick and make it bloom, could make anything grow in her hillside fields, could heal by touch and voice. Her remedies were in demand as far away as Arden. The clans were known for their leatherwork, their metalwork, their tradition of creating amulets and other magical objects.

Bayar had made much of the fact that Dancer had no named father. How did he know that, and why did he care? The way Han saw it, Dancer didn't need a father. He was totally embedded in the clan, surrounded by aunts and uncles who doted on him, cousins to hunt with, everyone connected by blood and tradition. Even when Willo was away, there was always a hearth to welcome him, food to share, a bed to sleep in.

Compared to Dancer, Han was more the orphan, with only his mother and sister and a father dead in the Ardenine Wars. They shared a single room over a stable in the Ragmarket neighborhood of Fellsmarch. The more he thought on it, the more Han felt sorry for himself—magicless and fatherless. Without prospects. Mam had told him often enough he'd never amount to anything.

They were about a half mile from camp when Han realized they were being followed. It wasn't any one thing that caused him to think so: when he turned to inspect some winter burned seed pods at the side of the trail, he heard footfalls behind them that stopped abruptly. A squirrel continued to scold from a pine tree long after they'd passed. Once he swung around and thought he saw a flash of movement.

Fear shivered over him. The wizards must have doubled back after them. He'd heard how they could make themselves invisible or turn into birds and strike from out of the air. Ducking his head just in case, he looked over at Dancer, who seemed absorbed in his own gloomy thoughts.

Han knew better than to allow an enemy to choose the time and place of an attack. Just as he and Dancer rounded a curve of the hill, he gripped Dancer's arm, pulling him off the trail, behind the massive trunk of an oak tree.

Dancer jerked his arm free. "What are you . . . ?"

"Shhh," Han hissed, putting his finger to his lips and gesturing for Dancer to stay put. Han loped back the way they came, making a big circle so as to come in behind any pursuers. Yes. He glimpsed a slight figure clothed in forest colors gliding from shadow into sunlight up ahead. He put on speed, lengthening his stride, thankful that the wet ground absorbed the sound of his footsteps. He was almost there when his quarry must have heard him coming and cut sharply to the right. Not wanting to allow the charmcaster time to conjure a jinx, Han launched himself, crashing into the intruder and hanging on as they rolled down a small slope and splashed into Old Woman Creek.

"Ow!" Han banged his elbow against a small boulder in the creek bed and lost his hold on the charmcaster, who twisted and wriggled and seemed incredibly slippery and soft in unexpected places. Han's head went under, and he sucked in a lungful of water. Coughing, half panicked, he pushed himself to his feet, slinging his wet hair out of his eyes, worried he'd be jinxed before he could act.

Behind him, someone was laughing, gasping with merriment, scarcely able to speak. "H-H-Hunts Alone! It's still too cold for s-swimming."

Han swung around. Dancer's cousin Digging Bird sat in the shallows, her mop of dark curls plastered around her face, her wet linen blouse clinging to her upper body so the light fabric was rendered nearly transparent. She grinned at him shamelessly, her eyes traveling up his body in turn.

He resisted the temptation to duck back under the freezing water. His face burned, and he knew it must be flaming red. It took him a minute to get his voice going. "Bird?" he whispered, mortified, knowing he would never hear the end of this.

"Maybe we should change your name to Hunts Bird," she teased.

"N-no," he stammered, raising his hands as if to ward off a curse.

"Jumps in the Creek? Red in the Face?" she persisted.

That was all he needed. Clan names constantly changed to fit until you were grown and thought to be stable. You might be Cries in the Night as a baby, Squirrel as a child, and Throws Stones as an adult. It was always confusing to flatlanders.

"No," Han pleaded. "Please, Bird . . ."

"I'll call you whatever I want," Digging Bird said, standing and wading to the shore. "Hunts Bird," she decided. "It can be our secret name."

Han stood there helplessly, waist-deep in the water, thinking she was the one who needed a new name.

He and Bird and Dancer had been friends since he could

remember. Every summer since he was small, Mam had sent him up from the city to live at Marisa Pines. They'd camped together, hunted together, and fought endless battles against imaginary enemies throughout the Spirit Mountains.

They'd studied under the ancient bow master at Hunter's Camp, chafing at the requirement that they build a bow before shooting it. He'd been with Bird when she took her first deer, then burned with envy until he got his. When he did, she'd taught him how to slow smoke the meat so it would last through the winter. They were twelve at the time.

They played hare and wolf for days on end. One of them—the hare—would set out through the woods, doing his or her best to throw the other two off, by walking over solid rock or wading miles in a streambed or detouring through one of the high-country camps. If one wolf found the hare, then they'd walk together until the third player found them.

Bird was great to travel with. She found the best campsites—sheltered from the weather and defensible. She could build a fire in the middle of a rainstorm and find game at any altitude. Many nights they'd shared a blanket for warmth.

The three of them had tasted hard cider for the first time at the Falling Leaves Market, and he'd washed the sick from Bird's face when she drank too much.

But these days he always felt awkward around Bird, and she was the one who had changed. Now when he walked into Marisa Pines Camp, she was likely to be sitting with a group of other girls her age. They would watch him with bold eyes and then put their heads together and whisper. If he tried to approach her, the other girls would giggle and nudge each other.

He'd once owned the streets of Ragmarket, and people made sure to get out of his way. He'd had his share of girlies, too—a streetlord could have his pick. But for some reason, Bird always put him off-balance. Maybe it was because she was so damnably good at everything.

When they were younger, wrestling in the creek would have been prelude to nothing. Now every word between them crackled with meaning, and every action had unintended consequences.

"Bird! Hunts Alone! What happened? Did you fall in the creek?" Dancer had appeared at the top of the slope.

Bird squeezed water out of her leggings. "Hunts Alone threw me in," she said to her cousin, a little smugly.

"I thought you were someone else," Han muttered.

Bird swung around to confront him, her face darkening. "Who?" she demanded. "*Who* did you think I was?"

Han shrugged and waded to shore. That was another thing. Where once they'd finished each other's sentences and all but communed mind to mind, now Bird had become unpredictable, given to bizarre fits of temper.

"Who?" she repeated, hard on his heels, intent on prying it out of him. "You thought I was some other girl?"

"Not a girl." Han yanked off his boots and dumped the water out of them. At least some of the mud had washed off. "We ran into some charmcasters in Burnt Tree Meadow. They spooked the deer, and we got into an argument. When I heard you following us, I thought you were one of them."

She blinked at him. *"Charmcasters,"* she said. "What would charmcasters be doing up here? And how do I look like one, anyway?"

"Well. You don't," Han said. "My mistake." He looked up, and their eyes met, and he swallowed hard. Bird's cheeks colored a deep rose, and she turned to Dancer.

"What words did you have to say to a jinxflinger, cousin?" she asked.

"None," Dancer said, shooting a warning look at Han.

"We would've each taken a deer if not for them," Han felt compelled to say, then was immediately sorry when Bird looked at him and raised her eyebrows. Bird always said that a deer in the smokehouse was worth a whole herd in the woods.

"So what happened?" Bird asked, leaning forward. "Was something burning? I smelled smoke."

Han and Dancer looked at each other, each waiting for the other to speak. "They set fire to Hanalea," Han said finally. "The charmcasters."

"So you confronted them?" Bird said, leaning forward, looking from one to the other. "And then what?"

"Nothing happened. They left," Dancer said.

"Fine," Bird said, angry again. "Don't tell me anything. I don't care anyway. But you'd better tell Willo about it, at least. They shouldn't be in the Spirits at all, let alone setting fires."

Han shivered. The sun had gone and he was covered in gooseflesh. In past days he'd have stripped off and laid his wet clothes out to dry. He glanced over at Bird. Not anymore.

"Let's go on to Marisa Pines," Dancer said, as if he could read Han's mind. "They'll have a fire going."

The sky had clouded over, and a chill wind funneled between the peaks, but the brisk six-mile walk kept Han's blood moving. Bird's lips were blue, and Han thought of putting an arm around her, to warm her, but it would have been awkward on the narrow rocky trail. Plus she might only snap at him again.

The dogs greeted them when they were still a half mile from Marisa Pines. It was a motley pack—rugged, long-haired sheepdogs, wolf mixes, and spotted flatland hounds bought at market. Next came the children, from solemn round-faced toddlers to long-legged ten-year-olds, alerted by the dogs.

Most had straight, dark hair, brown eyes, and coppery skin, though some had blue or green eyes, like Dancer, or curly hair, like Bird. There had been considerable mixing of Valefolk and clan over the years. And Valefolk with the blue-eyed, fair-haired wizard invaders from the Northern Isles.

But almost no direct mixing of wizard and clan. Wizards had not been allowed in the Spirit Mountains for a thousand years.

Questions flew from all directions, in a mixture of Common and Clan. "Where have you been? How did you get all wet? How long are you staying? Hunts Alone, will you sleep in our lodge tonight?" Even though Han came often to Marisa Pines, girls a year or two younger than him still dared each other to run up and touch his pale hair, so different from their own.

Bird did her best to shoo them off. One especially aggressive girl yanked out a strand of his hair, and Han stomped after her, scowling, pretending to chase her. That sent her and her friends scurrying into the woods, their laughter sieving through the trees like sunlight.

"What's in the bag? Do you have any sweets?" A tiny girl with a long braid made a grab for his backpack.

"No sweets today," Han growled. "And keep off. I've got a bag full of blisterweed." Excruciatingly conscious of the amulet in his bag, Han protected it under the curve of his arm. It was as if he had a large poisonous snake in there, or a goblet too fragile to touch.

By the time they came within sight of the camp, they had a large following.

Marisa Pines Camp stood sentinel at the pass that led through the southern Spirits to the flatlands beyond. It was large, as clan camps went—perhaps a hundred lodges of varying sizes, built far enough apart so they could be added onto as families grew.

The camp was centered by the Common Lodge—a large building used for markets, ceremonies, and the feasts for which the clans were famous. Close by the Common Lodge stood the Matriarch Lodge. Dancer and Bird lived there with Dancer's mother, Willo, Matriarch of Marisa Pines, and a fluid mix of friends, blood relations, and children fostered from other camps.

Marisa Pines prospered as a center for commerce, given its strategic location. Handwork from camps throughout the Spirits flowed into the camp, where brokers shopped its famous markets and funneled clan-made goods to Arden to the south, to Tamron Court, and to Fellsmarch down in the Vale.

Relations between the clans and the queen might be

strained these days, but that did not staunch the thirst of flatlanders for upland goods—silver and gold work, leather, precious stones set into jewelry and decorative pieces, hand-woven yard goods, stitchery, art, and magical objects. Clan goods never wore out, they brought luck to the owner, and it was said that clan charms would win over the most resistant of sweethearts.

The Marisa Pines clan was known for remedies, dyes, heal-ing, and handwoven fabrics. The Demonai were famous for magical amulets and their warriors. The Hunter clan pro-duced smoked meats, furs and skins, and nonmagical weapons. Other camps specialized in nonmagical jewelry, paintings, and other decorative arts.

Too bad it wasn't a market day, Han thought. On a market day they'd have got no attention at all. Which would've been fine with Han, who was growing tired of explaining his sodden clothes. It was a relief to duck through the doorway of the Matriarch Lodge and escape the relentlessly rattling tongues.

A fire blazed in the center of the lodge, hot and smoke-less. The interior was fragrant with winterberry, pine, and cinnamon, and the scent of stew wafted in from the adjacent cooking lodge. Han's mouth watered. Willo's house always smelled good enough to eat.

The Matriarch Lodge could have been a small market, all on its own. Great bundles of herbs hung from the ceiling, and casks and baskets and pots lined the walls. On one side were paints and dyes and earthenware jars of beads and feathers. On the other were the medicinals—salves and tonics and pungent potions of all kinds, many rendered from the plants Han gathered.

Hides stretched over frames, some with designs painstakingly drawn on them. Three girls about Han's age huddled around one of them, their sleek heads nearly touching, brushing paint onto the leather.

Hangings divided the room into several chambers. From behind one curtain, Han could hear the murmur of voices. Patients and their families often stayed over so the matriarch could tend them without leaving the lodge.

Willo sat at the loom in the corner. The overhead beater thudded as she smacked it against the fell of the rug she was weaving. The warp stretched wide and winter-dark, since weavers worked a season ahead. Willo's rugs were sturdy and beautiful, and people said they kept enemies from crossing your threshold.

Still shivering, Bird disappeared into one of the adjacent chambers to change into dry clothes.

Willo laid down her shuttle, rose from the bench, and came toward them, skirts sliding over the rugs. Somehow, Han's resentment and frustration faded, and it was a better day.

Everyone agreed that the Marisa Pines matriarch was beautiful, though her beauty went deeper than appearance. Some mentioned the movement of her hands when she spoke, like small birds. Others praised her voice, which they compared to the Dyrnnewater, singing on its way to the sea. Her dark hair fell, beaded and braided, nearly to her waist. When she danced, it was said the animals crept out of the forest to watch. She was a crooner, who could speak, mind to mind, to animals. Her touch healed the sick, soothed the grieving, cheered the discouraged, and made cowards brave.

When pressed, Han had trouble even describing what she looked like. He guessed she was in a category all on her own, like a woodland nymph. She was whatever you needed her to be to find the best in yourself.

He couldn't help comparing her to Mam, who always seemed to see the worst in him.

"Welcome, Hunts Alone," she said. "Will you share our fire?" The ritual greeting to the guest. Then her gaze fastened more closely on Han, and she raised an eyebrow. "What happened to you? Did you fall into the Dyrnnewater?"

Han shook his head. "Old Woman Creek."

Willo looked him up and down, frowning. "You've been in the mudpots as well, if I'm not mistaken."

"Well. Right." Han looked down at his feet, embarrassed that he'd been so careless with Willo's beautiful boots.

"He can have my flatlander breeches," Dancer offered. He studied Han's long legs. "Though he'll show some ankle, I guess."

Like most clan, Dancer owned the minimum one or two pair of leggings and one pair of breeches to wear into town. He'd be happy to give up the breeches. Dancer wore the uncomfortable flatlander garb under protest anyway.

"I think I have something that will work." Willo crossed to the assembly of baskets, bins, and trunks that lined the wall. She knelt next to one of the bins and dug through clothing. Near the bottom she found what she was looking for and pulled free a pair of worn breeches in a heavy cotton canvas.

She held them up and looked from Han to the trousers and back again.

"These will fit," she proclaimed, and handed them to him, along with a faded linen shirt that had been laundered into softness. "Give me the boots," she commanded, extending her hand, and for a moment Han was afraid she intended to take them back for good. She must have seen the panic in his face, because she added, "Don't worry. I'll just see what I can do to clean them up."

Han tugged off his muddy boots and handed them over, then ducked into the sleeping chamber to change clothes. He stripped off the wet leggings and shirt and pulled on the dry breeches, wishing he could wash the mud off his skin. As if his unspoken wishes caught the ear of the Maker, Bird pushed the hangings aside and entered with a basin of steaming water and a rag.

"Hey!" he said, glad he'd got his trousers on. "You could knock." Which was stupid, really, because there wasn't any door.

She'd changed out of her wet trail garb into skirts and an embroidered shirt, and her wet hair was drying into its usual intriguing tangle. Han still had his shirt off, and she kept staring at his chest and shoulders as if she found them fascinating. Han looked down to see if he'd got mud smeared under his shirt as well. But he was clean there, at least.

Bird plopped down on the sleeping bench next to him, setting the basin on the floor between them. "Here," she said, handing him a chunk of fragrant upland soap and the rag.

Rolling his breeches above his knees, Han soaped the rag

and washed the mud from his bare feet and lower legs, rinsing in the basin. Then he began scrubbing his arms and hands. The silver cuffs around his wrists kept turning when he tried to wipe them clean.

"Let me." Bird picked up a boar-bristle brush, gripped the cuff on his left wrist, and took the brush to it. She leaned in close, getting that familiar frown on her face that said she was concentrating. She'd used some kind of scent—she smelled like fresh air and vanilla and flowers.

"You should take these off if you're going to get into the mud," she grumbled.

"That's helpful," he said, rolling his eyes. "*You* try to get them off." He tugged at one of them to demonstrate. It was a solid three-inch-wide band of silver, and too small to slide over his hand. He'd had them on ever since he could remember.

"You know they've got magic in them. Otherwise you'd have outgrown them by now." Bird used her fingernail to dig out some dried mud. "Your mother bought them from a peddler?"

He nodded. It must've been during some prosperous time in the past, when there was money to spend on silver bracelets for a baby. When they weren't living hand-to-mouth, as Mam always said.

"She's got to remember something," Bird persisted. She never seemed to know when to leave off. "Maybe you could find the peddler who sold them to her."

Han shrugged. They'd had this conversation before, which he mostly got through by shrugging. Bird didn't know Mam. His mother never came to the camps in the mountains, never shared songs and stories around a fire. Mam didn't like to talk about the past, and Han had long ago learned not to ask too many questions, lest she slam her switch down on his fingers or send him to bed without supper.

The clans, they were all about stories. They told stories about things that had happened a thousand years ago. Han never tired of listening to them over and over. Hearing a familiar clan story was like sliding into your own bed on a cold night with a full belly and knowing you'd wake up safe in the same place.

Bird released his one hand and picked up the other. Her fingers were warm and soapy and slippery. "These symbols must mean something," she said, tapping the cuff with her forefinger. "Maybe if you knew how to use them, you could— I don't know—shoot flames from the palms of your hands."

Han was thinking he was just as likely to shoot flames from his rear end. "They look clan-made to me, but Willo doesn't know what the symbols mean," Han said. "And if she doesn't know, nobody does."

Bird finally dropped the subject. She rinsed off his hands and wrists and used the hem of her skirt to dry them. Pulling a small jar from her pocket, she uncorked it and smeared something onto the silver with her fingers.

He tried to pull away, but she had a tight grip on his wrist. "What's that?" he asked suspiciously.

"Polish," she said, rubbing the silver with a dry rag until it shone. She rubbed polish onto the other cuff. Han submitted, though he didn't really want to call attention to them these days.

"Are you coming to my renaming feast?" Bird asked abruptly, her eyes still focused on her work.

He was surprised by the question. "Well, I'd planned to. If I'm asked." It had never occurred to him that he wouldn't be. Bird's family was prominent among the clans, since she was niece to the Marisa Pines matriarch. Bird's coming-of-age would be celebrated with a huge party, and Han had been looking forward to it.

She nodded once, briskly. "Good."

"It's still a month away, right?" For Han, a month was an eternity. Anything could happen in a month. He never planned more than a day or two ahead.

She nodded again. "For my sixteenth name day."

Finally letting go of his hands, Bird dropped her own into her lap. She extended her bare toes out from under her skirts, studying them. She wore a silver ring on her right small toe.

"Have you decided on your vocation?" Han asked.

Among the clans, boys and girls to the age of sixteen were expected to train in all skills, from hunting and tracking and herding and use of weapons to weaving and metalworking and healing and singing.

At sixteen they were reborn into their vocations and began apprenticeships. Everyone was required to have a trade, though clan notions of a trade were more flexible than in the city.

For instance, storytelling was a trade.

When Han realized Bird hadn't answered, he repeated, "Have you decided on a trade?"

Bird looked up at him. "I'm going to be a warrior," she said, giving him a steely eye as if daring him to object.

"A warrior!" He blinked at her, then blurted, "What does Willo say?"

"She doesn't know," Bird said, digging her toes into the rug. "Don't tell her."

Willo might be disappointed, Han thought. Having no daughter of her own, she probably hoped Bird would follow her as matriarch and healer. Even though Bird wasn't exactly the nurturing type.

"How many warriors does Marisa Pines need?" he asked.

"I want to go to Demonai," Bird said, hunching her shoulders.

"Really?" Bird was aiming high. The Demonai warriors were legendary fighters and hunters. It was said they could survive in the woods for weeks on wind and rain and sunlight. That one Demonai warrior was a match for a hundred soldiers.

Personally, Han thought they were an arrogant lot who kept to themselves and never cracked a smile and tried to make you think they were privy to secrets that you would never know.

"Who are you supposed to fight?" Han asked. "I mean, it's been years since we've had a war in the uplands."

Bird looked annoyed at his lack of enthusiasm. "They're spilling enough blood down south," she said. "Refugees have been flooding into the mountains. There's always a chance the fighting will spread up here." She sounded almost like she hoped it would.

In the chaos following the Breaking, Arden, Tamron, and Bruinswallow had broken away from the Fells. Now the flatlands to the south were embroiled in an incessant civil war.

Han's father had signed on as a mercenary soldier, gone south and died there. But there had been peace in the north for a millennium.

"Willo's worried," Bird went on when Han didn't respond. "Some wizards are saying that they let go of power too easily, that it's time to return to having wizard kings. They think wizard kings could help protect us against armies from the south." She shook her head, looking disgusted. "People have such short memories."

"It's been a thousand years," Han pointed out, and received a scowl in return. "Anyway, Queen Marianna wouldn't let that happen," he added. "Nor would the High Wizard."

"Some people say she's not a strong queen," Bird said. "Not like the queens in the past. Some say the wizards are gaining too much power."

Han wondered who "some people" were, who had all these opinions. "Anyway, aren't you afraid of getting killed? Being a warrior, I mean?" He couldn't help thinking of his father. How different his life would be if he were still alive.

Bird snorted in disgust. "Don't tell me there's not going to be any war, and then warn me I might get killed."

The thing was, Han knew Bird would make a great warrior. Though she hadn't Han's muscle, she was better with a bow than he was. Better at woodcraft. Better at tracking. She could look over a broken landscape and know where the deer lay hidden. She was better at anticipating the moves of a possible enemy. She'd outfoxed him all his life.

And there was nothing she liked better than stalking things.

He looked up to find her watching him, as if eager for a response.

"You'll make a great warrior, Digging Bird," he told her, grinning. "It's perfect. Good choice." He took her hand and squeezed it.

She beamed at him, blinking back tears, and he was amazed that his approval meant so much to her. He was even more amazed when she leaned over and kissed him on the mouth.

She stood, picked up the basin, and ducked out between the hides.

"Bird!" he called after her, thinking that if she was in a kissing mood, he was happy to oblige. But by the time he got the word out, she was gone.

When Han returned to the common room, Bird was gone, and Willo and Dancer were sitting knee to knee on the floor, talking. If they weren't arguing, they were close to it. Han faded back into the doorway, embarrassed, not wanting to interrupt. But he could hear everything they said.

"Did you expect me to just stand by while they burned up the mountain?" Dancer was saying, his voice trembling with anger. "I'm not a coward."

Han was shocked. No one ever spoke that way to Willo.

"I expect you to remember that you are only sixteen years old," Willo replied calmly. "I expect you to use common sense. There was no point in confronting them. What did it accomplish? Did your bravery put the fire out?"

Dancer said nothing, only looked furious.

She reached out and stroked his cheek. "Let it go, Dancer,

as I have," she said softly. "This isn't like you. A grudge against wizards will only get you into trouble."

"They weren't much older than me and Han," Dancer countered stubbornly. "Haven't you said that wizards have to be sixteen to go to Oden's Ford? And didn't you say they aren't allowed to use magic until they get some training?"

"What wizards are *allowed* to do and what they actually do are two different things," Willo said. She stood and moved to the loom, fussing with the warp. "Who were they? Do you know?"

"The one was called Micah," Dancer said. "Micah Bayar."

Willo was looking away from Dancer and toward Han, so he saw the blood drain from her face when Dancer said the name. "Are you sure?" she asked, without turning around.

"Well, pretty sure." Dancer sounded confused, as if he'd caught something in her voice. "Why?"

"He's in Aerie House. That's a powerful wizard family," Willo said. "And not one to cross. Did they ask your name?"

Dancer lifted his chin. "I *told* them my name. I said I was Fire Dancer of Marisa Pines Camp." He hesitated. "But he seemed to know me as Hayden."

Willo closed her eyes and shook her head slightly. Her next words surprised Han. "What about Hunts Alone?" she asked. "Did he speak? Do they know *his* name?"

Dancer cocked his head, thinking. "I don't think so," he said. "I don't remember him introducing himself." He laughed bitterly. "They probably won't remember anything but his arrow, aimed at their black wizard hearts."

Willo swung around, facing Dancer, so Han could no

longer see her face. "He turned a bow on them?" she said, her voice cracking on the word *bow*.

Dancer shrugged. "The one called Micah, he had an amulet. He was jinxing me. Hunts Alone made him stop."

Han held his breath, waiting for Dancer to tell Willo that Han had taken the amulet, but he didn't.

Willo sighed, looking troubled. "I'll speak to the queen. This has to stop. She needs to enforce the Naéming and keep wizards out of the mountains. If she doesn't, the Demonai warriors will."

This was astonishing, Willo talking about what the queen needed to do. She made it sound as if speaking to the queen was an everyday thing. She *was* the matriarch, but still. Han tried to imagine what it would be like, meeting the queen.

Your Exalted Majesty. I'm Han Plantslinger. Mud-digger. Former streetlord of the Raggers.

Willo and Dancer had moved on to another topic. Willo leaned forward, putting her hand over Dancer's. "How are you feeling?"

Dancer pulled his hand free and canted his body away. "I'm well," he said stiffly.

She eyed him for a long moment. "Have you been taking the flying rowan?" she persisted. "I have more if you—"

"I've been taking it," Dancer interrupted. "I have plenty."

"Is it working?" she asked, reaching for him again. As a healer, she used touch for diagnosis and for healing itself.

Dancer stood, evading her hand. "I'm well," he repeated, with flat finality. "I'm going to go find Hunts Alone." He turned toward the doorway where Han was lurking.

"Tell him to eat with us," Willo called after Dancer.

Han was forced to beat a hasty retreat, ducking back into the sleeping chamber, so that was all he heard. But for the rest of that day, all through the evening meal, and sitting by the fire afterward, the conversation weighed on his mind.

He studied Dancer on the sly. Could he be sick? Han hadn't noticed anything before, and he noticed nothing now, save that Dancer seemed less animated, more somber than usual. But that could be left over from the afternoon's confrontation and the argument with his mother.

Han knew rowan, also called mountain ash. He gathered the wood and the berries, both of which were used in clan remedies. The wood was said to be good for making amulets and talismans to ward away evil. Flying rowan was especially valuable at clan markets. It grew high in the trees, and Han had learned better than to try to pass off regular rowan as the treetop kind. To the clan, anyway.

Willow had asked, "Is it working?" Had someone hexed Dancer? Were he and Willo worried that someone would? Was that why Dancer had a grudge against wizards?

Han wanted to ask, but then they would know he'd been eavesdropping. So he kept his questions to himself.

CHAPTER FOUR

A DANCE
OF SUITORS

It was late afternoon when Raisa finally climbed the curving marble staircase to the queen's tower. She ached all over; she was filthy and stank of smoke. Mellony was already in her bath. Raisa could hear her singing and splashing as she passed by her sister's chamber at the top of the stairs. Mellony was always so damnably cheerful.

Raisa had moved into new quarters since returning from Demonai Camp—larger, more elaborate, befitting a princess heir who was almost sixteen and so of marriageable age. Originally she'd been assigned a suite of rooms close to the queen's quarters, shrouded in velvet and damask and furnished with a massive canopied cherry bedstead and wardrobe. It felt crowded even when Raisa was all by herself.

Raisa had begged her mother to reopen an apartment at the far end of the hall that had lain barricaded and unused through living memory. There were many closed-off apartments in Fellsmarch Castle, since the court was smaller than it had been, but not many in such a prime location, with easy access to the queen.

Some longtime servants said the apartment had been abandoned because its walls of windows made it cold in the winter and hot in the summer. Others said it was cursed, that it was from this very room a thousand years ago that the Demon King had stolen Hanalea away, the incident that led to the Breaking. In this version, Hanalea herself had ordered the apartment sealed, vowing never to set foot in it again.

Legend had it that the ghost of Hanalea sometimes appeared at the window on stormy nights, hands extended, her loose hair snaking about her head, calling for Alger Waterlow.

That was just silly, Raisa thought. Who would wait at a window for a demon, let alone call his name?

When Raisa's mother finally gave in, and the carpenters broke down the barricades, they found a suite of rooms frozen in time, as if the previous occupant had meant to return. The furniture was huddled under drop cloths to protect it from the brilliant sunlight that streamed through dusty windows. When the drapes were removed, the fabrics gleamed, surprisingly vibrant after a thousand years.

The last occupant's possessions lay as she'd left them. A doll dressed in an old-fashioned gown gazed out from a shelf in the corner. She had a porcelain head with vacant blue eyes and long flaxen curls. Combs and brushes cluttered the dressing table, their bristles frayed by mice, and crystal perfume bottles stood arrayed on a silvered mirror, their contents evaporated long ago.

Gowns from a lost age hung in the wardrobe, made for a tall willowy girl with a very narrow waist. Some of the fabrics crumbled under Raisa's eager fingers.

Carved wolves graced the stone facing of the hearth. Bookshelves lined the public rooms. More books lay piled on the stand next to the bed. The ones in the bedroom were mostly romances, stories of knights and warriors and queens, written in a Valespeech with archaic phrasing. In the public rooms were shelved biographies and treatises on politics, including *A History of the High Country Clan* and a first edition of Adra *ana*'Doria's *Rule and Rulers in the Modern Age*. Raisa herself was just then plodding through it under the strict eye of the masters.

Hanalea or not, the suite had been occupied by a young girl, probably a princess. Perhaps she'd died, Raisa thought, and her parents had kept her room preserved as a shrine. That idea gave her delicious shivers.

Since the apartment was in one of the turrets, it was smaller than the rooms originally assigned to Raisa. But it felt spacious, since she had a view of the town and the mountains on three sides.

She'd dragged the bed into the space between the windows, and when it snowed, she felt like the fairy princess in the snow globe her father had brought her from Tamron years ago. On clear nights she pressed her face against the glass, pretending she was soaring in a winged ship among the stars.

Best of all, she'd discovered a sliding panel in one of the closets, which revealed a secret passageway. It snaked within the walls for what seemed like miles. The passageway led to a stairway, and the stairway led to the solarium on the roof, a glassed garden that was Raisa's favorite place in all of Fellsmarch Castle, even though it had fallen into disrepair.

When Raisa pushed open the door to her rooms, she found her nurse Magret Gray waiting for her. Magret was a formidable woman, tall and broad, with a lap that could accommodate several small children.

Magret wasn't really her nurse anymore, of course, but she still wielded an unwritten authority that came from changing royal diapers and scrubbing royal ears and even swatting royal behinds. Raisa's bath was already steaming on its little burner, and fresh underdrawers were laid out on her bed.

"Your Highness!" Magret said, looking aghast. "You are a terrifying sight, to be sure. The Princess Mellony said you were worse off than she was, and I did not believe it. I do owe that young lady an apology."

Right, Raisa thought. If there ever comes a day that I can't get into more mischief than Mellony, I'll cut my own throat.

Raisa's gaze fell on the silver tray just inside her door on which Magret left messages and mail and calling cards. Suitors had begun buzzing around like flies on a carcass as Raisa approached her sixteenth name day. On any given day there'd be five or six elaborate gifts of jewelry or flowers, mirrors and vanity sets, vases and works of art, plus a dozen engraved invitations and letters on embossed stationery, mostly proclamations of undying love and devotion, and proposals that ranged from bland to indecent.

Some of the gifts were too elaborate to accept. A pirate prince from across the Indio had sent a cunning model of the ship he proposed to build for her so she could sail away with him. The queen's secretary had answered on Raisa's behalf, politely declining.

Raisa kept the ship model, though. She liked to sail it on the pond in the garden.

Truth be told, Raisa had no intention of marrying anyone any time soon. Her mother was young—she would rule for many years yet, so there was no need to rush into the confinement of marriage.

If Raisa had her way, her wedding would be the culmination of an entire decade of wooing.

Which made her think of Micah. He would be at dinner. Her heart accelerated.

Centered on the wooing tray was a rather plain envelope. "Who's this from?" she asked, picking it up.

Magret shrugged. "I don't know, Your Highness. It was outside your door when I came back from the midday. Now sit so I can get you out of those boots." She said *those boots* in a decidedly disapproving way.

Raisa sat down in the chair by the door, still studying the envelope while Magret tugged at her boots. They left smears of mud and ash on the nurse's pristine white apron.

Raisa's name was written on the front of the note in a neat, upright hand—naggingly familiar. She tore it open and unfolded the page inside.

Raisa, I'm home. Come find me if you get this before dinner. I'll be in the usual place. Amon

"Amon's home!" Raisa cried, surging to her feet, one boot off and one on. She gripped Magret's elbows and danced her around the room, ignoring her outraged protests. She felt rather like a tugboat towing one of the big ships in Chalk Cliffs Harbor.

"In the name of the sainted Hanalea, *stop*, Your Highness," Magret said, struggling for dignity. Wrenching her arms free, she began pulling off Raisa's jacket.

"No!" Raisa said, twisting away. "Hang on, Magret, I need to go find Amon. I need to find out what he—"

Magret planted herself in front of the door. "You *need* to get into that bath and scrub off. If he sees you in this state, you'll scare him half to death."

"Magret!" Raisa protested. "Come on. It's just Amon. He doesn't care about—"

"Amon's kept this long, he'll keep a little while longer. You're expected at dinner in two hours and you smell like you just came out of the smoker."

Still grumbling, Raisa allowed herself to be stripped of the rest of her clothing and climbed into her bath. She had to admit, it felt wonderful. The hot water stung her many cuts and scrapes, but soothed and relaxed her aching muscles.

Magret dangled Raisa's charred shirt and leggings out at arm's length, wrinkling her nose. "These are going straight to Ragmarket," she declared.

"Please, Magret," Raisa protested, horrified. "You can't throw them away. They're the only comfortable clothes I own."

Scowling, Magret pitched them in the laundry basket.

It took all of the two hours for Magret to make Raisa what she called "presentable." Magret produced a new dress that she'd made over from one of Marianna's old ones. It was a pleasant surprise—less fussy than the dresses Marianna chose for Raisa, a simple fall of emerald silk that draped her body, cut low enough at the neck to be a bit daring.

Magret coaxed Raisa's still-damp hair into a coil and pinned it up on her head, then set her gold circlet on top. To finish, her nurse added Raisa's briar rose necklace—a gift from her father, Averill Lightfoot. Briar Rose was her clan name. He called her Briar Rose, he said, because of her beauty. And her many thorns.

When Raisa finally entered the dining room, it was already crowded. A string quartet tuned up in one corner, servers with trays circulated through the room, and the usual court grazers swarmed about a side table laden with cheeses, fruits, and wine.

She quickly scanned the room for Amon, though she didn't really expect to see him there. Unlikely that he'd be invited to mingle with the aristocracy.

Across the room, Raisa saw her grandmother, Elena Demonai, Matriarch of Demonai Camp. She stood with a small group of other clan, wearing the flowing, elaborately embroidered robes they reserved for special occasions.

She went and took her grandmother's hands, bowing her head over them in clan fashion.

"Good day, *Cennestre* Demonai," she said in Clan.

"Best to speak the lowland language here, granddaughter,"

Elena replied. "Lest the flatlanders think we're passing secrets."

"Have you heard anything of my father?" Raisa persisted, still in Clan. Annoying flatlanders was one of her few sources of entertainment these days.

"He'll be home soon," Elena said. "For your name day feast, if not before."

Her father had gone south on yet another trading expedition, crossing Arden to We'enhaven and beyond. Risky in wartime, but in wartime, trade goods brought high prices.

"I worry about him," Raisa said. "They say the fighting is fierce in the south."

Elena squeezed her hand. "Your father was a warrior before he was a trader," she said. "He knows how to take care of himself."

Take me back with you to Demonai, Raisa wanted to say. *I'm already tired of being here, displayed like a jewel in an ill-fitting setting.* But she only thanked her grandmother and turned away.

A dozen youngling courtiers had claimed space by the fireplace. Since Raisa's return, more and more of the nobility were sending their offspring to court, putting them under the nose of the princess heir, hoping to make—if not a marriage—connections that would benefit the family in the future.

Big-boned, gregarious Wil Mathis overflowed a chair by the hearth. The eighteen-year-old wizard heir to Fortress Rock, an estate along the Firehole River toward Chalk Cliffs, he was easygoing, unambitious, and a bit lazy, and so more charming than most of his kind. He preferred to spend his time hunting, dicing, playing at cards, and chatting up girls, avoiding the realm of politics.

Next to Wil was Adam Gryphon, who had parked his wheeled chair next to the fireplace. Adam was also heir to a powerful wizard house, but an accident in childhood had left his legs shriveled. He got about by using a wheeled chair or a pair of arm canes.

Raisa didn't know Adam very well. He'd been away at school at Oden's Ford for three years. Even when he was home, he seemed to prefer the company of books. His acid tongue drove off those who might otherwise pity him. His parents must have dragged him back to court for the season.

Raisa's cousins Jon and Melissa Hakkam were there, and Raisa's sister, Mellony, whose royal status gave her standing with the older crowd. The handsome, blond, vacant Klemath brothers, Kip and Keith, were stuffing down cheese, laughing loudly at nothing in particular. Their parents probably had hopes that one of the two would catch Raisa's eye. They'd been courting her with a clumsy enthusiasm, like a pair of sloppy-tongued golden retrievers.

"Could I bring you a glass of wine, Your Highness?" Keith asked.

"I'll bring you one too," Kip added, glaring at his brother. They bounded off.

As if she would marry anyone named Kip.

Micah leaned against the fireplace, flanked by his twin sister, Fiona, and surrounded by his usual coterie of admiring girls. Melissa and Mellony hung on his every word. Raisa had to admit, he'd cleaned up well—he wore a black silk coat and gray trousers that set off his falcon stoles. His hands were bandaged and he still looked rather pale against his mane of blue-black hair. As Raisa watched, he set an empty wineglass on a table and grabbed a full one from a passing server. Fiona leaned in and murmured something to him. Whatever it was, he didn't like it. He shook his head, scowling, and turned slightly away from her.

Both wizards, Fiona and Micah were like negative images of each other, each striking. They were the same height and shared the same lean bone structure, angular facial features, and acerbic wit. Fiona's hair was stark white, down to her eyelashes and eyebrows; even her eyes were a pale blue, like shadow on snow.

Fiona and Micah quarreled constantly, but cross one and you'd have both to contend with.

"Weren't you frightened when you saw the fire?" Missy asked Micah, her blue eyes wide and horrified. "I know I would have turned tail and run right back down the mountain."

Raisa struggled to keep from making a face or mimicking Missy's vapid demeanor.

A lady keeps critical thoughts to herself.

"*I* was frightened," Mellony put in, blushing. "But Micah came riding right into our midst and told us the fire was coming, that we should make a run for it. He was already burned from trying to put the fire out, but he wasn't scared at all."

Micah seemed uncharacteristically reluctant to talk about his exploits. "Well, good it came out all right in the end. Would anyone else like more wine?"

"Didn't Mellony say you came late to the hunt?" Missy said, putting her shoulders back to better display her oversized bosom. "How did you get between the queen and the fire?"

Good question, Raisa thought, amazed that Missy had come up with it. Keeping next to the wall, she sidled closer.

Micah seemed to think it was a good question too. He took a long swallow of wine, thinking about it. "Well, ah, we saw the fire from below, so we took a shortcut, hoping to catch them and . . ." Micah looked up and saw Raisa, taking full advantage of the distraction. "Here is Princess Raisa now," he said, sweeping down into an elegant bow.

Raisa extended her hand. Micah grasped it and raised it to his lips, then lifted his head and gazed into her eyes, sending a whisper of power through his fingers. She flinched and withdrew her hand. Young wizards sometimes leaked magic, but he smiled in a way that said he was showing off.

Raisa stepped on his foot and smiled at him in a way that said *that* wasn't an accident either.

Fiona glared at Raisa, somehow making herself even taller while delivering a chilly curtsy.

Well, all right, Raisa thought, feeling guilty. *Perhaps your brother's had a little too much wine. To be fair, he did save my life, he deserves to celebrate, and he's probably in some degree of pain.*

"Micah is being too modest," Raisa said, in a kind of backhanded apology. "The fire came on us like a downhill stampede. We were trapped in a narrow canyon with flames on all sides, and I thought for certain we would all burn to death. If not for Micah and his father and the Mander brothers, we would have. They put the fire out completely. It was amazing. They saved our lives."

"Oh, *Micah*," Missy exclaimed. She reached for his hands, recoiled at the sight of the bandages, then wound her arms around his neck and gazed up into his eyes. "You *are* a hero!"

Micah looked flustered enough to be charming, and untangled himself as soon as he could, shooting glances at Raisa.

Don't worry, she thought. *I'm not jealous. Only annoyed with Missy.*

"How do you suppose the fire started?" Missy asked, flicking her elaborate curls back into place. "It's been raining for weeks."

"Father thinks the clans might have had something to do with it," Micah said. "They're always keen on keeping people out of the mountains."

"*Wizards,*" Raisa said. "They're keen on keeping *wizards* out of the Spirits. But the clans would never set fire to Hanalea."

Micah inclined his head. "I stand corrected, Your Highness," he said. "You are familiar with their ways and I am not." He forced a smile. "It's a mystery, then."

"Well, I don't trust them," Missy declared, glancing about to locate the Demonai delegation before she continued. "They slip around like thieves, and they're always muttering to each other in that foreign language so you never know what they're saying. And everybody knows they steal babies and replace them with demons."

"Don't repeat nonsense, Melissa," Raisa snapped. "Children are fostered with the clans for their own good, to teach them the old ways. Besides, the clans were here first. If there's a foreign language spoken in the Fells, it's Valespeech."

"Of course, Your Highness," Missy said hastily. "I meant no offense. But Valespeech is a more civilized tongue. We use it at court," she added, as if that settled that.

The quartet had completed its warm-up, and now the first strains of real music floated over them.

"Would you care to dance, Your Highness?" Micah asked abruptly. Beyond him, the Klemaths were practically slapping their foreheads that they hadn't thought of it first.

Wil quickly offered his arm to Fiona. "Lady Bayar, it would be my honor."

Missy scowled, having been overlooked. She glanced around for other prospects.

Adam Gryphon smiled crookedly. "Would you care to dance, Lady Hakkam?" he said, making as if to swing his canes into position.

"Well—ah—perhaps I'll go and fetch some punch," Missy said, fleeing in the direction of the punch bowl.

Too bad Missy's disablity is between her ears, Raisa thought. She wanted to say something to Adam, but knew he'd come back with a cutting response.

Micah offered his arm, leading her to the small dance floor. She put one hand at his waist and cradled the bandaged hand carefully with the other.

They circled the floor, floating on the music. Raised at

court, Micah was an excellent dancer, despite his several glasses of wine and stomped-on foot. But then, he did everything relentlessly well.

"How are your hands?" Raisa asked. "Do they hurt very much?"

"They're all right." He seemed tense and unusually inarticulate.

"What happened this morning?" Raisa persisted. "Why were you so late?"

"Raider came up lame. We had to pull a shoe, and it took longer than expected."

"You must keep a dozen horses at court. You couldn't ride another?"

"Raider's my best hunter. Besides, like I said, it took longer than expected," he said.

"Your father was really hard on you today," Raisa said.

Micah grimaced. "My father is hard on me every day." And then, in the manner of someone who's intentionally changing the subject, he said, "That's a new dress, isn't it?" When she nodded, he added, "I like it. It's different from your other dresses."

Raisa glanced down at herself. Part of Micah's appeal was that he missed nothing. "Because it's not all layered with ruffles?"

"Hmmm." Micah pretended to think for a moment. "Perhaps that's it. Plus the color sets off your eyes. Tonight they're like pools in a forest glade, reflecting the leafy canopy overhead."

"Black sets off *your* eyes, Bayar," Raisa said sweetly. "They glitter like dying stars cast from the heavens, or twin coals from the bowels of the earth."

Micah stared at her a moment, then threw back his head and laughed. "You are impossible to flatter, Your Highness," he said. "I am helpless here."

"Just leave off. I was raised at court too, you know." She rested her head on his chest, feeling the heat of him through the wool, hearing the thud of his heart. They circled silently for a moment. "So you'll be going to Oden's Ford in the fall?"

Micah nodded, his smile fading. "I wish I could go now. They ought to send wizards at thirteen, like soldier pledges."

Micah would be attending Mystwerk House, the school for wizards at Oden's Ford. There were a half-dozen academies there, clustered on the banks of the Tamron River, on the border between Tamron and Arden.

There should be a school for queens in training, Raisa thought, where she could learn something more useful than table manners and pretty speech.

"The clans believe it's dangerous to put magic into the hands of young wizards," Raisa said.

Micah grimaced. "The clans should learn to relax a little. I know your father is clan, but I don't understand why they insist that everything remain the same. It's like we're all frozen in time, paying for an ancient crime that nobody else remembers."

Raisa tilted her head. "You *know* why. The clans healed the Breaking. The rules of the Naéming are intended to prevent it from ever happening again." She paused, then couldn't resist adding, "Didn't you learn that in school?"

Micah dismissed school with a wave of his hand. "There's too much to learn in a lifetime. Which is why they should give us our amulets at birth, so we can begin our training as soon as possible."

"They'll never do that because of the Demon King."

The song came to an end, and they drifted to a stop on the dance floor. Gripping her elbows, Micah looked down into her face. "What about the Demon King?" he said.

"Well. They say the Demon King was something of a prodigy," she said. "He took up wizardry—and dark magic— at a very young age. It destroyed his mind."

"Mmmm. That's what the *clans* say."

It was the argument they'd had a hundred times, packaged in different ways. "They tell those stories because it's the *truth*, Micah. Alger Waterlow was a madman. Anyone who could do what he did . . ."

Micah shook his head, a slight movement, his eyes fixed on hers. "What if it's made up?"

"Made *up*?" Now Raisa's voice rose and she had to make a conscious effort to lower it. "Don't tell me you've joined the Revisionists."

"Think what this story gets the clans, Raisa," Micah said, his voice low and urgent. "Wizards carrying around all this guilt, afraid to assert their inborn gifts. The clans controlling the objects that allow them to use their magical powers. The royal family, forced to dance to whatever tune they play."

"Of *course* the clans control amulets and talismans," Raisa said. "They're the ones who *make* them. It's the division of power between green magic and high magic that has kept us safe all these years."

Micah lowered his voice further. "Please, Raisa. Just listen a minute. Who knows if the Breaking ever actually happened? Or if wizards were the cause."

She glowered at him, and Micah rolled his eyes. "Never mind. Come on." Taking her elbow, he drew her into a windowed alcove overlooking the illuminated city.

Cradling her face in his bandaged hands, Micah kissed her, first lightly, and then with more intensity. Like usual, Micah was changing topics to something they could agree on. Most of their arguments ended this way.

Raisa's pulse accelerated, and her breath came quicker. It would be so easy to fall under his spell, and yet, she wasn't quite finished with the conversation.

Raisa gently pulled away from him, turned and stared out over the city. It sparkled below, perfect from a distance.

"Did you hear this theory about the Breaking from your father? Is that what the High Wizard thinks?"

"My father has nothing to do with this," Micah said. "I have ideas of my own, you know. He just . . ." He rested his hands on her shoulders and power sizzled through his fingers. "Raisa, I wish we could . . ."

He was interrupted by a rising clamor in the dining room. The band shifted smoothly into "The Way of the Queens." Raisa and Micah stepped to the doorway of the alcove in time to see Queen Marianna sweep the length of the room on Gavan Bayar's arm, dancers parting before them, sinking into curtsies and bows. Behind them came the Queen's Guard, resplendent in their Gray Wolf livery and led by Edon Byrne.

Raisa scowled at the sight of her mother processing arm in arm with the handsome master of the Wizard Council. She looked over and saw Elena Demonai watching, face stony with disapproval, and sighed. Lord Bayar might be a hero, but still. Tongues wagged well enough at court without encouragement.

The queen turned in a swirl of skirts and faced the room. She was dressed in champagne-colored silk that added highlights to her blond curls. Topazes glittered in her hair and on her neck, and honey-colored diamonds adorned her slender hands. She wore a lightweight diadem set with more topazes, pearls, and diamonds.

Queen Marianna smiled out at the assembly. "In a moment we'll go in to dinner. But first we shall recognize the heroes in the hall tonight. This day by their valor they saved the lineage of Fellsian queens." She extended her hand without looking, and someone placed a goblet into it. "Would Micah Bayar, Gavan Bayar, Miphis Mander, and Arkeda Mander come forward?"

Gavan Bayar turned gracefully and knelt in front of the queen. Micah hesitated a moment, hidden in the alcove, looking to either side as if he wished he could escape. Then he sighed and left Raisa to join his father. Arkeda and Miphis came and knelt as well.

Servers circulated through the crowd, distributing glasses to those who were without. Raisa accepted one and stood waiting.

"Today these wizards saved me, the princess heir, and the Princess Mellony from a disastrous wildfire through the use of extraordinary and accomplished magic. I therefore toast the unique and historic bond between the line of Fellsian queens and high wizardry that has long protected and sustained our realm in this time of war." The queen raised her glass, as did everyone else in the hall, and drank.

Mention Captain Byrne, Raisa mouthed to her mother, but Marianna did not.

"I would also like to welcome back to court a young man who has been like a son to us. After three years away, he has returned for the summer and will serve us on temporary assignment to the Queen's Guard." Queen Marianna smiled at the assembled soldiers, singling out one in particular. "Amon Byrne, come forward."

Raisa stared, amazed, as one of the tall soldiers stepped forward and knelt before the queen. Edon Byrne drew his sword and passed it to Marianna.

"Do you, Amon Byrne, swear to protect and defend the queen, princess heir, and all of Hanalea's descendants from our enemies, even to the loss of your life?"

"My blood is yours, Your Majesty," this strange, tall Amon said in an unfamiliar deep voice. "It would be my honor to spill it in defense of the royal line."

The queen tapped Amon on each broad shoulder with the flat of the blade. "Rise, Corporal Byrne, and join your captain."

The new corporal rose, bowed again, and backed away from the queen until he stood side by side with his father, who did not loose a smile.

Raisa stood transfixed, her hand at her throat. Amon's gray eyes were the same as she remembered, as was the straight black hair that flopped over his forehead. Much of the rest of him had been remade.

"Now," the queen said, "let's in to dinner."

Raisa had no chance to speak to Amon during dinner. She was seated at the head of the table, between Micah and his father. Arkeda and Miphis sat in positions of honor on either side of the queen, with Mellony on the far side, Fiona next to her. Also within speaking distance were the Demonais, and Harriman Vega, a wizard and court physician.

As captain of the Queen's Guard, Edon Byrne had a place near the foot of the table, but the Guard itself was stationed at the far end of the room, near the entrance to the ballroom. Raisa's eyes kept straying to Amon.

His face was thinner, the bone structure more prominent, any trace of baby fat worn away by his time at Oden's Ford. He had his father's intensity packaged in a rangier body, but he'd added a new layer of muscle in his chest and arms.

Now and again she saw flashes of the boy she remembered. He stood a bit self-consciously, back straight, one hand on the hilt of his sword. Once she caught him staring at her, but he looked away quickly when their eyes met, spots of color showing on his cheeks.

She felt flustered, disconcerted, almost angry. How could Amon have turned into this other person while he was away? If they did meet, what could she possibly say to him? *Sweet Leeza's teeth, you're tall?*

"Your Highness?" The words were spoken rather loudly almost in her ear, and Raisa jumped and turned toward Micah Bayar. "You've scarcely touched your food, and I feel like I'm talking to myself," he said as dessert was set before them. There was an edge to his voice that said he was irritated.

"I'm sorry," Raisa said. "I'm afraid I'm a little distracted. It's been a long day, and I'm tired." She poked at her pastry, wishing she were young again and could be dismissed from the table early.

"It's no wonder you're weary, Your Highness, after the scare this morning," Lord Bayar said, smiling. "Perhaps a walk in the garden after dinner would restore you. Micah would be happy to accompany you."

"Oh!" Raisa said. "Well. That's very kind of you to think of me, Lord Bayar, but I really . . ."

Micah leaned in closer, speaking into Raisa's ear so only she could hear. "Some of us are meeting later in the card room in the east wing," he murmured. "Should be entertaining. Please come." His hot hand closed over hers, pressing it to the table. A promise.

"What?" Raisa said distractedly.

Micah's breath hissed through his teeth. "You keep staring at the door. Are you that eager to leave? Or is it someone in particular you're looking at?"

Now Raisa was irritated. "I'll thank you to mind your own business, sul'Bayar. I'll look wherever I like."

"Of course." Micah released her hand and jammed his fork into his dessert. "It's rude is all I'm saying."

"Micah!" Lord Bayar glared at his son. "Apologize to the princess heir."

"Sorry," Micah said, staring straight ahead, a muscle in his jaw working. "Please forgive me, Your Highness."

Raisa felt hemmed in by wizards, oppressed by the tension between Micah and his father. It was quite wearing.

When dinner ended, the band reassembled. There would be dancing into the small hours, relentless drinking and flirting, underscored by a series of lame entertainments. In the card room awaited the dance of the would-be suitors. It was time to escape.

She pressed the back of her hand against her forehead. "I'm off to bed," she said. "I've a nasty headache." She pushed back her chair. When Micah and Lord Bayar made as if to rise, she said, "Please, sit. I'd like to slip out quietly."

"Are you sure you're all right?" Micah asked, glancing at his father, then back at Raisa. "Why don't I escort you back to your rooms?"

As if she needed help to find her way, but they'd often used that excuse to find time alone.

She stood. "No. You're the guests of honor. Her Majesty will be disappointed if you leave. Thank you again for every-thing."

Queen Marianna was looking at her, one eyebrow raised in inquiry. Raisa shrugged and again touched her forehead, the universal sign for headache. The queen nodded, blew her a kiss, and turned back to Miphis, who still looked thrilled and amazed to be sitting next to the queen.

Raisa walked the length of the dining room to the door. Hesitating, she looked back and saw the Demonais watching, a faint smile on Elena's face.

As she passed between Amon and his fellow soldier, she did not look to the left or right, but muttered, "The usual place, soon as you're able."

CHAPTER FIVE

OLD STORIES

Han put off leaving Marisa Pines as long as possible. It was late morning the next day when he said his good-byes and descended Hanalea, following the Dyrnnewater toward the Vale.

He'd sold or traded everything but the worthless snagwort, which would have to wait for the Flatlander Market. Coins jingled in his purse, and his bag bulged with trade goods—fabric and leatherwork he could sell at a profit, pouches of clan remedies, plus enough smoked venison to make a meal. And the amulet, hidden at the bottom.

He still mourned the deer he might have taken, but all in all, he'd done well for this early in the season.

He hoped Mam would agree.

On the way down the mountain, he stopped off at several solitary cabins to see if there was mail to go or goods to be carried down to market or orders for supplies that he would carry up the next time. Many of the cabin dwellers were clan who preferred life away from the bustle of the camps. There were also former flatlanders who liked solitude or had reason to avoid the notice of the queen's heavy-handed guard. Han earned a little money by carrying news and mail up and down the mountains and acting as agent for those highlanders who didn't care to visit the Vale.

Lucius Frowsley was one of those. His cabin stood where Old Woman Creek poured into the Dyrnnewater. He'd lived on the mountain so long, he looked like a piece broken off of it, with his craggy face and the clothes that draped his skinny body like juniper on a hillside. His eyes were opaque and cloudy as a winter sky—he'd been blinded as a young man.

Despite his blindness, the old man owned the most productive still in the Spirit Mountains.

Though Lucius could navigate the trails and ledges of the high country like a goat, he never went to Fellsmarch if he had a choice. So Han carried orders and containers and money up from the Vale, and product down. The containers were full when he carried them downhill and light and empty when he carried them up.

The best part: Lucius had books—not as many as in the temple library, but more books than any one man had a right to. He kept them locked in a trunk to protect them from the weather. What a blind man needed with a library, Han couldn't say, but the old man encouraged him to take full advantage, and he did. Some days he staggered down the mountain with half his weight in books.

That was another mystery—Han should have read them all

twice over by now. But Lucius always seemed to have new ones.

Lucius was cranky and profane and maybe siphoned off a little too much of his own product. But he was fair to Han, and told the truth, and always paid on time, which was rare. No one had dared steal from Cuffs Alister, streetlord of Ragmarket. But since he'd left the life, Han had been cheated more times than he cared to remember.

Lucius was also a nonjudgmental source of information. He knew everything, and, unlike Mam, he'd answer any question without a lecture.

The hillside cabin was empty, as was the distillery shack behind, but Han knew where to look. He found Lucius fishing in Old Woman Creek, which he did daily three seasons of the year. It was an excuse to sit and doze on the creek bank and sip from the bottle he always kept at hand. His dog, a rough-coated shepherd named Dog, sprawled by his feet.

As Han walked up the creek bed toward him, Lucius dropped his fishing pole and jerked around as if startled. The old man raised his hands as if for protection, his face pale and frightened, his blighted eyes wide under his wiry brows.

"Who's there?" he demanded, sleeves flapping around skinny arms. Like usual, he was dressed in mismatched clan castoffs and Ragmarket finds. Being blind, he wasn't fussy about color.

"Hey, Lucius," Han called. "It's just me. Han."

Dog raised his head and woofed approvingly, then rested

his head on his paws, twitching his ears to drive off flies.

Lucius's hands came down, though he still looked wary. "Boy!" he said. Lucius always called him *boy*. "You oughtn't to sneak up on folks that way."

Han rolled his eyes. He'd come along the water, same as always. Everybody was acting strange today.

Han squatted next to Lucius, touching his shoulder so he'd know where he was, and the old man started violently.

"Catching anything?" Han asked, beginning to feel aggravated.

Lucius squinted his rheumy blue eyes like it was a hard question, then reached down and hauled a clan-woven fish basket out of the creek. "Catched all of four, so far."

"Those fish for sale?" Han asked. "I can get you a good price at the market."

Lucius considered this a moment. "Nope. Going to eat these fish m'self."

Han settled himself back against a tree and extended his long legs in their flatland breeches. "Need anything to go with?" he asked, patting his backpack. "I have dried peppers and Tamron spice."

Lucius snorted. "Fish will do me fine, boy."

"Anything for Fellsmarch?" Han asked.

Lucius nodded. "It's set aside in the dog run."

Their business concluded, Han stared out at the rocks pricking the surface of the creek. Lucius still seemed jittery and unsettled. He kept tilting his head this way and that, as if to pick up a scent or a faint sound on the breeze. "You got your cuffs on, boy?" he asked abruptly.

"What do you think?" Han muttered. Like he could get them off.

Lucius seized Han's arm and dragged back his sleeve, fingering the silver band as if to read the runes by touch. The old man grunted and released Han's arm, still muttering to himself.

"What's with you?" Han demanded, yanking at his sleeves.

"I smell hex magic," Lucius said, in typically incomprehensible Frowsley fashion.

Han thought of the amulet in his carry bag, but decided there was no way Lucius could know it was in there. "What do *you* know about magic?"

"A little." Lucius rubbed his nose with his forefinger. "Not enough and too much."

Han tried again. "What do you know about wizards, then?"

Lucius sat motionless for a long moment. "Why do you ask?"

Han stared at him. Most adults answered questions with questions, but not Lucius.

When Han didn't answer immediately, the old man clamped his hand down on Han's shoulder. "Why do you ask?" Lucius repeated fiercely.

"Ow. Hey, take it easy," Han said, and Lucius let go. "Dancer and I had a run-in with some wizards up on Hanalea," Han said, rubbing his shoulder. He told Lucius what had happened.

"Bayar, you say?" Lucius scowled and found his fishing pole again. *"Thea's bloody, bloody bones."*

Lucius had been born on the mountain known as Thea, spiritual home of that legendary queen of the Fells. So he favored Thea when it came to swearing, even though most swore by Hanalea.

Han asked him about it once, and Lucius told him that *Hanalea* was too powerful a word to be flinging around.

"Do you know him?" Han asked.

Lucius nodded. "Know *of* him. His father more so. Gavan Bayar. He's the High Wizard, you know. Heart as cold as the Dyrnnewater. Ambitious too. You don't want to get in his way."

Micah Bayar had mentioned his father's high office, like bluebloods always did. "What else could he want?" Han asked. "Besides being High Wizard?"

"Well." Lucius lifted the tip of his pole, trying the line. "Fellow like Bayar, he's never satisfied. I'm guessing he wants to be High Wizard without all the tethers and restrictions put in place by the Naéming. Some say he wants the queen as well."

Han was confused. "He wants the queen? She already has a consort, doesn't she? Somebody from Demonai?"

Lucius wheezed with laughter. "For a street rat, you got no idea what's going on, do you?" He shook his gray head in amazement. "You got to keep your ear to the ground and your nose in the wind if you want to survive in these times."

Han couldn't picture how that physical feat could be accomplished. He could never figure out how Lucius knew everything that was going on, when he stayed up on the mountain all the time. It was a mystery.

Lucius's laughter finally wore out, and he wiped tears from his eyes. "Averill Demonai is Queen Marianna's consort. But he's a trader, and traders travel a lot. Spends too much time away for his own good, if you ask me. But nobody does."

Han struggled to control his impatience. All this talk of politics was boring, and had nothing to do with him. "About wizards," he prodded Lucius. "How do they get magic?"

"It's in their blood," Lucius said, stroking Dog's head. "It's like they get the raw talent, but they ain't really powerful until they study up and learn to store and control it with an amulet. In fact, they're dangersome until then, like a colt that ain't well broke and don't know its own strength."

Han thought of Micah Bayar, face black with anger, gripping his fancy jinxpiece and muttering charms. "Why? Do they have to say spells or something to make it work?"

"That's part of the learning up," Lucius said, nodding. "That Bayar, he's from Aerie House. Maybe the most powerful wizard family there is, since the fall of the Waterlows."

"Who are the Waterlows?" Han asked. "I never heard of them."

"Never mind. That house died out years ago." Lucius yanked up the tip of his fishing pole, felt his way down the line to the lure, then shook his head. "Guess they've stopped biting," he said. "Maybe it's time to pack it in."

"*Lucius,*" Han persisted. He knew from experience that things people didn't want to tell you were likely to be the most interesting. "Who were the Waterlows? Why did they fall?"

"Boy, you can pester a body near to death." Lucius grabbed up his bottle and took a swig, then wiped his mouth with a grimy sleeve. "It all happened a thousant years ago and it don't matter anymore," he said. When Han said nothing, Lucius snorted. "Y'know, most boys your age ain't interested in digging up old bones and old stories."

Han still said nothing.

Lucius released a gusty sigh and nodded, as if coming to a decision. "So a thousand years ago there was this powerful wizard house. Named Waterlow House. Signia was a raven and wizard crest was a twined serpent."

Han blinked at him, then dug in his bag, unearthing the parcel containing the serpent amulet he'd taken from the jinxflinger on Hanalea. He weighed it in his hand, recalling what Bayar had said. *If you even touch it, you'll be incinerated.*

Lucius turned his sightless eyes on Han. "What you got there, boy?" he demanded, extending his hand as if he could feel the heat of it too. "Give it over."

Han hesitated. "I don't know if I . . ."

"Give it here, boy." The old man's voice rang out, startlingly loud and compelling. It was like Lucius had been possessed by some other, irresistible being.

Han pressed the leather bundle into Lucius's hand. "Be careful, Lucius. It might . . ."

Lucius ripped open the leather wrapping and pulled free the jinxpiece.

Han leaned away, tensing against any possible explosion. None came.

Lucius ran his weather-beaten hands over the amulet, and

his lined face went slack with shock. "Where did you get this?" he whispered.

"Bayar had it." Han hesitated, unsure how much to share. "He tried to use it to jinx Dancer. I took it from him. I don't think he was supposed to have it."

Lucius laughed, a harsh barking sound. "Sweet Thea's kiss. I would guess not."

"Why? What is it?"

Lucius kept stroking the carving with his thick fingers as if he couldn't believe what his senses were telling him. "It's from the Waterlows, all right. Their treasury of magical artifacts was legendary. An armory, more like. No one ever knew what happened to it after the Breaking." The purple vein over his right eye pulsed dangerously. "I'll wager that snake Micah had no idea what he had." He nodded once. "And now you have it." Lucius extended the amulet toward Han. When Han hesitated, Lucius said impatiently, "Take it, boy. It won't bite."

Han took it warily, weighing it in his palm. It felt pleasantly heavy and warm, vibrating with a power Han could feel in his breastbone and in the cuffs at his wrists.

Warring emotions tracked across the old man's face, finally fading to an expression of alarm. Once again he gripped Han's arm, his long nails biting into Han's flesh. "Does Bayar know who you are, boy? Does he know you have this?"

Han shrugged uneasily. "I didn't tell him my name, if that's what you mean." When Lucius didn't look reassured, he added, "Look. I'll give it back, if it's that important. All right?"

Lucius let go of his arm and drummed his fingers on his

thighs, furiously thinking. "No," he said finally. "Don't give it back. It's too late for that. Keep it hid. Keep it safe. Better Aerie House don't have it." He chuckled bitterly. "Stay out of their way, the Bayars."

Han had never seen a Bayar before now, and doubted he would again unless Micah returned to Hanalea. Hopefully he wouldn't. "Fine," he said, rewrapping the necklace and stowing it back in his bag. What good was asking questions if you didn't understand a word of the answers? "You were saying? About the Waterlows?"

"If you want to hear a story, don't interrupt." Lucius rubbed his bristled jaw and returned to his story voice. "The wizards came from the Northern Isles. They landed on the east coast and conquered the rest of the Seven Realms with their high magic. Clan magic couldn't hold against it. It's green magic, subtle stuff, not good in a fight. Strongest magic they is, but made for healing, not destroying. Clan has it because they in harmony with nature. The matriarchs and the amulet-makers, they've learned how to draw on it.

"These wizards chose to live in the Vale. They married theirselfs to the blooded queens and reined as kings, but they wasn't bound to the queens the way they are today. The succession still came through the true female line. The trouble started during the reign of Hanalea, the most beautiful woman who ever lived."

Han nodded. Lucius had finally strayed onto familiar ground.

"Hanalea was handfasted to a wizard name of Kinley Bayar, of Aerie House, which was powerful then as now.

Bayar was set to be king. But there was this young wizard, name of Alger, heir to Waterlow House. He fell hard for Hanalea—that wasn't unusual. Only problem was, Alger was terrible powerful and used to getting what he wanted. He saw no reason why he shouldn't have Hanalea all to hisself.

"The council said no, and Aerie House especially said no. But Hanalea, she had a mind of her own. She disliked Bayar, who was an old man to her, cold and heartless as any snake. And she fancied young Alger, who was as handsome as she was beautiful. She run off with him, and they holed up in the Spirits with his allies—an army of wizards from Waterlow House and some of his friends—the best and brightest wizards of a generation.

"Alger proclaimed himself king and married Hanalea. The council couldn't put up with that, so the other wizard houses marched on Waterlow and laid siege to their hold. Anyone could see it was a lost cause, but not this boy. He was a longtime student of dark magic, and he thought he could conjure a spell that would end the siege and scare the council off.

"Hanalea tried to talk him out of it. She wanted to give herself up to Aerie House, but he was headstrong and wouldn't listen." Lucius smiled sadly. "Boy was a fool for love. Too much power and too little knowledge. They was together only three months."

Han shifted impatiently. Stories about Hanalea and her many suitors were like lengths of old cloth, so worn down by the telling, you couldn't tell one from another or even see the individual threads anymore.

Lucius stared into space, his milky blue eyes like painted-over windows that hid what lay within. Han was good at reading people—he had to be—but he could never read Lucius.

"So? What happened?" Han asked dutifully.

Lucius flinched, as if he'd forgotten Han was there. "They killed him, a'course. After. They took him to Aerie House and tortured him for days and forced that young girl to listen to his screams. But it was too late. The damage was done."

Han blinked, caught by surprise. "What damage? What are you talking about?"

Lucius raised bushy eyebrows. "The Breaking, a'course. You've heard of that?" he asked sarcastically.

"I've *heard* of the Breaking," Han said irritably. "What's that got to . . ." His voice trailed off and he stared at Lucius, wondering if the old man had sipped a little too much product. "Hold on. You're talking about the *Demon King*?" He whispered the last two words, which people tended to do, and resisted the urge to make a sign against evil.

"His name was Alger," Lucius said softly, his whole body slumping into a puddle of wrinkled skin and drab cloth.

The sun went behind a cloud, and it was suddenly cold on the creek bank. Han shivered and drew his jacket closer around him.

Lucius's unfortunate Alger Waterlow was the Demon King? Not possible.

The Demon King was the monster in every scary story. The devil you wouldn't name for fear of calling him to you.

The one that waited in the dark down a crooked street for bad children to come his way.

"That's not true!" Han burst out, fueled by righteous indignation and a lifetime of stories. "The Demon King stole Hanalea away on her wedding night. He chained her in his dungeon when she refused him. He tortured her with dark sorcery, trying to win her heart. When she resisted, he broke the world."

"He was a boy," Lucius muttered, fumbling for his flask. "They were in love."

"He was a monster," Han countered, shying a rock into the creek. "She destroyed him." He'd seen the frieze in the temple at Fellsmarch. It was called *The Triumph of Hanalea* and consisted of a series of scenes: Hanalea in chains, defying the Demon King. Hanalea, beautiful and terrible, holding the world together with green magic as the Demon King tried to shatter it. Hanalea standing over the Demon King's lifeless body, a sword in her hand.

If it's carved in stone, it has to be true, Han thought.

"They killed him," Lucius said. "And that released a destructive power like the world has never known, before or since." He sighed, shaking his head, as if it hadn't been the Demon King's fault at all.

"Afterward, the wizards meant to marry Hanalea off to Kinley Bayar." The old man sat up straighter, his eyes oddly clear and focused. His usually quavery voice rang out like a temple orator's, and his highland accent fell away. "But they had their hands full. The world was breaking, crumbling into chaos. Earthquakes shook their castles down. Flames erupted from the ground. The oceans boiled away and forests turned to ash. Night fell and stayed for months, lit only by the fires that burned day and night. The air was too thick to breathe. Nothing they conjured would stop it. Finally they had to turn to the clans for help."

Disappointment flamed within Han. How had they strayed so far afield from his original question about wizardry? He'd asked a serious question, and been repaid with this dreamer's tale. He'd wasted half the morning on the creek bank, the unwilling victim of an old man's fantasies. Now Mam would skin him alive for being so late.

"Thanks for the story and all," Han said, "but I've got to go. He scrambled to his feet and slid his backpack over one shoulder. "I'll pick up the bottles at the dog run."

"Sit, boy!" Lucius commanded. "You got this story started, now you got to hear me out."

Fuming, Han settled back on the creek bank. He'd never signed on for a monologue.

When Lucius was satisfied he'd held his audience, he continued. "The clans recognized the lineage of queens, so Hanalea acted as go-between. Think of what that must've been like. Negotiating with the clans on behalf of your sweetheart's murderers." Lucius smiled sadly. "But Hanalea had grown up. She was strong and smart as well as beautiful. She reclaimed the power of the Gray Wolf line. What grew out of those talks was the Naéming."

Lucius ticked off the tenets of the Naéming on his gnarled fingers. "In exchange for healing the world, the clans put wizards on a short leash. High magic and wizards were forbidden in the Spirits. They're confined to the Vale and the flatlands. The clan speakers have temples in Fellsmarch, and the queens got to go to temple once a week to learn the true faith. The Wizard Council chooses the most powerful wizard in the Fells as High Wizard and head of the council, but he is magically bound to the land and the queen, and ruled by her. The queens are fostered in the camps as children." Lucius smiled faintly. "And wizards ain't allowed to marry our queens anymore, because that gives them too much power."

"Hanalea agreed to that?" Han said. Guess they put the queen on a short leash too, he thought.

Lucius nodded, as if he'd read Han's mind. "The queen of the Fells is both the most powerful and the least free person in the entire queendom. She is a slave to duty once she comes of age."

"But she's the *queen*," Han said. "Can't she do whatever she wants?"

"Hanalea had learned the price of following her heart," Lucius said. He paused, his face settling into sorrowful folds. "So she bent her knee for the greater good, and married somebody she didn't love."

Han frowned. The stories always ended with the destruction of the Demon King and the triumph of Hanalea. "So, who did she marry, then? Bayar was a wizard, so . . . ?"

Lucius shook his head. "Poor Kinley Bayar met with an accident soon after the Breaking. She married somebody else." After the rich details of the story so far, he seemed rather sketchy on that point.

Han stood again, then hesitated, shifting from one foot to

the other, compelled to say something. "You know, Lucius, I'm practically grown. I'm too old for fairy stories."

For a long moment the old man didn't respond. "Don't ask for the truth, boy, unless you're ready to hear it," Lucius said, staring sightlessly out at Old Woman Creek. "Just remember what I said. Keep the amulet hid, and stay out of the way of the Bayars. They got too much power as it is. If they find out you have it, they'll kill you for it."

CHAPTER SIX

FELLSMARCH

The city of Fellsmarch nestled at the edge of the Vale, a fertile valley where the Dyrnnewater shouldered its way between the rocky cliffs of Hanalea and the rippling skirts of Alyssa, her sister peak. The Spirit-dwelling clan often referred to residents of the Vale as flatlanders. The Valefolk in turn looked down on the city of Delphi and the plains of Arden to the south.

The Vale gleamed like an emerald set high in the mountains—protected by the frowning peaks said to be the dwelling places of long-dead upland queens. It was warmed year-round by thermal springs that bubbled under the ground and broke through fissures in the earth.

True flatlanders—citizens of Tamron and the kingdom of Arden beyond Southgate—whispered that the Spirit Mountains were haunted by demons and witches and dragons and other fearsome things—that the very ground was poison to any invader.

Highlanders did nothing to dispel this notion.

Han's teacher, Jemson, claimed that before the coming of the wizards and the breaking of the world, the Seven Realms were one great queendom ruled from Fellsmarch. Grain from Arden and Bruinswallow and Tamron filled her bread baskets. Fish from the coasts, and game from the Spirits, and gems and minerals from the mountains added to her prosperity. The queen and her court were patrons of the arts, and the city built music halls, libraries, temples, and theaters all over the queendom.

Though it had fallen on hard times in recent years, the city of Fellsmarch still hung raggedly on the bones of its glorious past. It was studded with elaborate buildings that predated the Breaking. Fellsmarch Castle had somehow escaped the widespread destruction, as had the temples of the speakers and other public buildings.

So when Han rounded the last curve of the Spirit Trail and looked down on the city of his birth, an urban forest of temple spires and gold-leafed domes greeted him, gleaming in the last rays of the dying sun. He couldn't help thinking it looked better from a distance.

Lording over all was Fellsmarch Castle, with its soaring towers, a monument of marble and stone. It stood isolated, surrounded by the Dyrnnewater, untouchable as those who lived within its walls.

The City of Light, it was called, despite its long winter nights. There was even a period of time, around solstice, that the sun never rose at all. But on every other day, the sun flamed over Eastgate in the morning and kindled Westgate at the end of the day.

The Spirit Trail snaked down into the city and emptied into the first of a series of squares, the legacy of some long-ago royal architect. Connecting the squares was the Way of the Queens, the broad boulevard that ran the length of the city and ended at Fellsmarch Castle.

Han did not follow the Way of the Queens. Like it or not, he had business in Southbridge. He turned off into a series of ever-narrowing streets, burrowing deeply into a part of the city the queen never traveled to. As he left the Way behind, the buildings grew shabbier. People swarmed the streets, pinch-faced and wary-looking, prey and predators. Garbage moldered in the gutters and spilled out of bins.

The air reeked with the mingled stinks of cooking cabbage, wood smoke, privies and slop jars dumped into the street. It would be worse come summer, when the heat thickened the air into a dangerous soup that gave babies the croup and set old people coughing up blood.

At Southbridge Market, Han managed to unload the snagwort for a decent price, considering it was worthless. He could've sold it at Ragmarket, but didn't want to risk it so close to home, where someone might remember him.

Leaving the market, he put on his street face and strode quickly and purposefully past the fancy girls and grifters and street-corner thugs that would be on you at any sign of weakness or fear. "Hey, boy," a woman called, and he ignored her, as he ignored the glittery nobleman who tried to entice him into an alley.

Southbridge was the infection that festered under the seemingly healthy skin of the city. You didn't go there at night unless you were big and well armed, and surrounded by big, well-armed friends. But daytime was safe if you used your head and kept aware of your surroundings. He wanted to clear Southbridge before it got dark.

To be fair, some might call Han's own neighborhood a dangersome place. But in Ragmarket he knew who to watch out for and where they stayed. He only needed a few steps on anyone to disappear into the labyrinth of streets and alleys he knew so well. No one would find him in Ragmarket if he didn't want to be found.

His destination was The Keg and Crown, a decrepit tavern that clung like a mussel to the river's edge. The bank underneath had been undercut by centuries of spring floods, and it always seemed in imminent danger of tipping into the river. His timing was good—the common room was just filling up with the evening trade. He'd be out of the way before things got too rowdy.

Han handed Lucius's bottles to Matieu, the tavern keeper, and received a heavy purse in return.

Matieu stowed the bottles in the back bar, out of reach of his more aggressive customers. "Is that all you have? I'll have this lot sold in a day. Goes down smooth as water, it does."

"Have a heart. I can only carry so much, you know," Han said, pulling a pitiful face and working his aching shoulders with his fingers.

Every tavern in Fellsmarch clamored for Lucius's trade. Lucius could triple his production and sell it all, but he chose not to.

Matieu eyed him speculatively, then groped under his massive belly for his purse. Extracting a coin, he pressed it into

Han's hand, closing his fingers over it. A princess coin, by the shape and weight of it, called a "girlie" on the street. "Maybe you could speak to him. Convince him to send more bottles my way."

"Well, I could *try*, but he has a lot of long-standing customers, you know . . ." Han shrugged his shoulders. He'd spotted a plate of meat buns on the sideboard. His sister, Mari, loved meat buns. "Uh . . . Matieu. Got any plans for those buns?"

Han left The Keg and Crown whistling, a girlie richer, with four pork buns wrapped in a napkin. It was shaping up to be a good day after all.

He turned down Brickmaker's Alley, heading for the bridge over the Dyrnnewater that would take him into Ragmarket. He was nearly through when the light died in the passageway, as if a cloud had passed before the sun.

He looked ahead to see that the exit from the alley was now corked with two bodies.

A familiar voice reverberated off the stone buildings to either side. "Well, now, what have we here? A *Ragger* on our turf?"

Bones. It was Shiv Connor and his Southies.

Han spun around, meaning to beat it back the way he came, and found two more grinning Southies blocking his escape. This meeting wasn't random, then. They'd been laying for him, had chosen this place on purpose.

There were six Southies altogether, four boys and two girlies, ranging in age from a year or two younger than Han to a year older. He'd have no room to maneuver in the narrow alleyway, no way to protect his back. It was a mark of respect, recognition of his name in Southbridge.

That was one way to look at it.

In the old days, he'd have had his seconds with him. He'd never have allowed himself to get in a fix like this.

He thought of saying he wasn't with the Raggers anymore, but that would just mark him as an easy victim, someone without protection or turf of his own.

Han's hand found the hilt of his knife and he pulled it free, palming it, though he knew it would do him no good. If he was stripped of his purse and badly beaten, that'd be a lucky outcome.

Han put his back to the alley wall. "Just passing through," he said, lifting his chin, feigning a confidence he didn't feel. "Meaning no disrespect."

"Yeah? Well, I mark it different, Cuffs." Shiv and his gang formed a loose semicircle around Han. The streetlord was redheaded and blue-eyed, his face pale and beardless as a fancy girl's, marked only by the purple gang symbol on his right cheek and an old knife scar that dragged his left eye down at the corner.

Shiv wasn't big, and he was no older than Han. He ruled by virtue of his skill with a blade and his willingness to cut your heart out while you slept. Or any other time. A complete lack of a conscience made him powerful.

Shiv's blade glittered in the light that leaked from the street. His hands were scarred; he'd been badged as a thief by the bluejackets before he'd smartened up. He was the best blade man in Southbridge, and the only one better in

Ragmarket was a girlie—Cat Tyburn—who'd replaced Han as streetlord of the Raggers.

"You been doing business in Southbridge, and we want a whack of the takings. You've been told," Shiv said. The rest of the Southies jostled forward, grinning.

"Look, I'm not the bag man," Han said, falling into his old patter flash. "Who'd trust me with that kind of plate? I just deliver. They settle up on their own."

"Product, then," Shiv said, and the other Southies nodded enthusiastically. Like Shiv would be sharing.

Han kept his eyes on Shiv's blade, adjusting his stance accordingly. "Lucius won't pay a tariff or a dawb. And if I short anybody, I'm gone."

"Fine by me," Shiv said, grinning. "He'll need somebody to take over. No reason it can't be us."

Oh yeah? Han thought. Lucius is particular about who he partners with. But now wasn't the time to say it. "All right," he said grudgingly, as if giving in. "Let me talk to him and I'll see what we can work out."

Shiv smiled. "Smart boy," he said.

That must've been some sort of signal, because suddenly they were all over him. Shiv's blade slashed up toward Han's face, and when he parried that, those on either side seized his arms, slamming his wrist against the wall until he dropped his knife. Then an older boy, a southern islander, took to smashing Han's head against the wall, and Han knew he'd be done, maybe for good, if the boy kept that up. So he went limp, dragging him to the ground. Shiv kicked him hard in the ribs and somebody else punched him in the face. Nasty but not deadly.

Finally he was yanked upright by the arms and held there while Shiv patted him down. Han resisted the temptation to spit in his face or kick him where it counted. He still hoped to survive the day.

"Where's your stash?" Shiv demanded, turning out Han's pockets. "Where's all those diamonds and rubies and gold pieces everybody talks about?"

It would do no good to tell Shiv that the legendary stash never existed, save in street tales. "It's gone," Han said. "Spent, stolen, and given out in shares. I got nothing."

"You got these." Shiv scraped back Han's sleeves, exposing the silver cuffs. "I heard you was a fancy boy, Cuffs." Seizing Han's right forearm, Shiv yanked at the bracelet, practically dislocating Han's wrist. Furious, the gang leader pressed the tip of his knife into Han's throat, and Han felt blood trickling under his shirt. "Take 'em off."

The cuffs had been Han's trademark during his time as streetlord of the Raggers. Shiv wanted them as trophy.

"They don't come off," Han said, knowing with a numbing certainty that he was about to die.

"No?" Shiv breathed, his face inches from Han's, alive with anticipation, tears leaking from his damaged left eye. "That's a shame. I'll take off your hands, then, and see if they'll slide over the stumps." He looked around at his audience, and the other Southies laughed in a ragged sort of way. "But don't worry, Stumps. We'll give you begging rights this side of the bridge. For a cut of the takings, that is." His laughter was shrill and slightly mad, like an out-of-tune song.

Shiv withdrew his knife from Han's throat and continued

the search, giving him time to think about it. He found Han's purse and cut it free, taking a little skin with it. Stuffing the swag under his shirt, he grabbed Han's carry bag and began sorting through it, tossing his trade goods on the ground. Han's spirits sank even lower. There was no way Shiv would overlook Matieu's purse. And no way Han could make up that kind of money.

It wouldn't be his problem after he bled to death.

But it wasn't Matieu's purse that Shiv pulled out of the bag. It was Bayar's amulet in its leather wrapping.

"What you got here, Cuffs?" Shiv asked, his eyes alight with interest. "Something pricy, I hope?" He unfolded the leather and poked it with his finger.

Green light rippled through the alleyway, burning Han's eyes, temporarily blinding him. With an ear-splitting blast, Shiv and the Southies were flung back against the opposite wall like rag dolls, smacking the stone with a solid thud. Han went down hard, ears ringing.

He rolled to his knees. The amulet, apparently undamaged, lay on the ground just in front of him, still emitting an eerie green glow. After a moment's hesitation, Han dropped the leather wrapping over it and slid it back into his carry bag.

As he scrambled to his feet, he heard shouted orders and boots pounding over the cobblestones at the Southie end of the alley. He looked back. A clot of blue-jacketed soldiers jammed the entryway. The Queen's Guard. Han had a history with the Guard. Time to be gone.

He glanced at Shiv, who had heaved himself upright, shaking his head dazedly, surrounded by his cronies. No way to get his own purse back, but he still had Matieu's, and the Guard might slow the Southies down. It was a chance to come away alive. He'd take it.

Han sprinted down the alley, away from the guard and toward the river. Behind him, he could hear screamed threats and orders to halt. He thought about taking refuge in Southbridge Temple at the west end of the bridge, but decided he'd better try and get clean away. He cleared the alley, ran past the temple close, fought his way through the line for the bridge, and pounded his way across. He didn't stop running until he was well into Ragger turf. Then he took a circuitous route, careful to make sure no one was following.

Finally he turned onto Cobble Street, limping over the uneven pavers. Now that he felt safe, he surveyed the damage. He hurt all over. The skin stretched tight over the right side of his face said it was swelling, and he could scarcely see out of his right eye. A sharp pain in his side suggested a rib was broken. He carefully explored the back of his head with his fingers. His hair was matted with blood, and there was a goose egg–sized lump rising.

Could be worse, he told himself. Ribs could be wrapped, at least, and nothing else seemed to be broken. There was no money for doctors, so anything broken would stay broken, or heal any way it pleased. That's how it worked in Ragmarket. Unless Han was fit enough to climb back up Hanalea and put himself in Willo's hands.

He stopped at the well at the end of the street and sluiced water over his head, rinsing off the blood as best he could and combing his hair down with his fingers. He didn't want to scare Mari.

All the while, his memory tiptoed around what had happened in Brickmaker's Alley. Maybe he was addled. He'd hit his head, after all. He could swear he'd seen Shiv take hold of the amulet and then it sort of exploded. Just as Bayar said it would.

He could feel the ominous weight of the jinxpiece in his carry bag. Maybe Dancer was right. Maybe he should've buried the thing. But the fact was, if not for the serpent talisman, he'd be in a world of trouble. Maybe dead.

Ha! he thought. *Don't fool yourself. You're in a world of trouble anyway.*

He'd reached the stable at the end of the street, so there was no putting it off any longer. Inside the stable, Han sniffed the air experimentally. There was nothing of supper. Instead it stank of manure, damp straw, and warm horses. He'd have to muck out the stalls tomorrow. If he could even get out of bed.

Some of the horses poked their heads out of their stalls and whickered in recognition, hoping for a treat. "Sorry," he murmured. "I got nothing." Haltingly, he climbed the old stone staircase to the room he shared with his mother and seven-year-old sister.

Han eased open the door. From force of habit, his eyes flicked around the room, meaning to locate trouble before it came flying at him. The room was chilly and dark, the fire nearly out. No sign of Mam.

Mari was lying on her pallet by the hearth, but she must have been awake because her head popped up as soon as he came in. A big smile broke on her face and she flung herself at him, wrapping her skinny arms around his legs and burying her face at his waist. "Han! Where've you been? We've been so worried!"

"You should be asleep," he said, awkwardly patting her back and smoothing down her ragged tow-colored hair. "Where's Mam?"

"She's out looking for you," Mari said, shivering, teeth chattering with fear or cold. She returned to her bed by the fire and wrapped the threadbare blanket around her thin shoulders. She never seemed to have enough fat on her to keep warm. "She's in a right state. We was scared something happened to you."

Bones, he thought, feeling guilty. "When did she go?"

"She's been out all day, off and on."

"Did you have supper?"

She hesitated, considering a lie, then shook her head. "Mam'll bring something home, I reckon."

Han pressed his lips together to keep from spilling his thoughts. Mari's faith was somehow precious to him, like a dream he couldn't let go of. She was the only person in all of Ragmarket who'd ever believed in him.

He crossed to the hearth, pulled a stick from their dwindling supply, and laid it on the fire. Then he sat down on the thin mattress next to his sister, keeping his face turned away from the firelight. "It's my fault you got nothing to eat," he said. "I should've come home earlier. I told Mam I'd bring you something." He dug in his pocket and fished out the napkin with the buns. He unwrapped them and handed one to Mari.

Her blue eyes went wide. She cradled it in her fingers and looked up at him hopefully. "How much of it do I get?"

Han shrugged, embarrassed. "All of it. I brought more for me and Mam."

"Oh!" Mari pulled apart the bun and downed it in greedy bites, licking her fingers at the end. Sweet, spicy sauce smeared her mouth, and she ran her tongue over her lips, trying to get the last little bit.

Han wished he was seven again, when all it took was a pork bun to make him happy.

He handed her another, but as she took it, she got a good look at him. "What happened to your face? It's all swollen." She reached up and touched his face with her small hand, like it was delicate as an eggshell. "It's getting purple."

Just then he heard the weary clump, clump, clump up the stairs that said Mam was home. Han eased into a standing position, bracing himself against the wall, concealing himself in the shadows. A moment later the door banged open.

Han's mother stood in the doorway, her shoulders permanently hunched against a lifetime of bad luck. To Han's surprise, she was wearing the new coat he'd picked up in Ragmarket a week or two before, thinking it would serve him well the next winter. On her it nearly swept the ground, and she had a long scarf wrapped around her neck. Mam wore layers of clothes even in fair weather, a kind of armor she put on.

She unwound the scarf from her neck, freeing her long plait of pale hair. There were dark circles under her eyes, and she looked more defeated than usual. She was young—when

Han was born, she'd been no older than Han was now—but she looked older than her years.

"I couldn't find him, Mari," she said, her voice breaking. Han was stunned to see tears streaking down her cheeks. "I've been everywhere, asked everyone. I even went to the Guard, and they just laughed at me. Said he was likely in gaol, that was where he belonged. Or dead." She sniffled and blotted her face with her sleeve.

"Um, Mam . . ." Mari stammered, looking over at Han.

"I've told him and told him to stay off the streets, not to run with the gangs, not to carry money for that old Lucius, but he don't listen, he thinks nothing can touch him, he . . ."

I'm dog dirt, Han thought. I'm scum. The longer he waited, the worse it would get. He stepped out of the shadows. "I'm here, Mam." He cleared his throat. "Sorry I'm late."

Mam blinked at him, pale as parchment, her hand flying to her throat as if she'd seen a ghost. "W-where . . . ?"

"I slept over at Marisa Pines," Han explained. "And then I ran into some trouble on the way home. But I brought supper." He mutely held out the napkin with the remaining pork pies. An offering.

Crossing the space between them, she struck the napkin out of his hand. "You brought supper? That's it? You disappear for three days and I'm out of my head with worry, and you brought *supper*?" Her voice was rising, and Han waved his hands, trying to shush her. They didn't need to rouse the landlord, who lived next door, and remind him they hadn't paid their rent.

She came forward, and he retreated until he was up against

the hearth. She thrust an accusing finger into his face. "You've been fighting again. Haven't you? What have I told you?"

"No," he said unconvincingly, shaking his head. "I'm just . . . I stumbled over a curb and fell flat on my face in the street."

"You should put a cold rag on it," Mari said from the refuge of her bed. Her voice quavered, like it did when she was upset. "Mam, you always say that takes the swelling down."

Han glanced over at Mari, wishing he and Mam could take their fight somewhere else. But when you live in one room over a stable, there's nowhere to go.

"Who was it this time?" Mam demanded. "The gangs or the Guard? Or did you pick one too many pockets?"

"I an't lifting purses anymore," Han protested, stung. "Nor diving pockets, neither. I wouldn't—"

"You *said* you were going after plants for the Flatlander Market," Mam said. "Did you even go up on Hanalea? Or were you out running the streets the whole time?"

"I went up on Hanalea," Han said, struggling to control his temper. "Me and Dancer spent all day gathering herbs on the mountain."

Mam eyed him narrowly, then extended her hand. "You should have some money for me, then."

Han thought of his purse, now in Shiv's possession. He still had Lucius's money, but—like he kept saying—he wasn't a thief. He swallowed hard, looking down at the floor. "I don't have any money," he said. "It got taken from me in Southbridge."

Mam's breath hissed out, like he'd confirmed all her worst

fears. "You're cursed, Hanson Alister, and you'll come to a bad end," she said. "It's no wonder you're in trouble when you're out on the streets all day long. When you run with street gangs, thieving and robbing . . ."

"I'm not with the Raggers anymore," Han interrupted. "I promised you back in the fall."

Mam plowed on as if he hadn't spoken. "When you take up with ill-favored sorts like Lucius Frowsley. We may be poor, but at least we've always been honest."

Something broke loose inside Han, and when he opened his mouth the words came spilling out. "We're *honest*? Well, honest won't fill our bellies. Honest doesn't pay the rent. It's been me supporting us for the past year, and it's a lot harder without slide-hand. Be my guest if you think you can keep us out of debtor's prison taking in washing and picking rags. And if we do go to prison, what do you think will happen to Mari?"

Mam stood speechless, eyes very blue, her lips as white as the rest of her face. Then she snatched up a stick from the kindling pile and swung it at him. Reflexively, he gripped her wrist and held it. They glared at each other for a long moment, married by blood and anger. Slowly the anger drained away, leaving only the linkage of blood.

"I'm not going to let you hit me anymore," Han said quietly. "I've already had one beating today. That's enough."

Later, Han lay on his straw mattress in the corner. He could hear the soft, regular breathing that said Mam and Mari were finally asleep. Every bone in his body ached, and his face felt like it might split open. Plus, he was hungry again. He and Mam had shared the last two meat buns, but these days everything he ate seemed to evaporate before it reached his stomach.

His mind bounced off corners like a mouse in a maze. He was no philosopher. He had few spaces of time in which to dream. He was not the sort to try and reconcile the warring souls that lived inside his body.

There was Han Alister, son and big brother, breadwinner, deal-maker, and small-time conniver. There was Hunts Alone, who'd been adopted by Marisa Pines and wished he could melt into the clans for good. And finally, Cuffs, petty criminal and street fighter, onetime streetlord of the Ragger gang and enemy of the Southies.

From day to day he slid out of one skin and pulled on another. No wonder it was hard to sort out who he was.

He shifted on the hard floor. He usually used his carry bag as a pillow, but he wasn't sure if he ought to, with the amulet inside. The jinxpiece occupied his mind like a toothache. What if it exploded and killed them all? Or worse, left them alive with no roof over their heads.

Lucius's words came back to him. *Keep the amulet hid, and stay out of the way of the Bayars. If they find out you have it, they'll kill you for it.*

Finally he pulled the amulet in its wrapping out of his bag. Wearing only his breeches, he slipped down the stairs, past the horses in their stalls, and into the cold stable yard. Some distance from the building stood a stone forge built when there was a blacksmith in residence. It had been Han's hiding place since he was old enough to have secrets. Han lifted a loose stone at its base and tucked the amulet underneath, replacing the stone. Feeling more at ease, he returned to the stable and climbed the stairs, his mind working furiously.

Tomorrow he'd go back to Lucius, deliver his purse, and hopefully get paid. That might be enough to hold off the landlord for a while, especially if he mucked out the barn again.

Sitting down on his mattress, he dug in his breeches pocket, pulling out the princess coin Matieu had given him a lifetime ago. He turned it toward the dying fire, and the reflected flames picked out the silhouette engraved on it.

It was Princess Raisa *ana'*Marianna, heir to the Gray Wolf throne of the Fells.

"Hey, girlie," he whispered, running his dirty forefinger over the image. "I'd like to see more like you."

She was in profile, captured in cold hard metal—her graceful neck extended, her hair swept back from her face and caught into a coronet. No doubt proud and haughty as her mother, Queen Marianna.

No, Han thought sarcastically. It's far too much trouble to come into the highlands to hunt. We'll just have the deer delivered, even if it means setting fire to the mountain.

A princess wouldn't have to worry about keeping a roof over her head, about where her next meal was coming from, or if she was going to be cornered and beaten in the street.

A princess would have nothing at all to worry about.

CHAPTER SEVEN

IN THE GLASS GARDEN

Raisa hurried down the corridor, her dancing slippers whispering over the marble floors. She'd intended to return to her chambers and change clothes, but was at a loss for what to put on. Her clan leggings and tunic were filthy dirty. She had no play clothes anymore, and anyway, this new solemn Amon in his dress uniform seemed to call for something more formal. But what if he'd changed into breeches and shirt? She'd feel foolish in her gown.

Hold on. She was the princess heir, come from a dance. Why should she feel foolish at all? What was the matter with her?

Magret was waiting up, nursing a cup of tea, her graying

hair taken down and plaited. "You're back earlier than I expected, Your Highness," she said, rising and dipping a curtsy. "I thought it would go later."

"It will. I'm going to see Amon now," Raisa said, sitting in front of her mirror and removing the circlet. She'd leave the gown on, she decided, but take down her hair. Then she'd . . .

"Now?" Magret stared at her. "At this hour?"

Raisa blinked up at her. "Well. Yes." And when Magret continued to frown, added, "What?"

"You can't go off meeting a young man on your own in the middle of the night!"

What didn't Magret understand? "It's *Amon*. We used to stay out overnight all the time. Remember when Cook found us under the baker's table at sunrise? We wanted to be ready when the cinnamon buns came out of the oven." Raisa tugged a brush through her resistant hair, thinking Amon would never fit under the baker's table now. Not with those long legs.

"You'll not go out without a chaperone at this hour," Magret said stubbornly.

"I already said I'd meet him," Raisa said, plaiting her hair into a loose braid. "No one will know, anyway."

"If you go, I'll speak with Lady Francia, who will interrupt the queen," Magret said, thrusting her chin forward trumphantly.

"You wouldn't," Raisa said, now thoroughly sorry she'd not gone directly to her rendezvous.

"I would, Your Highness. You'll be sixteen in July, and eligible for marriage. It will be my head if anything happens to you. I mean, he's a *soldier*, after all."

"Blood. Of. Hanalea. I'm not marrying anyone, Magret.

Not for a long time." *I'll take a hundred lovers before then, just for spite*, she wanted to say. Besides, I'd be more likely to get into trouble in the card room with Micah or under Mother's nose in the banqueting hall than with Amon, Raisa thought.

They glared at each other for a long moment, at an impasse.

"Fine," Raisa said. "Come with me, then."

Magret looked down at her chamber gown. Obviously, she'd thought she was in for the night. "Really, Your Highness, I don't think . . ."

Raisa put on her imperious princess face. "If you insist on coming, you might as well make up a tray for Amon. He stood guard at the door all during dinner, so he's not eaten."

A quarter hour and much grumbling later, they left Raisa's rooms, Raisa in the lead, Magret following, radiating disapproval, carrying a large silver tray.

They climbed several flights of stairs that grew narrower and steeper as they ascended.

"Are you meeting him on the roof, then?" Magret wheezed, two flights behind Raisa.

"We're meeting in the glass garden," Raisa said, pausing at the top of the last flight to let Magret catch up. It would've been much easier to go up via the secret staircase, but that was one secret she didn't intend to share with Magret.

She'd not shared it with Micah, either. Once disclosed, it couldn't be taken back if it became awkward or inconvenient.

The greenhouse must have been a showplace once, designed by someone with a love for gardens. They entered through tall bronze doors decorated with cunning vines, flowers, animals, and insects cast into the metal. The air inside was moist, fragrant with earth and flowers and the breath of growing things. The dark slate floor gathered up sunlight all day long and gave heat back during the night. Hot water from thermal springs circulated through pipes, controlled by a series of valves so the temperatures could be adjusted to meet the needs of tropical, desert, and temperate plants.

Queen Marianna had little use for gardens, preferring her flowers to be arranged in vases, but Raisa shared a passion for digging in the dirt with her father. On those rare occasions he stayed at Fellsmarch Castle, they spent hours in companionable silence, rooting cuttings and thinning seedlings.

With both of them gone these past three years, the garden was overgrown and neglected, the more aggressive plants crowding out the weaker, more delicate kinds. Panes were broken here and there, stuffed with wool or crudely mended with ill-fitting patches. Some areas of the garden were too cold now for any but native plants.

Raisa led Magret to the entrance of the maze. Amon would be waiting in one of the side passages, in a pavilion next to the fountain.

Guess we'll have to find a new place to meet, Raisa thought, now that Magret knows about this one.

Although she might not be able to find her way back.

Raisa confidently threaded her way through the leafy tunnels, Magret tight on her heels, as if afraid Raisa might sprint away and leave her stranded. The boxwood walls had nearly grown together in some places, and more than once they had to push through tangles of branches.

"You're going to ruin that dress on the first wearing," Magret complained, licking her finger and rubbing it over a prick in Raisa's satin skirt.

Raisa heard Amon before she saw him. He was pacing back and forth, muttering to himself. At first she thought he was grumbling because she was late, but it seemed he was practicing some sort of speech.

"Your Highness, may I say how honored I am that you . . . ah . . . how pleased I am to be remembered . . . gaaaah." He shook his head in disgust and cleared his throat. "Your Highness, I was astounded—no—surprised when you spoke to me, and hope that you might consider our friendship . . . Hanalea's bloody bones!" he exclaimed, smacking himself in the forehead. "What an idiot."

Raising her hand to indicate that Magret should stay where she was, Raisa moved forward. "Amon?"

He jumped and swiveled around, his hand automatically going to the hilt of his sword. He tried to change it into a kind of elegant gesture, extending his hand toward her and bowing low. "Your Highness," he croaked, straightening and staring at her. "You're . . . um . . . you look well."

"Your *Highness*?" She strode toward him, satin swishing, chin lifted imperiously. "Your *Highness*?"

"Well," he said, flushing furiously, "I . . . ah . . ."

She gripped both his hands and looked up—way up—past the square Byrne chin and straight nose and into his gray eyes. "Bones, Amon, it's me. Raisa. Have you ever in your life called me 'Your Highness'?"

He studied on it. "As I remember, there were several times you *made* me call you that," he said dryly.

Her face grew hot. "I never did!"

He raised an eyebrow, an expression she remembered well. Very annoying.

"Well," she conceded, "all right. Maybe a few times."

He shrugged. "It's probably best if I get used to calling you that," he said. "If I'm going to be at court."

"I suppose," she said. They stood like that, hands linked awkwardly for a moment. She was suddenly very aware of the contact. Her heart stuttered.

"So," he said. "You look . . . well," he repeated. He couldn't seem to decide where he should be looking, which gave him a rather shifty-eyed appearance.

"And you look . . . tall," she replied, briskly withdrawing her hands. "Are you hungry? Magret brought supper for you."

He flinched and glanced around, his gaze lighting on Magret, sulking next to an ancient jade tree. The eyebrow again. "You brought Magret along? Here?"

Raisa shrugged. "She wouldn't let me come otherwise. It's hard these days."

"Oh." He hesitated. "Well, I *am* hungry," he admitted.

Raisa motioned to Magret, who set the tray on a small wrought-iron table at the waterside, lit the torches, and then withdrew to a bench close enough so she might still overhear what they were saying.

"Please," Raisa said to Amon. "Sit." She settled into a chair and chose a small bunch of grapes to nibble on, though she was still stuffed from dinner. She was glad of the distraction of the food, glad it gave them something to focus on besides each other.

Amon carefully removed his uniform jacket and hung it on the back of his chair. Underneath he wore a snowy white linen shirt. He rolled the sleeves past the elbows, exposing tanned and muscled arms.

"Sorry," he said, finally sitting. "I'm used to doing my own laundry at Wien House, so I try to keep my cuffs out of my soup."

He enthusiastically tucked into the bread, cheese, and fruit Magret had assembled, washing it down with cider. He looked up once and caught Raisa staring at him. "Excuse me," he said, hastily swiping at his mouth with a napkin. "I rode a long way today, I'm starving, and I'm used to eating in a barracks. It's kind of a free-for-all."

To Raisa, it was a relief to talk to someone who didn't try to flatter her. Who said what he thought. Who wasn't so smooth that she felt clumsy and ill-spoken herself.

"So," she said, "you're assigned to the Guard this summer?"

He nodded, chewed, and swallowed. "And every summer from now on."

"Will you be working a lot?"

"Aye, my da'll make sure the queen gets her money's worth from my sorry hide." He rolled his eyes. "I might get to see you if I'm assigned to your personal guard. But that's unlikely as a first year in the Guard."

"Oh," Raisa said, disappointed. She'd been lonely since

returning to Fellsmarch from Demonai. There was Micah, of course, but being with him wasn't exactly relaxing, not even with a chaperone.

She'd looked forward to a summer knocking about with the Amon she remembered. It hadn't occurred to her that he'd be so different. Or that he wouldn't have any free time.

"I hoped we could ride up to Firehole Falls again. I heard there was a new geyser that shoots fifty feet in the air."

"Really?" Amon cocked his head. "You haven't gone to see it?"

"I was waiting for you. Remember that time we went swimming at Demon Springs?" They'd fished for trout in the Firehole and cooked their catch in one of the steam fissures that crazed the landscape.

"Ah." He looked uncomfortable. "The queen may not like the notion of us riding off on our own anymore."

"Why not?"

"Several reasons." He paused, and when she didn't respond, added, "For one thing, it's more dangerous than it used to be."

Raisa twitched impatiently. "Everybody keeps saying that."

"Because it's true."

"And why else?" Raisa persisted.

"I'm a soldier, and I'm of age. You'll be of age by midsummer. It's different. People will talk."

Raisa made a disgusted noise. "People will talk regardless." But she knew he was right. After an uncomfortable silence, she changed the subject. "Tell me about Oden's Ford."

"Well." Amon hesitated, as if to be sure she really meant it. "The academy is split by the Tamron River: Wien House, the warrior school, is on one side, and Mystwerk, the wizard school, on the other. Guess they thought it best to keep the two separated, in the beginning. Those were the first two, but these days there are other schools as well.

"There are fifty plebes in Wien House each year. They come from all over, from Tamron, and the Fells, and Arden, and Bruinswallow. Some of 'em are actually at war with each other, but they're not allowed to bring it onto campus. There's something called the Peace of Oden's Ford that's enforced really strictly. Oden's Ford itself is like a small realm all on its own. It's on the border between Tamron and Arden, but it doesn't belong to either."

"Where do you stay?" Raisa asked, kicking off her shoes and drawing her feet up under her gown while Magret scowled disapprovingly.

"Each class stays together until we're proficients," Amon said. "Then we can choose our own housing."

"Is it pretty evenly balanced in Wien House, girls and boys?" Raisa asked casually.

He shook his head. "We send girls from the Fells, but in the south things are different. They have strange notions about what girls can do. Some say it's the influence of the Church of Malthus."

"Ah." Raisa nodded wisely, pretending to understand. Amon seemed so informed, so worldly next to her, and she was princess heir of the queendom! Shouldn't she know about these things? Did her mother, the queen, know about them? Maybe not. Marianna had never traveled outside the queendom, either.

Raisa was seized by the sudden desire to go somewhere, anywhere, out of the Fells.

"So it's about three-quarters boys, one-quarter girls," Amon went on. "The girls hold their own, though. Being a soldier isn't all about brute strength, as some of the southerners have found out." He laughed.

"What do you do, then?" she asked. "Do you do seat work or—or drill, or what?" Right, she thought, eying him sidelong. Seat work didn't put that muscle on your arms and chest.

"Some classroom, some applied," Amon said, seeming pleased by her interest. "We train in strategy, geography, horsemanship, weaponry, that sort of thing. We study great battles in history and analyze the outcome. The further along you are, the more practical application."

"I wish I could go," Raisa blurted.

"You do?" Amon looked surprised. "Well, it'd be too dangerous, I think. These days, just getting to and from school is a challenge."

"Why is that?" Raisa fingered her briar rose necklace. Maybe her yearning for foreign lands came from her trader father.

"You know there's the civil war in Arden—five brothers fighting over the throne, each with an army. So if you're of military age in the south, even if you're just passing through, you're at risk of being ganged into somebody's army. And military age is defined broadly—age ten to eighty, or thereabouts."

He pushed back from the table, stretching out his legs, massaging the muscles in his thighs as though they hurt. "Plus, you never know when you're crossing enemy lines or walking straight into a battle. Deserters and bands of mercenaries between patrons are everywhere. These days, people don't even try to identify you before they run you through."

"My father's in Arden," Raisa said with a shiver. "Did you know?"

He nodded. "Da told me." He paused, looking like he wished he could take back what he'd just said. "He's Demonai, and he was a warrior once. I'm sure he'll be all right. When's he coming home?"

She shook her head. "No idea. I wish he'd come. I just feel . . . uneasy, you know? Like something's going to happen." Raisa thought of what Edon Byrne had said, about the lawlessness in the countryside and the need for a guard on a simple hunt. What else was going on that she didn't know about?

"What do you think we should be doing differently?" she asked. "About the wars, I mean?"

He colored. "It's not my place to—"

"I don't care if it's your place or not!" She leaned across the table toward him. "I want to know what you *think*. Just between us."

Amon studied her, as if not sure whether to believe her or not.

When I'm queen, Raisa thought grimly, people won't be afraid to speak their minds.

"Just between us?"

She nodded.

"Well," he said, his gray eyes steady on hers, "Da and I have been talking. The civil war in Arden isn't going to last forever. If nothing else, they'll run out of soldiers. One of those bloody Montaigne brothers is going to come out on top, and when he does, he's going to need money. He'll look north, south, and west for new territory. We think there's things we could be doing now that would help protect us in the future."

"Such as?" Raisa prompted.

"Get rid of the mercenaries," Amon said bluntly. "They're always for sale, and the Montaignes are bloody treacherous. We need an army that's unquestionably loyal, made up of native born. Even if it's smaller. Otherwise the queen could be overthrown by her own soldiers."

"But"—Raisa bit her lip—"where would we get recruits? Times are hard. Who would volunteer?"

He shrugged. "Men from the Fells are selling their swords to Arden," he said. "Meanwhile, we're importing trouble from the south. Why pay foreigners to fight for us? Give people a reason to stay home where they belong."

"What reason?" Raisa persisted.

"I don't know. Something to fight for, to believe in. A decent living." He threw up his hands. "Like I'm an expert. I'm just a cadet, but it's what my father thinks."

"Do you know . . . has Captain Byrne discussed this with the queen?" Raisa asked.

Amon looked away from her, unrolling his sleeves with exaggerated attention. "He's tried. But Queen Marianna has lots of advisers, and Da's just the captain of her Guard." Raisa had the feeling he'd left as much unsaid as said.

"What about General Klemath? What does he think?"

Raisa asked. Klemath was father to Kip and Keith, her persis-
tent suitors.

"Well," Amon said, rubbing the bridge of his nose, "he's the
one who brought in the mercenaries in the first place. He's
not likely to support a change."

"We have wizards," Raisa said, thinking this was the kind
of conversation she should be having with her mother. "We
have Lord Bayar and the rest of the council. They'll protect us
from flatlanders."

"Aye." Amon nodded. "If you can trust 'em."

"You've become a cynic in the south," Raisa said, rubbing
her eyes and realizing it had been a very long day. "You don't
trust anyone."

"That's how you stay alive in the south," Amon said, staring out at the fountain.

Raisa smothered a yawn. "That's how you deal with
suitors too. You don't trust any of them."

Amon's head jerked up. "Suitors? Has that started already?"

"Already?" Raisa shrugged. "I'm nearly sixteen. My
mother married when she was seventeen."

Amon looked appalled. "But *you* don't have to marry right
away, do you?"

Raisa shook her head. "I'm not getting married any time
soon," she declared flatly. "Not for years and years," she added,
when Amon didn't look reassured. "My mother's still young,
and she'll rule for a long time yet." Raisa was glad to be in the
role of expert for once. She looked forward to courtship, but
marriage was another thing altogether.

"Rai. Will you have to marry an old man?" Amon asked,

with that familiar Byrne bluntness. "Not that I think your da . . . well, he *is* a lot older than the queen is all I'm saying."

"It depends. I could marry clan royalty or even some king or princeling from Tamron or Arden. It could be an old man, I guess. That's a good reason to put marriage off as long as possible."

Had her mother ever loved her father? Raisa wondered. Or had it been purely a political match? Before she'd gone to Demonai, it seemed like they'd been more of a family. How much did Raisa's current aversion to marriage have to do with what she saw between her parents?

She looked up to find Amon watching her. He looked away quickly, but she'd seen the sympathy in his gray eyes.

He was so different from Micah. Micah was intoxicating, always challenging everything she believed. Amon was comfortable, like a pair of broken-in moccasins. And yet, the changes in him were intriguing.

She glanced over at Magret. Her nurse was sound asleep, stretched out on one of the park benches, mouth open, snoring.

"Well," Amon said, following her gaze, "we've lost her." He stood. "And I'm on duty at sunrise. With your permission, I'll say good night."

He looks dead on his feet, Raisa thought with a rush of guilt. "Of course. But first, I've got something to show you," she said, still unwilling to let him go. Still wanting to negotiate some new kind of treaty. "There's a secret passageway. It's like a shortcut. We can go that way."

Amon hesitated, frowning. "Where does it let out?"

"You'll see," Raisa said mysteriously.

Amon tilted his head toward Magret. "What about her?"

"Let her sleep," Raisa said. "She looks comfortable enough."

"She may never find the way out on her own," Amon said.

"I promise I'll fetch her in the morning," Raisa said. Lifting free one of the torches, she marched off, between the walls of greenery, not looking back to see if Amon was following, but soon hearing the crunch of his boots on the gravel path.

They circled around and around until they reached the center of the maze. There, an exquisite wrought-iron temple stood forlornly amid a tangle of old roses and overgrown fragrance gardens. Honeysuckle and wisteria twined over trellises and covered the roof, dangling nearly to the ground, giving it the look of a living cave or a lovers' bower. Even Raisa had to duck her head to enter.

Leaves and twigs littered the floor. At one end stood an altar to the Maker, centering a semicircle of stone benches, with room for no more than a dozen worshippers.

A stained-glass window at the other end depicted Hanalea in battle, sword drawn, hair flying. In daylight, when the sun shone through it, it sent rivers of color washing over the stone floor.

Amid the stone pavers in the floor was set a metal plate engraved with wild roses. Raisa knelt and brushed away the debris with her forearm.

"Under here," she said, pointing. "You have to lift it."

Setting his torch into a bracket in the wall, Amon grasped a ring set into the plate and pulled, rocking back on his heels.

Hinges screeching, the plate swung up, followed by a rush of dank, stale air.

Amon looked up at Raisa. "When's the last time you were down here?"

Raisa shrugged. "Maybe two months ago. It's hard because there are always people around."

"I'd better go first," Amon said, eying her gown skeptically. "Who knows what's moved in here since your last visit."

"There's a ladder along the side," Raisa said helpfully.

Bracing his hands on either side of the opening, Amon lowered himself until his feet found the first rungs. He climbed down until his head and shoulders disappeared below floor level. He stopped at that point and reached his hand up. Raisa handed him a torch, and he resumed his descent until he reached the floor two stories below.

He looked up, and she could see his face in the torchlight. He seemed far away. "It's a long way down," he said. "I don't think this is such a good idea."

"It's fine," she said, with more confidence than she felt. "I've been up and down before."

Only not in slippers and a tightly fitted satin dress, she might have added, but didn't.

"Let's go back out the way we came," Amon argued, putting his foot on the lowest rung. "You can show me the passage another time, when you're ... um ... dressed for it."

"When are we going to get another chance?" Raisa said stubbornly. "Like I said, there're always people around, and you're going to be working every day."

She knew she was being unreasonable, but she was tired,

and she felt cheated. She faced the prospect of a summer on her own again, for all intents and purposes, when she wanted to adventure with Amon.

"I'm coming up," Amon warned, taking hold of the ladder with both hands.

"I'm coming down," Raisa said loudly, turning and feeling for the first rung with her extended foot.

"Just wait a minute, all right?" He disappeared from sight, but she could hear him moving around down there, see torchlight reflecting off the damp walls.

He reappeared at the foot of the ladder, looking up at her, a big smear of dirt on his right cheekbone. "It's clear. A few rats is all. Come on down, but be careful."

That was easier said than done. The rungs were far apart, difficult to manage by someone her size in the best of circumstances, nearly impossible in her dress. Her silk slippers gave her no purchase on the metal rungs. She hitched her skirt up above her knees, clutching it in one hand and holding on to the ladder with the other, wondering what kind of sight she presented to Amon below.

She was halfway down when she lost her single-handed grip on the slippery metal ladder, teetered a moment, arms flailing, then fell screaming through space.

She landed with a *whump* in Amon's arms. He staggered back a few steps, and for a moment she thought they'd both go down, but he regained his balance and ended leaning against the wall, breathing hard, cradling her close against the damp wool of his uniform jacket. She could hear his heart hammering next to her ear.

"Hanalea's bloody bones!" he swore, his face inches from hers, his gray eyes dark and roiled as the Indio Ocean in winter, his face chalk white. "Are you *crazy*, Raisa? Do you want to *kill* yourself?"

"Of *course* not," she said fiercely, her fright making her snappish. "I just slipped is all. Put me down."

But he seemed bent on lecturing her at close range. "You *never* listen. You always have to have your way, even if it means breaking your bloody neck."

"I do *not* always have to have my way," she said.

"Yeah? What about the time you just had to ride that flat-lander stallion? What was his name? Deathwish? Devilspawn? You had to climb the fence to mount him, and his back was so broad your legs stuck straight out, but nothing would do but you had to give him a try." He snorted. "*That* was the world's shortest ride."

She'd forgotten about Amon's annoying habit of repeating old stories she'd rather forget. Raisa struggled and kicked, trying to get free. He was definitely a lot stronger than she remembered. Even though she was smaller, she'd always been able to hold her own through force of personality, if nothing else.

"You never think about the mess you'd leave behind," Amon said. "If you bust your head and I'm in any way involved, my da won't leave enough of me for the crows to find."

"What happened to 'If you please, Your Highness' and 'With your permission, Your Highness'?" Raisa demanded. "For the last time, *put me down,* or I'll call the Guard."

Amon blinked at her, and she couldn't help noticing he

had really thick eyelashes smudging the gray of his eyes. Carefully, he set her down on her feet and took a step back. "My apologies, *Your Highness,*" he said, his face gone blank and hard. "Shall I go, then?"

And just that quick, her anger was gone, replaced by remorse. Her cheeks flamed. How could they possibly be friends if she kept pulling rank on him?

"I'm sorry," she whispered, putting her hand on his arm. "Thank you for saving my life."

He continued to stare straight ahead. "My duty, Your Highness, as a member of the Queen's Guard."

"Will you *stop*?" Raisa said desperately. "I said I was sorry."

"No apology is necessary, Your Highness," Amon said, looking down at her hand on his sleeve. "Now, if there's nothing else . . . ?"

"Please don't go, Amon," Raisa said, releasing his arm and staring at her ruined slippers. "I could really use a friend, even if I don't deserve one." She cleared her throat. "Do you think that's possible?"

There was a long pause. Then Amon put two fingers under her chin, and she lifted her head and looked at him, and the movement sent tears spilling down her face. He was leaning down toward her, his face was very close, and before she knew what she was doing, she slid her arms around his neck and kissed him on the lips.

Maybe he was thinking about kissing too, because he pressed his hands against her waist, lifting her tightly against him so her feet nearly left the ground. He returned the kiss with surprising skill and intensity. His lips were a bit rough and wind-burned, but in a good way, and Raisa wasn't ready to stop when he broke it off and backed away, gray eyes wide with alarm.

"I'm sorry, Your Highness," he gasped, reddening, raising his hands, palms out. "Forgive me. I . . . I didn't mean . . ."

"Call me Raisa," Raisa said, moving toward him again, reaching for him.

"Please . . . Raisa." He gripped her shoulders, holding her at arm's length. "I don't know what I . . . We can't do this."

Raisa blinked at him. "It's just a *kiss*," she said, feeling rather hurt. "I've been kissed before."

There was Micah, of course, and then there'd been dark-eyed, intense Reid Nightwalker Demonai, one of the warriors at Demonai Camp. Mush-mouthed Wil Mathis, Keith Klemath (not Kip), and probably one or two others.

"It should never have happened. I'm a soldier, and I'm in the Queen's Guard. If my father—"

"Oh bother your father," Raisa grumbled. "He doesn't have to know everything."

"He knows things. I don't know how. And I would know it." Awkwardly, Amon groped in his pocket, produced a hand-kerchief, and handed it to her.

Raisa knew the kissing was over. For the time being, any-way.

"When I saw you at dinner, you *looked* like a princess," he said, graciously averting his eyes from her tear-blotched face. "I mean, I always knew that, but you seemed different than I remembered. Kind of . . . remote. Not what I expected."

"You looked different too," Raisa said, blotting her eyes. "I didn't even recognize you until Mother called your name." She managed a damp smile. "You . . . you're very handsome, you know. You must have lots of sweethearts." She couldn't help thinking he'd had some practice kissing since she'd last seen him.

He shrugged, looking embarrassed. "There's not much time for sweethearts at Oden's Ford," he said.

"Magret says I'm willful and spoiled. My mother says I'm stubborn. I do try to get my own way, but I think it's because I'll never get my way on anything that matters." She looked up at him. "I won't get to choose where I live, or who I marry, or even who my friends are. My time will never be my own." She blew her nose, feeling bad about Amon's handkerchief. "It's not that I don't want to be queen, I do. I guess I don't want to be my mother."

"Then don't be," Amon said, like it was the simplest thing in the world.

"But most girls would love to be her," Raisa said, glancing around guiltily, as if someone might overhear them in the dank tunnel. "And I don't know how to be anything different. I don't want to be at the mercy of advisers. But how do you find things out? Other than how to play the lute or embroider, I mean. At least I know how to ride a horse and get along in the woods and shoot a bow from my time in Demonai. My father's got me well on the way to being a trader. But that and embroidery's not enough to be a good queen."

"Well, I'm no scholar," Amon said, leaning against the wall, seeming reassured that Raisa wouldn't attack him again. "But there are people in Fellsmarch who know things. The speakers in the temple, for instance. There's a huge library there."

"I guess," Raisa said. "It's just such an ordeal to even go there. Sometimes I'd like to be invisible." She twitched irritably. "I don't even know what's going on in the world. My mother's advisers either tell her what she wants to hear, or they're promoting their own agendas. People say she listens to them too much."

People being her grandmother Elena, among others.

"Now who's the cynic?" Amon said. "Maybe you need to find yourself some honest eyes and ears." He yawned and rubbed his eyes.

"Oh!" Raisa said, stricken. "I'm sorry. You said you have to get up." Half an hour into reform, she was being as self-centered and inconsiderate as always. She tried to ignore the voice in her head that said, *That's what queens do.*

"Come on, let's go." Seizing one of the torches, she led the way down the tunnel, trying to ignore the rustlings of rats and the reflected eyes of the creatures that stared down at her from the imperfections in the walls and scattered ahead of her at each turning.

Amon had no trouble keeping up, with his long legs. "How did this passageway get here?" he asked. "And who else knows about it?"

Raisa swiped a cobweb from her face. "I found it after I came back from Demonai," she said. "It's really old. I don't know who made it, and I don't think anybody knows about it. I haven't told anyone but you."

At last they reached the roughly circular stone chamber that meant the end of their journey.

"Here we are," Raisa said, setting the torch into a bracket by the door. She slid back the panel and pushed aside the wardrobe she'd positioned in front of the entrance.

"Where are we?" Amon asked, mystified.

"You'll see," Raisa said, picking her way through a mine-field of shoes and boots, pushing aside fluffy dresses on racks.

Her bedroom was chilly and dark, the fire dying in the hearth, her nightgown still laid out on the bed.

Amon emerged from the closet behind her and glanced about. His eyes widened and he looked a little panicked. "Raisa . . . is this your bedroom?"

"Yes," Raisa said in an offhand fashion. She crossed to the hearth and poked at the fire, laying on another log.

"Blood of the demon," Amon swore. "There's a secret passage in the walls leading to your bedroom? That doesn't worry you?"

She looked up at him. "No. Why should it?" In truth, it hadn't. She'd been focused on the convenience of having a means to come and go without passing under the eyes of everyone in the busy palace corridors.

"Somebody made this," Amon said. "Who else might know about it?"

"This apartment has been shut up for hundreds of years," Raisa said. "Maybe a thousand. You should have seen the way it looked before we cleaned it up. Someone made it, but whoever it was would've died a long time ago."

Amon was examining the sliding panel, running his hands over the wood molding surrounding it. "You should have it boarded it up, Raisa. Close it off permanently."

"You worry too much," Raisa said. "I've been here three months and no monsters have come through."

"I'm serious. I'm going to talk to my father about it."

"You will not," Raisa said. "You promised you wouldn't tell anyone."

He tilted his head, frowning. "I don't remember promising anything."

"Anyway," she went on, "I'll see if there's a way to put a lock on it. That should do." She crossed to the small pantry, suddenly reluctant to see him go. "Do you want anything else to eat?"

He shook his head, smiling ruefully. "I'd better go. We don't want anyone to find me here."

Raisa shook her head. "I guess not," she said. She felt conflicted, confused. On the one hand, she mourned the Amon she'd known in childhood, a friendship that would never be the same. On the other, she felt a thrill of possibility, a breathless fascination with this new Amon and anything he might do or say.

She walked him to the door and they stepped out into the hallway.

"Thanks for dinner," he said. "I'm really tired of southern food." He paused, cleared his throat. "Don't forget about the tunnel."

"Sorry I kept you out so late," Raisa said, committing to nothing. "But I'm really glad you're home." Putting her hand on his arm to steady herself, Raisa went up on her tiptoes and kissed him on the cheek.

"So this is where you've been all evening," someone said in a voice as cold as a demon's kiss.

Raisa jerked away from Amon and turned, knowing as she did so it was the wrong thing—the guilty thing—to do.

It was Micah Bayar, dark eyes glittering in the light from the sconces. A strong odor of wine said he'd been drinking.

"What are *you* doing here?" she demanded, knowing the best defense is a good offense. "Skulking about the queen's tower in the middle of the night?"

"I might ask this soldier the same question," Micah said. "He seems rather . . . out of place."

"Her Highness asked me to escort her back to her rooms," Amon said, stumbling onto the excuse that she and Micah always used. "I was just leaving."

"I see that," Micah said. "I thought you had a headache," he said to Raisa.

"I did," she replied. She turned to Amon. "Good night and thank you, Corporal Byrne."

She turned to enter her room, but Micah grabbed her arm, the loosed power in his grip stinging her flesh. "Hold on," he said. "Don't rush off. I need to understand something."

Raisa tried to pull free. "Micah, I'm really tired. Can we talk about this tomorrow?"

"I think we should talk about this now," Micah said, glaring at Amon. "While we're all here together."

"Let go!" Raisa said, trying to peel away his fingers with her free hand.

Suddenly Amon's sword was in his hand and pointed at Micah.

"*Sul*'Bayar," Amon said. "The princess heir has asked you to let go of her. I suggest you do so."

Micah blinked, then looked down at his hand on Raisa's arm as if surprised to see it there. He let go and took a step back. "Raisa, listen, I didn't mean . . ."

"You listen," Raisa snapped. "You don't own me. I don't think I need to be interrogated if I want to spend some time with a friend. I don't owe you any explanations."

Amon stowed away his sword. "Your Highness, it's late and we're all tired. Why don't you go on to bed, and we'll both be on our way, *all right?*"

Raisa swallowed hard and stepped into the shelter of the doorway. Amon planted a hand on Micah's shoulder and propelled him down the corridor. But the look Micah fired at Raisa over his shoulder said this wasn't the end of it.

CHAPTER EIGHT

LESSONS TO BE LEARNED

"Mari, hurry up or we'll be late!" Han said. He could hear the clamor of temple bells throughout the city, marking the half hour. "And pull a comb through your hair, will you? It looks like a rat's nest."

"But I don't *want* to go to school," Mari grumbled, lacing up her shoes. "Can't we go see Lucius? He's teaching me to fish."

"It's raining out. Besides, Mam doesn't like you to visit Lucius," Han said. "She thinks he's a bad influence."

"Mam doesn't like *you* to visit Lucius," Mari countered, struggling to disentangle the snarls in her hair. "And you still go."

"When you're old as me, you can aggravate Mam on your own," he said, thinking Mari was too smart for her own good.

Plus, she had a mouth that would get her into trouble. He should know.

He took the comb from Mari and used that and his fingers to put her hair in order.

"Mam won't know, anyway," Mari persisted, flinching when he pulled too hard. "She won't be back from the castle 'til late."

"Just shut it, Mari," Han said unsympathetically. "If you can't read and write and do figures, you'll get cheated all your life. And how are you going to learn anything else?"

"Mam can't read and write, and she has a job working for the queen," Mari argued.

"That's why she wants you to go to school," Han said.

It had been two weeks since Han brought the amulet home, and their lives had settled into a different cadence. Mam had a new job in the laundry at Fellsmarch Castle. It was reliable money, but she had to leave long before dawn to walk the length of the town across multiple bridges to get there. She never got home before dark, either, so they were on their own for supper. But at least there was supper to be had.

It had become Han's job to take Mari to and from school, which made it hard for him to work his route for Lucius. Once or twice he'd taken her with him on his rounds. Today he meant to leave off Mari, stop in at The Keg and Crown and several other Southbridge taverns, and get to and from Lucius's place before Mari was done at school. It was a risk—the Southies might be laying for him, but it had to be done.

Han dampened a rag in the basin to scrub off Mari's face, so the speakers at the temple wouldn't think she was neglected. He couldn't do much about her clothes, but she wasn't the only one who shopped from the rag bin.

"Let's go."

It was still dark in the narrow streets and alleyways of Ragmarket. It had rained hard overnight—Han had awoken to water dripping on his face through the leaking roof. There were puddles everywhere and the gutters ran full, but the rain had diminished to an irritating drizzle. Han pulled Mari under the shelter of his too-large coat, and they staggered along like some poorly designed four-legged animal.

"I don't see why it has to be so *early*," Mari said. "They've got the whole day to have school."

Han pulled her out of the way of a bakery cart that splashed muddy water up to their knees. "This way the 'prentices can get schooling and still get to work," he said.

Southbridge Temple anchored the far end of South Bridge. Han often thought that whoever built Fellsmarch Castle might've had a hand in Southbridge Temple. Its soaring towers pricked the sky and reminded a person that there was a world beyond Ragmarket and Southbridge, even if you couldn't get to it.

The stone facing around the door was carved with leaves and vines and flowers. Gargoyles launched themselves from every side of the building, and the downspouts were capped with fantastical creatures that must've died in the Breaking, because you never saw them these days.

The temple close housed libraries and dormitories for the dedicates—gardens and kitchens as well. It was by no means a cloister, however, since it welcomed in the citizens of the surrounding neighborhoods, feeding their minds along with their bodies.

Anyone could come inside the temple buildings and see artwork that had been collected for more than a thousand years. There were paintings and sculptures and tapestries with colors so brilliant they seemed to vibrate.

Han and Mari walked in through the side door as the great bells overhead began tolling the hour. They shook like a pair of dogs, scattering droplets over the slate floor of the foyer.

Classes were held in one of the side chapels. When they entered, Speaker Jemson was at the podium, riffling through notes. Behind him stood a line of easels holding paintings drawn from the temple collections that would be used to illustrate his presentation.

His dozen students fidgeted on cushions pulled from the benches in the sanctuary. It was a motley group of girls and boys, ranging in age from Mari's seven to seventeen. Some were dressed for trade, meaning to go on to their jobs after class.

Jemson, Han thought. So the topic would be history.

"History," Mari muttered, as if she'd overheard his thoughts. "Why do we need to know what happened before we were even born?"

"So hopefully we get smarter and don't make the same mistakes again," Han said, grinning at Jemson. It was one of Jemson's favorite lines, and he knew his old teacher would appreciate it.

"Hanson Alister!" Jemson said, rounding his desk and striding toward them, his gown flapping around his thin legs.

"It's been a long time. To what do we owe this pleasure?"

"Well, I, um . . ." Han stammered, exquisitely conscious of Mari looking on. "Actually, I'm not staying. I have something I need to do . . ."

"He thinks he's already smart enough," Mari said, nibbling at a fingernail.

"That's not it," Han said. "It's just I'm working now and . . ."

"That's too bad," Jemson cut in. "We'll be discussing the Breaking and how it's been depicted in art through the ages. Fascinating stuff."

Jemson thought everything was fascinating. It was kind of catching.

Only this time Han had his own reasons for being interested in the Breaking. The story Lucius had told was still rattling around in his brain, kindling little fires wherever it landed. And buried under the forge in the yard was something that might be a piece of that history. Han wanted reinforcement of what he knew to be true.

Except . . .

"The thing is, I've got business in Southbridge and I can't bring Mari along," Han said. "So I thought I'd go while she's in class."

Jemson eyed him, no doubt taking in his still-purple eye and bruised cheekbone, but not feeling the need to mention it. Which was one of the things Han liked about Jemson.

"I see. Well, most business in Southbridge doesn't get up this early anyway," the speaker said dryly.

Exactly. Han was relying on the Southies sleeping in. At

least it seemed less likely he'd run afoul of them at this time of day.

You never used to go out of your way to avoid trouble, he thought. *You used to go looking for it.*

"Tell you what," Jemson said, displaying his usual persistence, "sit in on class, and afterward Mari can stay with the speakers in the library while you go about your business. We'll give her supper, if need be." He paused, then couldn't resist adding, "You *will* be careful, won't you? For Mari's sake, if not your own?"

"I'm always careful," Han said, glancing at Mari. "And I guess I can stay a little while." It wasn't like he'd outgrown the temple school. There were boys older than him in the class.

"Excellent. Spectacular, in fact." Jemson put on his teacher face and turned to the rest of the class. "Yesterday we discussed the events leading up to the Breaking. Today we'll talk about some of the people involved. Who can name one of them?"

"Well, there was Queen Hanalea," one small girl ventured.

"*Good work*, Hannah!" Jemson said, as if she'd just demonstrated how to change dung into gold. "There was Queen Hanalea, for whom we thank the Maker every day."

He turned one of the easels to reveal a painting Han recognized immediately as *Hanalea Blessing the Children*. In it, the legendary queen looked to be thirteen or fourteen. She was seated at a harp, dressed all in white, like a dedicate, her glittering hair gathered into a loose plait, her complexion creamy pink, like rose porcelain. She looked like one of those fancy dolls in the shop windows along the Way of the Queens. The ones Mari pined for and would never have.

In the painting, Hanalea extended her hands toward a group of younger children, smiling benevolently, the glow from her skin illuminating their rapt upturned faces.

"This is Hanalea as a young girl, before the terrible events that we've—"

"Excuse me, Speaker Jemson," Han said. "The painter— was that someone who knew Hanalea?"

Jemson blinked at him, caught midsentence. "Say again?"

"When was that painted?" Han asked. "Was it painted from life or is it just somebody's idea of what Hanalea looked like?"

Jemson grinned. "Master Alister, we have missed your presence in these classes. This was painted by Cedwyn Mallyson in the New Year 505. What does that tell us?"

A serious-looking boy in threadbare clothes and a clark's collar said, "It was painted more than five hundred years after the Breaking. So the painter couldn't have known her."

"So it's possible she looked entirely different?" Han said.

Jemson nodded. "It is possible. What are the implications of that?"

This launched a discussion of something Jemson called *social context*: how religion and politics influence art, and art in turn shapes opinion. Jemson's enthusiasm rolled right over some of the younger students, who looked bewildered and excited at the same time.

"Since Hanalea carried clan blood, what are the chances that she was blue eyed and fair haired?" Jemson asked. "It seems more likely she was dark haired and dark skinned."

"Are there any paintings of Hanalea done by people who actually knew her, sir?" Han asked.

"I don't know," Jemson said. "There may be, right here in the archives. Why don't you look into that and report back to the class?"

That was Jemson, always snaring you into projects that involved time in the library; that would bring you back to class another day.

"Well. Maybe," Han said.

Jemson nodded, knowing better than to push. "So we have our Hanalea, as she's represented in history and art. Who else played a role?"

"The Demon King," Mari said, shivering a little. Several of the other students made the sign of the Maker, to ward off evil.

"Yes, indeed. We have the Demon King, who single-handedly changed the course of the world by nearly destroying it." With a flourish, Jemson turned another easel to display another painting. If Han recalled correctly, this one was called *The Demon King in Madness*. Painted in lurid reds and purples, it depicted a hooded, robed figure outlined in flame. His arms were raised, his fanatical eyes glowed in the shade of the hood, the only aspect of his face that was visible. But Han's eyes fixed on the demon's skeletal right hand, which was hold-ing aloft a glowing green amulet. A tangle of serpents. Han's stomach did a sickening backflip.

"Some say he was the Breaker incarnate," Jemson was say-ing. "Others that he was seduced by evil, made drunk by the power associated with dark magic. No one doubts that he was incredibly gifted."

"What's that in his hand?" Han asked.

Jemson glanced over at the painting. "It's an amulet often

seen in paintings of the Demon King. It's thought to be a direct link to dark magic."

"What happened to it?" Han asked. "Where is it now?"

Jemson turned and frowned at Han, as if trying to parse out the source of the rapid-fire questions. "I have no idea. Likely it was destroyed by the clans immediately after the Breaking, as were many of the most powerful magical pieces. In any event, it's lost to history."

"When was this painted?" Han asked. "And who did it?"

Jemson bent and examined the brass plate at the base of the painting. "The artist was Mandrake Bayar, painted in New Year 593." He squinted at the engraved lettering. "It was a gift of the Bayar family."

"Bayar?" Han's heart stuttered. "But how would the artist know about the amulet if it was painted so long after the piece was destroyed?" The other students were staring at him, but he didn't care.

Jemson shrugged. "It's a common element in paintings of the Demon King. I'm assuming it was copied from an earlier work."

Maybe, Han thought. Or maybe it was painted directly from the object itself.

"What was his name?" Han asked.

Jemson's brow furrowed. "Whose name?"

"The Demon King. Did he have another name? From before." Han persisted.

"Well, yes," Jemson said, still looking puzzled. "His birth name was Alger Waterlow."

For Han, Southbridge Temple was in every sense a sanctuary. It was a toehold in enemy territory, a refuge from the streets when he needed one. He couldn't help feeling edgy as he left the safety of its walls and ventured into Southbridge, his first visit since the confrontation with the Southies in Brickmaker's Alley.

Mari begged to come with him. Everything he did seemed to fascinate her, no matter if it was tedious or dangerous or on the hush. Before he left Mari at the library, he extracted a promise from her that she'd stay put. The last thing he needed was to be searching Southbridge for her.

He avoided Brickmaker's Alley, just in case, and followed the river west from the bridge, wrinkling his nose against the stench. If the Southies came after him, he reasoned, he could jump into the Dyrnnewater. No one who wasn't in fear for his life would follow him into that cesspool. The pristine river that emerged from the Eastern Spirits became an open sewer in Fellsmarch. It was a thorn in the side of the clans, who considered the river sacred.

The streets were strangely quiet, even for this time of day, and the Queen's Guard was unusually visible. Han faded away from several bluejacket patrols and had to continually adjust his route to avoid clusters of soldiers on street corners. In Southbridge, guilty or not, you avoided the Guard. It was a tradition handed down through generations.

By the time he reached The Keg and Crown, it was nearly midday. It should've been prime for the lunch trade, but only about half the tables were occupied. Matieu stood at the bar, glumly carving plate-size slices off a leg of mutton.

"Hey, Matieu," Han said. "I've come for the empties."

Matieu froze, staring at Han as if he'd seen a demon. Sliding the knife into his apron pocket, he retrieved the bottles from behind the counter and set them on the bar, never taking his eyes off Han.

"What's going on?" Han asked, sliding the bottles into his carry bag. "It's strange outside. Nobody on the streets except for the Guard, and plenty of them."

"You haven't heard?" Matieu squinted at Han.

Han shook his head. "Heard what?"

"Half a dozen Southies went down last night," Matieu said, pulling out his knife again. "And that's a lot, even for this neighborhood. The bodies was scattered all around the waterfront, left for show. So people are jumpy, thinking the gang war is starting up again."

"Went down how?" Han asked, staring at him.

"Now isn't that the odd part," Matieu said. "Wasn't your typical knifing or clubbing. They looked like they'd been tortured, then garroted."

"Maybe somebody looking for their stash," Han said, trying for casual, though it wasn't easy with his mouth gone dry.

"Mayhap." Matieu waggled his knife at Han, curiosity wrestling with caution all over his face. "Thought as you might know something about it."

"Me?" Han fastened down the flap on his bag. "What would I know about it?"

"Ever'body knows you're streetlord of the Raggers. And ever'body knows the Southies roughed you up th'other day. Looks like payback to me."

"Well, ever—everybody's wrong," Han said. "I'm out of that."

"Ri-ight," Matieu said. "Just remember—I don't want no trouble."

Han hoisted his bag over his shoulder. "Believe me, I don't want trouble either."

But trouble had a way of finding him. As he walked out of The Keg and Crown, he just had time to notice it had begun to rain again, before someone grabbed him by the collar and slammed him up against the stone wall of the tavern.

Bloody Southies! he thought. He kicked and struggled, trying to make himself a moving target, expecting at any moment to feel a knife slide between his ribs. But his captor kept him pinned to the wall with one hand while ripping his bag free with the other. The bottles clanked as the bag hit the ground. Then he was crudely patted down one-handed, and relieved of his several knives. And his purse.

Finally his attacker slung him around and smashed him against the wall, face out this time. Han found himself staring into a familiar face, sallow and unhealthy-looking, with thin cruel lips drawn back from yellow rotten teeth. His breath was staggeringly bad.

It was his old nemesis, Mac Gillen, sergeant in the Queen's Guard. And behind him, another half dozen bluejackets.

"Hey! Give me back my purse," Han said loudly, figuring it was best to raise the topic early and often.

Gillen punched him hard in the stomach, and the breath exploded from Han's lungs.

"Well now, Cuffs, you've done it this time," Gillen said,

taking advantage of Han's inability to speak. "I knowed just who was responsible, and I knowed just where to find you. Had to wait a bit is all."

"I . . . don't know . . . what you're talking about," Han gasped, doubled over, arms wrapped protectively over his midsection.

Gillen gripped Han's hair and yanked his head up so they were eye to eye. The sergeant had put on weight since Han had last seen him, and now his soiled uniform gaped between the buttons.

At least somebody's eating well in Southbridge, Han thought. "Who's been beating on you, Ragger?" Gillen demanded. "Wasn't the Southies, was it?"

"Nah," Han said, falling into his old habit of making a bad situation worse. "It was the Guard. I wouldn't pay up."

Everybody knew the bluejackets would leave you alone if you paid protection to the right person. And Mac Gillen was the right person.

Wham! Gillen brought his club down on Han's head, and he fell to his knees, biting his tongue and seeing stars. He covered his head with his arms.

"Stop it!" someone shouted, Han didn't see who. It must've been one of the other bluejackets. Or Matieu, come to his aid?

But Gillen was in a blood rage, totally focused on Han. "You did for those Southies, didn't you, Alister? You and your friends." *Wham!* This blow fell on Han's forearm with bone-shattering force, and he screamed.

"Now you're going to confess, and then you're going to

swing for it, and I'm going to be there to watch."

"I said *stop* it!" The same voice, but right on top of them now. Startled, Han wiped blood from his eyes and looked up to see the club descending again, but it never connected. It flew sideways and Gillen yelped in pain. Han slumped back against the wall, eyes closed, head lolling sideways, at the same time gathering his feet under him.

"You hit him again and I'll crack your skull," his bene-factor said. "Back off."

"What the bloody hell do you think you're doing?" Gillen bellowed. "*I'm* in command here. *I'm* the sergeant. You're just a corporal."

"Back off, Sergeant Gillen, *sir,*" the corporal said sardon-ically. "In the Queen's Guard, *sir,* we don't beat confessions out of prisoners on the street."

"Naw," one of the other bluejackets said, snorting with laughter. "We usually take 'em back to the guardhouse first."

"Are you all right?" A soldier squatted next to Han, look-ing anxiously into his face. Peering through his lashes, Han realized to his surprise that his benefactor was young, no older than he was. The baby bluejacket's face was pale with anger, and a lock of straight black hair fell down over his forehead.

Han blinked away a double image, and said nothing.

"You could've killed him," the corporal said, looking up at Gillen, his face twisted in disgust. Huh, Han thought. This one must've missed his Guard orientation. He had starch, at least, to cross Gillen.

"You listen to me, Byrne," Gillen said. "Maybe you're the son of the commander, and maybe you go to the academy.

155

That don't mean nothin'. You're still just a boy. You don't know these streets like we do. This 'un's a cold-blooded killer and a thief. Just never been caught red-handed before."

Byrne stood and faced Gillen. "Where's your proof? He got beat up? That's *it*?"

Good one, Han thought, silently rooting for the blueblood corporal, but knowing better than to say anything aloud.

Gillen nudged Han with a foot, none too gently. "They call him Cuffs," Gillen said. "He's the leader of a street gang named the Raggers. They been feuding with the Southies for years. Two days ago, the Southies caught Cuffs on his own in Brickmaker's Alley. If the Guard hadn't showed up, he'd be dead a'ready."

Gillen grinned and ran his pale tongue over his cracked lips. "Would've been a service to the community if we'd let them finish the job. Them poor devils we found yesterday— you saw what was done to 'em. Had to be the Raggers. No one else would take the Southies on. It's a revenge killing for sure, and this 'un's responsible."

Corporal Byrne looked down at Han, swallowing hard. "Fine. We take him in for questioning. He confesses or he doesn't. No beatings. Any confession you beat out of a person doesn't mean anything. They'll say anything to make you stop."

Gillen spat on the ground. "You'll learn, Corporal. You can't coddle a street rat. They'll turn on you, and they have teeth, believe me." He turned to the watching bluejackets. "Bring 'im along, then. We'll see to him back at the guard-house." The way he said it gave Han the shivers. This do-gooder Corporal Byrne wouldn't be there every hour of every day.

"One other thing, *sir*," Byrne said. "Maybe you should give him back his purse."

Gillen leveled a look of such vitriol at Byrne that, despite everything, Han had to stifle himself to keep from laughing. Gillen reached into his coat and pulled out Han's purse, made a show of digging through it to make sure he didn't have any weapons in there, then jammed it back into Han's jacket pocket.

No telling how long it'd stay there.

Two bluejackets grabbed Han's arms and hauled him upright, and the pain was blinding. His left forearm felt like it was packed with shards of glass. They draped his arms over their shoulders and began dragging him between them. Han hung, limp as a rag, trying not to pass out, his mind racing furiously, leaping from thought to thought.

Could the Raggers have done for six of the Southies? Why would they? Not on his account, not even for old time's sake. Anything that splashy always brought unwanted attention from the Guard. Everybody knew that.

If not them, who?

Whatever had happened, he couldn't expect fair treatment at the guardhouse. They needed someone to pin this on. He'd dance to whatever tune they played, and he'd end up at the end of a rope. He thought of Mari waiting for him back at the temple, of Mam scrubbing laundry at Fellsmarch Castle. They'd be the ones to pay. He couldn't let that happen.

By now they were passing Southbridge Temple, turning

onto the bridge over the river. Han groaned loudly, scuffling his feet in the dirt as if to gain a purchase.

"Hey! Watch yourself," one of the bluejackets said, tightening his hold on Han's upper arm.

Han groaned again. "Ow! My head! It hurts. Leggo!" He struggled to free his arms. "I don't feel so good," he said, allowing a trace of panic to enter his voice. "I'm serious! I'm going to spew!" He clamped his mouth shut and blew out his cheeks suggestively.

"Not all over me, you're not!" his bluejacket captor said. Gripping Han's collar and the waist of his breeches, the guardsman propelled him to the stone wall that lined the bridge. "Spill it into the river, boy, and make it quick."

Han braced his good hand on the wall, then slammed his head back into the guardsman's face. The bluejacket screamed and let go of him, blood pouring from his broken nose. Han boosted himself atop the wall and squatted there, looking down at the debris floating on the water.

"Stop him!" Gillen screeched behind him. "He's getting away!"

Hands clutched at him as Han launched himself from the wall, executing a flat, shallow dive that took him as far as possible from the stone piers of the bridge. Somehow he managed to miss hitting any of the boats crowded together in the narrow channel, and sliced into the water closer to the north shore. He surfaced, spitting out a mouthful of the filthy water, gagging for real this time.

Good he could swim, courtesy of his summers with the clans. Not many city boys could.

"There he is!" He heard Gillen's voice carrying across the water. "You on the water! Five girlies for the one what catches him."

Five girlies! He'd just about turn himself in for that.

Han submerged again and swam blindly toward the Ragmarket shore, kicking strongly to compensate for his useless right arm, eyes closed tight against the murky water. When he raised his head to check his position and correct his crooked progress, a clamor of voices said he'd been spotted. Then he went under again and managed to lose himself amid the motley of watercraft and floating garbage.

Finally he reached the docks on the Ragmarket side, slid underneath, and waded through the shallows to where the dock met the shore. There he huddled between the pilings, shaking, teeth chattering.

The noise of the search faded as the Guard spread its net wider and wider. Until finally Han couldn't hear it at all. Still, he waited for dark before he slipped out from under the dock and waded to shore.

CHAPTER NINE

EYES AND EARS

The day after the fire on the mountain, Raisa spent all morning with her language tutor, trying to wrap her tongue around soft southern vowels. Tamric was a sloppy language, given to imprecision and double meanings. Made for politics. Raisa much preferred the hard focus of Valespeech, or the subtle nuances of the clan tongue.

As they were finishing, the queen's messenger brought a request that Raisa join her mother for midday in her suite. This was unusual enough that Raisa wondered what kind of trouble she was in.

When the privy chamberlain ushered Raisa into her mother's rooms, she found a table set for two. Her mother was seated by the fire, her pale hair loose, a glittering silk shawl draped around her shoulders. The queen always seemed to be cold. She suffered like a delicate flatland flower transplanted into an inhospitable climate. By contrast, Raisa felt like a tough alpine lichen, dark and stubborn and low to the ground.

Raisa bobbed a curtsy, looking around as she did so. "Mama? Is it just us?"

Marianna patted the seat beside her. "Yes, sweetheart, it seems as though we've scarcely had a chance to talk since you returned from Demonai."

Praise the Maker, Raisa thought. Lately it seemed she never had the chance to be alone with her mother. Lord Bayar was always around. This was her chance to speak to the queen about the issue of the mercenaries. Maybe she could even persuade her mother to intervene and order Captain Byrne to assign Amon to Raisa's personal guard.

Raisa sat down next to her mother, and Marianna poured tea from a thick jug on the table.

"Are you quite all right after that dreadful scare up on Hanalea?" the queen asked. "I had trouble sleeping last night. Shall I ask Lord Vega to come attend you?" Harriman Vega was the court physician.

"I'm fine, Mother," Raisa said. "A few bumps and bruises is all."

"Thanks to the Bayars," Marianna said. "We are so fortunate in our High Wizard, and young Micah seems to have inherited Lord Bayar's talent, don't you think? *And* his good looks," she added, laughing girlishly.

"They are impressive, those Bayars." Raisa took a long sip of tea, recalling her encounter with Micah in the corridor, and wondering when and whether to bring it up.

"How are your studies going?" Marianna asked. "I worried you might have forgotten everything you knew, having been isolated up in the camps so long; but I've had good reports from the masters." She sounded mildly surprised.

"Well." Raisa shifted uncomfortably. You married a clansman, Mama, she thought. Do you remember why? When her parents were together, it seemed like she did. But now her mother sounded like a mouthpiece for Gavan Bayar's continual digs and slanders.

"I don't think I suffered for being at Demonai," Raisa said. "You know the clans are great for reading and storytelling and music and dance," she said. "Even ciphering. I spent a lot of time working in the markets."

"Well, I can't say I approve of that," Marianna said, frowning. "The future Queen of the Fells, learning to be a shopkeeper?"

"Oh, Mama, I learned so *much*," Raisa said. "It's all about learning to read people, and knowing when to give in and when to stick to a price. You have to be able to judge quality on the fly and decide what your high price is. Plus, you learn to walk away from a bad deal, no matter how much you want something."

Raisa leaned forward, gripping her skirts, willing her mother to understand how the delicate give and take of trade and negotiation fueled her. How the flicker of an eye or a sheen of sweat on a trader's upper lip revealed more than he intended. And how letting go of greed and desire allowed her to present an unreadable face in the tough and tumble world of the markets.

The queen listened, fingering the bracelet on her slender wrist, but Raisa could tell she wasn't in a buying mood. Raisa forced herself to settle back into her chair. "Anyway, it wasn't a waste of time," she said lightly.

"I'll take your word for it," Marianna said. She paused as Claire carried in a silver tray, set it on the table, and left again. The queen stood. "Well, then," she said. "Let's eat, shall we?"

Raisa's mother seemed to find it easier to say what was on her mind with food between them. "Your sixteenth name day is coming," she said abruptly as Raisa picked apart her puff-pastry fish pie.

"Is it really? I hadn't realized," Raisa said, rolling her eyes. "Magret is going swaybacked carrying in the suitor gifts."

Her mother smiled. "We expect your debut to attract considerable interest," she said, in her element now that the discussion was about marriages and parties. "Given the war in the south, the successions are, shall we say, in question. Many southern princes will see marriage to a northern princess as a means of solidifying their position in the south, and also as a kind of refuge in case the worst happens." She looked directly at Raisa. "We don't want to fall into that trap."

"What do you mean?" Raisa asked, pausing with a sweet bun halfway to her mouth. She'd never heard her mother say two words together about politics.

"Well, you won't know how things will turn out. Depending on how the war goes, you may be marrying a king or a fugitive."

Raisa shrugged. "I'll be queen on my own account. I don't need to marry a king."

"Precisely!" Marianna said, smiling and taking her first bite.

"I don't understand," Raisa said. "Precisely what?"

"We should avoid a southern alliance," Marianna said. "Things are just too unsettled. There's little to gain and much to lose. We could be drawn into their wars."

"Well," Raisa said, thinking of what Amon had said, "the southern wars won't last forever. Maybe we should wait and see who wins. Then decide what alliance would be most advantageous. A southern marriage may be just what we want. We may need friends when they turn their attention to us."

Marianna blinked at her as if she'd begun speaking Tamric. "But we don't know when that will *be*," she said. "We cannot afford to sit on our hands in the meantime."

"We could be preparing for it now," Raisa said. "A lot of our people have gone as mercenaries in the south, since the money's good. Wouldn't it be a good idea to try to bring them home and use them to build up our own army?"

The queen wrapped her shawl more firmly about her, as if it were armor. "We have no money for that, Raisa," she said.

"We could get rid of the foreign mercenaries we have now," Raisa said. "That should free up some money."

"That's easier said than done," the queen said. "They hold positions of command. General Klemath relies on them to—"

"I didn't say it would be easy," Raisa said. "I just think it's something to consider. It costs more to *buy* foreign soldiers, and people fight better when they're defending their own homes and families. And having all these foreigners here might be risky."

"Where did this come from?" Marianna asked, frowning.

"Is this something you heard at Demonai Camp?"

That was royal code for *Is this something you heard from your father? From your grandmother Elena?*

Just between us, Amon had said. And she didn't want to get him or Captain Byrne into trouble. "No, it's just something I've been thinking for a while."

"Right now you should be focusing on your studies," Marianna said. "I'll be considering who might be the best match for you and the Fells. We can't delay your marriage until the southerners stop fighting. That may never happen."

"But there's no hurry," Raisa said. "You married young, but there's no reason I should. You'll rule for a long time yet. I'll probably be an old crone with my grandchildren around me by the time I come to the throne."

Marianna fussed with her shawl. "I don't know," she said softly. "Sometimes I think I'm not long for this world."

It was an old weapon, familiar since Raisa was a little girl. Still effective.

"Stop that!" Raisa snapped, then added, "Please don't say those things, Mama. I can't stand it."

When she was little, Raisa used to creep out from the nursery to watch her mother sleep, afraid that she would stop breathing if Raisa wasn't there to intervene. The fact that there was something ethereal, almost otherworldly about her mother only reinforced Raisa's fears. Yet she knew Marianna wasn't beyond using this tactic to get her own way.

"It would just ease my mind if I knew the question of your marriage was settled," Marianna said with a sigh.

Raisa had no intention of seeing anything settled very

soon. Marriage was just another kind of prison to put off for as long as possible.

She'd been looking forward to a long season of flirting and wooing and kissing and clandestine meetings involving desperate declarations of love.

Negotiation. Give and take. Redirection.

Ah, redirection. That had always worked well with the queen.

"I've been thinking about my name day party," Raisa said, though she hadn't been, really. "I have some ideas about a dress, and I wanted to see what you thought."

And so they spent a half hour discussing the pros and cons of satin versus lace and black versus white versus emerald green, flounces versus overskirts, tiaras versus beaded snoods and glitter net. Then moved on to debating a tent in the garden versus a party in the Great Hall.

"We'll need to meet with Cook to discuss the matter of the menu," Marianna said, when they'd about worn the topic out. "If we make some decisions now, it will save us considerable trouble in the end. Now, some of it will depend on the guest list, of course . . ."

"Amon's looking forward to the feast," Raisa said, thinking to turn the conversation in a direction she favored. "I'm glad he's back."

"I've been meaning to talk to you about Amon Byrne," the queen said in a tone of voice that never meant good news.

"What about Amon?" Raisa asked, already defensive.

"Magret said you and Corporal Byrne had a secret meeting late last night in the glass house," Marianna said, absently turning a ring on her finger.

"It was hardly secret," Raisa said. "We haven't seen each other in three years. We wanted to catch up, and I didn't get a chance to talk to him during dinner."

"You told Lord Bayar you had a headache," Marianna said.

"I *did* have a headache," Raisa lied. "What of it?"

"And then you slipped away to meet Corporal Byrne," the queen said. "How does that look?"

"I sat with him in a public place with my nurse along," Raisa said, her voice rising. "You tell me. How *does* that look?"

"Magret says the two of you left her in the maze and slipped off on your own," Queen Marianna said.

"Magret fell asleep on the bench, and we chose not to disturb her," Raisa said. "You know how she gets when you wake her up. I had to go back to get her this morning."

That was gratitude for you. Magret *had* been rather testy, complaining about aches and pains in her old bones from sleeping on the stone bench all night. Which maybe explained why she'd run to Queen Marianna to tell tales. Raisa had counted on her to stay quiet to cover up falling asleep on the job. You never could tell what people would do.

Marianna cleared her throat. "And then Corporal Byrne was seen leaving your room later that night."

Raisa shoved back her chair, which made a loud scraping sound. "*Who* said that? Did you get a *report* on me this morning or what? Were you having people follow me *around*?"

"I was not having you followed," Marianna said in her very reasonable voice. "But the High Wizard came to me this morning. He said that Micah went to look in on you because you'd not been feeling well, and he saw you and

Corporal Byrne outside your room . . ."

And this merited a visit from the High Wizard? What business was it of his? "So it's all right if Micah Bayar comes creeping around my room, but Amon—"

"Micah was concerned about you, darling. It was understandable that—"

"Micah practically attacked me in the hallway, Mother! He'd been drinking, and he grabbed my arm, and Amon had to escort him back to his room."

"Don't be overdramatic, Raisa," Marianna snapped. "Micah was surprised, that's all, to find that you and Corporal Byrne had . . . arranged a *tryst*."

The irony was, Raisa and Micah *had* been meeting on the sly. And a marriage between them was expressly forbidden by the Naéming. This whole conversation made no sense.

Raisa stood, her napkin falling to the floor. She should have known better than to think her mother would support her against the Bayars. She was on her own, as usual.

"We're talking about *Amon*," Raisa said. "He's eaten at our table hundreds of times. Why do you keep calling him Corporal Byrne? And as for Micah, ask around. He's cut quite a swath among the ladies-in-waiting and the serving girls. In fact, there are stories that—"

"Micah Bayar comes from Aerie House, a well-respected, noble family," the queen said. "They've been on the council for over a thousand years. On the other hand, the Byrnes—"

"Don't say it!" Raisa interrupted. "Don't you dare. Edon Byrne is captain of your Guard. Are you saying Amon doesn't come from a respected family?"

"Of course he does, Raisa," Marianna said, twisting a strand of hair around her finger. "But he's a soldier, and his father's a soldier, and *his* father, back generations. They're good at what they do. But that's all they'll ever be."

Marianna paused to allow this to sink in. "I know Amon has been your friend. But now that you're older, you need to appreciate the differences between you, and how impossible this all is."

"How impossible *what* is?" Raisa quivered with indignation. "I'm not planning to *marry* him. I know all about my duty to the line. But Amon's my friend, and even if it turned into more than that, it's nobody's business but my own, as long as it doesn't affect the succession. Which it won't."

"But it might," her mother went on. "Do you have any idea how this looks, at a time when we're planning your marriage?"

Raisa opened her mouth and the words came pouring out as if they'd been dammed up in there for years. "If you're worried about how things look, you should worry about you and the High Wizard."

Marianna surged to her feet, the shawl spilling to the floor. *"Raisa ana' Marianna! What do you mean?"* The reasonable voice had disappeared.

"I'm just saying that people are talking about you and Lord Bayar," Raisa said. "They're saying he has too much influence. People say . . . people say it's time my father came home." She swallowed hard, tears welling up in her eyes. "I wish he would too." She got off a curtsy. "By your leave, Your Majesty."

She didn't wait for leave, but turned and fled from the

room. But before she got out of earshot, the queen called after her, her voice high and shrill, "I'm going to speak to Captain Byrne about this."

Like everything else in Raisa's life, her time in temple was prescribed by the Naéming. Four days a month, the Naéming said, the queen and princess heir would go to temple. That could mean one day in a week, or four days in a row.

At Demonai Camp, time in temple was a privilege and not an obligation. Four days in the Matriarch Lodge, in the company of others, or four days in the temple of the forest, meditating on the Maker and all of the works in the natural world. Raisa always ended those days feeling more powerful, more hopeful, somehow more centered in herself and certain of what she needed to do.

But in Fellsmarch Court there were many distractions. Raisa's mother came to temple as required, but she made it into a sort of party, surrounded by her ladies-in-waiting, musicians, entertainers, and servants bearing food and drink. After all, Marianna said, music and food and drink and gossip were the works of the Maker, weren't they, and worth celebrating. About the only difference from a typical day at court was the conspicuous absence of wizards and the presence of the speakers, who might look on disapprovingly, but had little to say. Marianna and her ladies made fun of them behind their backs.

Sometimes it seemed to Raisa that life at court was designed to keep a person from thinking too much about anything in particular.

But there were some things that needed thinking about.

After the argument with her mother, Raisa was in no mood to talk to anyone, so she took refuge in the small temple in the glass house maze on the roof. The sun poured down through the roof, and she slid open the glass panels, which allowed the spring air to pour into the garden.

For a time after she settled herself on the stone bench, her mind raced madly, chasing images of Micah Bayar and Amon Byrne, her mother and Gavan Bayar. Gradually her mind slowed and picked over thoughts more carefully.

Take charge of the horse you're riding before you try to rein in someone else's, Elena Demonai always said. And make sure you have a good seat before you do.

In the space of a day, she'd kissed two different boys— Amon and Micah. Both were intensely appealing, in different ways. Both were forbidden to her.

Was that why they drew her—because they were forbidden? Because she didn't have to confront the ugly matrimonial issue? Because she was tired of doing as she was told?

In a way, she was being true to her heritage. The Gray Wolf queens were famous for their dalliances. The most famous of all, of course, was Hanalea. There was even a book about Hanalea's conquests. She'd caught Magret reading it.

Raisa's mind drifted from romance to policy. Eyes and ears, Amon had said. She needed eyes and ears of her own.

Future possibilities rolled toward her. Straight before her lay a wide road that extended into the distance—what might happen if she followed the plan laid out for her. She saw a marriage to someone of her mother's choosing, and sooner rather than later. She could not see the end of it. It was lost in shadow.

To either side lay diverging passages, as narrow and overgrown as the ways in the maze, some difficult to find, each with its own risks and unknowns. So there were other possibilities, but never easy ones.

As she sat, eyes half closed, someone settled next to her on the bench. She knew without opening her eyes who it was, and she released her breath in a long sigh.

"Good afternoon, Raisa," Elena Demonai said. "May I join you?"

"Good afternoon, Elena *Cennestre*. Welcome," Raisa said, using the clan word for *Mother*. She opened her eyes. "How did you find me?"

"This is a very old place, *lytling*," Elena said, her caramel face crinkling into a smile that framed the green eyes of the seer. "It is one of the few places in the Vale with power. You will have need of it."

Raisa considered this. At Demonai she'd learned not to ask every question that came to mind, knowing some things would be understood in their own time.

"I'm worried, Grandmother," Raisa said. "The way ahead seems clear enough, but I'm not sure it's the right way."

"In the Spirits, we find our way by sun and stars and other landmarks," Elena said. "They tell us if we are on the right road, and keep us out of trouble. How do you avoid danger in the flatlands?"

Raisa thought a moment. "The same as in the markets. I look for a mismatch—when someone tells me one thing and their eyes and hands and bodies tell me something else."

"And are you seeing mismatches now?"

"I hear Lord Bayar's words coming out of my mother's mouth," Raisa said bluntly. "She used to speak for herself. And now . . . I don't know."

Elena nodded. "And what else?"

"I feel that a trap is closing around me, and I don't yet know what it is." Raisa hesitated. "I saw wolves on Hanalea the day of the fire, but Mama didn't seem to notice."

"Wolves," Elena murmured. "The Gray Wolf line is in danger, and the queen does not see it." She looked up at Raisa. "Under the Naéming, the High Wizard is magically bound to the queen. Lord Bayar does not act like a bound wizard. Something is amiss."

"What can I do?" Raisa asked.

"Would the queen be willing to come to Demonai Camp?" Elena asked. "Could you persuade her?"

Raisa shook her head. "I don't know," she said. "I don't think so. She's not very happy with me right now. Every time I try to talk about Lord Bayar, she gets angry."

"You must continue to try, *lytling*," Elena said. "Try to convince her to come to temple at Demonai. And you be wary of the Bayars. The young Bayar is charming and handsome, but keep your distance. Don't be ensnared."

"Yes, Grandmother," Raisa said.

"I have a gift for you," Elena said. She pulled a deerskin pouch from the pocket of her overtunic and handed it to Raisa.

Raisa untied the cord and spilled the contents into her

hand. It was a heavy gold ring on a chain, dulled with age, engraved with images of running wolves, endlessly circling. She could tell it that it was too large for any of her fingers.

Raisa looked up at Elena. "It . . . it looks very old," she said, which was all she could think of.

Elena took it from her, undid the clasp with amazing dexterity, and fastened the chain around Raisa's neck. "This once belonged to Hanalea," Elena said abruptly.

"Hanalea," Raisa said. "But it looks too big for—"

"It is what we call a talisman. It offers some protection against wizard charms. Never take it off.

"Now," Elena said, rising, "I will do what I can to bring your father home."

Sometime later, Raisa yawned and opened her eyes. She was alone in the maze, slumped in a corner of the bench, a warm south wind stirring her hair. Had she fallen asleep? Had it all been a dream?

But the Running Wolves ring hung heavy from the chain around her neck.

CHAPTER TEN

BACK IN THE MAZE

Raisa sent a messenger to the barracks, asking Amon to meet her in the maze temple at evensong time that evening, but he sent a reply back saying he was on duty. She tried again the next night, with the same result. After the third rejection, she threatened to visit him in his quarters in the barracks, and he finally agreed to come.

Meanwhile, Micah sent her an extravagant bouquet of flowers and several notes suggesting a meeting. She ignored them. She'd teach him to run to his father, telling tales.

That night she traveled through the stone passageway with more confidence, carrying a lighted taper and making enough noise to scatter the rats ahead of her. Her attire was more practical as well—she wore one of her divided riding skirts, boots, and a close-fitting jacket. This made it much easier when she ascended the ladder, clenching the taper in her teeth like a pirate.

When she slammed open the metal door from the

passageway, Amon leaped up from the bench, ripping his sword from its scabbard. He pivoted on his heel, scanning the room.

"Hanalea's bones, Rai," he said, shaking his head and sliding his sword home again. "I thought you were going to block that tunnel off."

"I never said I would," she replied, flopping down on the bench. "I like having a back door." She raised her hand as he opened his mouth. "Don't start. Please sit down. You're looming over me like a flatland priest."

He sat down on the bench, squeezing into the farthest corner as if she might be catching, his body stiff and formal, his hands carefully placed on his knees.

"Why have you been avoiding me?" Raisa asked bluntly.

"I haven't been . . ." He stopped when she glared at him. "All right. It's just . . . my Da had a talk with me."

"And said what?"

"Well." He flushed. "He said a lot. The main thing is, I'm in the Guard now, and that means I'm on duty all day, every day. If we're to do our job protecting the royal family, we have to keep a certain . . . distance." He cleared his throat. "And, well . . . I could see his point."

"See what point? I'm not allowed to have friends?" Raisa knew she was being unfair, but she was in no mood for fair play, and he was the only available target. Plus, the only time he left off his military correctness and turned into the Amon she knew was when she got him angry.

"Of course we're friends, but we—"

"We're not allowed to talk to each other, is that it?" Raisa pulled her long plait of hair forward and rebraided it.

"We can *talk* to each other, but—"

"Only across a crowded room?" She scooted closer. "Is this too close?" And closer. "How about this?" Until her hip was pressing against his.

"Raisa, will you let me finish a sentence at least?" he growled, but didn't move away. "I don't know where it's coming from, but Da said people are talking about us. He threatened to post me to Chalk Cliffs if he hears any more about it."

Raisa put her hand on his arm. "He wouldn't." Chalk Cliffs was a port on the Indio Ocean, hundreds of miles away.

He lifted an eyebrow. "Aye. He would. So if that's what you want . . ."

"Are you going to let Micah Bayar dictate who I see and talk to?"

He stared at her. "What?"

"Micah spoke to his father about seeing us outside my room the other night. Lord Bayar spoke to the queen, and the queen spoke to your father."

"The queen's involved in this?" He raked back his hair, looking bewildered. "I don't get it." He paused. "I was wondering if you and Micah were, you know . . ." He couldn't seem to find the word he wanted and stopped, cleared his throat. "Last night, I didn't know if . . ." He ran out of words again and stared down at his hands.

That wasn't really a topic she wanted to discuss with Amon Byrne.

"Never mind Micah," Raisa said. "He's just used to getting

his own way. But something's going on. I just haven't figured out what, yet. I need friends I can trust. I need somebody on my side."

"I'm on your side, Rai," Amon said quietly. "Always. You know that."

Raisa took his hand in hers. "Then help me."

He eyed her warily. "Help you how?"

"I need eyes and ears. I need to know what's going on—in the queendom, in the Wizard Council house on Gray Lady Mountain, everywhere. I feel like a canary in a cage. I see only the four walls around me, and meanwhile the castle is surrounded and my enemies are closing in."

"What?" He gazed into her face, no doubt looking for signs of madness or drink. "What are you talking about?"

"You know the blooded queens have visions sometimes that foretell the future." Amon nodded. "Well, I feel the way I did the day of the fire on Hanalea. I'm trapped, with the flames rushing toward me and nowhere to go."

"Well." Amon cleared his throat. "How can you tell if it's a true vision? I mean, I have nightmares sometimes, but that's all they are."

"It's possible that I'm imagining things," Raisa said. "But I can't take that chance."

"Have you told the queen? Seems like that'd be the place to start."

"The thing is, I think she may be part of the problem," Raisa said. "I've tried to talk with her, and we just end up arguing."

Her voice trailed off at Amon's conflicted expression. She

and Amon had always shared grievances with each other. But now it felt as though she were asking him to side with her against the queen he'd sworn himself to.

"That's not much to go on. A feeling," he said finally.

"*And* the peculiar way people are acting," Raisa argued. "My mother went on and on the other day about how I shouldn't marry a southerner, that things are just too unsettled down there."

"Maybe it's just jitters about you getting older, making your debut, and the like." Amon extended his hands, palms up. "All parents have trouble with that. I remember when my sister, Lydia, had her name day. Da interrogated and terrorized any boy who came near her."

"I don't know. At the same time, it seems like she's in a hurry for me to get married. She says she'd like to see things settled, that she may not be around too much longer, like maybe she knows something I don't. Even though I've not reached my name day and there's no candidate in sight."

"*You* said it wouldn't be for years and years," Amon said, almost accusingly.

Raisa shrugged. "If I have anything to say about it." She shuddered. "I don't want to get married. I'm only fifteen years old."

"Well, I'm just seventeen," Amon said. "And I'm going back to the academy in the fall. What do you want me to do? Who do you want me to spy on?"

"Not spy, exactly. For instance, I get information from Demonai Camp that I don't get from anywhere else. They don't flatter me. They don't treat me like an empty-headed icon. In a way, they respect me more than anyone else does."

"What kind of information do you want from me?"

Raisa sat up straighter. "Well, if there's trouble coming, I'm thinking it must be coming from one of two places—from the wars in the south, or from the Wizard Council."

"What about the people of Fellsmarch? What if they were planning some kind of rebellion?" Amon asked.

"Why would they do that?" Raisa said, frowning. "People love the queen. Whenever we go out in the city, they all cheer and throw flowers at our feet."

Amon was shaking his head, wearing a look that was almost pitying.

"What?" Raisa snapped, instantly annoyed.

"Well, they're miserable, for one thing, and starving, and from what I've seen, the Queen's Guard spends most of their time pushing them around."

"No," Raisa said with conviction. "The Guard is there to protect the people."

"Raisa, have you ever been to Southbridge?"

"Of course I have. I've been to the temple there, and I've ridden through dozens of times. It's kind of run-down, but ..."

"Let me guess. You rode in a carriage with an entourage down the Way, with your Guard lining the streets to either side."

She nodded reluctantly. "Pretty much."

"You can't tell what's really going on when you're so ... insulated. I've been on foot patrol in Southbridge and Ragmarket for the past two weeks. Let me tell you what happened this week. Yesterday, six people were murdered in

Southbridge. Four boys, two girls, all about our age. They were tortured and strangled."

"Sweet Hanalea," whispered Raisa. "I didn't hear about this. Who would do something like that?"

"Good question. They were all in a street gang called the Southies. Sergeant Gillen thinks a rival gang called the Raggers did them for revenge."

"Revenge for what?" Raisa asked, leaning forward, fascinated in spite of herself.

"The Southies beat up the leader of the Raggers a few days ago, a boy by the name of Cuffs. He wears these silver bracelets, kind of his trademark. Gillen knew where he might be so we grabbed him coming out of a tavern earlier today."

Amon raked back his hair with both hands. "He's *our* age, and Gillen thinks he murdered six people."

"So you questioned him?" Raisa prompted. "What did he have to say for himself?"

"Well, the first thing Gillen does is steal his purse and beat him senseless with a club," Amon said.

"*What?*" Raisa shook her head as if she could deny it was so. "Why would he do that?"

Amon shrugged. "Gillen's a bully and a thief. I finally put a stop to it, so now I'm on Gillen's dirt list for sure. If my da wasn't captain, I think Gillen would've beat the boy to death. He told me how I was new and didn't know the streets, and I'd learn."

"So they do this kind of thing all the time?"

Amon nodded. "Several times, just since I've been with them."

"So what happened? With Cuffs, I mean?"

"I insisted they take him back to the guardhouse and question him properly. But he broke away and escaped while we were crossing South Bridge. Jumped into the river, so he may be drowned." Amon smiled sourly. "This Cuffs isn't stupid, whatever he's done. If I was being dragged back to the guardhouse for interrogation by Mac Gillen, I'd do whatever it took to escape too. 'Course, now Gillen and them think it's my fault he escaped. And it probably is." He sighed.

Raisa leaned forward, trying to read Amon's face. "Do you think he was guilty?"

Amon stared out at the water. "Seems likely. But you don't find out the truth by torturing somebody." He looked up at Raisa. "The point is, people in Southbridge and Ragmarket are scared to death of the Queen's Guard, and for good reason." His gray eyes went flinty hard. "Me, I'd like to tie up Mac Gillen and leave him in a Ragmarket alley overnight. See what's left of him in the morning."

Amon's changing, Raisa thought. I hardly know him anymore. He's seeing things, and doing things, and learning things while I'm penned up here like a hothouse flower, learning what fork to use.

She put her hand on his arm. "I'll see that Gillen's dismissed," she promised.

Amon grinned, his first real smile of the evening. "So you'll tell the queen you were chatting with me and I suggested Gillen be let go? I don't think so." He shook his head. "No need. I already spoke with my da. If there's anything can be done, he'll handle it. But the Guard is full of Gillens. It's a haven for thugs. There's only so much a captain can do. It didn't used to be this way."

Raisa stood and paced back and forth. "This is exactly what I'm talking about. How can I be princess heir of the queendom and not know what's going on?" She stopped midturn. "You say people are starving?"

He nodded. "You know we don't grow much here. The Vale is fertile, but there's not much other suitable land and our winters are too long. We can't eat gold and silver and copper. We've always depended on trade with Arden and Tamron and the other kingdoms to the south for our grain. With the wars dragging on, what little food comes north costs too much for most people to afford." He paused, then forged ahead, blunt to the bone. "You can't assume that because you have plenty to eat that everyone does."

Raisa was mortified. "I don't want to be that kind of queen," she said. "Thoughtless and selfish and shallow and . . ."

"You won't be," Amon said quickly. "That's not what I meant."

"Yes it is. And I deserve it. I need to find a way to help people." But what could she do about it? She might live in a palace, she sat down to a feast every single night, and she had a wardrobe full of clothes—but no money of her own.

She could try speaking with the queen, but she'd had little luck pressing her suit earlier in the week. Based on that conversation, her mother probably planned to spend any extra money she had on a wedding.

Besides, Raisa wanted to do something on her own. Something important. Something emblematic of the queen she meant to be.

She'd felt totally useless since returning to Fellsmarch from Demonai.

Maybe she could empty her closet and sell some of her frilly dresses in Ragmarket and use the proceeds to buy food for people who had none. Though that wouldn't bring in much money.

And then she had an idea. The more she thought about it, the better she liked it.

She looked up at Amon. "Thank you for telling me the truth. Now that you've done that, will you help me?"

He squinted at her suspiciously. "Help you how?"

"Could you carry a message to Demonai and tell them to give it to my grandmother, Elena?"

He hesitated. "I'd need to know what it was about," he said.

"I'm going to ask her to send one of her best traders down to meet with me at Southbridge Temple day after tomorrow."

"Why Southbridge?" Amon asked. "Couldn't they come here?"

"I'm unlikely to be recognized there. And there's someone at Southbridge Temple I want to talk to. Have you heard of Speaker Jemson?"

"Well, yeah," Amon said, as if surprised Raisa had heard of the outspoken speaker. "Anyone who's been to Southbridge knows about Jemson. Only . . . how are you planning on getting there?"

She shrugged. "I'll go in disguise. You said I should get out more and see what's really going on in the city."

"What?" Amon raised his hands, looking alarmed. "I didn't exactly . . . You can't walk into Southbridge by yourself. I don't care what kind of disguise you've got on."

"Then come with me," she said, grinning at him. It could be an adventure, just like the old days.

"One person isn't enough to keep you safe." Impulsively, he gripped her hand, as if he could pull her over to his side of the argument. His hand was warm, the palm callused. "Come on, Raisa, why do you have to go on your own? Just make up a story. Say you're going to temple to worship."

She shook her head. "That'll mean an entourage, remember? Armed guard, carriage, and procession? I don't want that. I want honest answers, and I won't get that with an escort."

"If you're going to Southbridge, you'll *need* an armed guard." When she said nothing, he added, "What *are* you up to?"

"I don't want to say until I know if it'll work."

"What if I can't get away? I'll likely be on duty the rest of the week."

She stood. "Well, I'm going, with you or without you. If you want to come with me, meet me day after tomorrow at evensong at the far end of the drawbridge."

"You're planning to go at *night*?" Amon said, staring at her as if all his worst fears were being realized.

"Well, yes," Raisa said. "I'm less likely to be recognized in the dark."

"You're also more likely to get your throat cut. Or worse." He stood also, towering over her, hoping he could intimidate her into changing her mind. "This is a really bad idea. Drop it, Rai, or I'll tell my da, and he'll have someone waiting to intercept you."

Raisa met his gaze directly, though she had to tilt her head back to do so. "And if you do, I'll just wait and go another time on my own."

It was their pattern from childhood, and difficult to break. She came up with the bold, dangerous ideas, and he provided the muscle to see them through.

They stood glaring at each other for a long moment.

"I might not be able to reach Elena," Amon grumbled. That's how Raisa knew she'd won.

Only—why was he giving up so easily? She scanned his face. He wouldn't look at her, which meant he was hatching some scheme or other.

Fine. Whatever it was, she'd deal with it. She leaned in, intending a rather chaste kiss on the cheek, but he turned his head and it landed rather close to the corner of his mouth. She jerked back and they stared at each other. Close up, his face was pleasantly stubbled.

"Well then." She stood, feeling flushed and flustered. "Thank you for coming tonight. I feel like you're the only friend I have."

She crossed to the tunnel opening at the center of the temple. "Even if you can't come to Southbridge, let's meet here a week from now, and I'll let you know how it went."

"If you're still alive a week from now," he grumbled.

She grinned at him. "Close the hatch for me, will you?" She began to descend the ladder, feeling more alive than she had since her return to court.

Not that she didn't feel a twinge of guilt. It wasn't fair, what she was asking of Amon, and she knew it. He had much more to lose than she did. He was a member of the Queen's Guard, sworn to her service. His own father, the captain of the Guard, had told him to keep his distance from Raisa.

Then again, it wasn't like she was asking him to commit treason. She was the princess heir, after all, and he was in her service too.

But he was already in trouble on her account. The Bayars were known to be dangerous enemies, and Micah would be looking for a chance to get back at him. And all her excuses didn't change the fact that Amon would be the one to suffer if they were found out. A posting to Chalk Cliffs would be the least of it.

CHAPTER ELEVEN

SANCTUARY

The Southbridge Temple bells bonged four times. The sound reverberated on the cobblestones, proclaiming that it was four in the morning and any sensible person should be safe in bed. The torches to either side of the blessing entrance still blazed, however, welcoming anyone at need any hour of the day. At this particular moment, Han would have preferred to be hidden in darkness.

Pressing himself into the shadow of the building, Han lifted the elaborate knocker and allowed it to slam against the wooden door a second time. He looked over his shoulder, expecting at any moment to feel the hard grip of the Guard on his arm or the prick of cold steel.

He heard footsteps within, then the rattle of the latch as the door swung in. A white-robed dedicate blinked at him, her pale hair tousled from sleep. She looked to be the same age as Han. "The Maker bless you," she said, yawning; then her eyes went wide as she focused more closely on him. "What happened to you, mate?" she demanded, her Southbridge accent surfacing. "You been in a fight?" she asked, avid curiosity driving away sleep.

"I need a place to stay," Han said, and added, "please," when she still stood frozen. "I swear by the Maker, I'm not here to hurt anybody." He swayed a bit, and she draped an arm around his waist and helped him to a stone bench in the entryway.

She drew back quickly, brushing at her robes. "You stink," she said, making a face.

"Sorry. I fell in the river," he said, closing his eyes as a wave of dizziness swept over him.

"What's wrong with your arm?" she asked.

He ignored the question. "Could you wake Speaker Jemson, please? It's important."

"Well, I don't know as he'd like bein' waked at this time of night," she said. "Can I give him a message in the morning?"

Han kept his eyes closed and said nothing. Eventually he heard her pad away down the corridor. He was nearly asleep when he heard the rumble of Jemson's voice drawing nearer.

"How badly is he hurt, Dori? You're sure he's not one of our students?"

"I don't know as I'd recognize him, even if I knew him, Master Jemson. He's right mangled, he is."

Han opened his eyes to see Jemson looking down at him, tall and severe.

"Master Alister. Thank the Maker you're alive. I feared the worst."

"Where's Mari?" Han asked.

"She's sleeping, safe in the dormitory. The dedicates have taken charge of her. I sent word to your mother so she wouldn't worry."

Han struggled to sit up one-armed. "You got to get her out of Southbridge and back to Ragmarket," he said. "Nobody can know where I live or that I even have a sister."

Jemson looked over at Dori, who was listening with great interest. "That will be all, Dori," he said. "Go on to bed. I'll manage from here."

Dori shuffled out reluctantly, with many backward looks.

The speaker knelt in a whisper of fabric so he could look Han directly in the eyes. "Tell me, Hanson, did you have anything to do with those killings?" he asked sternly. "I need to know the truth."

"No, sir," Han whispered. "I swear it."

"Any idea of who might have done it? Or why?" Jemson asked.

Han shook his head. "No. But I'm being blamed. The Queen's Guard is hunting me." He looked down at his shoes. "I'm sorry to get you mucked up in this, and I'll leave if you want me to. It's just . . . I got to get off the street and I have nowhere to go. If I can make it up to Marisa Pines, I can stay out of sight up there for a while, but first, I got some business here."

"I don't like the sound of that," Jemson said. "You left this morning *on business*, and came back bloodied, on the run from the Guard. I think you'd best leave well enough alone."

"But I have to find out who did the Southies," Han said.

"If it was the Raggers, I need to know. I can't stay in the mountains forever. I can't leave Mam and Mari on their own."

"We'll see," Jemson said. "In the meantime, you need healing. If I'm not mistaken, that arm is broken."

Han had been cradling his injured arm with his other one. It was swollen from elbow to wrist, and turning a nasty blue-green color. His silver cuff was tight, the flesh bulging around it.

"I can't pay for a healer," Han said. "Maybe if we bind it, it can wait till I get to Marisa Pines."

"Actually, there's someone here who can help, I think," the speaker said. "Are you able to stand?"

When Han nodded, the speaker said, "Come with me." Jemson helped Han to his feet and led him down the hall, supporting his good elbow with one hand and carrying a lamp in the other. The usually bustling corridors were eerily silent, the temple sleeping around them. Jemson led him past the sanctuary and classrooms to the stone dormitories where the boarders and dedicates stayed.

They crossed a moonlit courtyard, and Jemson pushed open the door to a room that gave onto the healer's garden. Inside were two single beds, a table, a straight chair and a rocker, a tub for bathing, a trunk, and a dry sink and basin.

Jemson set the lamp on the table. "Lie down and rest. I'll be right back."

Han sank gratefully onto the bed, feeling guilty because he was still filthy from the river, but too tired to do anything about it. Just having a refuge, someplace to sleep for a few hours, was a blessing. His arm throbbed, but he was so tired he fell into a kind of worried waking sleep. It seemed only minutes later that he woke, startled, when someone entered the room and sat on the edge of his bed. He groped for a knife that was no longer there.

"Hunts Alone, what have the flatlanders done to you?" Willo set her healer's bag next to him and put her cool hand on his feverish forehead.

"Willo?" His mouth was so dry he could scarcely force out the word. "What are you doing here?" Willo never came to the city. She claimed it drained all the magic out of her.

"I had business in Fellsmarch," she said. She gently examined his arm, and the touch of her hand was like cool water flowing over it, washing away the pain. Rising, she poured water from the pitcher into a cup and sprinkled the contents of a beaded pouch into it. "Here," she said. "Drink. It's willow bark. It will help with the pain."

It was willow bark and turtleweed, and maybe something else, too, because then it seemed he began hallucinating.

A door opened and closed, and he thought he heard Dancer say, "What happened to Hunts Alone? Who did this? Let me see him."

Then Willo's voice, some kind of argument, like she was trying to persuade him to leave. Quick footsteps, then Dancer loomed over him, breathing hard, eyes wild, his face gleaming with sweat, his hair hanging in long damp strands. He wore a dedicate's robe, bright against his dark skin.

"Hunts Alone," he whispered, extending his hand toward Han's face.

Dancer's skin kindled and blazed, and flames pinwheeled

out from his body. Han threw his good arm over his face to protect it. Then Willo and Jemson were dragging Dancer back, out of Han's sight.

"You can't help him, Dancer," Willo was saying urgently. "Go with Jemson, and let me work. Please."

"Dancer!" Han shouted, trying to rise, but the drug made him helpless. Dancer was sick. Dancer was on fire. Fire Dancer.

Moments later, Willo returned. He tried to speak to her, to ask her what was going on, but he couldn't articulate the words. He was vaguely aware of Willo straightening his arm, saying words over it, splinting it, binding it to his body. And he knew nothing else after that.

He awoke in the late afternoon. Sunlight slanted through the windows, birds were singing, and the scent of flowers wafted through the open door. All good.

He looked down at himself. Somehow they'd bathed him and dressed him in a dedicate's white robe. His purse was sitting on his bedside table, but his clothes seemed to be missing. The swelling in his arm had gone down dramatically. It was bound tightly to his chest, and there was only a dull ache to remind him of the blinding pain of the day before. With any luck he'd have full use of it by the end of the week. Willo had worked on him before.

Images swirled through his mind like smears of wet paint. Gillen's club coming down on his head. Dancer on fire. Willo's worried face.

He swung his legs off the bed and stood shakily, realizing

he was starving. That was another thing about rapid healing—it left you ravenous. He shuffled barefoot to the door and peered out into the garden in time to see Dori heading his way with a likely-looking tray.

"Mother Willo said you'd be wanting something to eat," Dori said. "Good to see you up and about." She carried the tray into Han's room and set it on the table, then sat down on one of the beds and drew her knees up, propping her feet on the bed frame as if she meant to stay awhile. She had a round, pretty face marred by rather narrow blue eyes and a small, unhappy mouth. He couldn't tell much about the shape of her under the robes, but she looked rather plush.

"Well, thanks," Han said, sitting down on the other bed and pulling the napkin off the tray. He'd worried it might be porridge or some other invalid food, but it was a good slab of cheese, a hunk of brown bread, and some fruit. He tucked into it, washing it down with cups of water.

"I'm Dori," she said, leaning forward and sticking her face in close as if jealous of the attention the food was getting. "An' you're Cuffs Alister," she added, nodding wisely. "I've heard of you. Everybody has."

"Good to meet you," Han said with his mouth full.

"I'm a first-year dedicate," she said. "Before that, I lived in Blackberry Alley."

"Hmmm," Han said, and when she continued to look at him expectantly, added, "How'd you decide to become a dedicate?"

"Oh, 'twas my mother's idea," Dori said. "One less mouth to feed at home, she said. It was that or lady's maid."

"Ah. How do you like it?"

"It's all right, I guess." She tugged dispiritedly at her robe. "I get tired of wearing these all the time," she said. "I wish they came in colors, at least."

She leaned forward and said conspiratorially, "What's it like, being leader of the Raggers? I heard there was a thousand-girlie price on your head."

"That's not me," Han said, thinking he should letter it across the front of his robe. "People make that mistake all the time. I don't run with gangs."

"Oh," Dori said, disappointed. "So you never killed nobody, I guess." Then, after a pause, "But you got fair hair like him. I never seen a boy with hair so fair as yours. It's near as light as mine. See?" She wound a strand of her hair around her forefinger and held it out for his inspection.

Han finished off the last of the bread and cheese and licked his fingers. "Thanks for dinner," he said, yawning and lying back on his pillows, hoping she would get the hint and leave.

But instead she came and sat down on the edge of his bed, seized hold of his good hand, and pushed back his sleeve. "You're wearing the silver," she said, glaring at him like he'd tried to pick her pocket. "You're Cuffs Alister, you got to be."

"What's it matter?" he said, wishing for the thousandth time he could get the bloody bracelets off.

"They say you got the bluejackets in your pocket," Dori said. "They say that in your secret hideout you got treasure lying around all over the place—di'monds and rubies and emeralds stole from the nobility, and you dress all in gold and keep beautiful rich women for ransom, and they all fall in love with you and don't want to be let go."

"I don't know how that rumor got started," Han said, desperately wishing her gone.

"And so, when you let them go, you tell them to pick anything they want from your treasure to take with them, and they choose a ring or necklace or something and won't give it up, not for nothing, and they sleep with it under their pillows. And some of them take temple vows after that because they i'nt interested in anybody after you."

Han would've busted out laughing if it wasn't for the fact his instincts were screaming *Danger* at him. "Use your head," he said. "I'm only sixteen. How could any of it be true? Besides, I'm out of all that."

She blinked at him with eyes as vacant and blue as a cloudless sky. "I don't believe it. Why would you get out of it?"

Han had no interest in trying to explain it to Dori—the war that had gone on within him most of his life. Street life was seductive. It made you feel powerful, because you controlled life and death and commerce within a few city blocks. Because people crossed the street when they saw you coming. Because girlies wanted to be with a streetlord.

Eventually, your story grew into a legend until you didn't know who you were anymore and what you were capable of. The violent battle for turf, swag, and survival became addictive, so that school and family life seemed a dull backdrop for the adrenaline reality of the streets.

He'd been good at it. Crazy good, or maybe just crazy.

He'd done things he didn't like to think about now.

Dori's breathless voice broke into his reverie. "Do you have a sweetheart?" she asked, holding fast to his hand. "'Cause I don't have a sweetheart."

Han knew this was straying into treacherous territory, but just then someone appeared in the doorway like a small-sized angel sent from heaven. "Han!"

It was Mari. The reason he'd left the life.

Dori snatched back her hand and retreated to the other bed. Han propped himself up, and his little sister flung herself into his arms—or *arm*, rather. "They said you were hurt. What happened to your arm? Where did you go yesterday? Why didn't you come back?"

"I got jumped in the street," Han said, which was perfectly true. "I may have to go away for a while. But first I'll get you back home."

"Where do you live?" Dori asked, looking from Han to Mari.

"On Cobble Street, over the stable," Mari said, before Han could stop her. He wasn't sure why he should stop her, he just felt like he didn't want Dori knowing where to find him. Assuming he ever got to go home.

"You look funny in those robes," Mari said. "And your hair is sticking up." She wet a finger and tried to smooth it down. "Master Jemson sent me to see if you were awake. You're supposed to go see him in his study. Right now, he said, if you're able." She tugged at his hand.

"Ah. Well. See you later, Dori," Han said, thinking, *Not if I see you first.*

Speaker Jemson's study was all over books—stacked on every level surface and shelved in bookcases that stretched to the ceiling. Parchments were rolled and stored in niches and spread out on his desk, anchored with stones. Maps of far-away places were pinned to the walls. It smelled of leather and dust and lamp oil and learning.

When Han was a small boy, he used to bury himself in Jemson's library for hours at a time. Jemson never fussed at him to wash his dirty fingers before touching the gold-stamped bindings or to be careful turning the fragile pages. The speaker never warned him not to spill ink when he was transcribing passages, or told him not to touch the hand-painted illustrations. He never took books away because they were too complicated, too grown-up, or too thick for him to look at.

Jemson's love of books was catching, and Han took care of them even though he'd never owned one himself.

The speaker sat at his desk, inking something onto parchment, his teapot on a little burner beside him. Without looking up he said, "Sit down, Master Alister. Mistress Mari, Speaker Lara is holding forth in the art studio this afternoon. Please join her while I speak with your brother."

Mari stiffened and opened her mouth to protest, but Han patted her shoulder awkwardly. "Go on," he said. "Don't worry. I'll come find you when I'm done."

Han sat in silence for a few minutes while Jemson continued with whatever he was writing. When the master had finished, he sifted sand over the page and set it aside. Then he looked up at Han for the first time.

The speaker looked somehow older than he had the day before, his face hollowed by new pain and disappointment. "Would you like some tea, Master Alister?" he asked, fetching down a mug from the shelf behind his desk.

Han sat forward in his chair. "What is it? What's happened?"

Jemson poured for him, anyway. "They found two more bodies this morning," he said.

"Southies?" Han asked.

Jemson nodded.

Han licked his lips, his dinner sitting heavily in his stomach now. "Same as before?"

Jemson nodded again. "They'd been tortured. Burned in different places. It was kind of hard to tell what actually killed them. Maybe they died of fright."

"You saw the bodies?"

Jemson turned his mug in his hand. "They brought them here, hoping we could identify them. I knew both of them. Josua and Jenny Marfan. A brother and sister. They used to come to temple before I lost them to the streets. I always hoped they'd leave that life. Like you have."

The speaker gave him a long significant look, and Han knew he was waiting for him to volunteer something. Jemson could make a person confess any crime with his silences. Han often thought the Guard would do better if they'd hire him for interrogations in place of beatings.

"Like I told you before, I don't know anything about it," Han said. "You know I had no personal hand in it, since I was here all night. The Guard will blame the Raggers, but it doesn't make sense to me. Whatever point they were trying to make, six dead Southies would do fine. No reason to kill two more. Unless they mean to clean the Southies right out of Southbridge."

Jemson lifted an eyebrow. "Is that a possibility?"

Han shrugged. "Unlikely. Ragmarket is the better territory. Closer to Fellsmarch Castle, more money passing through, more easy marks with fat purses. Over here they got Mac Gillen wringing them dry. He's been on the dawb for years. Gillen claims to be buyable, but he'll double-cross you in a heartbeat if he needs a scapegoat. He has high-up connections, I hear, so I'm guessing he'll never get the sack. So what I'm saying is, it's just not worth the aggravation of trying to take Southbridge over."

Han blew on his tea and took a cautious sip. "Over in Ragmarket, the Guard's workable. They're mostly locals, and they'd rather sit in their garrison houses and dice and play cards. Nobody's trying to make a name for himself. If you make a deal with them, they honor it. If they're on the dawb, they won't come after you, unless you do something they can't ignore. Which is why all these murders are stupid."

"Stupid." Jemson stared at Han as if he'd been speaking a foreign language.

"Well, yeah. There's no swag in it except bragging rights, and it brings out the bluejackets. You got to play it smart. When I ran the Raggers, we'd never . . ." His voice trailed off as he took in Jemson's expression. "Say it," he growled. "Whatever you're thinking."

"I'm thinking that there are other reasons not to murder

people beyond the fact that there's no *swag* in it, as you say," Jemson said mildly.

"Yeah, well. I can sing any song you like, you know that," Han said. "I'm just being straight with you here."

"I know, and I appreciate that." Jemson rubbed his forehead with the heel of his hand. "Forgive me. I just get frustrated sometimes. Master Alister, I see that your reputation as a leader and strategist is fairly earned. And all those qualities that made you a stellar streetlord could take you wherever you want to go. The trades. The army. The court at Fellsmarch." He sighed. "*Should* take you. But too many of the children I care about end up dead. It's such a waste."

"The *lytlings* that come to Southbridge Temple are the smartest anywhere," Han said, thinking of Mari. "But there's nothing for them except the gangs. Some get into it because they're thugs at heart. A lot do it because it's how you can survive. You can feed a family on a gang share if you have the right streetlord." He half smiled. "And if you get killed, at least you aren't watching your family eating clay to fill their bellies.

"Do you know how hard it's been since I quit the game? I work three times as hard for half the swag. The Southies still have it in for me, and the Raggers don't know what to make of me. Not a day goes by that I don't wonder if it might have been better to stay."

"Why'd you leave it, then?" Jemson asked. He cleared his throat. "Since you were so . . . successful at it."

"Mari," Han said bluntly. "I didn't want it for her. And when you're in the gangs, loving somebody is like putting your heart on a plate and serving it up to your enemies. When

I ran the streets, I never went to see Mam and Mari, and I acted like I hated them. I sent them money, but I had to be careful about that. I had Raggers watching the house, but still. All it takes is one careless moment, one street runner who wants to make a name. The time was coming that Mari would have to join up for her own protection."

"What are you hoping for, for Mari?" Jemson asked softly.

"I dunno. Depends on what she wants." Han gestured, indicating their surroundings. "She likes it here. Maybe she'd want to be a speaker someday. I think she'd be a good teacher or clerk. Maybe she could find a good castle job. She's musical. I wish she had the money to go to the conservatory at Oden's Ford." Han looked up at Jemson. "That's the thing. I want her to have a choice."

Jemson nodded. "Mari's very smart. Like you." He paused. "But right now your choices are limited. The Guard's going to be looking under every rock, trying to find you. Even though the victims are street runners, eight dead bodies is a lot."

"I'm planning to go up to Marisa Pines and stay up there a while," Han said. "But first I need to find out who really did the murders."

"Master Alister, it is not your job to find out who killed those children," Jemson said. "I've put too much time and effort into your education. I don't want to be burying you in the temple close."

"I can't afford to hide up in the Spirits forever," Han said. "Unless I find out something, the Guard won't look any farther than me. It's hard enough to make a living without bluejackets on my back." Jemson said nothing, so Han rushed on. "I want to talk to the Raggers, see what they know. If I can make contact with the Southies, I will. Maybe they've got new enemies I don't know about."

Jemson let go a great sigh. "I assume I can't talk you out of this."

"Somehow I have to clear my name. I don't know how else to do it."

"All right." Jemson pulled a cloth bag from under his desk. "This is for you." He handed it over.

Han weighed it in his hand. "What is this?"

"It's from Willo."

"Where is she?" Han asked, looking about as if she might suddenly appear. She had a way of not being seen if she didn't want to be. He'd kind of hoped she'd take another look at his arm. Maybe a second laying on of hands might heal it up even faster.

"She's gone back to Marisa Pines. Her business is done. But she says to come and stay with her as long as you like."

Han frowned. "Dancer was here too." He looked up at Jemson. "Wasn't he? I thought I saw him."

Jemson hesitated, then nodded. "Yes. Dancer was here with his mother. They've both gone now."

"He's sick, isn't he?" Han asked. "There was something . . . It was almost like he was burning up in front of me. Or I'm going crazy," he added.

Jemson straightened the folds of his robe, not meeting Han's eyes. "You *were* rather out of it, my boy. You'd had a hard blow to the head."

Speakers weren't supposed to lie, but they could sure talk around a subject.

"So what's this?" Han asked, struggling with the drawstring one-handed.

Jemson took the bag back and untied it for him. "Willo apparently knows you as well as anyone. She said you wouldn't come right away, that you'd want to get things settled here first." Groping in the bag, Jemson pulled out a smaller pouch.

"This is henna and indigo, to dye your hair," Jemson said. "You should get a red-brown color out of that. Hopefully that will make you harder to spot. There's also some money and clan clothing in there." He smiled wryly at Han in his dedicate robes. "Assuming you don't want to stay and take vows."

CHAPTER TWELVE

BREAD
AND ROSES

Raisa discovered that the palace laundry was a good place to troll for disguises. Everyone's clothes, save those too fancy to submit to washing, came through there. And just now she had no need of fancy clothes.

She hoped to pass for a ladies' maid or somebody's governess, but it wasn't easy to find such clothes to fit her slight figure. After digging through the freshly washed laundry, she settled on a long skirt and white linen blouse with a snug-fitting bodice layered over. She had to lace the sleeves tight to keep them from sliding over her hands, and the skirts dragged on the ground. Even after she bundled her long hair into a lacy snood, she still felt utterly recognizable. She was princess heir of the realm. Everyone knew her. How could she possibly carry it off?

Hanalea hadn't been afraid, she told herself. The legendary queen with the common touch had often walked anonymously among her subjects. If she could do it, well . . .

Raisa practiced a timid shuffling gait, trying not to trip over her long skirts, dipping curtsies every few feet. She kept her eyes downcast, murmuring, "Yes, ma'am," and "No, sir." She hid her disguise in the secret chamber at the foot of the garden stairs.

As luck would have it, Magret took to her bed at midday with one of her blinding headaches. Raisa saw that as a sign from the Maker, and sent word to her mother that she'd be having supper in her rooms. Then, in late afternoon, Raisa ventured into the Room of Romantic Entanglements.

That was Raisa's name for it. It was a small locked closet off her bed chamber where Magret stored the gifts sent by Raisa's would-be suitors after recording the particulars in a ledger Raisa called the Great Book of Bribes.

The presents ostensibly honored Raisa's sixteenth name day, her official entry into adulthood and, coincidentally, the marriage market.

Jewelry spilled out of a silver casket sent by Henri Montaigne, recently assassinated heir to the throne of Arden. At least he wouldn't be expecting a return on his investment. The other Montaigne brothers had contributed their own gifts, each no doubt hoping that a marriage to the princess heir of the Fells would prop up their claims or provide a reliable source of revenue for the festering war.

Markus the Fourth, King of Tamron, had sent a set of priceless enameled jewelry boxes and an invitation to visit his waterside cottage at Sand Harbor. The boxes were inscribed with the initials *M* and *R* intertwined. Markus seemed completely undeterred by the fact that he was sixty years old and had three wives already.

Aerie House had gifted her with a tiara and necklace set with emeralds and rubies, their strong colors more suited to her dark hair and green eyes than the moonstones and topazes her mother favored. The pendant on the necklace was the image of a snake with glittering gold-and-silver scales. They were in an old-fashioned style, and Raisa wondered if they were family heirlooms.

We'enhaven's gift was an inlaid and jeweled desk set made of tropical woods. Demonai sent clan ceremonial robes made of softest doeskin, painted and beaded with her Gray Wolf totem, and Marisa Pines contributed matching dancing shoes and a fur throw for her bed.

Which reminded Raisa that, though her father came from clan royalty, the camps had not yet put forward a candidate for her hand. She wondered if they would.

Setting the Aerie House and clan items aside, Raisa shoveled jewelry and small art pieces into her carry bag until it was bulging. She focused on smaller, less distinctive items from foreign sources that would be least likely to be recognized.

This will do for a start, Raisa thought. Shouldering her carry bag, she left the treasure store and crossed her bed chamber to the other closet and the entrance to the tunnel. There she changed into her disguise and climbed the ladder into the solarium.

By the time she descended into the palace proper, the lanterns were lit along the corridors, and the mouth-watering scent of roasting meat emanated from the kitchens. Raisa kept to the servants' hallways, but they were unfamiliar, so she kept getting turned around. She walked briskly, looking straight ahead as if she were on some important mission that couldn't be interrupted. It wasn't easy since she didn't really know the way.

She was just passing the pantries when ahead of her she saw the imposing figure of Mandy Bulkleigh, Mistress of Kitchens, standing, arms crossed, her eyes scouring the corridors like those of some predatory bird.

Bones, Raisa thought, quickening her pace and lowering her head still farther.

Bulkleigh allowed her to get almost past, then said in her booming voice, "You! Girl!"

Raisa didn't slow down, didn't even look up. Three more steps, and she heard Bulkleigh coming after her.

She might have made it, but her feet got caught in her too-long skirts, and she stumbled. Bulkleigh's hamlike hand closed on her upper arm, jerking her upright.

"You! Girl! Are you deaf?" she demanded.

Raisa resisted her first instinct, which was to wrest herself free and ask Bulkleigh just who she thought she was, assaulting the princess heir of the realm in such a manner, and if she'd like to spend the night in gaol.

Instead, Raisa kept her face turned away as best she could, hoping to somehow salvage the situation. "Yes, ma'am?" she mumbled.

But Bulkleigh seized her chin and jerked her face up so she was looking her in the eyes. "Look at me when I'm talking to you, girl."

Raisa looked into the cook's eyes, dumbly waiting for

recognition to flood into Bulkleigh's face, waiting for the premature end of her ill-fated adventure.

"What's your name, girl?" Bulkleigh demanded, giving her a little shake. "I'm going to report you to the steward, I am. Impertinent little snip."

Raisa was so astonished, it took her a while to get her voice going. "Um . . . R . . . Rebecca, ma'am," she said. "Rebecca Morley, if't please you," she said, trying for a curtsy.

"Where were you going in such a hurry?" Bulkleigh asked, steely-eyed.

"Well. I was . . . ah . . . going to market for—"

"Whatever you were doing, it in't as important as this." Releasing her, the cook turned and picked up a covered tray and thrust it into Raisa's hands. "The princess heir is taking her supper in her rooms," she said. "Carry this up and leave it in the upstairs pantry."

Raisa blinked at her. "This is for the Princess Raisa?" she asked.

"The princess heir to you," Bulkleigh said. "Now be off with you; it's getting cold. If I get a complaint about it, I'll skin you alive. The princess is very particular about her food, she is."

"She is?" Raisa said, before she could stop herself. "And you want *me* to take her supper to her?" She would have added, *Aren't you worried about poison or assassins, or . . .* but the cook's expression stopped her.

"Do you see anyone else waitin' for the assignment?" the cook said sarcastically. "Queen Marianna is hosting dinner for fifty in the main dining room, and sure it would've been more convenient if Her Highness had troubled herself to come down to eat with the rest of 'em," Bulkleigh said. "But she didn't. Now go on."

Squaring her shoulders, Raisa turned and hurried back the way she came. As soon as she was out of sight of the cook, she stowed the tray behind a statue of Queen Madera feeding the multitudes, and left the servants' corridors for the safety of the main hallways.

Raisa felt relieved, yet oddly disappointed. She was the blooded princess heir, yet in servants' clothes she was apparently unrecognizable. In the stories, rulers had a natural presence about them that identified them as such, even dressed in rags.

What's the nature of royalty, she wondered. Is it like a gown you put on that disappears when you take it off? Does anyone look beyond the finery? Could anyone in the queendom take her place, given the right accessories? If so, it was contrary to everything she'd ever been taught about bloodlines.

Without further incident, she passed through the gate tower, past the dour guardsmen at the entrance, under the dangerous-looking portcullis, and into the chill of the evening. Day workers who lived outside of the castle grounds streamed across the drawbridge, heading home. The younger servants were laughing, joking, and flirting with each other. Some of the older ones plodded along, obviously weary.

Torchlight flickered on the river below as she crossed over the bridge. At the far end, she stopped and looked back at

Fellsmarch Castle, trying to imagine how the people of the city might view it, remote and brooding, lording over the city.

Amon was waiting by the gatehouse at the city end of the bridge, surveying the flow of people off the drawbridge. To her surprise, he'd shed his blue Guard uniform and was dressed in a long cloak and dark breeches. As he turned, though, she could see the hilt of his sword poking out through the front of the cloak.

If she'd hoped to fool Amon, she was disappointed. He fixed on her before she got within fifty feet of him, watching her as she pushed through the crowd. She paused in front of him and curtsied low, grinning.

"You're late," he grumbled. "I was beginning to hope you'd changed your mind."

"Call me Rebecca Morley, young sir," Raisa said, rising. "How do I look?"

"It'd be better if you'd dressed as a boy," Amon said. "It'd be better if you were ugly."

She guessed that was some kind of compliment.

"I fooled the mistress of kitchens, you know," she said, rather smugly.

"Hmmph," was Amon's comment.

"Let's pretend we're sweethearts meeting after work," she said, taking his arm. "Why didn't you wear your uniform?"

He snorted. "One guardsman on his own is more a target than protection." Amon steered her onto the Way of the Queens. "We'll take this through Ragmarket all the way to the bridge," he said.

"I was hoping we'd get to see something of the neighbor-hood," Raisa said as he marched her straight down the middle of the street.

"You'll see more than you want to see, before we're done." He gently extricated his right arm from her grip and moved her to his left side. "So I can get at my sword," he explained when she looked up at him questioningly.

Blood and bones, he's jumpy, Raisa thought.

"What did Mother Elena say?" Raisa asked, nearly trotting to keep up with Amon's long legs. "Will she be able to send one of the traders to meet with us?"

"She said she'd see what she could do," Amon said. "She wouldn't promise more than that."

I can't do this on my own, Raisa thought. It was hard enough to sneak out this one time.

There was little of twilight in the Vale. Once the sun extinguished itself behind Westgate, darkness ran in rivulets through the streets, quickly flooding the entire city. Close to Fellsmarch Castle, the lamplighters circulated, igniting the magical lanterns that lined the Way. But as they proceeded south, even on the Way, there were fewer street lanterns, and many of them appeared to be broken or disabled or simply not attended to.

Near to the castle, garbage was picked up and stowed away. But here, people pushed it out their doors, and it sat on the sidewalks, stinking.

At first there were people all around them, but the others peeled away in twos and threes into side streets and alleys, and soon Raisa and Amon were walking alone. Every block or two, a tavern spilled light and music onto the street, and patrons huddled in the doorways, talking loudly, spitting into the gutter, clutching mugs of ale.

Sometimes girls stood on the porches, watching them pass by. They wore flashy clothes and lots of paint, but Raisa guessed that some were younger than her. They looked at Amon appraisingly but did not speak to him with Raisa on his arm.

"Are those fancy girls?" she asked Amon.

He only grunted in reply. Raisa tried to imagine walking this street by herself, and shuddered. She shifted her carry bag on her shoulder, acutely conscious of its valuable contents and feeling more and more like a target.

The houses seemed to be buttoned up tight, shades drawn, as if unwilling to draw attention to themselves by leaking light into the streets.

A fine rain began to fall. Amon ignored it, but Raisa shivered, pulling her cloak more closely around her. "Where is everyone? It's not late. There should be people on their way home."

"Most people are too smart to be out in this neighborhood after dark," Amon said, sliding her a significant sideways look.

"How do people get around, then?" Raisa asked.

"They don't." Amon was in one of his monosyllabic moods.

"What about the Guard?" Raisa asked.

"The Guard can't be everywhere," Amon said. "And in Ragmarket, some say the Guard's been bought off."

"Bought off?" Raisa frowned. "By whom?"

"Like I told you before. Streetlords." Amon seemed distracted, focused on the streets around them. What with the rain and the lack of streetlights, it was dark as a cellar. Raisa was beginning to think Amon had been right: this wasn't such a good idea. A rat skittered across the cobblestones ahead of them, and Raisa flinched backward.

"Just a rat," he said calmly. "You get used to them."

Just a rat, she repeated to herself. After all, there were rats in the palace. Human and otherwise. Could be worse. Could be much, much worse.

But when the wind slammed a shutter against a building, Amon ripped his sword free in a heartbeat. When he'd identified the source of the noise, he rolled his eyes and stowed his blade away again, but kept his hand on the hilt.

As they neared Southbridge, Raisa glanced aside, into an alleyway where an unshuttered window splattered light on the wet pavement. She saw a flicker of movement, as if someone were walking parallel to them a block over. Now she watched, and down the next cross street she definitely saw someone slipping from shadow to shadow. And there! The same thing, on the other side.

Raisa's heart began to hammer. "Someone's following us," she hissed, gripping Amon's arm.

But this time he seemed unconcerned. "It's all right," he whispered back. "We're almost to the bridge. Raggers won't follow us into Southbridge."

"But didn't you say the Raggers just killed a half dozen Southies? In Southbridge?" she persisted, struggling to remember the gang names.

"Just stay close," he murmured.

Raisa was annoyed at his muted reaction. "Amon Byrne! Did you hear me? We're being followed! There's two or three of them on either side of us. I'm sure of it." Raisa groped under her cloak and drew her belt dagger.

Amon's eyes widened. "Where did you get that?" he asked.

"At Demonai. It's clanwork."

"Well, put it away. You won't need it."

And then it hit her like a runaway horse cart, and she stopped dead in the street. "You know who's following us, don't you?" she said, swinging around to face him. "*Don't* you? Who are they?"

"Who are who? I don't know what you're talking about," he said, his gaze flicking to left and right.

"Who is it? The Guard?"

He adopted what he probably took for an innocent look, but Amon had always been a hopeless liar. "Why would the Guard be following us?"

"You there!" Raisa called. "Show yourselves! I command it!"

"Shhh," Amon hissed a little frantically.

"Then tell me who they are."

"Well." He cleared his throat. "They're . . . friends of mine. Cadets in my triple."

As a corporal, he commanded a triple of nine guards.

"I told you, I—"

"They don't know who you are." Amon said. "I told them I needed to walk my sister to temple through Ragmarket and asked if they would provide escort. I said you were rather shy around young men, and so they should try and do it unobserved."

215

Raisa could tell he was rather proud of the story he'd created.

"Your sister! How could they possibly believe I'm your sister? She'd make two of me." Amon's sister, Lydia, was near as tall as he was.

He flexed his hands nervously. "Well, you're my other sister. The . . . ah . . . short, religious one. I told them you'd gone as a dedicate at a young age. " Amon seemed to realize he wasn't doing himself any good. "So, shall we . . . ?"

"You may as well call them in," Raisa said, her voice brittle and cold. "No need for them to skulk down alleys."

"All right." He whistled a long low sound. It must have been a preplanned signal, because moments later, Raisa heard running feet as the guard closed on them. She couldn't say what made her do it, but she waited until they were about ten feet away, then gripped Amon's lapels and pulled his face down for a long passionate kiss.

She found she liked kissing Amon. His lips were warm and firm—not hot like Micah's, and not at all like Wil Mathis's sloppy, wet technique. It took Amon a while to break away, and when Raisa looked up, they were encircled by six gawking young cadets in civilian dress, all close to their age.

"So . . . ah . . . Corporal," one of them said. "You're right fond of your sister, I guess?"

Amon's face was flaming. "Sorry. She has these fits sometimes," he growled. "She got hit in the head when she was little."

"I'm Rebecca Morley," Raisa said, delivering a little curtsy to the cadets. "Who are you?"

"We call ourselves the Gray Wolves," a cadet said. She was

a tall sturdy girl a few years older than Raisa. "Or sometimes the Wolfpack. I'm Hallie Talbot."

The others gave their names—Garret, Mick, Keifer, Talia, and Wode.

Now traveling as a group, they crossed South Bridge without further incident and entered the temple close.

It was like crossing into another world. The temple was surrounded by herb, vegetable, and dye gardens, quilted with torchlit pathways, a serene sanctuary amid the squalor of Southbridge.

A fair-haired girl in a long dedicate robe greeted them at the door, with a bobbing curtsy.

"We're expected," Raisa said. "We're here for a meeting with Speaker Jemson."

"There's a trader already arrived," the dedicate said, eying the guardsmen in their dripping cloaks as if they were sweet buns on a plate. "He's with Speaker Jemson in the study. It's just down the hallway on the right. May I take your cloaks?"

They piled their sodden rainwear into her arms, and she practically staggered under the weight.

"Shall we wait out here?" Garret asked Amon, obviously leery about being drawn into some kind of philosophical discussion.

"Yes," Raisa answered for him.

Amon looked at Raisa. "Shall I . . . ?"

"Come with me," she said. "I think you should know what I'm up to."

"Finally," he muttered ungraciously as they turned into the hallway. "That would be a first."

"You should talk," she said back. "*Brother* of mine."

Speaker Jemson's study reminded Raisa of the temple library in Fellsmarch Castle—lined with bookshelves, warmed by a cheerful fire. Two men were seated by the hearth in large comfortable chairs—one in the garb of a clan trader, the other in speaker's robes. They seemed to be immersed in a lively discussion—almost a debate.

When they entered, the trader rose and turned toward them.

Raisa stopped in her tracks. "Father! You're back!"

"Briar Rose!" Averill crossed the space between them with a few long strides, folding her into his arms. She pressed her face against his doeskin shirt, breathing him in. He always smelled exotic—of deerskin and spice and fresh air and far-away places. By the Maker, she'd missed him.

"I reached Demonai Camp day before yesterday. When Mother Elena said you'd sent for a trader, I couldn't resist coming," he said. Holding her out at arm's length, he grinned at her. "Raisa, I've seen you in leggings and I've seen you in court dress, but I can't say I've ever seen you quite like this."

"I'm in disguise," she confessed happily, setting her carry bag on the table and stripping off her wet cloak.

"But you're wearing Elena *Cennestre*'s gift?" he said, touching the Demonai amulet he wore around his neck.

So her father and grandmother had been talking about her. She nodded and fished the Running Wolves ring from under her bodice.

"Good," he said. He took a breath as if he wanted to

say something more, but apparently thought better of it. He looked travel weary, and his graying hair needed cutting.

Speaker Jemson had stood also, and when Raisa turned her attention to him, he bowed respectfully but somehow warily. "Your Highness, Lord Demonai wouldn't tell me the purpose for your visit, but we are honored to have you here at Southbridge Temple."

Raisa extended her hand, and he kissed it. "We've never officially met," she said, "but I've heard you speak at temple several times. I was impressed with what you had to say about your school and about our responsibility for ministering to the poor. You suggested that the aristocracy could be doing much more. "

Jemson colored slightly, but he did not flinch, which Raisa liked. "Ah. Well, Your Highness, I hope you did not take my words as too harshly critical of the queen and council. It's a topic I'm passionate about, however, and—"

"Your words *were* critical, Speaker Jemson, and maybe rightly so," Raisa said. "In Fellsmarch Castle, we're insulated against the hardships our people experience every day. We don't ask questions as we should, and if we do ask questions, those who surround us often tell us what we want to hear."

"I suppose that must be true," Jemson said, in the manner of a man who knows he should guard his tongue but can't restrain himself. "But it's frustrating to those of us who are immersed in this city, who see how great the needs are, every day. We can't help but wonder why so much money goes to support the army and the wars in the south. It seems to me that we have no dog in that fight."

"I don't know much about it," Raisa admitted, embarrassed. "I want to learn more so I can make good decisions when the time comes. That's one reason I'm here. But I'd also like to do something in a small way to aid your ministry."

"Aid us how?" Jemson asked, looking nonplussed.

She glanced at Amon, who stood by the door as if guarding it. "Corporal Byrne has been very . . . ah . . . frank with me about the problems in Southbridge and Ragmarket." She put her hand on her carry bag. "I would like to provide funds to support your school and to feed the hungry."

Jemson raised both eyebrows. "You've brought a bag full of gold through Southbridge?" he asked.

"Well, not exactly." She looked at her father. "This is where you come in."

"I was sure I had a purpose here," Averill said.

Raisa unfastened the flap on her bag and dumped the contents onto the table.

Jemson, Averill, and Amon gaped at the pile of jewelry and art objects.

"Father, you're the best trader I know," Raisa said. "Could you take these things to market and sell them for as much as they will bring? Then give that money to Speaker Jemson for his ministries."

Averill leaned over the table, fingering the jewelry, holding precious stones up to the light, picking up one object, then another. He looked up at Raisa. "This is high quality, most of it," he said. He held up a diamond brooch, a gift from some minor lord in Tamron. "Except for this one. It's cut glass." He tilted his head. "Where exactly did these come from?"

"Well . . ." Raisa hesitated. "They're gifts for my name day. They're coming in by the wagonload, so . . ."

Averill laughed, that deep belly laugh she loved. "So you're selling off the dreams of your hapless suitors, Raisa?"

"Well." Raisa shrugged. "It's not like I'd marry someone because they gave me a bauble." She frowned and nudged the Tamron brooch with her forefinger. "Though I will *not* marry someone who takes me for a fool."

"Then my work is done, daughter," Averill said, laughing again.

It was such a relief to hear someone laughing for a change. It made Raisa feel that maybe things weren't so bad after all.

"It's not like I'll have much to say about who I marry anyway," Raisa said, half to herself. She looked up at Averill. "So, Father, how long do you think it will take you to turn this lot into money?"

He thought a moment. "Marisa Pines market day is a week away. That attracts more flatlander traders, so you might get a better price. Though I'll take them to Demonai Market if you want me to sell them a greater distance away. Perhaps you don't want anyone to recognize their hand-chosen gifts on the sale table."

"I don't care," Raisa said bluntly. "I kept back the pieces that had historic, personal, or political value. Most of these were probably chosen by proxy. None of these gifters have even met me, so it's not like they're emblems of undying love. This is a better use for it than sitting in my vault."

Speaker Jemson's face was alight with plans. "Even a little money could make a huge difference. There are so many things we need at school, so many students who could attend with a little help. We'll put books into the hands of children who've never owned one before. We'll call it the Briar Rose Ministry in honor of you, Your Highness."

"Oh, no," Raisa said, wondering how her mother, the queen, would react to this. "I'd rather keep this quiet. It's just something I thought I could do on my own . . ."

"But don't you see, Raisa," her father said, "if people know you're contributing to Southbridge Temple school, it will make it the stylish thing to do at court. It will attract more donations, beyond your own. People will even donate in your name. If you're willing to let them know about it, that is."

"Oh." Raisa hadn't thought of that. Once again she felt caught between her two strong-willed parents. "Well, I suppose. If you think it would help."

"Splendid," Jemson said. "Perhaps you could come back during the day and meet some of the students. It would do them good to see their benefactor. It would send the message that they are important, that their rulers haven't forgotten them."

Raisa nodded. "Well, right. I'd like that. And maybe we could eventually connect them with apprenticeships and clarkships in the castle close."

"We'll need to speak with your mother about that," Averill said. "When the time is right."

Raisa couldn't help wondering what would happen now that her father was home; how much her father knew about Marianna's relationship with Gavan Bayar.

How much did she know about it herself?

She took Averill's hand. "Are you coming back with me to court, Father? Does Mother know you're back?"

Averill nodded. "Aye. I've sent word to the queen." He hesitated for a heartbeat, then added, "I'm to be at Kendall House until space can be found in the keep."

Kendall House was within the castle close, but at some distance from Fellsmarch Castle itself.

Raisa blinked at him. "Until space can be . . . What about your old apartments? What's wrong with them?"

"Apparently they are being redecorated and are, for the present, uninhabitable." Her father had his trader face on, signaling that now was not the time for this discussion.

But Raisa couldn't help herself. "Then they should make somebody else leave," she said. "This is unacceptable. I'm going to speak with Mother as soon as I . . ."

"I will speak to Queen Marianna on my own behalf, daughter," Averill said. "Give me some credit, will you? I am a trader, after all." And he smiled, looking into her eyes. "Briar Rose. Your mother needs to get used to having me home again."

He knows more than he's saying, she thought. My father was never a fool.

"All right," Raisa said, nodding and forcing a smile of her own. "But any time you need a place to stay within the keep, you can stay with me. And come to supper tomorrow night."

She embraced her father, reluctant to let him go after his long absence.

She glanced over at Amon, who shifted his weight, looking eager to be on his way. "I guess that's it for now," she said.

"Corporal Byrne will let you know when I have more, um, things to go to market.

They turned toward the door, but before they could reach it, somebody barreled through. It was a young man, Raisa's age, or a little older, with muddy red-brown hair, dressed in clan leggings and shirt.

"Jemson! Three of the Raggers have been nabbed by the bluejackets. Seems they mean to make an example of . . ." His voice trailed off when he saw the people gathered in the room. "Oh. Sorry, sir. I didn't know you had company."

His eyes flicked to Averill, then Amon, and widened in alarm.

He recognizes them, Raisa thought.

"Let's discuss this later, Hanson," Jemson said quickly, jerking his head toward the door.

Hanson began backing from the room, but Amon said, "Wait! What's that about Raggers?"

The boy blinked at him, blank-faced. "Raggers? I didn't say nothing about Raggers."

"Yes, you did," Amon said, walking purposefully toward Hanson. "Have we met? You look familiar."

"Ah, no," the boy said. "Not likely." He was tall, nearly as tall as Amon, though more slender in build, with brilliant blue eyes. His face bore evidence of a recent beating. His right eye was blackened and there was a blue-and-yellow bruise over one cheekbone. His right forearm was splinted, but he didn't favor it. He seemed to be trying to keep his face turned away from them, as if he were embarrassed by his injuries.

This must be one of Jemson's students, Raisa thought with a rush of sympathy.

"What happened to you?" she asked, moving closer so she could examine his face at close range. She touched his arm. "Who did this?"

Hanson flushed. "Wasn't nothing. Just ... my da. Gets mean sometimes when he's in his cups."

Just then Amon's hand snaked forward. He gripped the boy's splinted arm and raked back his sleeve, exposing a wide silver cuff. "So, *Hanson*," he said. "I think we have met after all. You ever go by the name Cuffs?" he said.

Cuffs? Raisa looked from Amon to the other boy. Wasn't that the gang leader who'd killed all those people?

Then it seemed like everything happened at once. The boy slammed his free fist into Amon's face and twisted away with the ease of long practice. Amon drew his sword and stepped between the boy and the door, yelling for the other cadets. And then the boy called Cuffs grabbed hold of Raisa, drawing her back tight against him. She felt the prick of a blade at her throat and tried hard not to swallow.

"Hanson, no!" Speaker Jemson shouted, pale with horror.

"Now then," Cuffs said, close to her ear. "Back off or I cut the girlie's throat." His voice shook a little—with fear or nerves or excitement, Raisa couldn't tell.

Raisa thought of the six, dead in the street. Tortured, they'd said. Done by this pretty blue-eyed boy holding the knife.

"Please," Jemson pleaded. "In the name of the Maker, let her go. You don't know who—"

"No." Averill raised a hand to shush the speaker, his eyes fixed on Raisa. He wouldn't want Cuffs to know who it was he held captive. "Listen," he said to the boy, "perhaps we can make some kind of trade."

"Here's a trade," Amon said, stepping away from the door. "Let her go and leave, and you'll stay alive."

"With all you bluejackets snapping at my heels?" Cuffs snorted. "I'd not make it far as the bridge."

Amon's face had gone stony hard, his gray eyes like chips of granite. "If you hurt her, I swear on Hanalea's blood and bones you'll regret it."

By now the other Gray Wolves had arrived and were clustered in the doorway, gawking.

"You, there," Cuffs said to the new arrivals. "Get over with the others."

"Do as he says," Amon ordered.

As the cadets shuffled to the back of the study, Raisa could hear the Ragger's heart thumping against her back, feel his breath hot on her neck. He kept adjusting his grip on the knife as if he was nervous.

Don't startle him, Raisa thought, looking from Amon to Averill to Jemson, sending messages with her eyes.

"I don't mean to hurt anyone," Cuffs said. "Just don't mean to go to gaol and be tortured into admitting something I didn't do."

Raisa stiffened, and the boy's grip on her tightened. "The Queen's Guard doesn't torture anybody," she blurted. "You'll receive a fair trial. If you're innocent—if you really didn't murder all those people—you can clear your name."

The boy laughed softly. "Ah, girlie," he said. "Would that was true. There's lots that go into gaol and are never seen again."

Raisa felt stupid and naive. What was it that Amon had said? *If I was being dragged back to the guardhouse for interrogation by Mac Gillen, I'd do whatever it took to escape too.*

Cuffs wrapped an arm around Raisa's middle and dragged her past the others to the door of the study.

"Your keys, sir," Cuffs said to Jemson. He was polite, well spoken, like the gentleman thief from the stories. "Hand them to the girlie."

He has a trader face, Raisa thought. He puts it on at need.

"Hanson," Speaker Jemson said. "This is a mistake. You know it is. You're better than this. Let the girl go."

Cuffs shook his head stubbornly. "I been in gaol. Not going back."

Despite everything, Raisa couldn't help wondering, what was the relationship between Speaker Jemson and this streetlord? Jemson seemed to know him, seemed to believe in him, for some reason. Maybe Hanson/Cuffs had fooled him, though the speaker didn't come off as gullible.

Jemson dug in his pockets, fetched out a ring of keys, and passed them to Raisa while Cuffs kept her pinned tightly to him, her head locked under his chin, his knife in the ready position. Sweat trickled down between her shoulder blades, dampening her linen blouse.

"Please," Jemson said again. "Don't do this. There's another way."

"I'm sorry, sir," the boy said, and he did sound sorry. "If there's another way, I don't see it."

Cuffs backed out through the doorway, dragging Raisa with him. "Now. Pull the door shut behind us and lock it," he said, as if they were coconspirators. "That'll slow them down a bit. Then give me the keys and we'll be off."

"No!" Amon shouted. "Leave the girl here. Take me instead."

Cuffs looked from Raisa to Amon and shook his head, grinning. "Nuh-uh. I'm guessing she'll be less trouble. And she's prettier, besides."

Trader face, Raisa thought.

Amon's expression promised death, for a start. "I should have let Gillen beat you to death," he said. "What I get for being a bleeding—"

"Mercy is never unbecoming, mate," Cuffs said. He pointed at the door with the tip of his knife. "Go on, girlie. Do as I said. We haven't got all day."

Raisa complied, pulling the door shut and locking it, her hands shaking so much she could scarcely fit the key into the keyhole. It was a stout wooden door to a windowless room built like a fortress. Behind the door, she could hear faint shouts and cries for help, followed by a muffled thud of bodies against wood.

Cuffs was right. It would slow them down for sure. The dedicates were fast asleep across the courtyard. It was unlikely anyone would hear them until morning filled the corridors again. A lot could happen before morning

Cuffs gripped her wrist hard and tugged her down the corridor, toward the door.

"Leave . . . me . . . be!" she shouted, trying to set her heels on the stone floor, then collapsing into a heap.

Swearing under his breath, Cuffs stowed away his knife and slid his hands under her, slinging her over his shoulder like a sack of turnips. He was surprisingly strong. "Now be quiet," he muttered. "Don't make me do something I don't want to do."

He obviously meant to take her someplace and torture her, as he had the others. Raisa groped at her waist, found the hilt of her knife, and yanked it free. Could she really stick it into him? Gripping the hilt with both hands, she aimed for the center of his back, closed her eyes, and went to drive it home.

Instead she found herself flat on her back on the floor, seeing stars from slamming her head on the slate. He'd unceremoniously dumped her. Cuffs seized her wrist and took the knife from her. "Next time you go to stab someone, do it quick," he advised her. "Don't study on it so long."

He expertly patted her down, running his hands over her bodice, down her sides and back, and up and down her legs, even pulling off her lace cap, looking for other weapons. Although he was businesslike about it, the blood rushed to her face at the touch of the streetlord's hands.

He was good at it, and very quick, his hands deft and sure. He found Elena's ring, with its circling wolves, on the chain around her neck, but didn't take it. And the little velvet purse, heavy with coins, she'd tucked into her bodice. He weighed the purse in his hand, then handed it back to her. She blinked at him, surprised.

He then hauled her to her feet, handed back her cap, dusted her off with mock chivalry, and finished with a rude pat to her behind.

Despite the grim situation, there was something about him, a kind of wild untamed humor and bravado and dogged stubbornness that tugged at her. He expects nothing, she thought, because he's never had anything. And nothing was expected of him. He was free in a way she never would be.

You're a fool and a romantic, she thought. A worse fool than Missy. And you'll likely end up ravished or dead at the hands of a street thug.

He looked her up and down speculatively, as if devising a plan of attack. "You're not heavy," he said. "But you are bloody awkward to carry."

She extended her purse toward him. "Take my purse. But leave me here."

"I don't *want* your purse," he said, scowling. The words hung between them.

Well, if he didn't want her purse . . . Raisa swallowed hard. One thing she knew—there was more chance of escape if she were on her own two feet.

"I can walk," she muttered, trying to recover some dignity.

"Right, but can you run?" he asked, grabbing her wrist and yanking her out the temple door. A moment later they were racing through the rain across South Bridge toward Ragmarket. Halfway across, he dropped the ring of keys into the river.

Once on the Ragmarket side, he led her off the Way, onto a side street. They turned again, into an alley, and he pulled a large handkerchief out of his pocket and tied it over her eyes.

"You always carry blindfolds, do you?" she said, trying to keep a quaver out of her voice. For once he didn't reply, but took her hand and led her forward.

You'll never get away with this, she thought of saying. But it seemed likely that he would, whatever "this" was.

CHAPTER THIRTEEN

THE RAGGERS

Han couldn't say what possessed him to take the girlie along. She was inconvenient and uncooperative. She only slowed him down, not to mention trying to stick him with her fancy knife. No doubt he'd have been across South Bridge and into the safety of Ragmarket sooner without her. With any luck, Jemson and the others wouldn't be freed from the study until morning, so he didn't really need a hostage. And now he had the problem of what to do with her.

At least she wasn't actively fighting him anymore, but trotted obediently beside him as he led her deeper into Ragmarket, twisting down streets and alleys so she'd never find her way back on her own. He found his way by the map in his head. It was dead dark away from the main street, so it wouldn't have done the girlie much good to have the blind-fold off. Still, he could tell from the way she cocked her head and counted under her breath at each turning that she was trying to keep track. She'd be looking for another chance to escape.

There was something about the girl that intrigued him. She was dressed like a blueblood servant in overlarge clothes, carried a heavy purse, and had the manners of a duchess. So sure of herself. Entitled, even.

Where does that come from, he wondered. The idea that you deserve to take more than your share from the world?

The Queen's Guard doesn't torture anybody, she'd proclaimed, like she was some kind of expert. *You'll receive a fair trial.*

Sorry, girlie, he thought. I'm the expert on that, and I'm not buying what you're selling.

He pondered what he knew about her. She'd been closeted up with Jemson and a clan trader who might be Averill Lightfoot Demonai, Patriarch of Demonai Camp. It had been three years since he'd seen him—Han's visits to Marisa Pines had been sporadic these last three years on the streets, and Lord Demonai rarely visited Marisa Pines. But his wasn't a face you forgot.

That tall, dark, intense boy—the one who'd recognized him—he was that Corporal Byrne who'd been with the blue-jackets that had grabbed him outside The Keg and Crown. Plus there were those other baby bluejackets who'd come running when Byrne had called. What were they all doing there, out of uniform? Jemson wasn't in the habit of enter-taining the Guard.

'Course, it could be just his usual bad luck. That, at least, was consistent.

Corporal Byrne—was he the girlie's sweetheart? He'd guess so, the way he'd acted. Han had another thought: maybe they'd come there to be married, with his mates as witnesses. The speakers did marriages all the time.

Han pushed that idea away. He didn't like it.

The girlie was beginning to wear out—breathing hard, lagging behind so he had to tug her along. He needed a place to hide for a little while. He felt cut loose and vulnerable, having lost the shelter of the temple. He'd probably ruined whatever chance he had of solving the mystery of the murders.

"Here." He pulled her into an alley, then turned down a passageway between two buildings that was so narrow they had to slide through sideways. It ended in a small brick-paved courtyard, half-roofed against the rain. Up against one of the buildings was a set of wooden cellar doors, set into a stone pad, and secured by a sturdy-looking padlock.

Han had it open in a heartbeat. It pleased him to know he was still a deft gilt with a pick.

The hinges protested as he pulled the doors open, and a rush of dank cellar air swept over him. Didn't look like anyone had been there since he'd left the life. He led the girlie to the steps. "It's a dozen steps down." He took her elbow so she wouldn't fall. "Feel with your foot."

She hesitated on the edge. "Please," she said, lifting her chin and squaring her shoulders. "Have mercy. Just kill me now. I've not done anything to you."

"I'm not going to kill you," Han blurted out, surprised.

"I don't want to be tortured. Or ravished."

"I'm not going to torture you," Han said desperately. "Or . . . or anything. I'm cold and wet and tired, and I just want to quit walking for a while, all right?"

"I don't want to go down there," she persisted, shuddering. "Please don't make me."

"Look." He reached over and untied her blindfold, then pulled it off. "Here we are." He smiled at her, his best, most charming smile. "This is . . . kind of a hideout. I promise you, it's more comfortable than it is out here in the rain. And I'm coming down with you."

"That is *not* reassuring, Mr. . . . . Cuffs," she said, with some of her old spirit.

"Look, what's your name?" he asked.

"R . . . Rebecca Morley," she said, trembling, teeth chattering from either cold or fear.

"Rebecca, I can't turn you loose in Ragmarket in the middle of the night," he said. "Hang on. I'll light a lantern, but you have to promise not to take off on me."

"Hold it over the steps to light my way down," she commanded, then added as an afterthought, "Please?"

She descended the steps with great dignity, head high, like a saint walking into the flames. He followed after her, setting the lantern in the center of the room and pulling the cellar doors closed after them.

It was really quite cozy, for a cellar. No golden thrones or heaps of jewels and coins or captive women, as Dori had imagined, but there were three sleeping cots and blankets and a stout wooden chest that contained spare clothing and candles and several jars of dried beans, jam, biscuits, sugar, and grain. The grain had gone moldy, but the rest looked all right.

Even better, this cellar had a back door, a narrow staircase into the warehouse beyond. Han always liked having a back door.

"So this is your hideout?" Rebecca said, looking disappointed. She seemed rather the worse for wear—like a street waif gone wrong. The hair that had been tucked under the cap had come down and hung in long wet strands around her shoulders. Green eyes shone out from an olive-skinned face suggesting a mixture of bloods: clan and Vale, maybe. A lush, kissable mouth was centered over a stubborn chin. Her long skirts were smeared with mud all around the hemline, and her blouse appeared to be soaked through.

But when she turned her head—in profile—she looked somehow familiar. Perhaps he'd seen her at the markets, or . . .

"Have we met?" he asked.

"I am sure we have not," she said, sniffling a little, looking miserable.

Blood and bones, he thought. Please don't go crying. As if things aren't bad enough.

"Hey now," he said. "I'm the one should be crying. Thanks to your bluejacket, I've got no home, no job, no prospects."

"May . . . maybe you should have thought of that before you killed those people."

"I didn't kill anyone," he said, stung. "I told you. That wasn't me."

She said nothing, only wrapped her arms around herself and shivered a little.

"If you'd like some dry clothes," he said, "you can look through the trunk and see if anything fits. I could . . . um . . . turn my back or go back outside." Into the rain. He was really going above and beyond with this girlie.

"I'm fine," she said, too quickly. She sank into a puddle of skirts in a defensible corner, watching him with big, wary eyes.

"Would you like something to eat? Biscuits? Or biscuits with jam?" He gestured expansively, the proper host. "Biscuits with sugar on?"

"No."

He sat, cross-legged, at a distance that he hoped would make her comfortable. "What were you doing at Southbridge Temple?" he asked.

She paused long enough to make up a lie. "Applying for a job."

"Really? What kind of job? What are you good at?"

Her expression said, *Cutting the hearts out of thieves and kidnappers.*

He tried again. "Where do you live?"

Another pause. "Near the castle close. On Bradbury Street."

"That's rather posh," he said, surprised.

"I'm a servant. A . . . um . . . tutor. In the . . . Bayar household."

She lied in little fits and starts, making it up as she went. Either she wasn't very good at it, or she didn't care to be convincing.

But she'd got the name Bayar from somewhere.

"Lord Bayar's the High Wizard, right?" he said, aiming for casual.

She nodded, looking surprised that he'd heard of him.

"So what are they like, the Bayars?" he asked, gnawing on a hard biscuit. "Is it true they're really decent sorts, once you get to know them?"

She narrowed her eyes, reappraising him. "Why did you bring me here?"

"Well, like I said, I thought we could rest until morning, and—"

"No," she said impatiently. "Why didn't you lock me in with the others back at the temple?"

Han had to admit, she had starch. It was a risky question to ask, when she didn't know what the answer would be.

"I thought I might need you to get across the bridge and . . ."

She hunched her shoulders and glared at him. She wasn't buying it.

"I don't know," he said simply. "Just a spur of the moment thing, I guess. Does everything have to have a good reason?"

In fact, he'd been asking himself that same question. There, in the study, she'd come toward him, saying, "What happened to you? Who did this?" with this kind of fierce look on her face, like she was totally on his side, ready to do battle on his behalf. She'd touched his arm, and it had warmed his center like a coal fire.

Then Byrne had named him a murderer, and she'd yanked

her hand back with this look of revulsion. And the next thing he knew, Han was dragging her across the bridge. Like he might somehow drag her back into his corner.

Well, if she was on his side before, he'd ruined it now. Six or eight murders was a big hurdle to overcome. Plus, he'd end in gaol if he showed his face in Fellsmarch again. There was another barrier, right there.

To what? What did he expect from this girlie? Did he think they'd go walking out together? Would she call on him in his palace over the stable?

Rebecca kept sliding glances at him, as if memorizing every detail. Probably so she could pick him out of a lineup.

"Where'd you get the wrist cuffs?" she asked unexpectedly. "Did you steal them from somebody?"

It was almost like she was trying to provoke him, to end the suspense.

"No," he said. "I didn't."

"You know they're looking for us," Rebecca said, just full of good news. "They won't rest until they find us."

"Try and get some sleep," he suggested. "That's what I'm going to do. Tomorrow, I'll figure out a way to turn you loose." He rooted in his trunk and tossed her a blanket that wasn't too smelly. And a pair of breeches and shirt that were way too small for him now, just in case. Then he dragged one of the cots over to the bottom of the stairs and curled up resolutely.

Sleep was a long time in coming. He heard rustling from Rebecca's corner, the whisper of fabric sliding over the floor. She'd apparently decided to change out of her wet clothes after all. He stared out into the darkness, trying to keep *that* image out of his head. It would only cause trouble.

Eventually she quieted, and he could hear a soft rhythmic breathing that said she was asleep.

Every time he closed his eyes, he saw the green serpent amulet, like it was engraved on his eyelids. He was beginning to think it was a bad-luck charm. His recent troubles had started when he'd found the thing. Maybe Micah Bayar had cursed it when it came into Han's possession. Maybe he should ignore Lucius and dig it up and return it to its rightful owner.

Only, according to Lucius, the Bayars weren't the rightful owners.

But why wouldn't they be? They'd killed the Demon King and taken it from him, hadn't they?

Maybe that was it. Maybe it was only good for dark magic. But all the tools of dark magic would have been destroyed after the Breaking, right?

Finally he slept. And Corporal Byrne's face haunted his dreams.

Somehow, Raisa slept, though she'd have said it wasn't possible, trapped in this dirt-floored cellar with a multiple murderer. She woke early, unravished, though stiff and aching all over from sleeping slumped in the corner.

The lamp had gone out, but pale morning light leaked around the cellar doors. Cuffs was asleep, sprawled on his cot at the base of the steps.

Raisa watched him for a bit, to make sure he was really

out. He slept fitfully, muttering and twitching as if troubled by dreams.

Or a guilty conscience.

Raisa creaked to her feet, padded across the cellar, and looked down on him. He looked younger, somehow, when he was sleeping, his splinted arm over his chest, his other arm flung out to the side, his eyes moving under his bruised eyelids. His knife lay half underneath him.

He was handsome under the bruises, though his muddy red-brown hair didn't match his coloring. She resisted the urge to reach out and run her fingertips over his fine-boned face.

Why would he be wearing clan garb? she wondered. It was just one of many mysteries she'd never have the answers to.

Could she trust her instincts—the ones that said he wasn't capable of doing the crimes he was accused of? Did he really mean to let her go? He hadn't harmed her yet, but that didn't mean he wouldn't.

Then again, maybe it would be better just to let him cut her throat. When her mother heard about this adventure, Raisa would be locked up for sure. Amon would be exiled to Chalk Cliffs, and it would be her fault. Even now, the whole of the Queen's Guard was probably combing the city.

She'd spread her cloak, skirts, and petticoats over a chair to dry. When she fingered them, she found they'd gone from dripping to stiff and only damp. She considered changing back into them, but worried she'd wake Cuffs in the process and be caught betwixt.

The breeches were overlong and loose at the waist, so she found a length of rope and threaded it through the loops, rolling the hems to fit. The shirt was dingy white and hung nearly to her knees. She buttoned it up to her neck, wrinkling her nose at the scent of boy sweat. She found a brightly colored rag on a pile of clothes and tied her hair back with it, then draped her cloak around her shoulders.

Would she be able to slip up the stairs and out the doors without waking him? She'd need a good lead, since he knew this neighborhood and she did not.

Heart pounding so loud she felt sure it would wake him, she stepped over his prone body and put her foot on the first step. She shoved off with her other foot and climbed the steps as quickly as she could, expecting at any moment to feel his hand close around her ankle. When she reached the top, she looked down, taking a long slow breath. He was still sleeping in his rowdy fashion.

Raisa reached up with both hands and shoved at the double doors.

Scr-e-e-e-ch! The squeal of the hinges split the early morning silence. Below her, she heard Cuffs's measured breathing break off, followed by a sleepy exclamation.

Well, there was no going back now. She thrust herself upward, slamming open the doors, squinting against the light outside. After a moment's panicky tangle with her cloak, she was out of the cellar and sprinting across the courtyard. She heard a muffled shout behind her as she slid into the sliver of space between the buildings.

She popped out the other side like a cork from a bottle,

and then she ran, twisting and turning through the narrow streets, not knowing or caring where she was or where she was heading, just wanting to put distance between her and her former captor.

She ran until a stitch in her side and a lack of breath forced her to stop and huddle in an alleyway. She stood for a time catching her breath, listening for pursuit, looking up and down the street.

Then she began to walk. She'd try to find an inn or shop that was open. Perhaps someone there would be willing to go for help, if she could convince them there was a reward in it.

But the taverns were locked up tight, the houses too, the streets deserted at this early hour. She tried pounding on the doors of some of the more prosperous-looking dwellings, but no one answered. If anyone saw her, it was unlikely they'd let her in. She must look a fright—a ragged filthy creature of indeterminate gender.

To the east, the towers of Fellsmarch Castle pricked the horizon, silhouetted against the rising sun. It was several miles away at least, somewhat farther than they'd walked the night before. Was it really just a day ago she'd crossed Ragmarket with Amon and her secret escort?

There was no choice but to leg it. She headed for the towers, navigating the twisting streets and alleys, feeling as if she walked two miles for every one in a straight line. It was like the maze in her rooftop garden, only walled in with decrepit dwellings and paved with cobbles, broken brick, dirt, and debris.

She was crossing a courtyard when a young girl ran out of an adjoining alleyway, all in a panic. She was thin, maybe a year or two younger than Mellony, with long blond hair scraped back into a plait. "Young miss! In the name of Madeleine the Merciful, help, if you please. It's my baby sister! She's sick!"

Raisa looked around to see if she might be speaking to someone else, but there was no one in the courtyard. "Me? What's wrong with your sister?"

"She's choking! Turning purple!" The girl tugged at Raisa's hand. "Please come."

Raisa followed the girl down the alleyway, her mind racing. Maybe here was a chance to do some good. The choking sickness had been going around. There were healers in Fellsmarch Castle Temple who had been successful in treating it. Maybe . . .

Suddenly she and the girl came up against a brick wall. Raisa turned and saw that they were no longer alone. Five others came out of the adjoining streets, four boys and another girl, surrounding them. Her stomach did a nauseating flip.

"Hey now," the new girl said, squinting at her. "Where you going in such a hurry?"

Her accent said she was from the southern islands. She was older than the first girl, maybe sixteen, with dark skin and long, wavy black hair wrapped with thread into sections. She had high cheekbones, and a generous mouth. She wore breeches and a sleeveless vest, exposing muscular tattooed arms.

The girl reached out and ripped Raisa's makeshift scarf

from her hair. "What are you doing with this?" she demanded, shaking it in front of Raisa's face. "Where'd you get it?"

Raisa saw then that all of them wore bandannas of similar weave and color knotted around their necks.

"Raggers!" she blurted. "You're Raggers!"

The girl flinched and looked up and down the alley before she replied. "Are not. Who says?"

"Did Cuffs send you?" Raisa demanded, furious at being taken so easily. "Well, you can tell him for me that I don't care how many cutthroat street ruffians he sets after me; I'm not—"

"Shut it!" Now the girl looked angry and frightened at the same time. "We've got nothing to do with whatever Cuffs Alister be up to. He not in the Raggers anymore. He don't give the orders in Ragmarket. Now let's see what you got in your carry bag, hmm?"

The Raggers closed in on Raisa, and she backed away until she came up against the wall of the building.

An older boy in a faded red velvet coat reached out and fingered her hair, and she slapped his hand away. He smiled, revealing a tongue bright red from chewing razorleaf. "You got any family, girlie? Somebody who might pay to get you back?" He leaned closer, and his razorleaf breath made her eyes water. He seemed jumpy and jittery, like leaf users often did.

"*There* you are, Rebecca!" Everyone swiveled, and Cuffs came swaggering down the alley like some pirate prince, in his clan leggings, fancy clan-made boots, and a beat up deerskin jacket overtop.

He nodded to the other Raggers. "Hey, Velvet, thanks,

mate, for looking after my girlie for me. I tell you, she's been nothing but trouble."

As Velvet gawked at him, Cuffs grabbed Raisa's arm and shoved her behind him, planting himself between her and the others. He pressed something into her hand, and she felt cold metal. Her knife. She palmed it and peeked out from behind his back, head spinning with confusion.

The Raggers stared at Cuffs with the avid interest given murderers, adulterers, kings, actors, and other notorious people.

All except the tattooed girl. The expression on her face was more complex: a mixture of anger, desire, and betrayal.

She's sweet on him, Raisa thought. And he's jilted her.

"Get off, Alister," the tattooed girl said to Cuffs. "The girlie's ours."

"Nuh-uh, Cat," he said. "I saw her first. Not much swag for a flimper like you, but she's pretty, at least."

"Is she the one that beat you up?" Cat sneered. "Or was it the Southies, like everyone says?"

"What's all that in your hair, mate?" Velvet asked. "Blood or dirt?"

Cuffs touched his head, looking momentarily puzzled. "Oh. Right," he said, his confusion clearing. "Just trying out a new color. What d'you think?"

"He's in disguise, mates," Cat said. "Can't even walk the streets as himself anymore."

"Are you coming back, Cuffs?" a younger boy piped up hopefully. "Shares was always good when you was streetlord." He clapped his mouth shut and darted a nervous glance at Cat.

"No, he's *not* coming back," Cat said, stepping out in front of the others, her hand on the dagger shoved into the waistband of her breeches. "It's his fault Flinn and the others got pinched. Cuffs is poison. We gang up with him, the blue-jackets'll be all over us."

"The bluejackets is all over us now," an older boy pointed out. "We can't move for the Guard. Cuffs always kept 'em bought off, at least."

"Shut up, Jonas," Cat said, glaring at him, and Jonas shut his mouth.

"There's eight Southies down on the bricks," Cuffs said. "That was a daft move. You can't dawb your way out of that."

It was like Cuffs had slid into his streetlord skin and began speaking a foreign language.

Cat glared at him. "You act like *we* did the Southies."

Cuffs shrugged. "Who else?"

Raisa, feeling ignored, had been shifting from one foot to the other, debating her chances of making a run for it. Now she focused more closely on the conversation.

Cat snorted. "Us? *We* had nothing to do with it. We figure it was you. That's who the Guard is blaming, anyway."

"The bluejackets are blaming all of us," Cuffs said. "Look, how could I have done the Southies? All by myself?" He grinned. "*You* maybe, Cat. Me, I'm good, but not that good."

Cuffs is a charmer, no doubt about it, Raisa thought.

Cat studied him suspiciously. "You're not with anyone else? The Keepers? Widowmakers? Bloodrunners?"

Cuffs shook his head.

"We heard you was bringing leaf up from We'enhaven,"

Jonas said. "Heard you'd made a killing selling it off to pirates in Chalk Cliffs."

"I don't do business with pirates anymore," Cuffs said. "They're more likely to cut your throat than pay up."

"How you getting on, then?" Cat asked, rolling her eyes.

Cuffs cleared his throat, as if embarrassed. "This and that. I'm a runner for Lucius Frowsley. Do some trading. Shine the gentry's shoes." He touched his knife. "Get in a little barbering."

Laughter rippled through the Raggers. All except for Cat.

Cuffs noticed. "Look," he said, going serious, "I got no idea who's doing the Southies, but we're all paying for it. I need your help. If you know anything . . ."

"How about this?" Cat said, leaning toward Cuffs. "We'll hand you off to the bluejackets. Then maybe they'll leave us be."

"You can *try*," Cuffs said. His voice was calm, his manner unruffled, but Raisa noticed that he straightened and gripped the hilt of his knife. "'Course, I'd not sell *you* out. I think mates need to hang together. But that's just me."

The Raggers shifted nervously, stealing glances at one another, some of them nodding.

I can learn something from Cuffs Alister, Raisa thought. He's been here ten minutes, and he has them all in the palm of his hand. Except for Cat, who has a grudge against him.

Cuffs moved in closer to Cat, fixing her with his blue eyes, his voice soft and persuasive. "Give me a moment, will you?" He looked from her to the other Raggers, raising his eyebrows. "Please?"

She hesitated, then waved the rest of them off. They

shuffled to the open end of the alley and huddled there. Velvet scowled, shooting dark looks their way.

"What about her?" Cat hissed, nodding at Raisa.

Cuffs gave Raisa a little push toward the closed end of the alley, keeping himself between her and the way out. "Stay there," he growled, then withdrew a few paces to talk to Cat. Raisa pretended to ignore them, all the while straining to make out their conversation.

"Who is she, and what's she to you?" Cat tilted her head toward Raisa.

"Just some girlie who happened to be in the wrong place at the wrong time," he said. "I gave my word I'd let her go."

"Your word?" Cat laughed bitterly. "Good luck to her, then."

"Cat," Cuffs said, extending his hands, then dropping them, "I never made any promises."

"No. You didn't." Her expression said promises were implied, if not spoken.

"I had to leave the life. I had no choice. It had nothing to do with you."

Cat stared at him incredulously. "Had . . . nothing . . . to do with *me*? How do you figure that?"

Cuffs tried to patch it over. "What I mean is, I didn't leave because of you."

"You didn't *stay* because of me neither," she spat. "Anyways, what makes you think I care where you go or what you do?" Cat shook her hair back. "The bluejackets pinched three of my runners because of you. They'll be torturing them now, trying to make 'em tell where you are. They'll torture them *dead*, because they got no idea."

Cuffs stilled and focused. "I heard there was three Raggers taken. Flinn and who else?"

"Jed and Sarie too," Cat said.

Cuffs glanced toward Raisa, lowered his voice. "Where are they keeping them?"

"Southbridge Guardhouse," Cat said.

Raisa heard Cuffs's intake of breath. "Bloody bones. Gillen?"

Cat nodded. "As if you cared." There was a certain challenge in her stance, an expectation of disappointment. "You know I don't spill nothing to the bluejackets. But I'd give you up to save them."

Cuffs stared out into space, a muscle working in his jaw. "First, I need to settle the girlie. Will you let us go then?" Raisa understood the gesture. He was submitting to Cat, recognizing her status as streetlord.

"Fine," she said, her face expressionless, her voice flat. "Off you go. Just don't ever—"

"Meet me at the far end of South Bridge tonight," he interrupted. "I'll help you spring Sarie and the others."

Cat studied him appraisingly. "How do I know you won't bring the Guard with you?" she said. "How do I know you won't sell us out?"

He gripped her elbows, looking into her face, his voice low and fierce. "Because this time I *am* promising."

Ragmarket was waking up around them as they headed uptown. Somehow, Han needed to shed the girlie before they ran across a nosy bluejacket or some other troublesome person. Only now he felt somehow confident she wouldn't turn him in.

Every time he looked at Rebecca, she was studying him through narrow green eyes, like he was a cypher that needed solving. He was beginning to think he preferred the wide-eyed terrified look. How much of the conversation with Cat had she overheard?

"That Cat, she was your sweetheart, wasn't she?" she asked him, as if she were privy to his thoughts.

"Not exactly," he replied.

She rolled her eyes, in that way girlies had.

"What?" he said irritably, skirting a large pile of potato peelings at the curb. Could be worse, in Ragmarket.

"Obviously *she* thought so."

"Well, she's with Velvet now." Why was he telling her this? Han decided to change the subject. "You know, you look good in breeches," he said, running his eyes over the display. "Very—ah—shapely," he added, grinning and demonstrating with his hands.

That shut her up. She blushed bright pink, and there was no more talk of sweethearts.

She *did* look good in breeches, in fact, and it wasn't that he was dazzled by the novelty of it. Clan girls wore leggings, after all.

In the camps they told stories of tiny beautiful wood nymphs that would catch you in their snares and challenge you with riddles. Rebecca could've been a character in any of those. Her waist was so small, he could have spanned it with his hands, but there was a wiry toughness to her that appealed to him.

Glancing sideways at her, he wondered what it would be like to kiss her.

Leave it alone, Alister, he thought. You got trouble enough. Whoever she was, she had powerful friends.

"I'm going to leave you on the Way," he said, pulling her by the hand, pushing between the delivery wagons and crowds of laborers and shopkeepers in the narrow street. "There's lots of traffic this time of day, and it should be safe. You can easily walk back to the castle close."

"I'm fine on my own, you know," she said, putting her nose in the air.

He snorted. "Right. You were fine when I found you in the alley. Cat and them would've eaten you alive."

"Why'd you save me?" she asked. "I mean, I ran away."

Sometimes Rebecca seemed plenty sharp, and other times she'd say the stupidest things. "I was the one that dragged you off from Southbridge Temple," he said. "You end up with your throat cut, I'll get the blame. I got enough problems as it is."

"You're going to try to rescue the Raggers, aren't you?" she said. "The ones taken by the Guard."

Hanalea's teeth! He had to get shed of her while he had any secrets left.

"Where'd you get that idea?" he asked.

"You are, aren't you?" she persisted.

"Well, that'd be bloody stupid, wouldn't it?" Han said. "Do you think I'm stupid?"

"No. You think it's your fault they were taken. But it's not, if you're innocent."

She nearly tripped on her long breeches, and he grabbed her arm to right her.

"So. Now you think I'm innocent, do you?"

"Of murdering the Southies, at least," she said, giving him the evil eye that said he was still guilty of plenty. "They'll catch you if you try, you know. They've got to be expecting this sort of thing. That's probably why they took them in the first place. To lure you out of hiding."

As if he didn't know that. "Well, not your worry, is it?" A few more blocks, and he'd take his leave and . . .

She suddenly set her heels, practically skidding to a stop, her eyes alight with some new scheme. "Take me back to Southbridge Temple," she commanded, like the bloody Duchess of Ragmarket. "I forgot something."

"Are you out of your *mind*?" He said it louder than he intended, and passersby turned and stared at them. "We just came from there," he said, forcing his voice down. "I only just got away, and I'm not going back."

"You'll have to go back anyway, to free the Raggers," she said. "Southbridge Guardhouse is right by the temple close," she added.

As if he didn't know *that*. "No. You're going home. If you really want to help me, you'll keep your mouth shut about everything that's happened."

She set her lips into a thin line and drew herself up to her puny best height. "Fine. I'm off to Southbridge Temple on my own, then."

It was like one of those nightmares that gets worse and worse until you think you'll die or bust a vessel, but you still can't wake up. It was his bloody bad luck to take a crazy person hostage.

He looked around, but there was no dragging the girlie anywhere with the streets so crowded.

He had a notion to pitch her in the river and see if she sank. Instead he turned up his collar and trailed after her, grumbling, back toward Southbridge.

CHAPTER FOURTEEN

ON THE
WRONG SIDE
OF THE LAW

Despite all the troubles she'd had over the previous two days—the kidnapping and threats and robberies and rain and dirt and all—Raisa was intoxicated, bewitched, and bemused by freedom. She strode through the streets in her breeches and shirt, anonymous to the citizens around her, drinking in the details of the colorful neighborhood known as Ragmarket.

Colorful was a word for it. It was also stinking and clamorous and spicy and terminally interesting. Pregnant with possibilities and risk. The bubble that usually protected the princess heir of the Fells had burst, and multiple sensations flooded in—the sights and smells and raw emotions of the queendom she was to rule one day.

She grappled with the notion that it was only context and

clothing that made her recognizable. Was that really all she was—the random occupant of a spot in the lineage of queens? Could any girl be chosen off the streets, dressed up, and put in her place? Did she have any natural ability to do this job?

The Guard was thick on every street, bristling with weapons and bravado. Yet no one recognized her. There was no undercurrent of rumor as there would be if her disappearance were common knowledge. Puzzled, she stopped and asked a shopkeeper sweeping his steps to tell the news.

"Somebody said there was a kidnapping," she said. "Is that why the Guard's all about?"

The shopkeeper shook his head. "Don't know nothing about a kidnapping. It's those murders in Southbridge. The Guard is searching every tavern, inn, and warehouse in Ragmarket. Bad for business, it is. I say, if the street rats want to murder each other, let them." He glanced about, lowering his voice. "They say it was that Cuffs Alister. He's as bloodthirsty as they come."

Raisa couldn't help glancing over her shoulder. Cuffs was trailing half a block behind her, as if he hoped he wouldn't be seen—*by* her or *with* her, Raisa wasn't sure.

It was somehow thrilling to know he was back there, in pursuit of her, like in the story of Hanalea and the highwayman.

But this wasn't a story. This was real. And she meant to find out what was really going on.

The towers of South Bridge loomed ahead of her. The guardhouse crouched hard by the bridge, on the Southbridge side. It was a squat, sturdy, stone building with tiny barred windows. A paved courtyard surrounded it, with stables behind for the horses. The Gray Wolf banner flew overhead, proclaiming that this was the queen's outpost, even amid the squalor of Southbridge.

The line for the bridge was longer than usual. A half-dozen fully armed guardsmen stood at each end, questioning all who sought to cross. Raisa's stomach did a sickening flip. Surely she'd be recognized by anybody who'd been sent out specifically to find her.

On impulse, she turned aside into a bakeshop. Inside, it was relatively clean and well kept, with displays of sticky buns and meat pies and pastries. The boy behind the counter wore a slouched red wool muffin cap to contain his hair.

"Good morning to you," she said. "I would like eight sticky buns, wrapped for travel. And your hat."

After a brief negotiation, Raisa left the shop with eight sticky buns in hand, her hair tucked up under the boy's cap.

I'll probably end up with the itches, she thought.

Cuffs was waiting for her outside. He gripped her wrist and yanked her into a doorway. "What. Are. You. Doing?" he hissed, his face inches from hers. Close up, she saw that his blue eyes were flecked with gold, his lashes thick and pale, the angry bruises on his face fading into pastels, a bit of blond stubble on his chin.

She held up her sack of buns. "I'm a bakeshop girl," Raisa said.

"This an't a game," Cuffs said. "You need to turn yourself in to the bluejackets on the bridge. Tell them you're the girl that was stolen from the temple. And go home."

"I've got something to do first."

"Look. I can't cross the bridge while it's swarming with

bluejackets," he said. "I can't help you if you get into trouble in Southbridge."

"Fine. You're done with me. I'm on my own, all right?" Raisa said, thinking, You can't help me where I'm going.

She wrested free of him and headed for the near end of the bridge. She looked back once to see him staring after her, hands stuffed into his pockets, a scowl on his face.

It took a good ten minutes to get through the line. Raisa tapped her foot impatiently, anxious for the encounter to be over. She wasn't used to having to wait.

At the checkpoint, she bowed low before the guardsmen, as she'd seen others do.

"What's your name and business, girl?" the guardsman demanded, scratching himself in a rude place.

"Rebecca Morley, Your Honor," Raisa said, staring at the ground, still worried about being recognized. "Mean to sell bakery goods cross the river."

"Bakery goods, you say? Let's see."

Raisa mutely opened the sack of buns and extended it toward the soldier. He reached a filthy paw in and removed one. He bit into it, grinned approvingly, and took another.

Raisa's cheeks flamed, and it took all of her self-control to keep from snatching the bag back. If she were truly a bakery girl, the cost of the buns would come out of her own pocket.

"These is good," the soldier said, handing back the depleted sack and swiping at his mouth with his sleeve. "Save me a couple for when you cross back." And he waved her on, grinning.

Raisa fumed all the way across the bridge. So *this* was the queen's face to the people. A common thief and bully. No wonder Amon considered rebellion a possibility.

On the Southbridge side, the temple stood on one side of the Way, the guardhouse on the other, like emblems of good and evil. Raisa leaned against the temple wall and studied the guardhouse. It looked impregnable, its windows like slitted eyes sneering at her. There was no way Cuffs and his gang were getting in and out of there.

At least she could find out if what they said was true—were they really holding three Raggers in the guardhouse, and were they really being tortured?

She took a deep breath and tried to center herself in her work, as Elena always said. Then she crossed the Way to the guardhouse door.

The lone guard at the door surveyed her in a bored fashion. In the guardroom beyond, several soldiers diced and played cards.

"What do you want?" he barked.

"I . . . ah . . . it's my sister, Sarie," Raisa said in a whiny voice. "She got ta'en by the bl . . . the Queen's Guard th'other day. In Ragmarket. I was told she was here. I brung her some dinner is all." She shook the bakery bag.

The guard grabbed it away from her. "We'll see she gets it," he said, dismissing her.

Well. That wouldn't do at all.

"Please, sir," Raisa persisted. "I was hoping as I could see her, you know. It's been three days, an' I wondered how she was getting on. She's been sick lately, and three days in gaol can't be doing her good."

"No visitors." He squinted at her suspiciously. "You should know that a'ready."

Raisa snatched at his sleeve, and he slapped her hand away, gripping the hilt of his sword. "Stay off! You bloody little—"

"Please. I've got some money, sir," Raisa quavered. "Not a lot, but some, and . . ."

The guard turned back to her, interest lighting his face. "If you've got money, let's see it, then."

"I will. You'll see, sir. Only maybe after . . ." Raisa began.

The guard's hand snaked forward. He gripped the neck of her shirt and yanked her toward him. "Don't play games with me, girl." He drew back his huge fist, and Raisa's mouth went dry with fear, but then a voice came from behind him.

"Let the girl in, Sloat. Lemme see her."

Sloat released her and stepped aside.

The man who'd spoken sat at a table by the fire, with greasy plates, playing cards, and several empty mugs arrayed before him. He had a thin, cruel face and muddy brown eyes, lank hair that hung to his shoulders. He wore the blue uniform of the Queen's Guard, and the bars on his collar said he was a sergeant.

"Come here, girl," the sergeant said, motioning to her with a smile that turned Raisa's bowels to water.

Reluctantly, she crossed the room and stood before him, keeping her eyes downcast. Why had she thought this was a good idea?

"You're Sarie's little sister, are you?"

She nodded mutely.

He gripped her wrist, twisting it hard. "Speak when you're spoken to, girl."

Raisa gasped in pain, tears springing to her eyes. "Yes, sir. I'm Sarie's sister." She held up the bakery bag with the other hand, like a shield. "I brought her dinner, sir."

"The Sarie what's in the Raggers?" the sergeant continued.

She glanced up quickly, then away. "The Raggers, sir? What's that?"

The sergeant laughed. He let go of her wrist and took a swig of beer. "What's your name?"

"Rebecca, sir."

"You're a right pretty little thing, Rebecca. How old are you?"

Raisa cast about desperately for an age. Younger was better she decided. "Th-thirteen, sir," she said, hunching her shoulders, trying to remember what thirteen looked like.

"Ah." He grinned wider. "Would you like to see your sister, then?"

"I would, sir."

The sergeant stood and took her by the arm. "Come on, then."

Sloat began muttering a protest. "Sergeant Gillen, I a'ready told her, No visitors."

"Shut it, Sloat," Gillen said. "We'll make a special exception, in this case."

He hauled her down a long corridor lined with stout-looking wooden doors, her feet touching the floor only at every third step. And all the way, Raisa kept thinking, This is the brutal Sergeant Gillen. The one the Raggers whispered about. The one Amon spoke of, who beats people in the street. What have I gotten myself into?

At the end of the hall was a metal gate, and beyond that another wooden door that Gillen unlocked with a large metal key. Gillen took her through both, stopped long enough to light a torch, and then propelled her down a narrow staircase to the cellar.

Raisa shivered from fear and cold. It was chilly and damp on the cellar level, and she knew they must be close to the river, because of the stink.

Or maybe it was the stink of death all around her. This was an evil place, where evil things were done. Images of disaster circulated through her head. She felt panicked, claustrophobic, and she knew she had to get out.

"You know, sir, I'm thinking maybe it's best I come back tomorrow," she said, turning back toward the stairs.

"Come on, missy, we're almost there." Gillen seized the scruff of her neck and yanked her forward so hard she nearly fell.

Instinctively, she knew that any sudden claim to royalty would be disregarded. In the unlikely event he did believe her, he would not hesitate to throttle her to death and drop her in the river to prevent her from carrying this story back to Fellsmarch Castle. Gillen had a killer's heart under his royal blue uniform.

She'd thought of it as an adventure, like something Hanalea would do. She'd thought she understood the stakes she'd be playing for, and she'd been wrong.

Had Hanalea been frightened when she confronted the Demon King? Raisa felt plenty frightened now.

Ahead was a metal grillwork bolted into the stone with a massive metal lock at one side. As the torchlight bled through the cage door, Raisa could see movement in the gloom beyond, a shuffling of bodies.

It was a girl and two boys, fifteen or sixteen, maybe, though it was difficult to tell. They were thin and filthy, and they'd been beaten so badly they were scarcely recognizable as human. They did not crowd forward, as one might expect, but pressed themselves back into the corners as if hoping to escape Gillen's notice.

Raisa was sickened—and furious to know that what Cuffs Alister had said was true.

"Hey, Sarie," Gillen crooned, unfastening the door. "I've brought you some company."

"Go *away*," came a whisper from the dark. "We can't tell you what we don't know. We an't seen Alister in months."

"Come now, don't be like that," Gillen said, his voice silky. "Someone's here to see you."

"Who'd come to see me?" she demanded.

"I've got little Rebecca here, luv. She's brought some supper."

"*Who?*" Overcome by curiosity, Sarie shuffled out of the shadows and into the light. She was tall for her age, and broad of hip and shoulders. She looked like no relation to Raisa.

"Now your baby sister is here, I think we'll get some-where," Gillen said with a bone-chilling smile. He tightened his grip on Raisa. "Maybe it'll loosen your tongue when we put her on the rack."

Sarie gaped at Raisa, then back at Gillen. "Who the bloody hell is this?"

In stories, Queen Hanalea fought off the powerful Demon King through strength of character and the power of good.

In the clan camps, they spoke of the small overcoming the mighty through the force of a focused mind.

Amon Byrne had shown Raisa street-fighting techniques meant to disarm a bigger and stronger opponent.

Raisa was smart enough to know that her chances of

overpowering someone like Mac Gillen were slim to none. But when a person gives no quarter, if she's fighting for her life, it can make a difference.

When she slammed both feet into Mac Gillen's kneecaps, she knew it was unlikely to disable him. She hoped it would be enough to distract him.

In that she succeeded. He screamed like a stuck pig and went down, clutching at his knees, swearing.

"Get him!" Raisa shouted recklessly, rolling to her feet. "To me! Come on!"

With the strength born of desperation, the three Raggers jumped on Gillen, dragging him to the floor, kicking and punching for all they were worth. Gillen was like a massive bear set upon by coyotes who were snapping and biting and growling, but doing very little damage.

Gillen's hands fastened around Raisa's throat, and he squeezed, stopping her breath. She twisted and turned but could not break free. The blood roared in her ears, and spots swam before her eyes, coalescing into wolflike shapes.

Then somebody plowed into them, and the pressure on her throat was released.

Greedily gasping for air, Raisa snatched up the fallen torch and jammed it, still burning, into Gillen's face. He screamed with pain and rage and left off pounding one of the boys. Suddenly he seemed less interested in beating them to death and more interested in getting to the door. Raisa hooked a foot around his ankle and sent him sprawling, and Sarie lifted a heavy iron chamber pot and slammed it into his head.

Gillen finally lay quiet.

CHAPTER FIFTEEN

STRANGE BEDFELLOWS

Amon Byrne was not the kind of person who dwelled on things. He usually made a decision and moved on. But this time was different. He'd done more second-guessing over the past two days than he'd done in his lifetime before then.

They'd not been released from Speaker Jemson's study until the morning after Raisa's abduction.

By then the trail was cold. Amon had sent his Gray Wolves racing into Ragmarket to search for any trace of Cuffs or Raisa, while he went straight to his father to confess what he'd done.

He found his father at breakfast, dining alone, as was his habit. Once the first few words were out of Amon's mouth, Captain Byrne stopped eating, sat back, and listened stone-faced, firing a question here and there.

When Amon finished, his father threw his napkin on the table and sent his orderly to fetch his duty officers to the garrison room.

Amon extended his sword to his father, hilt first. "I'm sorry, sir," he said stiffly. "I hereby resign my comm—"

"Keep that," his father growled. "You'll likely need it."

"Sir?" Amon stammered, confused. "But . . . when the queen hears . . ."

"They are headstrong, the Gray Wolf queens," his father said. "No one knows that better than me. The most difficult task a guardsman faces is to say no to his sovereign when he knows it may result in his own dismissal, imprisonment, or death." He fixed Amon with his hawklike gaze. "But sometimes you have to say it. You should have said it to the princess heir."

"But how can we do that, sir?" Amon restored his sword to its scabbard. "I mean, we serve the queen, and so—"

"We serve the *line* of queens," his father said. "We serve the throne. Sometimes an individual makes a bad choice."

Amon stared at his father. "But isn't that . . . isn't that . . ."

"Treason?" Captain Byrne smiled thinly. "Some would say so. Who are *we*, after all?" He rose, walked to the hearth, and prodded the fire with a poker. The careful arrangement of logs collapsed in a fountain of sparks.

"We Byrnes are here by a covenant made with Hanalea, the first of this stubborn line," his father said, staring into the fire. "It is a tricky business, for sure, but we'll be all right as long as we keep our eyes on the good of the line and the good of the realm."

"But . . . not everyone in the Guard is there for the good of the realm," Amon said, thinking of Mac Gillen.

His father nodded. "Time was, the captain chose every

man and woman who went into the Guard. That's no longer true. Politics have come into play. I did not choose Mac Gillen, and I've been unable to dismiss him, much as I've tried."

Who chose Mac Gillen? Amon wanted to ask. But didn't. "What . . . what are we going to do, sir?" he asked.

His father continued to gaze into the flames, his face hard and unreadable. "We're going to risk everything to protect the line."

"What do you mean?"

"The princess heir has her name day this summer, after which she'll be eligible for an alliance by marriage." He turned and leaned against the mantel, looking as grim as Amon had ever seen him. "It may be best for the long-term defense of the Fells if the princess heir marries a southern prince. But they're conservative in the southern kingdoms. If they find out our princess was held captive overnight by a street thug, it may affect her prospects for a match."

Amon's stomach clenched. He thought of Cuffs Alister, his knife at Raisa's throat, declining a hostage switch. He found himself actually spluttering. "He wouldn't . . . if he's touched her, if there's—"

His father held up a hand. "The facts are less important than the perception when it comes to marriage contracts, Corporal."

The facts are important to me, Amon thought. "They . . . they wouldn't name Mellony heir, would they? If Rai . . . if the princess heir is tainted," he said, not really sure who "they" might be.

Amon shook his head. "They may try, but we cannot allow that. Mellony is not the blooded heir, as long as Raisa lives. The Naéming does not recognize politics. I hope Her Majesty won't be influenced . . ." His voice trailed off. "We are direly in need of a strong queen," he said softly, rubbing his forehead as if it hurt.

"Da," Amon said, anxious to get back to his subject, "when you said we'd risk everything to protect the line, what do you mean by that?"

His father fixed back on him. "Here it is. We will *not* announce that the princess has disappeared. We will set the Guard looking for one Rebecca Morley—that was the name you said she used, wasn't it—who fits the princess's description, taken from Southbridge Temple by Cuffs Alister. Rebecca, we'll say, comes from a wealthy family but wanted to do good works for the poor. We'll offer a very generous reward for information."

Amon wasn't sure he understood. "But . . . we'll tell the queen the truth?"

His father looked him straight in the eyes. "No."

Amon couldn't believe it. His father, the soul of duty and propriety, was proposing a massive deception, one that could have dire consequences if it went bad. It would be perceived that the captain of the Guard had risked the princess heir to protect his son. It could be his career.

"Da! We can't do that. If you're found out . . ."

"Remember what I said. We are bound to preserve the line, no matter the cost. If this Cuffs knows who he holds, it will put the princess heir at greater risk. He might be frightened enough to kill her on the spot. He could carry her across the border and sell her off to some southern prince. Or align himself with the Gray Wolf's enemies."

"If she's even still alive," Amon forced himself to say. "It's been hours and hours."

"She's alive," his father said. "I would know if the line was broken. And you will too, once you're truly named." His father put his hand on Amon's shoulder, stopping his questions. "I know the queen enrolled you in the Guard, but anyone can be enrolled, as I've said. This is different."

He left it at that, but Amon was glad to take his father's word for it. Glad he wouldn't have to insert the language "If Raisa's still alive" into every speculation.

"But . . . but how will we explain Raisa's disappearance?" Amon persisted. He was half relieved he wouldn't have to face the queen right away, half convinced this scheme would never work. "She must have been missed by now. They're probably already in a panic."

"Averill Demonai will help us," his father said. "He'll say Raisa's gone back to Demonai Camp for a . . . a prenaming ritual. Very secret, very sacred. Lord Bayar will be furious, but we can live with that." A smile ghosted over his face.

"Why would Averill do that? He's her father. He has to be worried."

"He'll want to keep it secret for the same reasons we do— for the good of his daughter and the good of the line."

"What would you have me do?" Amon asked humbly, knowing he deserved no role in this, but desperately desiring one.

"You'll comb Ragmarket and Southbridge. You'll use all your contacts. You'll talk up the reward in taverns and inns. After all, you know the streets, and you know Raisa, and you can identify Cuffs, and that's important when most members of the Guard have never seen the princess in the flesh."

Over the next two days, Amon walked the streets around the clock, mostly in Ragmarket, since that was Ragger turf and Cuffs was seen crossing the bridge with Raisa immediately after the confrontation in the study. Amon threw money around in taverns, but never drank himself. He interviewed countless people, asking after "Rebecca Morley," describing her in detail, showing a secret sketch of Raisa that his sister, Lydia, had done for him.

Amon pushed himself so he wouldn't have to think. When he *did* think, guilt washed over him.

He was the one responsible for Cuffs's escape in the first place, that day they'd collared him outside of The Keg and Crown. And by going along with Raisa's plan to go to Southbridge Temple, he'd put her in Jemson's study when Cuffs barged through the door.

And finally, his decision to confront Cuffs then and there, in the temple, had resulted in his taking of Raisa.

Of course, there was a chance that by now Raisa had already told the streetlord who she was. Amon could picture that conversation, but he couldn't picture what would happen next, except sometimes in nightmares. So he did his best not to sleep.

Consequently, Amon was less than alert in the days after

Raisa's disappearance as he walked the narrow streets and alleys of Ragmarket, but he couldn't bring himself to care.

He'd arranged to meet the Wolfpack at the bridge at noon to see if anyone had news. He was not optimistic. He was nearing the river, walking a narrow alley, when someone behind him called his name.

"Corporal Byrne."

He swung around. It was Cuffs Alister, in a side courtyard, on the wrong side of a wrought-iron grillwork. A half dozen other Raggers stood in a cluster behind him. No Raisa.

Amon lunged toward Cuffs and came up against the grillwork, which was too fine to insinuate even his hand through. Still, Cuffs skipped back a step, as if he thought Amon might somehow manage it.

"Where is she?" Amon demanded, looking for some way over or around the fence. "What have you done with her? If you've touched her, I swear I'll—"

"Rebecca, you mean?" Cuffs frowned as if confused.

"Right. Rebecca." Amon's mind stumbled to a conclusion. So the streetlord still didn't know Raisa's true identity. "Who else would I be looking for, you murdering, thieving . . ."

"She's in Southbridge Guardhouse," Cuffs said, cocking his head right, toward the river.

"Southbridge?" Amon struggled to control his voice. "What's she doing in there?"

"I don't exactly know what she's doing in there," Cuffs fingered the silver at his wrists. "But she went in there yesterday and hasn't come out. Something's up. I was hoping you could, you know, take a look in. Make sure she's all right."

Amon was lost. There was something crucial the streetlord wasn't telling him. "Why wouldn't she be all right?" And why hadn't Amon heard she'd been found?

Cuffs shrugged. "Mac Gillen's in there, for one."

Mac Gillen was a brute on the streets, but what did that have to do with Raisa? "How did she come to be in there?" Amon asked, choosing his words carefully, trying to resist the impulse to beat on the metal door between them. "Did the Guard find her, or did she escape from you, or . . ."

"Well, I believe she went in to rescue some Raggers from the pits," Cuffs said. "She wasn't all that specific."

"She went in to rescue—why would she do that?" Amon gripped the ironwork, studying the streetlord's face. Was he lying? And if so, what was the purpose?

"Guess she's kind of taken with us," Cuffs said. "You know, the glamour of the gang life and all. Getting beat up every other day, arrested for crimes you didn't commit, long nights in gaol, sleeping in the cold and wet. It's . . . seductive." He raised an eyebrow.

Amon couldn't help thinking Cuffs had chosen that word on purpose. Yet despite his sardonic tone, the streetlord's face was pale and anxious under the dirt and bruises, and he practically twitched with tension.

Was he worried about Raisa?

No. He wasn't allowed.

"Why should I trust you? Why should I believe you about anything?" Amon asked.

Cuffs spat on the ground. "All right, then. If it's too chancy for you to walk into your own guardhouse and find your own girlie, I'll go myself. I just thought you might get a better reception." His face had gone hard, his blue eyes bright with anger.

Amon wavered, unwilling to lose Cuffs now that he had him in his sights. Even if he was tantalizingly out of reach.

"Look," Cuffs said, rubbing his chin. "I'm sorry I took your girlie. I don't want her to get hurt. And the longer you wait, the more likely that'll be. I don't know what else I can say."

"You wait here," Amon said. "Don't you move." As if he had some power to enforce it.

"All right," Cuffs said, smiling slantwise. "You go on. I'll be waiting here."

Amon turned and raced toward the bridge, but hadn't gotten more than a few paces when he heard his name again.

"Amon! Corporal Byrne! Where've you been? Wasn't we supposed to meet at noon?"

He turned and found his Gray Wolf cadets clustered around the bridge pillar.

On impulse he said, "Come on with me to the guard-house. I hear there's trouble."

They cut to the front of the line for the bridge. The guardsman on duty saluted.

"Are you the reinforcements?" he asked, eyeing Amon's companions.

"Right," Amon said. "Reinforcements. What seems to be the trouble?"

"Dunno. Some kind of prisoner riot."

Amon set a killing pace across the bridge, which cut down on the questions from the Wolfpack. The door to the guardhouse was ajar. Several guards stood around outside, armed with clubs. Amon slowed his pace and approached cautiously from the side. When he peered around the door frame, he saw a handful of guardsmen bunched at the end of the corridor that led to the cells.

"What's going on?" Amon asked, leading the others inside. "Where's Sergeant Gillen?"

"Corporal Byrne, thank the Maker," one of the guardsmen said, only too happy to hand over responsibility. "The prisoners took over the cell block yesterday morning. They have the gate barricaded and they're holding Sergeant Gillen and some others hostage."

Amon blinked at them. "How did all this happen?"

The man shrugged. "Search me. This young girl come in looking for her sister, said she was being held in the cells. Sergeant Gillen, he took the girl down to the pit."

"A young girl? Who did she want to see?"

"It was one of them Raggers what Sergeant Gillen's been interrogating. The next thing I know, all hell's broken loose and the prisoners are demanding a way out or they'll cut Gillen's throat."

Well, Amon thought, that'd be a shame, to sacrifice Sergeant Gillen for the good of the realm. Aloud he said, "Who's their spokesman?"

"That girl and her sister, I guess. We didn't know what to do, so we been waiting for word from the captain."

"Captain Byrne sent me to—um—investigate." Amon poked his head into the corridor. The prisoners had stuck torches on either side of the gate, blinding him so he couldn't see beyond them. "You! In the cells! This is Corporal Byrne. I need to talk to you."

"Corporal Byrne? Really?"

It was Raisa's voice, and Amon nearly collapsed from relief. He had no idea what she was up to, but she was alive at least, and out of Cuffs's hands. Now all he needed to do was get her out of there without giving away her identity and raising lots of questions they didn't want to answer.

"Yes," he said. "Ah—who are you?" It seemed like the safest question.

"I'm Sarie's sister, Rebecca," she said, hesitating a little over the name.

"I'm the officer in command," he said, feeling foolish as he said it. "Truce for a meeting?"

He heard a flurry of conversation, more like an argument, and then a new voice said, "*You* come to *us*. Unarmed. Hands raised. Try anything and I'll spit you like a pig."

"I wouldn't do it, sir," someone said behind him. "They'll just take you hostage too. We'd best starve them out, I say."

Amon unsheathed his sword and handed it to one of the guardsmen. "I'm coming," he called. "Unarmed. Under truce," he added, just as a reminder. All the while wondering how this would end. Wondering what his father would do.

He walked slowly down the corridor, hands in the air. When he reached the gate, he paused. A girl's rough voice said, "Come ahead," and he passed between the torches, skin tingling, expecting at any moment to feel the prick of a blade.

When he entered the cell block, Amon was nearly overwhelmed by the stench of urine and unwashed bodies and the metallic reek of blood. As his eyes adjusted to the dark, he saw that he was surrounded by nearly two dozen prisoners of all ages—from children to one cadaverous, matted-haired old man who stared down at his hands, muttering to himself. Several were slumped against the wall, looking ill or injured.

Two prisoners stepped forward. One was a taller girl wearing an ill-fitting guard uniform. Her face was layered in bruises, her nose badly broken, and those were just the injuries he could see. Alongside her was Raisa, carrying a short sword and clad in trousers and shirt, her hair stuffed under a boy's cap like some knight's errant page. Her neck was mottled with bruises and there was a jagged cut over her cheekbone. She looked up at him, green eyes wide, and her finger to her lips. "I'm Rebecca," she said, in case he'd forgotten. "This is Sarie."

At that point Amon didn't know whether to embrace her or throttle her. So he took a middle path. "Where are Sergeant Gillen and the other guards?" he asked.

"They're safe put away in the cages," the tall girl, Sarie, said, grinning smugly. "Like the animals they are."

"What is it you want?" Amon asked.

"We want safe out of gaol, for one," Sarie said. "We want the Guard to quit trying to make us confess to something we didn't do."

"We want Gillen reassigned," Raisa said. "Send him to the borderlands, where people fight back."

"Kill 'im!" somebody shouted from the back of the crowd. "Then there's no chance he'll come back."

"Ah." Amon cleared his throat. "Could I speak with Rebecca a minute? In private?"

Sarie looked from Amon to Raisa and shook her head. "If you got something to say, say it to all of us."

Amon's mind raced. "All right. I can bring you out of here, but you're going to have to give up your weapons, and I'm going to have to take you out under guard."

Loud protest erupted from all sides.

"Listen to me!" For a small person, Raisa had a commanding voice. "Listen," she repeated. "I know you've reason to hate bluejackets. But I know Corporal Byrne, and I know he wouldn't lie to you." Then she turned to Amon and demanded, "Why do we have to give up our weapons?"

Amon leaned in close and spoke so only Raisa could hear, ignoring the dirty looks from the others. "Because it can't look like I'm setting you free," he said. "The Bayars have eyes and ears everywhere. They don't care about dead Southies, but if it looks like I'm loosing criminals on the streets, they'll use it against my da."

Sarie pushed her way between them. "Who are you, anyway?" she asked Raisa. "How come you and this blue-jacket are so chummy? You say Cuffs sent you, but he may be dead for all I know. I've not even seen him for a year."

Amon was losing patience. "If you all don't want to come, fine. You stay here, but Rebecca's coming with me." There was more grumbling all around, and he added, "Take it or leave it."

This was followed by a clamor of "Put 'im in the cage with Gillen!" and "We're leavin' it, then!"

But Sarie raised her hand for silence, her eyes locked on Amon's face. "Fair enough," she said. "But we'll take our shivs wi' us, hid under our coats." She stowed her dagger under her jacket. "And I'm keeping the girlie close to me. Try anything, and she'll be the first one down." She put an arm around Raisa and drew her in close, her other hand resting on her weapon.

Amon's impulse was to rip Raisa free and drag her away with him, but she looked at him and shook her head, a movement so slight, Sarie missed it.

"All right," he said. "Let me . . . give me a minute."

He ducked through the doorway, between the torches, and walked back toward the front, painfully aware that his back made a tempting target.

Back in the duty room, the other guards peppered him with questions, and he had to hold up a hand for silence.

"They want an audience with the captain," Amon said. "To tell their grievances. I agreed. So we're going to bring them out under guard." Ignoring the muttering of surprise and muted protest, he scanned the crowd and chose out his cadets. "Mick, Hallie, Garret, Wode, Kiefer, come with me."

"You want us to jump 'em soon as you're clear of the cells?" one of the bluejackets asked, fondling his club.

"No." Amon looked around the room, meeting every eye. "Nobody so much as touches his weapon. I mean to get them out of here without spilling blood. Any soldier that makes a move on them will be brought up on charges."

There was another mutter of protest, but Amon thought they'd follow orders.

They made a rather odd procession, like refugees from some poorly planned and provisioned war. Twenty-five or so prisoners limped, shuffled, and swaggered at the center, loosely ringed by Amon's mostly beardless cadets. They marched through the duty room and out the door, crossed the court-yard, and turned onto South Bridge. Guards stared at them, perplexed, as they streamed across. Citizens cleared out of the streets ahead of them, but peered out of windows and leaned out of doorways after they'd passed.

Amon's racing heartbeat slowed a bit once they'd made it to the other side of the river. They marched straight down the Way of the Queens until they were out of sight of the guard-house.

"Turn here," he commanded, veering off into a side street. They walked a ways farther, made another turn, and Amon brought the parade to a halt.

"All right," he said. "You're free to go. Just don't land in gaol again, all right? That'd be hard to explain."

Most of the prisoners melted quickly into the shadows and were gone.

But Sarie blinked at him, then glanced around, suspicious to the bone. "Just like that? You're springing us? How come?"

Because your princess heir commands it, Amon thought of saying. *Because I'm a fool. Because I still haven't figured out how to say no.*

"Because you've been ill used," Amon said. "Because some of us don't believe in beating a confession out of a person."

"Such a pretty speech, Corporal." And just like that, Cuffs was there with the rest of the Raggers. The Gray Wolves bunched up, prickling with weapons.

"No worries," Cuffs said, grinning. "Cat and me just came to meet and greet." He nodded toward another Ragger, a tall Southern Islander with a scowl on her face.

"Let's go," Cat said, and all of the Raggers, including the three held by the Guard, bled into the surrounding streets. All of the Raggers but Cuffs.

He came and stood before Raisa, sketching out a little bow. "Rebecca," he said, "bravo. I do think you're a Ragger at heart."

"She's not," Amon said, pushing between them. "If by that you mean she's a thief and kidnapper."

"Amon," Raisa said, laying a hand on his arm.

"I'm thinking your girlie don't seem that happy to see you," Cuffs said, shaking his head sadly. "I thought she'd be all over you with happiness, and not even a chaperone kiss."

"I'm thinking you should answer for taking her," Amon said. "I want to know what you . . ." He swallowed hard. "I want to know if you've hurt her in any way."

"I'm *fine*," Raisa interjected, pressing her fingers into the flesh of his arm. "He never touched me."

Amon looked down into her face. She raised her eyebrows, signaling him to leave off.

"What about the dead Southies?" Amon went on, not able to help himself. "Convince me you weren't involved."

"You going to put me on the rack, then, like the others?" Cuffs asked, still smiling, though it looked kind of frozen to his face. "Yank out my fingernails? Smash my—"

"*You* stop it!" Raisa said sharply. "Amon is not a torturer. He was the one who freed your street runners from gaol. If not for him, I—"

"They're not *my* street runners," Cuffs interrupted.

"Fine," she said, glaring at him.

"Fine," he said, rolling his eyes.

Amon was beginning to feel a little extraneous. "You know Gillen's going to come after you again," he said to Cuffs. "It'd be better to turn yourself in."

"Would it? Let me think about it . . . No thanks," Cuffs said. "I'll be off, then. Good luck with your girlie, mate. I think you'll need it."

And before anything more could be said, he'd turned the corner and was gone.

Aflame with anger and embarrassment, dizzy with relief, Amon whistled for his triple, and they assembled around him, jittery as colts.

"First of all, great work, everyone," Amon said. "You should all be proud to have pulled this off without any bloodshed." The Wolfpack elbowed each other and grinned. "Second of all, nobody says a word to anybody about what happened over here. Don't ask questions, because I can't answer them. This is the queen's business. The fewer who know about it the better."

Their faces fell, and Amon knew hopes of tavern bragging and free rounds of drinks were evaporating.

"Now. We're going to take Rebecca back to the castle close," Amon said. "Fall in."

Amon marched his little army back to the Way and turned toward Fellsmarch Castle. The guardsmen walked a few paces ahead and behind, giving Raisa and Amon a little space in which to talk.

"What's going on?" Raisa whispered. "Is my mother furious or worried or both?"

"Furious," Amon said. "The queen is fuming, and Lord Bayar is making all kinds of threats. But not for the reasons you'd guess. My da and Lord Averill told her you went back to Demonai for a week for some kind of name day clan ritual."

Raisa blinked at him. "They did? Why did they say that?"

Amon cleared his throat. "My da is worried that if news gets out about you spending the night with a streetlord, your prospects for marriage might be . . . diminished."

She stared at him. "I'm the blooded princess heir of the Fells," she declared through gritted teeth, those green eyes dark as the deep ocean. "Any prince or noble in the entire Seven Realms should be *thrilled* to marry me. No questions asked."

Her voice was getting louder and louder, and Amon put his finger to his lips. "Shhh. I agree, and Da agrees, but the southern princes have . . . old-fashioned ideas about women," he said. "They think brides should be . . . pure . . . when they come to . . . Bones, Raisa, just trust me, all right?"

His face was flaming. He shouldn't be having this conversation with the princess heir of the Fells. It was just wrong.

"And we want to keep those options open since we think, I mean, *Da* thinks it might be more advantageous for you to marry south than to marry someone within the realm . . ."

"And he thinks this because . . . ?"

"Well. Because we may need allies when the Ardenine wars are over," Amon said lamely. *And Lord Bayar seems to be against it*, he added to himself.

"So now the captain of my Guard and one of his officers

are laying plans for whom I should marry," Raisa said in that quiet voice that meant trouble. "And dithering over my reputation like two old aunties."

"Anyway," Amon said hurriedly, hoping to bring this conversation to a quick close, "he thought it best if we avoid that whole thing by—"

"By lying to his liege queen?"

"Well, yes. Basically." Amon cleared his throat, feeling the blood rush to his face.

She paced along, taking two steps for his one, her dark brows drawn together. "So nobody knows about . . . about the trip into Southbridge, and the kidnapping, or anything?"

"Different people know pieces. The Queen's Guard has been searching for a girl named Rebecca. My triple thinks you're my . . . sweetheart." He looked over at Raisa. "What does Cuffs know?"

She shrugged. "He thinks I'm your sweetheart too, I guess," she said wryly.

Amon felt a spark of optimism. "So maybe this will work," he said. He glanced over at her, wanting to ask for a rundown of everything that had happened since she was grabbed from the temple.

Something had happened between them, of that he was certain, and he didn't like it. One overnight with Cuffs Alister, and Raisa had turned into some kind of outlaw. So he said, "Are you . . . are you sure you're all right? That . . . Cuffs . . . did he . . . ?"

"Me? I'm fine," she said distractedly. "But we've got to do something about the Guard. They're torturing people. That old man who came out with us? He had been down in the pit for fifteen years. Mac Gillen is a heartless brute."

"So you went into the guardhouse . . . to rescue them?" Amon was still trying to understand.

"I went in to see if what Cuffs said was true. He told me he wouldn't submit to the queen's justice because there *is* no justice. And he was right."

"Not everyone's like Gillen," Amon said, feeling the need to defend the Guard. "And you can't believe what Cuffs says. He's accused of murdering eight people."

"But it was *true*. What he said. And I don't believe he did those killings. He thought the Raggers did it. And he hasn't been with the Raggers for a year."

Maybe it was all an act for your benefit, Amon thought, but didn't dare say it aloud. "If not him, then who?" he asked.

"I don't know," she said irritably. "*You're* the one in the Guard."

"Don't forget," he said, "he sent you in to rescue his friends. How would it be if you'd escaped from a streetlord only to be killed by your own Guard?"

"I didn't escape. He let me go. And he didn't send me. I went on my own."

"But you can't take chances like this," Amon exploded. "Things are unstable enough as it is. We can't risk a change of succession."

"The succession, the *bloody* succession. Well, if you ask me, the lineage of queens is like a chain around my neck," Raisa muttered. "I'm no good to anybody if these kinds of things are being done in my name. And I expect you to help me stop it."

With that she strode on in silence, hands fisted at her sides.

CHAPTER SIXTEEN

DEMONS IN THE STREET

Han didn't know whether to hope his mother was home or not. It might be a long time before he saw her again, but he just didn't think he could deal with more drama.

He wrinkled his nose as he mounted the stairs, catching a whiff of cabbage cooking, a scent that always meant hard times.

When he pushed open the door, Mam and Mari looked up from the book they were reading.

A *book*?

"Han!" Mari squealed, scrambling to her feet. She charged across the room and fastened herself to his leg like the lamprey eels from faraway oceans he'd read about in one of Jemson's books. "I've got a book all my own! Speaker Jemson handed them out. He said the Princess Raisa bought them for us. He says I can keep it."

"That's great, Mari," Han said, distracted, looking over

Mari's blond head at Mam, hoping for a clue. His mother's expression mingled relief and apprehension.

"Thank the Maker," she said. She crossed the room and pulled him into her arms, awkwardly patting his back. "The Guard's looking for you," she said, smoothing down his hair. "They been all over Ragmarket, asking after you. Sergeant Gillen, he's in a fury. They said you busted some Raggers out of gaol."

How come he always got the blame? "Not exactly," he said, thinking Mam must have been really worried to skip the lecture. "Have they been here?"

She shook her head. "But you can't stay here, you know," she said. "He'll catch you sooner or later."

"I know. I'm going back to Marisa Pines. I'll stay up there until things calm down." He hesitated. "What are you doing home? I thought you'd be at work."

"I'm not working up at the castle close anymore," Mam said, releasing him and stirring the cabbage on the hearth. "But it's good, because it makes it easier for me to take Mari to school."

That had been his job. To convey his sister safely to Jemson's care.

"You're not working for the queen anymore?" Han gently detached Mari from his leg and led her over to the hearth, sat, and pulled her onto his knee. "Why? What happened?"

"I ruint one of the queen's gowns." Mam shrugged. "The seed pearls were made of paste, that was the problem. Didn't like it there anyway. Fellsmarch Castle, I mean. People were snooty. At least in Ragmarket they treat you like you're human."

"But what are you going to live on?" Han said. "It's going to be hard for me to come into town, to carry for Lucius, or sell what I glean up mountain."

"We'll get by," Mam said. "There's always rags and laundry. And now they're giving away food at Southbridge Temple two or three times a week. It's part of that Briar Rose Ministry Princess Raisa started."

"Princess Raisa?" Han repeated, surprised. Was she slumming in Southbridge or what? "Huh. I wonder how long that will last."

"She's doing good work," Mam said. "Everyone says it's a blessing. And it helps until I can find something steady again."

Han thought of the girl Rebecca Morley. She knew people in the castle close. Maybe she could pull some strings, help Mam get her job back, or get another job, just as good.

Or maybe it was just an excuse to see her again.

But no. He couldn't risk giving away his connection to Mam and Mari. He liked to think of them as safe, separate from his life in the gangs, hidden away in the room above the stable.

"Hanson," Mam said, in the manner of a person launching a prepared speech.

Han sighed. He should have known there'd be a lecture, by and by.

"You can't just hide in the mountains all the time," Mam said. "And you can't seem to be here athout getting into trouble. You're sixteen now, and you've got to find a vocation. You could go to Oden's Ford, enter the warrior school, and become a officer. That don't take no connections, and there's lots of call for soldiers these days, so they don't ask a lot of questions."

Officer? Most of the soldiers he knew were in the Guard, and they'd never take him. Plus he couldn't see himself smashing heads on the street. But what if he could be an officer in the regular army? He'd have armor and a sword, and his enemies would be out in front of him. He wouldn't always have to be looking over his shoulder.

Only there was one big barrier to all of this. "It costs money to go to Oden's Ford," he said. "And we don't have any."

And then he had a thought. He scraped back his sleeves, exposing the silver cuffs. "We could sell these," he said. "They ought to bring enough money to live on for a year or more."

Mam shook her head, looking from the cuffs up into his eyes, her face pale and strained. "I think you'd best leave well enough alone. They ain't meant to come off. Not ever."

Han stared at Mam. There was some knowledge in her eyes, and fear as well.

He wanted to grip her by the shoulders and shake her. He wanted to yell, *What do you want from me? It's that or thieving! I got nothing else.* But he couldn't, not with Mari in the room.

"I'll ask Willo about it again," he said, tugging his sleeves back into place. "There must be a way."

There *was* a way. One good taking, one good mark with a heavy purse, and Mam and Mari would be set for a while. A few more takings and he might have the swag to go to Oden's Ford.

He thrust the idea from his mind.

Fetching his rucksack from the corner, he stuffed his spare breeches and shirts into it. After a moment's hesitation, he pulled his Ragger neck scarf from under the mattress. He thought about the amulet buried out in the yard. His fingers itched, longing to touch it again. But no. It was safer where it was. If anything happened to him, it would rest there forever, out of reach of the Bayars. It gave him some small satisfaction.

Mam handed him a cloth bag. "Here's some bread and an end of cheese for the road," she said. "Tell Willo thanks for your keep," she said roughly. "Tell her . . . tell her I'm sorry I can't provide for my own son." Her lower lip trembled, and tears stood in her eyes.

"It's all right, Mam," Han said. "Willo doesn't mind. And it's my own fault I have to leave."

Mari was crying too, tears streaming down her cheeks. "You can't go away again," she said. "You only just came back."

Han attempted a smile and ruffled her hair. "I'll be back before you know it. And I'll expect you to read to me when I come back."

"I can read to you now," Mari said, grabbing up her book and extending it toward him. "Stay and I'll show you."

He shook his head. "I've got to go."

And there was nothing else to be said, so he left.

By now it was dead dark, so he wound his way through backstreets, alert for Guard patrols and other inquisitive folk. Once or twice he thought he saw movement in the spaces between buildings, or heard soft footfalls behind him. But each time he turned around, there was nobody there.

It had begun to rain, a cold constant drizzle that sucked up the light and added to his misery. Two blocks over from home he stopped in at Burnet's Meats. Out in back of the butcher shop, a long trough carried blood and offal into the gutters. Han soaked his spare breeches and shirt and neck scarf in the blood.

He came at the river a mile east of the bridge, where there'd be less traffic. Scrambling down the bank, he arranged his bloody clothes at the edge of the river, finishing with his gang scarf. He wrote "CUFFS—DUBL CROSSR" in the mud with a stick. It was crude, but it might fool the Guard anyway.

The bells in Southbridge Temple tower were sounding two as he trotted across the bridge, keeping close to the wall. Over the temple's side entrance hung a new banner, proclaiming, THE BRIAR ROSE MINISTRY. And, in smaller letters, BY THE GRACE OF HER HIGHNESS, PRINCESS RAISA ANA'MARIANNA.

Huh, Han thought. Seems like Her Worship is everywhere.

He kept in the shadow of the temple for two long blocks, thinking of Jemson, somewhere within its walls, probably sleeping.

"Sorry, Jemson," Han whispered. "Sorry I let you down. Don't let it keep you from believing in somebody else."

Tears came to his eyes, and he scrubbed them away, feeling sorry for himself.

The streets were deserted, unusually quiet, save for the Guard. They were thick. Twice he ducked into a doorway as a triple of guardsmen passed. Fortunately, they were loud as barroom brawlers and easy to avoid. So he turned east, away from the temple, meaning to travel through Southbridge on backstreets. He'd cut back to the Way as it exited the Vale and hope patrols were less frequent up that way. Once or twice he thought he heard footsteps behind him, but when he swung around, no one was there.

You're jumpy as a fellsdeer, he thought. Good thing you're leaving town.

He was just crossing a small cobblestone courtyard, when they materialized from the darkness, three tall cloaked figures who came at him from three directions, seeming to drift soundlessly over the pavement.

"Blood of the demon," Han muttered, backing away, his mouth going dry and metallic with fear.

Their hoods were pulled forward, obscuring their faces (if they even had faces), and they wore black leather gloves so there was nothing about them to even suggest they were human. They seemed to glow through the misting rain, smears of light all around them that spoke of sorcery.

He'd heard of things like this, demons who walked the streets, seeking souls for the Breaker when business was poor.

"Don't go so soon," one of them said, his voice as sibilant as a snake's. "We want to talk to you. We're looking for someone."

"I . . . I can't help you," Han said, his back coming up against a wall. "I . . . don't know where anyone is."

The monster's laugh was bone chilling. "I think you do. I think you can help us. In fact, you're going to be very, very eager to help us before we're through."

"If you help us, we'll let you go," the tallest demon said. "Such a pretty boy. A shame if anything happened to you."

"Who are you?" Han asked, his voice squeaky with fear.

"*We'll* ask the questions," the snake-voiced demon said. "We're looking for a boy named Shiv."

And then Han knew. The dead Southies. These were the ones responsible. He thought of the burned and mutilated bodies, and his insides seemed to liquefy.

"I never heard of him," Han said, sidling along the wall, trying to escape the circle they'd put around him; but the tallest demon stuck out his arm, preventing further progress.

"Oh, I think you have," he said. "And I think you'll tell. But first, we'll take you somewhere more private."

The three demons seemed edgy, looking over their shoulders, like they were worried about being interrupted. Which was odd. Why would demons be afraid of the Guard?

The third demon reached under his cloak, as if groping for a weapon, and Han knew it was now or never.

"Murder! Bloody murder on the streets!" he screamed. "Somebody call the Queen's Guard!"

The demons flinched, and the one with his hand inside his cloak reached out and grabbed Han's arm, but screeched and let go quickly like he was burnt, slapping his hand against his side.

Han kept screaming, and then he heard the pounding of feet and someone calling out, "Hold in the name of the queen!"

The demons hesitated for two long seconds, the dark holes of their hoods pointed toward Han, then, hissing, they melted into the nearby streets.

It was the second time in less than a month that he'd been

happy to see the Guard arrive. Which said something about how his life was going.

Only now he had to avoid being taken himself. He pulled his sodden cap low on his head and pointed in a random direction, forcing his voice into a plaintive whine. "They went that way. Bloody street rats took my purse and threatened to cut my throat, they did! Hurry or they'll get away."

Han reasoned that if demons were mentioned, the blue-jackets would be less likely to pursue.

The Guard charged off in the direction he pointed. "There's a reward in it if you get my purse back!" he called after them, for good measure.

Han stumbled away on shaking legs in a completely different direction, not really watching where he was going, focusing only on putting distance between him and the place he'd encountered the demons.

As he ran, he noticed that his wrists were warm. When he yanked back his sleeves, he saw that the silver cuffs were glowing. What was that all about? Had the demons done something to him, done something to his cuffs? Could they use the cuffs to track him? Desperately, he tried to pry them off, mangling up his hands in the process, but with no more luck than any time before.

Thoughts spiraled through his mind. Who were the demons and why were they looking for Shiv? Had his sins been so great that the Breaker sent a special team of servants to claim him?

Or was it some kind of war among the Southies themselves? Or between the Southies and another gang? If so, he'd put his money on the side with the demons.

Finally, exhaustion made him slow his pace to a walk, and his pounding heart began to quiet. By then he was thoroughly lost. He looked up at the sky, but got a faceful of rain for his trouble. He sniffed the air. The stink of the river seemed to be behind him, so he should strike the town walls before long if he headed the other way.

A sudden flurry of sound behind him made him fling himself sideways. A body flew past him and hit the ground hard. At first Han thought it was the demons come back again. But no. This figure was much smaller than the demons had been— only a boy with a knife in his hand. Han released a long breath in relief, but then realized his troubles were far from over. The other boy was up like a cat and moving toward him, leading with the blade.

This can't be happening, Han thought dispiritedly. *Oh, go away,* he felt like saying. *I'm at my limit.*

The boy came forward, passing under the streetlight, and Han started in surprise. It was Shiv Connor, looking gaunt and hollow-eyed, all of his manic confidence evaporated.

"What do you want?" Han demanded. "I don't have anything worth stealing this time." Unless you mean to chop off my hands again, he thought, but he wasn't going to bring that up.

"Call them off," Shiv whispered, glancing about as if they might be overheard.

"Call who off?" Han asked, bewildered. "I don't know what you're talking about."

"Those . . . those *things.*" Shiv licked his lips. "Your demons.

Call them off or I'll cut you. I'll kill you, I swear. I got nothing to lose."

"You're talking about those . . . those monsters?" Han asked, his mind clearing. "I can't call them off. I don't even know what they are."

"So it's coincidence, is it, that we beat you up in the street, and right after, they come hunting me?" Shiv tried to sneer, but sneering's not easy when you're as scared as Shiv seemed to be.

Han shook his head. It was like the Maker's hand was pointing at him all the time. *He's the one. Blame him.*

"I don't know who they are," Han said, lowering his voice. "I just ran into three of them, north of here."

"And you come out of it alive?" Shiv forced a laugh. "Fought 'em off, did you?"

Han just shook his head wordlessly, keeping his eyes on Shiv's blade, his hand on his own.

"I can kill you, you know," Shiv said wildly, cutting the air with his knife. "I'm better'n you with a blade, one on one."

Han knew Shiv was right, but he was not about to admit it. "I don't want to fight anybody," he said, and that was the absolute truth.

"Why would you? You got demons to do your fighting for you." Shiv swung his head from side to side, as if the monsters might suddenly appear. "The Southies, they'll turn on me, you know. Give me up to save themselves. There's eight dead a'ready, and they . . ." His voice trailed off and he swallowed hard, as if he'd said more than he meant to.

Han regarded his enemy with more sympathy than he'd ever have imagined possible. "Maybe you should leave," he suggested. "Hide out somewhere until things . . . cool off."

"You'd like that, wouldn't you?" Shiv snarled, on the defensive again. "All of Southbridge under your lordship." He raised his scarred hands, spreading his ringed fingers, indicating their surroundings. "I *built* this," he said. "I fought for it. It's my turf. Mine. I got no place else to go." His voice actually broke at the end.

Han recalled the demon's snakelike hiss, and shuddered. "There's some things you can't fight," he said softly.

Shiv stared at him a moment, his eyes narrowed. "What is it about you? People can't stop talking about you. Telling stories. It's all I hear about. Cuffs Alister this, Cuffs Alister that. It's like you're golden."

Han was speechless. Golden? He'd just faked his own death and was sneaking out of town with the Guard on his heels. He couldn't even support his mam and little sister.

Shiv rattled on. "I need to know. How'd you do it? Conjure them demons? Did you sell your soul to the Breaker? Did you make some kind of . . . of deal?"

Shiv looked desperate to make a deal of his own.

Han was growing impatient, eager to bring this awful encounter to an end. "Look, it don't matter how many ways you ask it; I got no idea what's chasing you."

Shiv stared at him defiantly for a long moment, then his body kind of settled, almost shrunk into itself. "All right. You win." He took a deep breath, then fell to his knees in the streaming street. He looked very small amid the shadows of the buildings. Bowing his head, he extended his knife, hilt-first, toward Han.

"I, Shiv Connor, pledge fealty to Cuffs Alister as streetlord of Southbridge and Ragmarket. I . . . pledge my loyalty and my blades and weapons to his use and place myself under his protection. I promise to bring all takings to him and to accept my gang share from his hands as he sees fit. If I break my promise, let me be torn apart by . . . by . . ." Here his voice faltered.

If it was possible to feel more miserable, Han did. "I can't protect you," he said. "I'm sorry. My advice is to run."

He left Shiv kneeling in the rain.

CHAPTER SEVENTEEN

PARTY WARFARE

There was a spate of name day parties in June, because most who shared Raisa's birth year preferred to avoid competing with the princess heir's festivities in July. Some, perhaps, hoped to secure matches before the stakes were raised by her entry into the marriage market, while the more optimistic among the boys might be saying, "Why not me for royal consort?"

The gifts still came thick and fast, and it gave Raisa a fierce pleasure to redirect them to her father and, through him, to the temple school. Not that it was easy. Queen Marianna was most displeased with her husband, following Raisa's supposed "visit" to Demonai Camp. She made it clear that Averill was not welcome at court in all the various ways available to queens.

So even though her father was back in the Vale, Raisa didn't see as much of him as she would have liked.

Would her own marriage be like this, Raisa wondered—

this constant sparring, shifting alliances, hidden agendas, the gaining and losing of ground? She loved both of her strong-willed parents, but it wasn't easy to be caught in the middle.

If Raisa had felt trapped before, she felt stifled now, the cage of expectations closing tightly around her. She was almost never alone, and there were always spies, servants, lords, and ladies ready to carry tales. Queen Marianna meant to make sure her headstrong daughter took no more unauthorized excursions.

Often Amon fell into the role of courier, ferrying messages and trade goods to Averill. Raisa worried about that, knowing she shouldn't be encouraging the Queen's Guard to go behind the queen's back.

It set a poor precedent for when she came to the throne herself.

The queen even ordered Magret to sleep in Raisa's room, which made it difficult for Raisa to meet Amon in the garden. She was able to slip out a few times, when Magret drank sherry for her aching bones and fell fast asleep. Once, though, Raisa emerged from the closet to find Magret awake and peering under the bed, looking for her lost charge. Raisa made up some story about drifting to sleep while fondling her new dancing shoes.

The only other name day party to rival Raisa's in extravagance would be the one thrown by the Lord and Lady Bayar in honor of Micah and Fiona. The fusion of magical and political power, glamour, and hints of wickedness was not to be resisted. Parents used whatever influence they had to make sure their offspring were included. Those invited were ecstatic; those not so favored were socially ruined.

Lady Bayar issued word that all guests were to be attired in black and white, in honor of her striking children. Tears were shed, plans and wardrobes scrapped, homes were no doubt mortgaged, and every bit of black and white cloth in the Vale was snapped up.

Dressmakers and tailors were called in from all over the queendom, and silks and velvets ordered from Tamron Court and We'enhaven, despite the price gouging caused by the wars. It was whispered that the fabric for the Bayars' clothing came from the Northern Isles, and had sorcery woven right into the cloth.

"What if I wore purple and green pantaloons," Raisa said, as she submitted to the final fitting. "Do you think they'd bar the door against me?"

"Hold still," Magret said, teeth gritted around the pins in her mouth. She stood on one side, the dressmaker on the other, pinning out the extra fullness in the hips. When they'd finished, the black dress fit like a second skin, and Raisa wondered if she'd ever be able to squirm in and out of it.

Secretly, Raisa was pleased with the fashion mandate. Approved colors for boys and girls on their name day were spun-sugar shades of blue, pink, and green. Black and white was deemed much too sophisticated for them.

She'd not been alone with Micah since their argument outside her room. They'd been at table together in the dining room, surrounded by courtiers, exchanging stiffly polite comments on the food and the weather.

He'd continued to ply her with small gifts, notes, and

proposals, but she'd never responded. She often felt the pressure of his eyes across a crowded room.

Holding a grudge against Micah had grown tedious, though. She'd decided it was time to forgive him, in honor of his name day. Her heart beat faster at the thought of seeing him again, of sparring with him in conversation and the possibility of stolen kisses. Life was much more interesting with Micah Bayar in it.

She was also pleased because it would be another opportunity to see Amon. Though there was no love lost between Micah and Amon, the Bayars wouldn't dare exclude the cadets.

Many of them were younger sons and daughters of the prominent nobility. Name day parties were a chance for them to connect with a fortune through marriage.

"Your Highness, it's nearly time," her comber complained. "And I need to get at your hair."

Raisa backed onto a high stool and sat while her comber coaxed her hair into a cascade of ringlets pinned high on her head.

Raisa heard a commotion in the corridor outside her room; then the door flew open and the queen swept in, resplendent in white satin sashed in black, wearing a necklace of pearls and black onyx.

Queen Marianna walked all the way around Raisa, inspecting her from every angle, a small frown on her face. She poked disapprovingly at Elena's battered ring, which hung on its chain above Raisa's bodice. "You don't mean to wear this."

Raisa shrugged. "Well, I thought I . . ."

"What about the diamond pendant, Your Highness?" Magret said, rummaging through Raisa's jewelry case. "Or your pearl choker, that'd be lovely."

"What did the Bayars send for your name day?" Queen Marianna asked. "Jewelry, wasn't it?"

"Here we are!" Magret pounced, seizing a velvet box. She opened it and turned it toward the queen. It was the emerald and ruby serpent necklace.

"Perfect!" Marianna said. "You can wear this in their honor."

"Well," Raisa said uncertainly. "Maybe I could wear both together." She'd grown used to the weight of the ring settled between her breasts. She liked having it there.

"Nonsense," Queen Marianna said. She lifted the chain over Raisa's head and set Elena's ring on the dressing table, then circled Raisa's neck with the emerald pendant, fastening the clasp with cool, dry fingers.

"You look lovely, darling," Queen Marianna said, kissing her on the forehead and slipping her arm through hers. "Now, let's be off; your father and Mellony are already waiting in the carriage."

There were times that Raisa thought all would be well between her parents if only her father's work as a trader didn't so often keep him away from the Vale. They complemented each other—he with his wiry, powerful build, wind-burned skin, brown eyes set under thick dark brows and silver hair, and she with her cool reserve and tall spare figure. He could always make her laugh, and the queen's cares seemed to fall away when he was home. When he was home, she seemed grounded. When he was gone, she was like one of the aspens on the slope of Hanalea—swaying and trembling in the political winds.

Tonight Averill wore clan robes, long black and white panels of rough-spun silk replacing his usual brilliant colors, and heavy rings of silver and onyx on his hands.

The royal carriage was bracketed on all sides by the Queen's Guard. Neither Amon nor Edon would be riding with them, since they were also guests.

A long line of carriages snaked up Old Road, which led up Gray Lady. Where the way broadened, other carriages pulled aside to let the Gray Wolf pass.

The Bayar estate nestled in the skirts of Gray Lady, named for a queen so ancient her name had been lost to the mists of time. Further up the mountain stood the Wizard Council house, frowning down on the city. From here wizards had once ruled the Vale.

The clatter of hooves on cobblestones said they'd arrived. The footmen swung open the double doors of the carriage and placed the steps. Averill emerged first, then turned to offer his arm to the queen.

The entire front of the Bayar mansion was ablaze with torches. Wizard lights pricked the darkness along the paths in the gardens and tangled in the trees, creating a fairyland. Servants in the Bayars' Stooping Falcon livery clustered in the entries, collecting wraps and directing guests.

Lord and Lady Bayar waited in the entry hall, resplendent in black and white. Raisa and her mother entered together, as was protocol, with the consort and Princess Mellony trailing a few yards behind.

Lord Bayar swept down into a deep bow as his lady curtsied. "Your Majesty," he said. "And Your Highness. This is indeed an honor. Micah and Fiona will be so pleased you've come. You'll find them in the ballroom." Lord Bayar nodded courteously to Averill. "Lord Demonai, welcome back," he said. "From everything I hear, your business is prospering."

Raisa wondered if this could be a dig at her father the tradesman, but if so, there was no evidence of it on the wizard's face. Indeed, Bayar continued, "I'm hoping we can do some business in the coming weeks. I'll send my factor around, shall I?"

"It would be my pleasure, Lord Bayar," Averill murmured, inclining his head.

The familiar ballroom had been transformed from a cold marble-floored room into an elegant space lined with dimly lit, cozy retreats. Servants circulated with platters of food and drink, and the room was fronted with tiers of small dining tables enclosed with black and white screens and centered with candles and black and white lilies. Falcon banners in black and white lined the walls.

"This . . . this is beautiful," Raisa exclaimed, enchanted. "I've never seen it like this."

Queen Marianna surveyed the scene, biting her lip, no doubt comparing it to her own plans for Raisa's name day.

Micah and Fiona stood at the far end of the room, greeting a procession of guests. As usual, they complemented each other. Micah wore a white coat that fit closely over his lean frame, black trousers, boots, and a rich black stole bearing the falcon crest. His black hair hung shining to his shoulders. Fiona wore a long black dress slit to her hip, black gloves, and a white stole of her own. Diamonds and platinum glittered around her slender throat and wrists.

Raisa couldn't help comparing her own small frame to Fiona's elegant height.

As they entered the room, the crier was announcing the arrival of other guests.

"Lady Amalie Heresford, Thanelee of Heresford, in Arden," he intoned.

Lady Heresford was a plump girl of Raisa's age with red hair, creamy skin, and a sprinkling of freckles, dressed in the covered-up southern style. With her flat black dress and black lace pinned into her hair, she might have been one of the professional mourners the wealthy sometimes hired for funerals.

She kept her head high, eyes straight ahead, like an old painting of Hanalea walking through the field of demons.

Raisa's heart went out to her. She looked scared to death.

Following after her, unannounced, was a tall, bulky woman upholstered in black, and a tall man shrouded in priest's robes. His face was twisted, as if he smelled something bad.

In the Fells, there was a saying, "Sour as a flatland priest." Well, Raisa thought, that's right on target.

"This is unusual," Averill whispered to Raisa. "Southerners sending their women north with only a governess and a priest for protection. In the south, marriage to a wizard would be scandalous. But it shows how desperate things are. Lady Heresford's father, Brighton Heresford, was executed by

Gerard Montaigne, one of the contenders for Arden's throne. She's the heiress to Heresford Castle, but needs to marry someone strong enough to help her hold it. She's a catch for the right person."

Raisa nodded, grateful to her father for the information, but thinking it should be her mother providing it.

"Her Royal Highness Marina Tomlin, Princess of Tamron," the crier said. "His Royal Highness, Liam Tomlin, Prince of Tamron."

"Ah," her father said, nodding. "Tamron is hoping for an alliance with the Fells, as some protection against Arden. They'll begin negotiations with the Bayars, but nothing will be settled until after your name day. They could match Liam with you, or Marina with Micah Bayar. Failing that, Liam could marry Fiona, and Marina will make a match in the south."

Raisa surveyed the Tomlins with interest. They were tall, copper-skinned, and graceful, fine-boned as race horses. Liam Tomlin had dark curly hair, a strong nose, and a brilliant smile. He wore lots of silver with his requisite black and white.

In their way, the Tomlins were as striking as the Bayar twins.

Now it was their turn. The crier went ahead of them announcing, "Queen Marianna *ana*'Lissa of the Fells, and her daughter, Raisa *ana*'Marianna, the princess heir."

To either side, courtiers dropped into bows and curtsies, like a field of black and white grass felled by a sharp blade.

Raisa and her mother swept forward, their skirts swishing over the marble floor. Behind them she could hear her father and Mellony announced. Ahead, Micah and Fiona knelt side by side in a nimbus of light, like a god and goddess come to earth.

At last they reached the front of the ballroom.

"You may rise," Queen Marianna said, and there was a rustle of silk and satin all around them.

Micah came gracefully to his feet. Queen Marianna extended her hand, and he lowered his head to kiss it.

He turned to Raisa; his eyes lingered for a long moment on her face, then traveled down, pausing again at the top of her bodice until her face grew warm with embarrassment.

"Ah," he said. "You finally wore it, Raisa. I was afraid you didn't like it."

"Of course I like it," she said, fingering the necklace. "It's beautiful. Is it a family heirloom?"

"Yes," he said, still looking at her with such intensity that she grew a little flustered. Micah was always forward, but tonight he'd shed his usual mocking edge.

She thrust out her hand. He pressed it to his lips, still looking into her eyes. His kiss burned against her skin, and she felt a little dizzy. "Am I finally forgiven, Raisa?"

"Yes," she whispered, her cheeks burning. "You're forgiven."

"Would it be bad of me to claim every dance?" he asked, still keeping hold of her fingers.

She withdrew her hand reluctantly. "You are the guest of honor," she said. "And you know you have a job to do. Winning the hearts of all the young ladies is the easy part. You'll need to dance with all the old ladies, and the aunts and grannies and mothers. Maybe even some of the fathers, now you're in the marriage market."

He laughed. "Save some dances for me, Your Highness," he said. "I'll need refuge from the aunts and grannies." He held her gaze for a long moment, then turned to greet Mellony and her father.

She danced with Miphis Mander and the wizard Wil Mathis, who spent the whole time looking over her shoulder at Fiona. Mick Bricker and Garret Fry, cadets from Oden's Ford, who made awkward small talk and towed her around the floor as if she were breakable. Then her father, who was as skilled at court dances as he was in the more challenging clan steps.

The entire time, she was aware of Micah's presence, drawing her attention like a lamp in a dark room. Whenever she looked for him, it seemed he was looking at her.

Kip Klemath asked her to dance. And then Keith. Then Kip again. The brothers apparently meant to pass her back and forth like a satin-clad kickball, but behind her someone said, "Your Highness, may I have the next dance?" while Kip and Keith were arguing over who was next.

She turned, and there was Amon Byrne, tall and broad-shouldered in dress blues that fit his frame perfectly.

She grinned at him and said, "Absolutely." And he spun her away as a storm of protest from the Klemath brothers erupted behind them.

"Where have you been?" she asked. "I was beginning to think you weren't coming."

"I got delayed," he said. "There was . . . some business I had to take care of in Ragmarket." He took a breath, like he was going to say something more, but then seemed to think better of it.

"Where'd you learn to dance?" she asked as they circled the dance floor. "I don't remember your knowing how."

"I've learned a few things in the past three years," Amon said.

If she thought he was going to elaborate on that, she was disappointed. They circled the room again in silence. He'd look into her eyes, then avert his gaze as if afraid he'd give too much away.

Amon had never been known for his flirtatious banter, but on this evening he had almost nothing to say.

She tried again. "Didn't you say you don't have time for dancing at Oden's Ford?" she said.

"I said I didn't have time for sweethearts," he said.

Raisa was surprised he recalled their conversation in such detail.

"Then where did you learn to dance?" Raisa asked, feeling like she was prying each word out of him, like mussels out of their shells.

"Tamron Court isn't far from Oden's Ford. We'd go over there if we had a day off duty."

Tamron Court, the capital of Tamron, had the reputation of being a wicked city, the place to go for fancy women and gambling and illicit entertainment.

"Oh, really, Corporal Byrne?" Raisa lifted her eyebrows. "And do what?"

"Well, *dance*," he said, as if it were obvious. "And play cards. I'm a fair cardplayer," he said almost defensively.

"Well," she said, "of course. You're a soldier." She tried to imagine Amon carousing in a tavern, and failed.

He didn't reply, seeming lost in thought, so she changed the subject. "How are things going in Southbridge? Did they ever find out who killed those Southies?"

He flinched as if she'd caught him out somehow. "Actually, I have some news," he said, avoiding her eyes.

"News? What kind of news?"

Amon glanced about as if worried they'd be overheard. The song was over, so he drew her aside, off the dance floor, and to one of the more private tables. A servant offered a tray. Amon took two glasses and handed her one.

Raisa flopped into a chair, a little relieved to be off her feet. "I need a drink to hear this news?" she asked wryly, taking a cautious sip of wine, aware that she hadn't had anything to eat.

"Well, first of all, my da tried to get Gillen dismissed again, and got nowhere." He grimaced. "He must have powerful friends."

Raisa slammed her glass down on the table, spilling her wine over her wrist. "Not more powerful than me," she said. "That's it. I'm going to my mother. This can't stand."

Amon reached for her hand, then hastily drew his back, glancing about again. "Please, Raisa, you can't tell the queen about that whole Southbridge thing. Trust me. You just can't." He drained his glass and set it down. "Don't worry. We Byrnes don't give up. We'll get him sooner or later."

That was unsatisfactory. What was the good of being the heir to the throne if you had no real power?

Raisa looked up, and Amon was still watching her with that peculiar expression on his face. Wary. Almost guilty.

"What?" she asked irritably.

"That streetlord. Cuffs," he said. He cleared his throat.

Images came back to her: Cuffs sitting cross-legged on the dirt floor of his cellar hideout, offering her stale biscuits to eat. Cuffs armored in his leggings and deerskin jacket, his blade in his hand.

She'd thought of him often, since her adventure in Southbridge. She'd hoped he'd managed to avoid the Guard. Even wished she could see him again.

"What about him?"

"He's dead. Murdered in Ragmarket."

"What?" She spoke louder than she intended, and he flinched, shushing her. "When? When did this happen?" she demanded, her insides funneling into her toes.

"Likely it was last night. They found his things this morning on the riverbank."

She felt ambushed. Betrayed. It wasn't possible. "His . . . things. They didn't find a body?"

He shook his head. "Just his clothes, and Ragger scarf. Whoever did it must have thrown him in the river."

"How did you know the clothes were his, then?"

"They scratched his name in the mud," Amon said. "A warning of sorts."

Cuffs Alister was dead. Raisa recalled the last time she'd seen him, on a street corner in Ragmarket, his sardonic bow on parting.

I think you're a Ragger at heart, he'd said.

It wasn't true. He'd been a free spirit, and Raisa was everybody's prisoner. Was death the price of freedom?

"You don't know he's really dead, then," she said stubbornly. "If there was no body."

"It was . . . there was blood everywhere," Amon said, glancing around, seeming to realize that this might not be the time or place. "I'm sorry, Raisa, I guess I shouldn't have said anything, but . . . the good news is, maybe now the killing will stop," he said. "You see, that same night they found another body. Boy named Shiv Connor, who's streetlord of the Southies. He'd been tortured and killed, like the rest. We think Cuffs was done in revenge for that."

"Or maybe he had nothing to do with it. Maybe the same people that killed this Shiv killed Cuffs. If he's even dead." She looked up, hope kindling. "He's tricky. What if he just wanted us to think he's dead? The Guard's been hunting him forever! Maybe he just decided to disappear for a while."

Amon didn't reply, but he wore a pitying expression that infuriated her.

"Fine!" she said, blinking back the tears that burned in her eyes. "You win. He's dead. Are you happy?"

Amon looked as if she'd struck him. "Rai, come on, I never wanted—"

"I'd better go finish off my dance card," she said, rising in a rustle of satin. "I'm sure I'm way behind."

She pushed blindly through the draperies separating the table from the dance floor and ran right into Micah Bayar.

He gripped her elbows to keep her from falling. "There you are," he said. "I was looking for you." He focused in on her face. "What's the matter? Are you crying?"

"Oh," Raisa said, swiping at her face. "I'm fine. I just ate some hot peppers is all."

"Hot peppers?" Micah laughed. "There is danger every-where tonight. For instance, that Lady Heresford is cold as Harlotsborg at solstice. I tried to steal a kiss, and those guard dogs of hers practically assassinated me."

"What about Princess Marina?" Raisa asked, thinking that Tamron's ways might be more to Micah's liking. "She's lovely."

Maybe a little *too* lovely.

"Right now I want to dance with *this* princess," he said, bowing gracefully. "I've just escaped from the aunts and grannies. Let's take advantage, shall we?"

He led her out onto the dance floor as the orchestra launched into a waltz.

"Why aren't you dancing with someone who might do you good?" Raisa whispered as they navigated their first cir-cuit of the ballroom. "Missy Hakkam looks positively sullen over there in the corner. And you know Princess Marina is here for the wooing."

All this was true, and yet she had the urge to keep Micah Bayar entirely to herself.

"You should make the most of your time tonight," she said dutifully. "This must have cost your parents a fortune."

"I *am* making the most of my time," he murmured, pulling her in closer than was entirely proper. His fingers burned through the fabric of her dress. Raisa felt dizzy again, as if the wine had gone to her head.

"Or have you already made your conquests?" she said

recklessly. "Any marriage contracts in the offing? Any trysts planned for later on tonight?"

"There's only one conquest I want to make," he said, leaning down and speaking into her ear. "Only one heart I want to win."

"Oh, no," she protested feebly. *Don't waste your time flattering me*, she wanted to say, but somehow she couldn't get the words out. It seemed that her wits had deserted her. So she gave in and rested her head on his chest, hearing his heart thump through the fabric of his coat. Even his scent seemed intoxicating.

I only had one glass of wine, she thought.

It seemed whatever she had to say, he had a clever answer. So they danced three more dances, and with each twirl she felt more weightless and insubstantial in his arms, like she was disappearing.

"Can we . . . can we get something to eat?" she asked, thinking maybe food would help.

"Of course," he said, leading her through a maze of black and white fabric to a secluded table. He settled her into a chair, resting his hot hands on her bare shoulders for a long moment.

He must have left, but she scarcely noticed. Even the music seemed diminished, as if everyone else were far away.

Then he was back, with plates of food and two more glasses of wine, and she startled awake, although she didn't think she'd been asleep. He pulled his chair next to hers and sat close, his leg pressing against hers. He draped his arm around her shoulders, pulling her head down on his shoulder, and fed her bits of food with his other hand.

He raised the glass of wine to her lips, and she tried to say no, but before she knew it, she'd drunk.

He cupped her chin in his hands and kissed her. And again, longer and sweeter. And again, and her resistance evaporated. He kissed her lips, her chin, her collarbone.

Wizard kisses, she thought murkily, are dangerous things.

And now she was kissing him back, snaking her arms around his neck, getting lost, wanting to somehow burrow into him. And he was laughing a little at her enthusiasm, but his breath was coming quicker too, and there were spots of color on his cheeks.

I don't care who you are, she thought. I don't care about who I'm supposed to be. I'm tired of following old rules.

Micah pushed his chair back and stood. "Come on," he said, gently lifting her to her feet, steadying her with a hand under her arm. "I know somewhere we can go."

She nodded mutely and gripped his one hand with both of hers to keep from swaying. He led her through the maze of silk tents, past candlelit tables and murmured conversations.

A sound insinuated its way into her clouded mind. A familiar voice, someone calling, as if from far away. *"Raisa! Where are you?"*

Micah's hand tightened on her arm. "Don't answer him," he said.

"But it's Papa," she said. "He sounds worried."

"He just wants to keep us apart," Micah said. "They all do. Come on." He pulled her in the opposite direction. "Let's go this way."

They ran, twisting and turning, toward the side exit, ducking away from Wil Mathis, who was chatting up a girl in the corner, and Mellony, who was edging close to the dessert tray again. It was exciting, like a game of hide-and-seek in dress-up clothes.

They slipped out into the corridor, and came face-to-face with Amon Byrne, who blocked the way.

"Oh!" Raisa skidded to a stop in her stocking feet. She seemed to have lost her shoes.

"You again," Micah said. "How is it possible you can be everywhere at once?"

Amon ignored him. "Your father's looking for you," he said to Raisa. "Didn't you hear him calling?"

"Well, ah . . ." She looked at Micah, somehow at a loss for what to say. "We're going . . . somewhere else."

"This is none of your business," Micah said, pulling Raisa forward as if he meant to bull right past Amon. "Out of our way."

Amon did not move, but looked from Raisa to Micah, scowling. "What'd you do to her?" he demanded. "She looks like she's in some kind of trance."

Again, Raisa heard her father's voice. Coming closer. "Raisa!"

"Lord Demonai!" Amon shouted. "She's here! In the corridor! With Micah Bayar. Hurry up!"

"Blood and bones," Micah swore. "When will you learn to stop meddling? You'll pay for this." He let go of Raisa's hand and chose a pastry from a nearby tray. Then leaned against the wall, waiting.

And suddenly her father was there, his face like a thunder-cloud over Hanalea.

"Ah. Well. I'll be going, then," Amon said, edging back toward the ballroom. The corners of his mouth twitched, as if he were pleased with himself.

"You! Stay where you are until I get this sorted out," Averill said, and Amon froze in place.

Averill picked Raisa's wrap up off the floor where it had fallen, and settled it over her shoulders. As he did so, he seemed to fix on Raisa's necklace. He stared at it for a long moment, then turned back to Micah.

"What are you two doing back here?" he demanded, glaring at him.

Micah shrugged and waved the pastry. He was trying to look casual, but his hand was shaking. "I was encouraging the princess to eat something. I think she's had a bit too much to drink."

"Oh, really? Is *that* what it is?"

Averill took hold of Raisa's chin and gazed into her eyes. He looked so peculiar. She laughed, then flinched when he gripped harder.

"Not so hard," she complained, wresting herself free. Why was he being like this? "Micah and I were just leaving."

"Were you?" Averill suddenly seemed very tall and imposing in his clan robes.

"I was going to show her the view off the terrace," Micah said, popping the rest of the pastry into his mouth and licking his fingers. He had powdered sugar on his lips, and Raisa impulsively pulled his head down and kissed it away. His kisses had been sweet-hot already, and who knew how much sweeter they might be now.

"Raisa," Micah whispered rather thickly, sliding his arms around her again, ignoring Averill's glowering expression.

Micah seemed a little intoxicated himself.

"Raisa!" Averill pulled her away and pushed her down into a chair. "You're not yourself. I think it's time we called for your carriage."

"It's early yet," Micah said. He cleared his throat, looking from Raisa to Averill, back to Raisa. "Please, Your Highness. Stay a while longer. It's my name day, after all."

"I think not," Averill said, his voice hard and even. "Go on back to the party, jinxflinger. But first I want to know where you got this." Averill's hand closed on Micah's wrist. He lifted Micah's hand, displaying an elaborately carved ring set with emeralds and rubies.

"Let go of me!" Micah struggled to free himself. "It's none of your business."

"It is my business, actually," Averill said, releasing him. "I've seen this design, but only in old manuscripts. It predates the Breaking, and it's forbidden these days."

Micah rubbed his wrist. "Someone sent it. A name day present. I've a whole vault full. What's it to you?"

Raisa squinted down at it, bleary-eyed. Somehow she hadn't noticed it before. And now that she looked closer, she saw that it was a ring in the form of a serpent, coiled around Micah's finger, with rubies for eyes. But there was something familiar about it.

She reached up and touched her necklace. The gold pendant that rested against her skin matched Micah's ring. It felt warm to the touch.

Averill's eyes flicked between the two pieces of jewelry. "Where did you get the necklace, Raisa?"

"Hmmm?" For a moment she couldn't remember. "Oh. It was a gift from the Bayars."

Averill gripped the pendant and lifted it away from her chest. Beneath it was a red mark burned into her flesh. A snake's head.

With a roar of anger, Averill ripped the necklace away, breaking the clasp and sending bits flying. He flung the jewelry into Micah's startled face.

"Just what was it you hoped to accomplish, jinxflinger?" he demanded.

Micah blinked at him, then glanced down at the necklace on the floor. He looked completely bewildered. "I don't know what you're talking about."

Raisa doubled over, pressing her hands to her breast, feeling as if her father had ripped out her heart. "Merciful Maker," she gasped.

Averill looked at her, then closed his eyes for a moment as if struggling for composure. He turned back to Micah. "I'm clan, remember? Demonai. Did you think I wouldn't recognize it?" Averill gripped the front of Micah's fancy coat and gave him a hard shake. "She's not for you, do you understand that? That will never happen."

Now anger flooded into Micah's face, replacing bewilderment. "Why not? I'm good enough for the princesses in Tamron."

"Then marry one of *them*," Averill said.

"Who said anything about marriage? Micah said, his black

eyes glittering. "But, now that you mention it, why can't we marry if we want? I'm tired of living by stupid rules made a thousand years ago."

"You try anything like this again, and the clans will go back to hunting wizards. Starting with you."

"They've never left off hunting wizards," Micah said bitterly. "We know what you're plotting, up in the camps. We know you're a Demonai warrior. We have spies of our own. As for the necklace"—he nudged it with his foot—"all these tales of evil magical amulets are just that—tales. You Demonais always see a magical conspiracy where there is none."

Micah stooped, scooped up the necklace, and put it in his pocket. "Take her home, then. I'm going back to the party." As he passed Raisa, he leaned down and kissed her lips. Then he looked up and grinned crookedly at Averill. "But I like kissing her, and from what I can tell, she likes it too. Just try to keep us apart."

And he was gone.

Averill stared after him for a long moment. Amon shifted his weight, as if unsure whether to stay or go.

Raisa's insides churned. It was as if her body were a battleground, sensations rushing out and rushing in like the surf at Chalk Cliffs. Her lips still tingled from Micah's kiss, and she wanted to run after him, to tell him she was sorry her father had gone barking mad. She felt dizzy, sick with need. Putting her head between her knees, she breathed deeply, determined not to faint.

Amon knelt in front of her, gripping her hands in both of his. "Rai . . . Your Highness," he said, his face drained and pale. "Can I . . . get you anything?"

She looked up into his face, and he looked wary, yet determined, as though he were afraid she might spit in his face, but willing to take the risk.

Instead she vomited all over him. And herself.

Horrified, she tried to apologize, but he looked so solemn and ludicrous with sick in his hair and all over his dress blues, that soon she was laughing. He glared at her, then pulled out a handkerchief and carefully wiped off her face.

Averill grabbed her wrap out of danger. "Where are your shoes, Raisa?" he asked, glancing about.

She shook her head helplessly. Now she was crying, big fat tears, shivering uncontrollably. What was wrong with her?

"Don't take my shoes," she said, struggling to rise. "I've got to find Micah. I need to . . . tell him something."

"Amon," Averill began, "go tell the queen . . ." He took a better look at Amon and reconsidered. "No. *I'll* go tell the queen that the princess heir has taken ill. You take Raisa back to Fellsmarch Castle. Don't let anyone see you. Take her to her rooms and keep her there. No matter what. Don't take your eyes off her for a moment. Stay there until I come."

He turned on his heel and stalked away.

Amon helped Raisa to her feet, but she nearly collapsed again, saved only by his grip on her arm.

Amon glanced around for witnesses, then whipped a tablecloth off a nearby table, flinging the devil weed and calla lily centerpiece onto the floor. He draped the tablecloth over Raisa, covering her head to toe, then tipped her into his arms.

"Amon! Put me down!" she protested, struggling feebly, her voice muffled by linen. "I've got to . . . I've got to go. . . ."

He put his lips next to her ear, and she could feel his warm breath through the fabric. "Come on, Rai," he said, desperation edging his voice. "Don't make this any harder, all right?"

He carried her through several twists and turns, the light changing as they passed through darkened hallways and brightly lit rooms. Finally, Raisa breathed in the night air and knew they were in the courtyard.

She recalled Micah's kisses, his hands on her shoulders, and her heart beat faster. Desire crashed over her again. "No!" She began squirming again. "I've got to . . . go back and get my shoes."

Amon whistled, and she heard the squeak of carriage wheels coming toward them.

"Wot you got there, soldier?" the driver asked, laughing. "Souvenir from the party?"

"My sister," Amon said, sounding unamused. "She's not well."

Raisa heard laughter. "Care to introduce us, Corporal?" someone shouted.

"I . . . am . . . not . . . your sister," Raisa growled. "Why do you keep saying that?" But Amon was wrestling her into the carriage, and she heard the snap of the reins, and they rattled off into the night, farther and farther from Gray Lady and the fascinating Micah Bayar.

She must have slept, because the next she knew, Amon was clumping up a flight of stairs, still carrying her in his arms.

He turned and walked a hundred paces down a corridor, then carefully set her down on her feet. He unwound her from her makeshift shroud like a corpse from its wrapping, keeping one hand fastened around her arm. They were standing in front of the door to her room.

"Let me go!" Raisa said, trying to pull away. "I forgot something. I need to go back to Gray Lady."

He pounded on the door. "Open up!"

Raisa heard Magret on the other side of the door, grumbling her way toward them.

Bam! The door slammed open, revealing Magret in her dressing gown. "A body can't catch a little sleep athout . . ." Magret's eyes focused on Raisa. "Your Highness! What happened to you?"

"She's not feeling well," Amon said.

"Phew!" Magret said, waving away the vapors with one hand. "Begging your pardon, but you both reek of sick!" She eyed Raisa suspiciously. "You've not been into the brandy, have you?"

"Lord Demonai asked me to bring her back here to you," Amon said. "He said you'd take care of her."

Magret puffed up with importance. "But a'course he'd say that; he knows old Magret, he does." She took Raisa's arm and drew her inside, then made as if to shut the door in Amon's face.

"Lord Demonai told me to stay until he comes," Amon said stubbornly, sticking out his boot to keep the door from closing. "She's . . . in danger. He told me to stay right with her."

"He did?" Magret said, flustered. "Well, I never thought I'd live to see the day, young men inviting themselves into a young girl's room in the middle of the night." She studied him for signs of depravity, then shook her head. "Well, come ahead, then."

"Magret," Raisa said desperately, "I need to go back to the party. Corporal Byrne has kidnapped me and dragged me back here against my will."

"Is that so?" Magret eyed Amon with new hostility.

"It's so," Amon said, with that direct Byrne look that could be so convincing. "But it was on Lord Demonai's orders. He'll be here soon."

"Well," Magret said grudgingly, "she can't go back to the party if she's sick, can she?"

Amon shook his head solemnly. "No, doesn't seem wise."

Raisa hated both of them.

"Come," Magret said, pulling her toward the bed chamber. "Let's get you into your bath, dearie." When Amon made as if to follow, Magret straight-armed him. "You sit here by the fire, Corporal Byrne."

"Lord Demonai told me to keep a close eye on her until he came," Amon said stubbornly. "She's not herself."

Magret scowled at him. "Where's she going to get off to, with you out here by the door?" she said.

"I gave my word," Amon said, and Raisa knew he was thinking of the passage that led from the closet to the garden. He wasn't about to give her the chance to escape that way. Raisa cursed the day she'd shared that secret with him.

Amon displayed the usual Byrne boneheadedness, and in

the end, Magret put up a screen around Raisa's tub, and Amon plunked himself down in a chair next to the window. It seemed strange to know he was just on the other side of the screen when she had no clothes on.

Once she was pronounced clean, Magret helped her into her nightgown, and Raisa emerged from behind the screen to find Amon, his shirt off, wet hair sticking up, scrubbing down using a basin and pitcher. His broad shoulders and muscular arms shone in the firelight. This image reverberated with memories of Micah Bayar's planed face and dark eyes until Raisa thought she might be sick again.

"Sweet martyred lady!" Magret said, actually blushing and closing her eyes to shut out the view, then opening them again and peeking back at Amon. "Come, Your Highness, let's get you into bed."

Raisa had just climbed under the covers when there was a knock at the outer door. Magret gave Amon the evil eye of warning and went to answer.

It was her father, Averill, and her grandmother, Elena, both still in their clan ceremonial robes from Micah's party. Elena carried a beaded remedy bag.

"Thank you for your help," Elena said to Magret, and somehow maneuvered the nurse out the door. Then she crossed to Raisa's bedside.

Smiling down at Raisa, she laid her palm on her forehead. "Briar Rose, granddaughter, how is it with you?"

"I don't know, Elena *Cennestre*," Raisa said with spirit. "I may be sick, but everyone around me is crazy." She glared at her father and Amon Byrne, who must have found a shirt somewhere, because he was covered up now.

Elena laughed, slapping her thigh, and Raisa immediately felt better. Elena would sort everyone out.

"Let's see this mark of yours," Elena said, untying the string at the neck of Raisa's gown. She spread the fabric and studied the mark at the base of Raisa's neck. There were blisters now, centered around an area of tender pink skin.

"Does it hurt?" she asked.

"No. I didn't even know it was there," Raisa admitted. "I must have reacted to the pendant."

"So it seems." Elena studied the wound some more, and then fished in her bag, producing a stone jar. "It doesn't seem to have gone too deep," she said. "I'm not the healer Willo is, but I have some skill." She yanked out the stopper and held out a jar of light green ointment. "It's rowan, and some other herbs. With your permission?"

"All right," Raisa said warily.

Elena dipped her fingers into the ointment and smeared it over the blisters on Raisa's neck. It smelled like pine and fresh air and seemed to cool her entire body. She settled back into her pillows, releasing a long breath. Her head stopped spinning. Where she had been feverish and agitated, now she felt calm and focused. Her mind slowly cleared of doubt and confusion and desire, like sediment settling from a mountain lake.

"Thank you, Mother Elena," she whispered. "That's much better."

Elena recorked the jar and dropped it into her remedy bag. "Your father said you were with the wizard Micah Bayar. What happened between you?"

Raisa wasn't certain exactly what her grandmother was asking. "Well, we danced. And . . . and kissed."

"Nothing else?" Elena's eyes were fixed on her face.

Raisa's face burned with embarrassment. This was not the sort of conversation she wanted to have with her grandmother. Much less the Matriarch of Demonai Camp. And not with Amon Byrne watching. At least he had the decency to look embarrassed.

"That's pretty much it," she said bluntly.

Elena and Averill exchanged meaningful glances.

"So I don't see what all the fuss is about," Raisa said. "If I want to dance with Micah Bayar, I will. He's . . . he's a good dancer," she finished lamely. "And charming."

Amon Byrne rolled his eyes, and Raisa resisted the urge to stick out her tongue at him.

"The necklace the Bayars gave you was a seduction amulet, Raisa," Averill said. "In common use before the Breaking, but forbidden these days. It works with the ring young Bayar was wearing to create a powerful attraction in both parties."

You finally wore it, Raisa, Micah had said, in his intense fashion. *I was afraid perhaps you didn't like it.*

"But why would he use it on me?" Raisa asked. "It does him no good." There was a plague of throat clearing, and her face went hot again. "I mean, aside from—you know. Whatever he said at the party, he knows we can't marry. He should be using it on Princess Marina or someone like that."

As soon as she said it, she realized he wouldn't need it for that purpose either. Political marriages were what they were, arranged by others to create alliances and build power. Seduction had nothing to do with it. And even if it did, Raisa had no doubt Micah Bayar would do quite well on his own.

"That's the question, isn't it," Averill said, looking grave. "Why would he use it on you?"

I know somewhere we can go, Micah had said. And yet . . .

"I don't think he knew what it was," Raisa said. "I think the whole thing took him by surprise."

"Raisa," her father began, looking troubled, "I know you like to think the best of people—"

Raisa put up her hand. "Just stop. I do *not* like to think the best of people. In fact, I often think the worst. Especially about Micah Bayar. But he looked completely blindsided when you ripped off my necklace and threw it at him. I think he had no clue there was a connection between his ring and my necklace. He thought he was charming me all on his own."

Amon spoke for the first time. "Let me get this straight. You think it was a coincidence that you were both wearing jinxpieces?" He raised that annoying eyebrow.

"If it wasn't him, someone else arranged it," Averill said. "The question is, why. And if they have this weapon, what else do they have? And where are they keeping it?"

"Where's the ring I gave you?" Elena asked abruptly. "I told you to keep it on."

Raisa frowned, remembering. "Oh. I was going to wear it, but Mother suggested I wear the emerald necklace instead."

They all stared at her.

"What?" Raisa asked irritably. "You think my mother the queen is involved in a conspiracy against her own daughter?

No. I'm sure it was a matter of fashion, not politics."

"Where is the ring now?" Elena asked.

Raisa struggled to remember. "It's on my dressing table." She waved vaguely toward the sitting room.

"I'll fetch it," Amon said, and bolted through the doorway as if glad to have a job to do. He returned moments later with the ring clutched in his large fist. He handed it to Raisa.

She hung it around her neck again. The ring felt cold against her heated skin.

"Micah questioned why he shouldn't be allowed to marry you," Averill reminded her. "He said he planned to continue to court you."

"*Kiss* me," Raisa said. "He said he liked kissing me and planned to keep it up."

"What about you?" Elena asked. "Do you plan to keep it up?"

Raisa was suddenly tired of the interrogation, tired of being made to feel foolish when she was doing the best she could. Tired.

"I don't know," she said, yawning. "I might."

As she fell asleep, her last recollection was Averill, Elena, and Amon Byrne, their heads together, whispering. No doubt planning a conspiracy of their own.

CHAPTER EIGHTEEN

ON THE BORDERLAND

It wasn't like Han expected to be the center of attention at Marisa Pines. But he wasn't used to being overlooked entirely, and that was the way it seemed. The renaming ceremony was bearing down on them—it was only a week away now. Bird spent long hours of every day in seclusion in the women's temple, meditating on her future. Han tried sneaking in for a visit once, figuring she would welcome the distraction, since she already knew what she wanted to be, after all. He'd had hopes they'd get back to kissing. And move on from there.

He got rudely evicted for his pains.

Even when Bird wasn't meditating, she was consumed in plans for her name day. She had no time for hunting, for fishing, for swimming in the Dyrnnewater or Old Woman Creek. She didn't want to hike up Hanalea to camp by the lake or take in the view from the top.

Like anything forbidden, she became fascinating to Han. When she walked through the camp in her summer skirts, he couldn't help noticing the sway of her hips, her rare brilliant smile against her dusky skin. Even often overlooked parts, like elbows and knees, seemed appealing.

But he was relegated to watching from a distance.

Dancer was different, but worse, in a way. He'd always been slender and fine-boned, but now he looked hollow-cheeked, almost cadaverous. Was he ill? Or was the anger he carried around burning away his flesh?

Whatever grievance lay between him and his mother seemed to have deepened. Han was staying with Willo and Dancer in the Matriarch Lodge. They scarcely spoke to each other in public, and within the lodge the tension was oppressive. Sometimes they welcomed his presence, as if it was an excuse not to deal with each other. Other times he would walk in on conversations that collapsed into stony silence. Sometimes he slept elsewhere just to avoid feeling like an interloper.

Willo also spent hours in meetings with the elders of the clan. A delegation came from Demonai, on the eastern slopes, and all of the elders closed themselves up in the temple for hours.

A dozen Demonai warriors accompanied the visitors, and Han found excuses to pass by their camp. They were proud, elite, mysterious—the stuff of legends that dated from before the Breaking, to the wars between the wizards and the clans.

In the old days, it was said that the Demonai put a braid in their hair for every wizard killed. Many of them still wore braids studded with beads, and some said killing a wizard and taking his amulet was still the price of admission to their ranks.

It's like any gang, Han thought. You have to show what you're made of to get in.

The Demonai warriors rode the best horses and carried the most powerful enchanted clan-made weapons. They wore the Demonai symbol around their necks—an eye radiating flames. It was said they floated over the ground, leaving no trace of their passing. Han often saw Bird sitting at their fires, eating from their common pot, raptly listening to what they had to say. Having little to say herself for once.

Han couldn't help feeling a twinge of jealousy. More than a twinge—a bone-deep ache. Truth be told, he felt left out. For the nobility in the city, name day parties proclaimed them of age and eligible for marriage. Some of them came into their inheritances then. Wizards received their amulets and left for the academy at Oden's Ford to explore the mysteries of their calling.

Among the clans, the renaming ceremony admitted the young to full membership in the lodge, launched their life's work, welcomed them to the temples, and often began the dance of courtship.

Han was in a kind of no-man's-land of existence. His sixteenth birthday had come and gone months ago, scarcely noticed. Mam had brought home a honey cake from the bakery on the corner and had reminded him that he needed to find a real job. No ceremony marked Han's transition from *lytling* to grown-up. He just oozed over the borderlands, like any creature close to the ground.

So Han was envious, yet Dancer seemed miserable. Was he having trouble choosing a vocation? Was Willo pressuring him into something he didn't want?

He tried to talk to Dancer about it, one day when they were fishing. At least Dancer would fish with him. In fact, he seemed eager to be out on the mountain and away from camp. He'd seize any excuse to do so.

"So," Han said, flicking the tip of his pole so his fly lighted on the water, "Digging Bird barely talks to me. She always has her nose in the air."

Dancer grunted. "She'll talk to you, don't worry. After the ceremony." Dancer set down his pole and lay back on the riverbank, closing his eyes. His eyelids looked like great bruises in his unusually pale face.

"If . . . if I had to choose, I don't know what I'd be," Han said, feeling like he was rattling on against Dancer's silence. "I've had lots of vocations already."

"A vocation is different from a job," Dancer muttered. "Trust me."

"How is it different?" Han asked, encouraged by Dancer's response.

"A vocation is not something you slap on, like a coat of paint, and change whenever you want. A vocation is built into you. You have no choice. If you try to do something else, you fail." This last was said with deep bitterness.

Han nodded. Sometimes it seemed like he'd never escape his past life as streetlord of Ragmarket. If you were good at something, if you made a name, that something stuck to you, haunting you all of your days.

He fingered the silver cuffs around his wrists. They seemed to symbolize his lack of options. If he could just get them off, he might turn into someone else. At least he wouldn't be so easily recognized.

"I guess it's important to figure out what it is you were meant to do," Han said. "What would you do, if you could choose anything?"

Dancer opened his eyes, squinting against the shafts of sunlight leaking through the trees. "I always thought I'd like to apprentice with a Demonai goldsmith, like Elena, and learn to make jewelry, amulets, and magical pieces."

Dancer had always gravitated toward the gold and silversmith tables at the markets.

"Have you asked her?" Han asked.

Dancer closed his eyes. "She won't take me on."

That was strange. Elena knew Dancer, would know him to be a hard worker, and honest. "Well . . . can your vocation change? Are you locked in? Do you have to do the same thing all your life?

"It depends," Dancer said. "Some of us have no choice at all." He swiped at his eyes with the heels of his hands. Then he stood and walked away, into the woods, leaving all his fishing gear behind.

A week after his arrival at Marisa Pines, Han decided to visit Lucius Frowsley's place. He had to let him know he'd no longer be able to deliver his product to Fellsmarch. He hoped

Lucius would give him some other kind of job, something he could do without going to town, but he knew that was unlikely.

He descended using the Spirit Trail, then cut away on the path leading to Lucius's place.

The cabin looked deserted as usual, no smoke curling from the chimney. But Lucius wasn't fishing on the creek bank, or tending his still on the hillside. In fact, the fire under the boiler had gone out and the brick liner was cold. That never happened. Lucius might be slow, but he was consistent.

Han piled wood under the boiler and replenished the wash, but didn't light it, and left the distillate where it was.

Perplexed, he walked back to Lucius's cabin, which was the last place he'd expect to find him on a sunny spring day. He could leave a note, but that'd do no good to a blind man. He had a last bit of money he owed Lucius, but he hated to leave it in the cabin when the old man wasn't there.

He knocked loudly. There followed a spatter of barking, and then Dog's solid body hit the door.

He must be here, Han thought. Lucius and Dog were always together.

"Hey, Dog," he said, pushing open the cabin door. Dog was all over him, slapping his face with his long wet tongue, all in a dog frenzy of joy. "Where's Lucius?" Han asked, feeling a twinge of worry.

His eyes adjusted to the dim light, and then he saw movement on the bed in the corner. "Lucius?"

There were no lamps, of course, but Han ripped the curtains open to admit some light into the room. The old man was sitting on his bed, curled up against the wall, cradling a bottle, sick or drunk or something.

Han glanced around the cabin. Dog's water dish was empty, and his food dish too.

"Lucius? What's the matter with you?"

"Who is it?" the old man quavered. Then his voice changed, grew shrill and defiant. "Cowards. Have you come for me too?"

"It's me. Han," Han said, hesitating in the doorway. "Don't you know me?"

Lucius slung his arm over his face as if he could hide behind it. "Go away. I know the boy's dead. I a'ready heard, so don't try to fool me. You've got what you wanted, so leave me alone."

Han crossed to Lucius and patted him awkwardly on the shoulder. The old man flinched away, clutching his bottle like a lifeline.

"What are you talking about? I'm not dead. You're talking crazy."

The old man opened his clouded eyes. "You don't have it, do you? The jinxpiece. The boy hid it good, did he?" Lucius cackled. "Well, I don't have it, if that's what you're after. Do your worst. You can torture me, but I can't tell you what I don't know."

"Just stop it, Lucius," Han said, losing patience. "I'm going to get you something to eat."

If Lucius hadn't fed Dog, chances were he hadn't fed himself either. Han went out to the pump in the yard and filled a bucket with water. He brought it in and filled Dog's water dish and dipped some into a cup for Lucius.

"Here," he said, gently wresting the bottle out of Lucius's hands. "Drink this instead." He dug in his carry bag and pulled out a biscuit, pressing it into Lucius's hand. When the old man just sat clutching it, Han broke off a piece and put it in his mouth.

Lucius chewed mechanically, his bristled jaw working up and down. Dog lapped noisily at his water. Han rooted through Lucius's cupboards and found an end of ham that he broke into pieces. He put part into Dog's food dish and fed the rest to Lucius, bit by little bit, alternating with sips of water.

Dog wolfed his down.

"They said you was dead," Lucius mumbled, and Han knew he was back to his senses. "I thought it was my fault, for telling you to keep the jinxpiece."

"Who said I was dead?" Han asked.

"They said you was murdered down by the river," Lucius went on. "Ripped apart by demons."

Understanding flooded in. "Oh. That was my doing. I wanted people to think I was dead."

Lucius stopped chewing. "Are they after you, then? The Bayars?"

Always the Bayars. "No. The bluejackets are after me. The Queen's Guard. They think I killed a dozen people."

"Ah." Lucius heaved a great sigh of relief. "Thank the Maker it's nothing worse."

"It's bad enough!" Han exploded. "I can't go home, I can't make a living. I'm stuck here on Hanalea."

"There's worse things," Lucius said, eating on his own now. "Did you kill 'em? Those people?"

"No, I didn't kill them! You know better than that. I'm out of that. Or trying to be."

"Well, then. Give the bluejackets time. Once the hoopla dies down, they'll be buyable again." Lucius licked his fingers and reached down, groping for the bottle.

Han put the cup of water in his hand. "I think you'd better stick with this."

Lucius sighed and said, "So you're going to stay at Marisa Pines?"

"For now. I'm not going to be able to deliver for you for a while, anyway. I'm sorry."

"Where's the amulet?"

"It's hidden. Back in town." Which was inconvenient, now that he thought about it. It would be difficult to get.

Lucius coughed and spat on the ground, the way old men do. "Maybe you should consider going south, to Bruinswallow or We'enhaven. Or east to Chalk Cliffs, and get a job on the docks. You'd be safer there."

"Well." Han fingered the cuffs around his wrists. "I was thinking of Arden, or Tamron. It's not so far away. I could get home to see Mari and Mam now and then."

"There's a war going on, boy, or hadn't you heard?"

"I thought I could go as a line soldier," Han said. This was his latest idea.

Lucius slammed down his cup. "A soldier? A *soldier*? What kind of fool idea is that?"

Han hadn't expected this reaction from Lucius.

"Well, it's good money, and I wouldn't need an apprenticeship, or schooling, or—"

"You've got schooling, boy! Schooling enough to know you don't want to go as a soldier. Here I just got done feeling guilty because I thought you was dead. Soldiers' lives are too cheap these days. If you was an officer, you'd have a chance, anyway."

"Officers come from the academies," Han said. "I've got no money for that. I thought I could save up some money from soldiering, and then go to the academy."

"'Course you can," Lucius said sarcastically. "You think Wien House'll take you one-legged? Blind like me? With your lungs burned out by the poisons the Prince of Arden uses? Do you want to end up like your father?"

"You're right, Lucius. I have all kinds of other options," Han said, wondering why everyone had a license to lecture him lately. "How to decide? I could be a ragpicker. I could keep mucking out stables. I could be a fancy boy; the money's good, and the clothes . . ."

"Doesn't Jemson want you for a teacher?" Lucius interrupted.

How does he know these things? Han thought. "Well, I'm not going into orders, if that's what you mean. Besides, I kind of burned that bridge," he added, thinking of Corporal Byrne and Rebecca with the green eyes that could pin you to the wall. It seemed a lifetime ago, but he'd bet no one had forgotten it.

They both fell silent, each wrestling with his own thoughts.

"Funny they've not come after you," Lucius said finally. "The Bayars, I mean."

"Maybe the jinxpiece isn't as valuable as you thought," Han suggested. Lucius scowled and shook his head, and Han added, "Or maybe they don't know who I am."

"Hmmph. Well, we can hope for that, boy," Lucius said. "We can hope for that."

CHAPTER NINETEEN

NAME DAY

Despite feeling left out of the ceremony itself, Han couldn't help getting excited as the name day celebration approached.

Every year at summer solstice, all the clan children who turned sixteen during the warm weather months were celebrated at a naming ceremony. It was one of the few times during the year that Marisa Pines and Demonai camps came together for dancing and flirting and matchmaking between the clan families. It was also a time for show-off cooking, so it was bound to be the feast of the year.

The guesthouses were full three days before solstice, and visitors spilled over into the other lodges. Even the Matriarch Lodge had its share of guests.

Bird had secluded herself in the Acolyte Lodge with the other oath-takers, as was custom, but Dancer disappeared into the woods two days before the feast without a word to any-one. Han could tell Willo was worried. She was busy with preparations for the ceremony, but several times she went to the door and peered out, saying, "I thought I heard someone coming." She flinched at every sound and slept fitfully.

Insignificant Han slept fitfully also, sharing the floor of the lodge with six young Demonai cousins, who giggled and whispered and yanked out strands of his hair.

When Han emerged from the Matriarch Lodge the morning of the ceremony, haunches of venison were already roasting on spits, and the succulent scent of roast pork wafted from fire pits in the ground. Long trestle tables had been set up under the trees. Han and the younger children brought back armloads of wild onions and garlic, and freshly baked pies were lined up on the cooling racks in the cooking lodge.

Han helped lay the fire in the outdoor temple, dragged more seating into place for clan elders, and flirted with some Demonai girls he hadn't seen for six months.

Willo dressed in her Matriarch's robes, then carefully laid out Dancer's clothes, unfolding them from the trunk at the foot of her sleeping bench—leggings and moccasins, a soft shirt and fringed buckskin jacket painted and beaded in her distinctive style. Han studied it for clues. It was a nontraditional, somewhat jarring design, incorporating the familiar Marisa Pines and Matriarch symbols with rowan and jinx signs.

Willo even pulled out a beaded buckskin shirt for Han, the lone hunter symbols embroidered on the back yoke. Han stammered out a thanks, and Willo smiled and shook her head.

"Thank you for being a friend to Fire Dancer," she said. "He will need you in the coming days."

Han blinked at her. "What do you . . . ?"

She shook her head. "You will see," she said, turning away, dismissing him, and sitting down at her loom as if it weren't a feast day.

And still Dancer didn't come.

"Do you want me to go look for him?" Han asked, unable to stand the suspense any longer and wanting to do something useful.

"He will come," Willo said, throwing her shuttle and catching it. "He has no choice."

The feast began in late afternoon, the long tables groaning with platters and bowls, dogs circulating hopefully underneath. Han wasn't as hungry as he thought he'd be, eating on his own. His friends were all sequestered, preparing to cross into the future.

Finally, at the last possible moment, Dancer slipped back into camp, looking haggard and dirty, like he'd slept for three days on the ground.

Willo silently handed him a basin, and he sluiced water over his head and face, scrubbing away the grime with a towel. He then dressed for the ceremony with quick fierce movements, making no comment on his new clothes.

Han opened his mouth, but his voice died in his throat. He was angry with Dancer for acting this way. Jealous of his friend's place in the world and the ceremony that would confirm it. Whatever vocation had been chosen for him, he needed to accept it. Han wished someone would tell him what to do with the rest of his life.

And then it was time to go. The torches were already lit as

they made their way along the path to the outdoor temple, even though the light would linger far into the night on this longest of days. A soft breeze kissed Han's skin, carrying the scent of night lilies and the promise of the brief upland summer.

Dancer left them when they reached the temple, circling around to join the others in the Acolyte Lodge. Willo split off too, to join the elders at the front of the temple. The grown-ups wore the ceremonial garb of their chosen vocations, a flower garden of colors. Han, feeling foolish, sat on the ground with the younger children, folding his long legs up out of the way.

The ceremony began with speeches from the elders of both camps. Han recognized Averill Lightfoot and resisted the urge to fade back into the woods. He'd last seen the trader during the disaster at Southbridge Temple, when he'd kidnapped Rebecca and escaped into Ragmarket.

It's all right, Han told himself. The trader hadn't recognized him then, and by now the red-brown dye had nearly washed out of his hair. Who would expect to find a Ragmarket streetlord at the Marisa Pines naming ceremony?

Cennestre Elena, Matriarch of Demonai Camp, told the familiar story of how the clans were carved from Spirit stone and the breath of the Maker brought them to life. And how, to this day, the queens of the Fells returned to the Spirits at the end of life, each claiming a peak as her final dwelling place.

Han found himself relaxing, the cadence of the familiar old stories soothing him as it always did. Why couldn't real life be that orderly? Instead it was a tangled fish line, with knots and connections you couldn't see.

For instance, Averill was the consort to the queen of the Fells, the father of the princess heir. Han couldn't help but think it strange, this linkage between those glittering Valefolk who lived within the frowning walls of Fellsmarch Castle and the members of the upland clans, whose camps seemed like an extension of the landscape, who walked so gently on the land.

It was time for the first of the summer born to be introduced by their sponsors. Iron Hammer, a blacksmith, came forward, followed by a tall, broad-shouldered girl in a leather vest and leggings, decorated by horses and flames burned into the leather.

She must be Demonai, Han thought, since I don't know her.

"Who do you bring before us, Hammer?" Averill asked.

Hammer cleared his throat. "The girl, Laurel Blossom, came to me, saying she dreams of metal and flame. She has been examined, and it is a true calling. I have agreed to be her sponsor. She has meditated on her name. I present to you Flame Shaper." And he grinned broadly, as if it were his own daughter he was presenting.

And so it continued. An apprentice basket maker was named Oak Weaver. A would-be storyteller was named Tale Spinner. A jewelry maker became Silver Bird.

Now two Demonai warriors came forward, a man and a woman, heads high, knives at their belts, bows slung over their shoulders, silver Demonai emblems hanging from chains around their necks. They were clad in the green and brown leggings and shirts that made them invisible in the forest. Anyone who went up against wizards had to have a bit of magic of their own.

Excited whispers rustled through the temple. The Demonai did not often sponsor a named warrior.

"Who is that?" someone behind him whispered.

"Reid and Shilo Demonai," someone whispered back. All of the Demonai warriors took the surname Demonai.

So that's Reid Nightwalker, Han thought. The tall, muscular warrior was only a year or two older than Han, but he was already famous, or as famous as a warrior can be during peacetime.

Shilo was smaller, with a bulkier build, but there was a resemblance among all the Demonai, a kind of shared veneer of arrogance.

"We have received a petition," Shilo said, as if the warriors required no introduction. "We have accepted it," she went on, as if the assembly deserved no explanation of Demonai warrior ways.

The two warriors turned, looking into the forest.

Bird emerged from the trees, eyes downcast, as befitted one humbled by such a great honor, yet the lightness of her step told Han she was practically floating. She was already dressed in Demonai green and brown, and her unconscious grace matched theirs.

She came forward until she stood just in front of the warriors.

Her sponsors did not bother to speak of her history. "We accept this girl, Digging Bird," Reid said, "a Demonai warrior candidate, under our sponsorship. If she is successful, she will receive a new name and the Demonai amulet before next solstice."

What if she isn't? Han thought, feeling a little resentful. What happens then? And what does she have to do to be successful?

Reid Demonai presented Bird with a bow, a quiver of arrows, and a knife with the Demonai emblem engraved into the hilt. She slid the knife into a sheath at her belt and stood, cradling the other weapons in her arms, then raised her head and looked around the circle. She allowed herself a brilliant smile, that familiar curl falling down over her forehead.

She's happy, Han told himself. It's what she wants.

Which made him think of Dancer. All of the other summer borns had come forward. Willo was conversing with Averill and Elena, their heads close together. Everyone looked solemn and grave.

"There is one final summer born to name," Averill said. "I call forward Fire Dancer, also known as Hayden, son of Willo, Matriarch of Marisa Pines."

After a moment's breathless pause, Dancer emerged from the woods and walked forward, all alone, his beautiful jacket reflecting the light of the torches. His face bore the stony expression that was becoming familiar.

Where is his sponsor? Han wondered, peering into the surrounding forest and seeing no one. Then Willo stepped forward and stood beside her son. Dancer glared at her but did not move away.

Now *Cennestre* Elena Demonai stepped forward, mother of them all. The firelight deepened the lines on her face, the map of her long life. Her eyes were like woodland pools, reflecting the common memory.

Her voice assumed the cadence of the storyteller. "I will tell you a story about a girl born and raised at Marisa Pines."

Typical clan, Han thought. The relevance of a story wasn't always clear until the end. And sometimes it was just a story that needed telling, and had nothing to do with the situation at hand. For Dancer's sake, he hoped that wasn't the case this time.

"This girl's name was Watersong, and the magic was strong in her," Elena went on.

Some of the elders in attendance exchanged significant glances. This story was known to some, at least.

"She was so beautiful that young men came from all over the Seven Realms to see her, hoping to catch her eye. And when the time grew close for her to choose her vocation, everyone paid attention, because she was good at everything. She had no lack of possible sponsors."

What's this all about? Han wondered. Isn't it bad enough that Dancer has no sponsors? Why bring this up now?

"Not long before Watersong's naming ceremony, she was out walking in the woods one morning when she encountered a young man, a handsome stranger, someone who was not clan, someone who *should not have been there*." She paused for effect, then went on.

"The young man wore an elaborate ring on his finger, studded with emeralds. He asked Watersong if she would like to try it on."

The word *No!* rippled through the temple. The storyteller Elena Demonai held them in the palm of her hand. Except

Han, who was distracted by Dancer's misery and the pain in Willo's face.

"She put on the ring and fell into a dream," Elena said. "When she awoke, she was alone in the woods. It was night-time and she was shivering with fear and cold. The young man had disappeared, and so had the ring. Watersong went back to camp, and soon after discovered she was with child.

"Watersong was big with child when she attended her naming ceremony. Because the magic was strong in her, she was apprenticed to Elena Demonai, Matriarch of Demonai Lodge. She was renamed Willow Song, and called 'Willo.'"

Elena paused and looked around, and everyone knew what she would say next. "Willow Song had a boy child, and they called him Fire Dancer. You see him before you."

Han sat stunned, looking from Willo to Dancer and back to Elena. So this was the story that had gone untold about Dancer's missing father. That Dancer's father must have been a wizard.

"Dancer inherited much from his mother," Elena said, smiling sadly at Dancer. "He is a beloved child of Marisa Pines. He has many gifts, and would have no lack of sponsors in choosing a vocation. But he has inherited gifts from his father as well, and so must follow his own path. Dancer has chosen a vocation none of us can sponsor."

Bird had apparently reached her limit for silence. "What are you saying?" she demanded, looking from Elena to Averill to Willo. "What have you chosen, Dancer?"

"It wasn't a choice," Dancer said, barely audible.

Comprehension dawned on Reid Demonai's face. "He's a *jinxflinger?*" he said, groping for his knife. "Here?"

Then everyone was talking at once, like a clamor of crows in a cornfield.

Willo stepped between Reid and Dancer, but spoke to the entire assembly, her voice clear and steady and nearly loud enough to rise above it all.

"Although we cannot sponsor him here, we have arranged for Dancer's training. He will go to Oden's Ford, to the charmcaster academy there, and learn to harness the magic he's inherited."

Han's head spun as scenes and images came back to him: Dancer's moodiness over the past months. The conversation Han overheard in the Matriarch Lodge, when he'd wondered if Dancer might be ill.

But no. He'd taken rowan—meant to protect against sorcery. Dancer had been trying to damp down the magic. Willo would have bent all her skill to that task. And if she couldn't do it . . . no one could.

He'd seen Willo and Dancer in Fellsmarch, when she'd healed him at Southbridge Temple. Maybe they were consulting the temple healers. Or maybe they were there to make arrangements for Oden's Ford.

Han studied his friend for any telltale signs of wizardry. Dancer looked the same as always, except for being desperately unhappy. There were the blue eyes which must be a gift from his father, so incongruous against his dark skin and hair.

"You're going to train up another wizard?" Reid spoke contemptuously. "When there are far too many already?"

Elena stood her ground. "We are going to give Fire Dancer what he needs to control the gift he's been given."

"That's not a gift," Reid said. "It's a curse. And the world would be better off with one less wizard in it."

Shilo nodded, regarding Dancer as if he were a viper she'd found under the porch. "He can't stay in the Spirits. The Naéming forbids it. You know that."

"The boy has stayed here this long," Averill said sharply. "He can stay until he leaves for Oden's Ford."

Han processed this in fits and starts, seemingly a few steps behind the others. Dancer was leaving? No, he was being exiled. Evicted like a tenant from a slumlord flat.

He remembered the meeting with Micah Bayar and his friends on Hanalea, when Dancer had confronted the young wizards with this very rule—wizards were not allowed in the Spirit Mountains.

But Dancer—couldn't an exception be made? He belonged here. This was his home.

Han stood, meaning to say as much, even though he had no right since he was only a guest himself. But Willo caught his eye and shook her head.

Confused, Han sat down again. Did Willo really mean to let this happen? Would she allow her son to be sent south to live among strangers?

Elena faced Dancer, thrusting her hand into a pouch she wore at her waist. She pulled out something glittering, which she dangled in front of Dancer.

It was an amulet—carved from a translucent caramel-colored stone. A glowing figure of a clan dancer ringed by flame. Dancer stared at it with a terrible fascination, as if it were a poison he was required to take.

"Fire Dancer," Elena said gently, "we in the clans have long been the makers of the tools of high magic, even though we are unable to use them ourselves. For hundreds of years we have been in an uneasy truce with those who can use them. When these gifts are abused, we control access to them. Each mistrusts the other, but each depends upon the other. The Maker in her wisdom has decreed that her gifts be distributed thus, to protect us all."

She slid the chain over Dancer's head so the amulet rested on his chest. He stood stiffly, hands clenched at his sides, as if moving might set it off. A long moment passed, and the amulet began to glow. In answer, something kindled under Dancer's skin, an incandescence that hadn't been apparent before.

"You are a summer born, a child of this camp. And so we bestow this gift directly on you, the amulet that you will take to Oden's Ford." Elena shrugged her narrow shoulders. "Still, we hope you will remember where you came from. Perhaps you will be the one who brings wizard and clan together."

The hatred on Reid's face said that would never happen. "You should hold the amulet until the jinxflinger leaves Hanalea," he said. "Else it isn't safe."

"The elders have spoken, Reid Nightwalker," Averill said. "Fire Dancer has no sponsor. The amulet will be the connection between us. It is all we can offer him now."

"You needn't worry," Dancer said. "I have no desire to use anything left to me by my father. And I'll be gone before you know it." With that, he ripped off the jacket Willo had made for him and flung it into the fire. Then he stalked off into the woods, leaving silence behind him.

CHAPTER TWENTY

WILLO AND BIRD

The backwash from the naming ceremony persisted for several days. Dancer disappeared again, and Han spent fruitless hours searching the woods surrounding Marisa Pines, visiting all their familiar haunts. When he did find him two days' walk away in a hunter's shelter on the shores of Ghost Lake, Dancer wasn't fishing, or hunting, or reading. Just sitting, staring out at the lake.

Dancer had little to say to Han's suggestions; he seemed to feel he'd exhausted all possibilities.

"We could go down to the temple in Fellsmarch," Han said. "The speakers know all sorts of things. Maybe they could help."

"We've been to see Jemson," Dancer said. He picked up a rock and sent it skimming over the water. "He tried some things, but none worked." Dancer glanced over at Han. "Besides, didn't you say you're a wanted man down in Fellsmarch?"

Well. Yes. There was that.

"What about one of the other camps? Maybe there's a healer there who would have a new idea."

"My mother's the best. You know that. And Elena knows the other matriarchs; she's always traveling. If there was something else to try, she would know about it."

"If you don't have an amulet, mightn't it just . . . stay dormant?"

Dancer didn't honor that with an answer.

Han felt compelled to offer increasingly desperate plans. "We could go to the Northern Isles. That's where wizards come from, right?"

"You think that's better than going to Oden's Ford?" Dancer asked. "Sailing across the Indio to someplace I've never been to find the people that invaded us centuries ago?"

"You could . . . you could talk to the Wizard Council. You could try to find your father."

"The only reason I would look for my father is if I decide to kill him," Dancer said, his blue eyes hard as topaz.

Stunned into silence, Han didn't say anything for a long time. He'd never seen Dancer so bitter. Dancer was the one who always saw the good in people, who was always the peacemaker.

"I'll go with you," Han said finally. "To Oden's Ford, I mean."

"And do what?"

"I'll go to the warrior school at Wien House."

Dancer looked him up and down and actually grinned. "You? In the army? It's all about rules. You wouldn't last a week. You'd be asking why all the time. You'd be better off going into temple orders."

"It could work," Han persisted. The more he talked about it, the better he liked it. "All the armies are eager to take on Wien House graduates. I could find one that I fit in with."

"How would you pay for that?" Dancer asked. "You don't have any money."

"How are you paying for Mystwerk House?" Han countered.

"The camps are sponsoring me, over the Demonai warriors' objection. It's one way to get me to go away."

"What's the Demonais' problem?" Han asked.

Dancer shrugged. "Ask them. But you're not a soldier. I'm not sure what you are, but you're not that."

When Han arrived back at camp, he told Willo where Dancer was, making it clear that Dancer was frustrated.

"It's all right, Hunts Alone," she said, looking up from her dye pot. She was stirring a cauldron full of bright blue yarn over the fire in front of the Matriarch Lodge. "Leave him be. Dancer needs some time alone. Hanalea soothes him."

"What's he going to do when he has to leave? What's going to soothe him then?" Han was angry with Willo, like this was all her fault.

"He will find his way. He has to," Willo said simply.

"How long have you known about this?" Han demanded. "That Dancer is a jinxflinger."

Willo blotted her sweaty forehead with her forearm. "I knew it was a possibility from the . . . from the beginning. But wizards don't manifest until they're older, and I had hopes it wouldn't happen. I began to see the signs three years ago. And finally he noticed too, and came to me."

"There has to be something you can do." After all, Willo

was a gifted healer. Couldn't she heal her own son?

It was like she read his mind. "Wizardry is a gift, not an affliction. It's not amenable to healing. I tried rowan, of course, and certain . . . talismans." Her voice trailed off, and she looked down at her blue-spotted apron. "I should have acted sooner, when he was just a baby. Sometimes wizardry can be held at bay if the intervention is early enough. Otherwise it's like a cancer that spreads until you can't cut it away without killing the host."

Right, Han thought. It's a gift. Like a cancer. Willo seemed as confused as everyone else.

Maybe now was the time to press his suit. He felt nervous—Willo had turned him down before—but surely she'd see the sense of what he suggested.

"I've been thinking," he said. "I need a trade, and I can't go back to Fellsmarch any time soon. I could go to Oden's Ford with Dancer and enroll in the warrior's academy. We'd be in different schools, but I bet we could see each other, anyway. And we could travel back and forth together. It would be safer for both of us."

Willo was already shaking her head. "You're no warrior, Hunts Alone," she said dismissively.

"It's my choice," he said. "I'm nearly grown. If I was clan I'd already be named."

"Why are you asking me, then?" Willo asked, sitting back on her heels.

"I'll need money to enroll. I asked Jemson about it, and it costs at least twenty girlies a year, plus board. That's not counting travel money."

Willo studied him. "Are you asking me for money? So you can throw your life away fighting in the flatlander war?"

This was not going well. Han extended his wrists toward her. "I can pay my own way. I just need you to take these off," he said. "I know traders who'd pay good money for thick silver like this. They should bring more than enough to keep me on the way south, plus get me enrolled once I'm there."

"No," she said. "I've told you already. I can't do that."

"Willo, I have nowhere to go," he persisted, perilously close to begging. "I need to make a living somehow, and I can't go back to Fellsmarch. There's nothing for me here. Dancer's going to Oden's Ford, and Bird is going to Demonai. Everyone else I know is apprenticed. Nothing's going to be the same."

"There are trades you can learn here at Marisa Pines," Willo said. "You're already good at plants and potions. I'll take you on, if no one else will."

"I can't hide out up here all my life," Han said, thinking there was little adventure in doing what he had been doing all along, only less.

"You're not a warrior, Hunts Alone," Willo said flatly. "And no amount of money will make you one." She tossed down her stirring stick and swept into the Matriarch Lodge.

Han spent the next several days sulking. The continuing presence of the guests from Demonai were as irksome as a pebble in his boot. It was like having houseguests in the middle of a family fight. You just wanted them gone so you could speak your mind.

Not that he was exactly family, as he kept reminding himself.

The Demonai warriors in particular frayed his temper. Bird spent all her time with them, of course, all solemn-faced, hanging on Reid Demonai's every word.

That was another thing—Han was disappointed in Bird. She could have defended Dancer when Reid Demonai attacked him.

Just like Han could have defended him too. No matter what Willo said.

The Demonai warriors fell silent when Dancer passed by, and left the fire circle when he joined it. They watched him constantly, like he was a mad dog or a venomous spider.

Han couldn't help worrying that the Demonai warriors might go after Dancer if they caught him on his own. So he became a self-appointed spy, lingering near their fire, watching their comings and goings from camp, and listening in on their conversations.

Until one day, he was slipping through the forest, following Reid Demonai, probably to the privy, when Bird stepped into his path. She was dressed in her Demonai clothing, and she seemed to materialize out of shadow and sunlight.

"What do you think you're doing?" she hissed.

"Doing?" He shrugged. "What does it look like I'm doing?"

"You're playing a dangerous game is what. Do you think they don't notice? They're *Demonai warriors*," she said, as if *he* hadn't noticed.

He gave her a "So what?" look. "I've been walking in these woods all my life," he said. "If it makes them jumpy, they should leave."

"It's only fair to warn you, Reid's patience is wearing thin. He's about ready to cut your throat."

"He can *try*," Han said, affecting indifference, though his heart beat faster. A confrontation with Reid Demonai seemed appealing.

"You don't understand," Bird persisted. "They've trained for this all their lives. They're dangerous."

"Really? Well, I'm dangerous too." He felt like he was bragging in the school yard, but he couldn't help himself. "Looks to me like they're all bristle and no brains."

"Shhh!" Bird glanced around, like Reid might be behind a nearby tree, listening. "Come on." Moving with her usual catlike grace, she led him off the trail, down into a small ravine, to a place where two slabs of rock had slid together, forming a small cavelike shelter. Maiden's kiss and columbine cascaded from the crevices, and a small stream tumbled along the floor of the canyon.

"Sit," she said, waving him to a flat rock.

He sat, and she sat across from him.

"I've tried to talk to Dancer," she said. "And he won't speak to me."

"Do you blame him?" Han asked. And then, after a pause, "I can't believe you'd want to be in a group that would treat your friend that way." There. He'd said it.

Bird bit her lip and stared down at her clasped hands. "It . . . it's nothing personal," she said. "But that's why the Demonai exist. To fight wizards. And the presence of . . . of any wizard on Hanalea is sacrilege."

"We're talking about *Dancer*," Han said, thinking of how Dancer had challenged Bayar and his friends. "He was born here. He belongs here."

"I know." She swallowed hard. "But think about when the jinxflingers invaded the Fells—they were ruthless. They put *lytlings* to the sword. They captured our queen and forced her into marriage. They evicted the priests from the temples and launched a reign of terror. But the clans held the Spirits, and they were our sanctuary. If not for that, we would have been eradicated as a people."

It was a pretty speech. Han wondered if it came from Reid Demonai. He imagined them sitting hip to hip by the fire, Bird looking into his eyes, spellbound. He blinked the image away.

"That was a long time ago," he said. "I'm not sweet on wizards either, but . . ."

"That was a long time ago, but these are dangerous times," Bird said. "We have a weak queen. The power of wizards is growing. We in the clan feel less welcome in the Vale. We wield less influence at court."

"Averill Demonai is consort to the queen," Han said. "And father to the princess heir. That sounds influential to me."

"Appearances can be deceiving," Bird said. "Reid says it's more important than ever to maintain the traditional boundaries against wizards."

And I'm not really interested in what Reid says, Han thought. "So what's the plan?" he asked. "Will you be going back to Demonai with them or what?"

Bird nodded. "We leave soon. It's just . . . Reid doesn't want to leave while Dancer's still here."

"Well, they won't have to worry about him much longer, will they?" Han said, his own guilt driving the knife home. "Once he leaves, we may never see him again."

Bird raked her curls off her sweaty forehead. "Do you . . . do you think it's a good idea? Dancer going to Oden's Ford? Training as a wizard?"

Han stared at her. "What choice does he have? You just said—"

"Maybe . . . maybe he should just move down into Fellsmarch," Bird said, not meeting his eyes.

Han leaned forward. "And do what? He's no flatlander. The things he's good at have no value in the city."

"He could learn a trade," she said. "And then . . . we could visit him sometimes." She looked up at him hopefully. "Maybe . . . without training . . . the magic would just . . . go away."

"You think so? Or is that what Reid says? Do you think Willo would send Dancer away if it was as easy as that?"

She shook her head. "No. Only . . . the Demonais don't want Dancer to go to Oden's Ford."

A great cold fury was growing in Han's middle, spreading into his extremities. "You don't want him here, but you don't want him to go to Oden's Ford. You just want him to disappear, is that it?"

"No! I love Dancer. It's just . . . Reid is worried about training up a wizard who knows the Spirits so well. Who is privy to clan secrets. What if he comes back . . . on the wrong side?" She looked at Han appealingly.

"I don't know much about politics," Han said, his voice brittle as river ice. "I just try to get by. But if you ask me, you're treating Fire Dancer like the enemy. And I can't think of a better way to drive him to the other side. You do what you want, but whatever side Dancer's on, I'm there."

That was what he'd been trying to tell Dancer. So he'd know he wasn't alone. That Han would go with him, and help him if he could.

Han looked up and saw that Bird was crying, tears sliding silently down her cheeks. Han couldn't recall ever seeing that before.

"Hey, now," he said after a few minutes of this. "Come on. We've been together forever. We'll work it out."

"All I ever wanted . . . was to be a Demonai warrior," she whispered. "And now, whatever I do, I'm betraying someone."

"You just have to remember who your friends are, is all," Han said. "Maybe you have something to teach the Demonais about loyalty."

"I didn't speak up for him at the ceremony," she said, swiping at her nose.

"I didn't either." He sat next to her and put an arm around her, and she turned toward him, burrowing her face into his shoulder. He patted her back awkwardly, trying not to notice her chest pressed against his. She smelled of pine and leather and summer in the uplands.

Bird raised her head and looked up at him, her lashes wet and clumped together. She slid her arms around his neck, pulling his head down, and suddenly they were kissing like desperate people, like it was the last kiss either one of them would ever get. He lowered her down to the rock, kissing her nose, her eyelids, every part he could reach, and she slid her hands under his shirt, pressing him closer, her hands warm and rough against his back.

It was the first thing in a long time that made him happy.

CHAPTER TWENTY-ONE

BLOOD AND ROSES

The day after the Bayars' party, word came down from the queen that since Raisa was ill, she was to stay in her room and rest. Raisa wasn't sure whether this was 1) Marianna's genuine concern about her daughter's well-being, and desire to have her well recovered in time for her own party, 2) punishment for being foolish enough to be ensnared by Micah Bayar, or 3) a strategy for building anticipation for Raisa's name day party to a fever pitch.

Raisa sent several messages to her mother, requesting an audience, but Marianna did not reply. Hadn't Lord Averill told her mother what the Bayars had done? Surely he had. Then why was *she* being punished? Raisa fumed and fretted, but it did no good.

A basketful of cards and invitations graced the table in Raisa's entry hall, but Magret had her orders and declined them all on the princess's behalf. As word of her purported illness circulated, gifts and flowers flowed in until the mingled fragrances made her half sick for real.

A dozen roses arrived each morning from Micah Bayar, a different color every day. When Magret refused them, they accumulated in the hallway until it looked like a shrine to some forgotten goddess. Soon Raisa was sending them out to all of her ladies-in-waiting and to the healers' halls at the temple.

Micah sent her several messages, asking permission to visit, but she did not reply. Magret continued to sleep in her room, and a member of the Queen's Guard always seemed to be lingering outside her door. Clearly the queen meant to prevent any clandestine trysts or further wizardly intrigue.

This prevented any meetings with Amon as well. Raisa wished she could slip out through the tunnel and climb up to the garden and find him there, pacing the cobblestones or waiting on the bench. She found herself dwelling on him more and more.

When she wasn't thinking of Amon Byrne, she was haunted by Han Alister. The streetlord ambushed her in her dreams, swaggering up the street as he had in Ragmarket, with his quick wit and sardonic smile. She remembered the way he'd pushed her behind him, pressed a knife into her hand, and faced down six Raggers on her behalf.

If you're going to knife someone, don't think about it so long, he'd said. And now he was dead. Had *he* hesitated at some critical moment, and been lost? Was there something she could have done differently that would have saved him?

Was it her job to save him?

I need to go to parties, Raisa mused, so I don't think so much.

Her only visitors were dressmakers and combers and her chattering ladies-in-waiting, who slept till noon, then spent the early afternoons in Raisa's chambers, going on and on about the parties they'd been to, and the dresses they'd worn and planned to wear, before retiring to their chambers to prepare for the evening ahead.

It was considered a social coup to host southern royalty, even if they had fallen on hard times. So, with Raisa unavailable, the Tomlins and Lady Heresford were swept from dance to dance and dinner to dinner with scarcely a chance to visit the garderobe between.

Raisa missed Melissa Hakkam's name day party, but Missy came the next afternoon to tell her all about it. Missy was all baggy-eyed and yawning, having stayed out till the wee hours.

"A shame you couldn't have been there. Mother was *so* disappointed," Missy said. "She kept pairing me up with this dreadful Arno Manhold. Can you imagine? Lady Melissa Manhold? How *awkward*."

"Who is he?" Raisa asked disinterestedly, to stop the flood of words.

"He's a ship owner from Chalk Cliffs—well, he's actually from the Northern Isles—and he's at least fifty years old. He does own ten ships, and he has loads of money and three houses, one in Fellsmarch, one in Chalk Cliffs, and an estate along the Dyrnnewater, but he's a *tradesman*, after all, and he trod on my feet all night, and he only knows two old dances."

"What if he owned *four* houses," Raisa said. "And a

hunting lodge in the Heartfangs. How many dances would he need to know then?"

Missy blinked at her, confused. "Well! I'm sure I don't know. Me, I am hoping for a southern match. I mean, Prince Liam is *so* handsome." Missy heaved a great sigh and batted her eyelashes. "And he says such wicked things. He's a wonderful dancer too, unlike the Klemaths. How does this sound?" She struck an elegant pose, tossing back her excessive hair. "Princess Melissa of Tamron."

"Some people say matters are rather—unsettled—in Tamron," Raisa said, unable to resist deflating Missy. "They say there's a chance the war in Arden will spread west."

"Some people are tiresome and gloomy," Missy said, completely undeflated. "We could both be princesses, wouldn't that be wonderful? I might even become queen before you."

"Prince Liam has declared himself, then? He's spoken to his father? What wonderful news!" Raisa said, stooping to cruelty.

Now Missy looked flustered. "Well, of course not. His father is in Tamron and Prince Liam is here, but no doubt when he returns home . . ."

Just then Magret tapped on the door to Raisa's bedroom, entered, and curtsied. "Lord Averill Demonai, Royal Consort, to see you, Your Highness." Magret always went formal when Raisa had company.

Good, Raisa thought. Maybe I'll finally find out what's going on.

"I'd best go, Your Highness," Missy said, rising and curtsying herself. "There's a tea this afternoon for Lady Heresford. I only wish you could come." She backed from the room under Raisa's scowl as Averill entered.

Raisa embraced her father. "Thank the Maker you're here. I am going crazy, not knowing anything. What's going on? Are the Bayars in trouble?"

Averill took a deep breath and shook his head. "Well, no. Not exactly."

"What?" Raisa backed away from him. "What do you *mean*, not exactly?" Then she noticed that he was wearing traveling clothes, his trader pouch slung over his shoulder.

"You're going away again," she said, her heart sinking.

"Briefly," Averill said, with a wry smile. "The queen has decided I should ride to Chalk Cliffs and speak with the garrison commander about port security. It seems there's a problem with pirates."

"Why you?" Raisa said. "And why now? It's the middle of the season, and my party is only four days away."

"Why indeed?" he said lightly. "Your mother is not pleased with me these days, I'm afraid," he said. "But don't worry. I'll be back in plenty of time for your celebration. I wouldn't miss it."

"Why doesn't she send Captain Byrne?" Raisa muttered. "Or General Klemath?"

"Captain Byrne is coming with me, in fact," Averill said. He paused, as if to let the weight of his words settle.

"She's sending you away, while I feel like I'm being held captive," Raisa grumbled, pacing the floor. "I haven't even had a chance to properly meet Prince Liam and Princess Marina. I don't get it. Isn't that what I'm supposed to be doing right now—going to parties? Meeting prospective suitors?"

"Why do you think she's doing this, Briar Rose?" Averill gazed out through the windows over a city without shadows, stark in the noonday sun.

Raisa pressed the heel of her hand against her forehead, trying to massage away the headache Missy always left behind. "Is she blaming me for what happened at the Bayars' party?"

"I told her about the amulet. She should know it wasn't your fault. But she seems angry with *me* for raising the issue."

"Angry with you? But why?" Raisa felt stupid. She hated feeling stupid.

Averill sighed. "When she confronted Lord Bayar, he explained to Her Majesty that the jinxpieces are harmless reproductions of old magical pieces; that they gifted you and Micah with matching jewelry to symbolize the long connection between the queens of the Fells and the Bayar family."

He turned away from the window and looked at her straight on. "Lord Bayar showed the queen the serpent necklace and ring, which were, indeed, very well-crafted reproductions."

Raisa's hand crept to her neck. A faint welt lingered where the pendant had rested. Was it possible? Could it really have been a matter of too much wine and Micah Bayar's kisses?

"Are you saying you were *mistaken*?" she said. "That the necklace wasn't really . . ."

"No." Averill shook his head. "I was not mistaken," he said without a trace of doubt in his voice or expression.

"Why hasn't my mother come to talk to *me* about it? Why is she asking Lord Bayar instead?"

Averill hesitated, as if debating how much to say. "Lord Bayar suggested that you and Micah simply got carried away. You violated the rules against congress between wizards and the Gray Wolf line, and so were looking for an excuse."

Raisa snatched up a bouquet off the mantel and flung it into the fireplace. The porcelain vase shattered, sending chips flying in all directions and scattering lilies and orchids across the hearth.

"Your Highness!" Magret exclaimed, poking her head in from her quarters next door. "Blessed lady!" she added when she saw the mess.

"Briar Rose," her father said, shaking his head and putting his finger to his lips. Raisa read the message in his eyes. *Trader face*, he was saying.

It wasn't easy. Raisa was in the mood for breaking things. But she mastered herself and said, "It's all right, Magret. It slipped. I'll clean it up later."

Averill waited until the door closed behind Magret before he went on. "Marianna has forbidden Micah to see you. He's restricted to Aerie House. She has confined you to your room. She seems to believe that's appropriate punishment."

"What is Micah saying?" Raisa asked glumly.

Averill shrugged. "He's saying nothing at all. That I know of, anyway."

Raisa gestured vaguely at the floral display. "He's been sending flowers. Asking to visit."

"You know your mother doesn't like trouble," Averill said. "She'd rather not know about some things so she doesn't have to confront them. It may be nothing more than that."

Raisa nodded. "I even thought maybe she wanted to keep me away from the other parties to, you know, make my party more special," she said. "She seems determined to make it the party of the year." It sounded foolish now that she was saying it.

"That may be," Averill said, though he didn't sound convinced. "Apparently Marianna sees no need to show you off before then." He hesitated, then plowed ahead. "Your mother may worry that I have a clan match in mind for you. There's been talk about you and Reid Demonai."

"Reid?" Raisa frowned. She and Reid had shared some kisses, some long walks in the woods, a few dances at clan gatherings. "I like Reid, but there's been talk of him and every girl at Demonai."

"It didn't help that I supposedly spirited you off to Demonai without telling her," Averill said.

"That's my fault, and I'm sorry," Raisa said. "It was a stupid thing to do, going to Southbridge Temple without an escort. It could have ended much worse."

She'd never have met Han Alister. She wouldn't have to feel bad that he was dead.

Averill waved her regrets away. "You have to take chances, Raisa. What seems safest on its face may not be in the long run. Your ministry is making a real difference in Southbridge and Ragmarket. Speaker Jemson is working wonders with the money you've provided."

"I've meant to go and visit," Raisa said, pacing again. "But everything is so hard right now. I feel like a prisoner."

Averill fingered the Demonai pendant that hung around

his neck. "Could it be that your mother already has a match in mind for you?"

Raisa stopped pacing and swung around. "I've told her I don't want to marry any time soon."

Averill shrugged. "Sometimes monarchs must act on a match, whether the timing is ideal or not. You've heard of child marriages among the nobility, I know, especially in the south. Not that you're a child any longer, Raisa."

Raisa studied her father's face, hoping he was teasing her, but he looked completely serious. "There's so much I want to do before I get married," she said. "With the war going on, I haven't even had the chance to travel. I'd like to go to Tamron and We'enhaven and Arden, and see how they do things there. I want to see Oden's Ford. I want to go sailing on the Indio and visit the Northern Isles."

"And get captured by pirates, no doubt." Averill held up his hand, laughing. "You are too much like me, daughter. Unable to keep still for very long. I take it your mother hasn't mentioned a specific suitor, then?"

Raisa shook her head. "She does seem to be opposed to a southern match, though. She said things were too unsettled, that I might marry someone who'd lose his throne the next week. I said, Fine, I have my own throne. I told her we should wait until the war is over and it's all sorted out."

"What did she say to that?" Averill asked.

"Well." Raisa thought back to her conversation with the queen. "She seems to be in a hurry. You know how she is. She wants to see me settled." A cold dread settled under Raisa's breastbone. Did the queen really intend to marry her off before she'd had a chance to *do* anything?

Who would it be? One of the Klemaths? Jon Hakkam? About the best that could be said for them was that they'd be easy to manage.

"I'm going to wait until after I'm crowned," Raisa said. "And then I'll marry whoever I like."

She scowled fiercely at her father, and he grinned back, shaking his head. They both knew that was unlikely to happen. Queens married for the good of the realm.

"Just . . . be careful, Briar Rose," Averill said. "You have good instincts. Listen to them."

"I will." Raisa nodded. "Well," she said shyly, taking his hands, "I guess this is good-bye for a few days."

"The next time I see you, you'll be officially grown," Averill said. "Named heir to the Gray Wolf throne. Breaking hearts all around, no doubt."

"Pursued by every spotty, ambitious lord and second son between twelve and eighty," Raisa replied, shivering. She'd been looking forward to this season in her life: to dancing and flirting and kissing and love poems and notes ferried by trusted friends, and secret meetings in the garden, but when it came down to it, who would she have if she had a choice?

Micah was intriguing, but she didn't really trust him, even if a marriage to him were possible.

No one else came to mind except Amon, and that would never be either.

She looked up to find her father gazing at her sympathetically, as if he could read her mind.

"Save at least one dance for me." He kissed her on the forehead, and was gone.

Following the incidents in Southbridge and his lack of success in having Mac Gillen booted from the Guard, Edon Byrne had proposed reassigning Amon to a less treacherous neighborhood, where there would be less opportunity for Gillen to take revenge.

Amon had refused the reassignment. Absent a posting to Raisa's personal guard (which carried its own risks and temptations), there was nowhere else he'd rather be than on the meanest streets of Fellsmarch. So instead of reassigning Amon, Edon transferred his Oden's Ford classmates to Southbridge Guardhouse, so he'd have someone to watch his back.

One thing was true—Southbridge was a great place to learn. Amon learned more in two months than in a year at Oden's Ford. Though, to be fair, it was a different curriculum, to a different purpose. He knew he'd need the theory and strategy and history he'd studied at Wien House as an officer.

In Ragmarket and Southbridge, he learned how to defuse a potentially violent situation without drawing his sword. He learned to look into a man's face and predict whether he would run or fight, whether he was lying or telling the truth. He learned how to put a victim at ease, so he could get the information he needed to track down a thief. When trouble was brewing, he could smell it in the air.

Amon developed networks of residents who began to trust that he wouldn't betray them if they fed him information about thieves or tipped him off to a gang fight. The other soldiers at the Southbridge Guardhouse—the good ones—learned that he wouldn't betray them either, and they began to turn to him for leadership of sorts.

All in all, Amon felt that he was doing some good, despite Mac Gillen. Best of all, his successes were a constant irritant to his sergeant.

One night he and his patrol returned to Southbridge Guardhouse to find his father waiting in the briefing room, maps spread over a long table. It was two a.m., and a rumble of snores came from the next room. Jak Barnhouse, the duty officer, was hovering, practically wringing his hands.

"I know Sergeant Gillen would want to speak with you, if he was here," Corporal Barnhouse said. "I don't know where he is just now."

"The rest of you, give your reports to Corporal Barnhouse and get some sleep," Edon said, waving off Amon's squadron. "I need to speak with Corporal Byrne in private."

They shuffled off with Barnhouse, looking over their shoulders like they were hoping Captain Byrne would relent, and they'd be asked to stay.

"Sit." Amon's father gestured to a chair. "At ease." The captain's face was etched with lines of weariness, and Amon felt a twinge of worry.

Amon sat, resting his hands on the table. "What is it, Da?"

"I need to ask a favor."

"Anything."

"I know you—ah—prefer your posting here in Southbridge." Here, a trace of a smile came and went. "But I need you and your triple to come back to the castle close and serve as personal guard to the princess heir."

Amon frowned, confused, then looked around to make sure no one could overhear. "But . . . but I thought you said it was best if I kept my distance since . . . since the complaint from the Bayars. That people would talk."

His father studied Amon's face for a long moment, then said, "People will talk, that is a risk, but greater risk has come up, so I'll deal with this one."

"What do you mean?"

"Queen Marianna is sending Averill Demonai and me to Chalk Cliffs to look into reports of pirates," Edon said. "Tomorrow."

Amon still didn't understand. "What does that have to do with the princess heir?"

"I have a bad feeling about it, that's all," his father growled, raking a hand through his salt-and-pepper hair. Then, after a long pause, he added, as if the words were difficult to say, "My connection with the queen has been . . . muddied. Usually I can predict what she'll do, guess what she's thinking, but lately . . . I don't know. Something's changed. I almost feel as though she wants to get us out of the way."

"Why would she want to do that?" Amon felt stupid, asking question after question, but he'd figured he rather know than take a guess. "And . . . if she does . . . I mean, she is the queen and all."

Amon pressed the heel of his hand against his forehead as if it hurt. "I'm just not sure she's making good decisions. She may have good reasons for doing what she's doing. I just don't understand them. But I'm going to do what I need to to protect the line. And if I'm wrong, then . . ." He shrugged.

"Well, then. You sent my triple to bed." Amon rose to his feet. "Shall I wake them and tell them to get ready to leave?"

His father shook his head. "There's something else. Something important." He waved him back to his seat.

Amon sat down again, waiting, smothering a yawn. He'd do whatever his captain, his father, wanted him to do. That was a given. So why couldn't they all get some sleep?

His father cleared his throat. "In the clan, as you know, there is a naming ceremony, in which the young are confirmed in their vocation. Among the gentry here in Fellsmarch, name day parties mark passage into adulthood."

"Right," Amon said, and was tempted to add, *I know*, but didn't.

"We Byrnes have our own rite of passage," his father said.

"We Byrnes?" Amon looked up at his father's face, thinking he was joking, but found no trace of humor there. "What do you mean?"

"Our family has a special bond with the queens of the Fells, going back to Hanalea. It often passes to the eldest in each generation. Unless he or she refuses. Then it goes to the next child."

"The captain of the Queen's Guard has always been a Byrne," Amon said. "Is that what you mean?"

"It's a Byrne for a reason," his father said. "A soldier named Byrne died for Hanalea when she was taken by the Demon King. That soldier's son helped to free her. When she returned to the throne, she proclaimed that henceforth the captain of her Guard would be bound to the queen, blood to blood, so he would be better able to do his job. That soldier's son was the first to be bound. Your many-greats-grandfather."

"So," Amon said, trying to understand, "you are . . . bound to Marianna. Is that what you're saying?"

"And my mother was bound to Lissa. And her father to Lucia."

"How does that work? Do you swear an oath, or . . ."

"It's more than an oath. There is a temple ceremony, a binding ritual. And after that, your destinies are linked. We serve the line of Gray Wolf queens. The bond cannot be broken. We cannot knowingly act contrary to the good of the line."

"It's *magic*, then?" Amon said, and his father nodded.

"What happens if you *do* act contrary to the good of the line?" Amon asked. His father shook his head. "We don't That's the thing. We are physically incapable of doing so."

This was more than surprising. Amon had always considered his family the least magical of any he knew. In fact, he'd always felt left out and rather colorless next to those that had it, like wizards, clan royalty, even the queens.

The Byrnes were dependable, steady, honest, hard-working, loyal—courageous to a fault. The kind of men and women you would want to have fighting beside you or covering your back or guarding the treasury. But magical?

Amon struggled to come up with something to say other than, *Are you sure?* Or, *You're not serious?*

"You have magical powers, then?" he asked.

His father laughed, rubbing his chin as if embarrassed. "Well, it's a subtle thing."

"The queen—she knows about this?"

Byrne shook his head. "The queens do not. That's the way Hanalea wanted it—she was more interested in preserving the Gray Wolf line than in supporting an individual queen."

"Are you bound to the line, or to an individual queen?"

"I'm bound to the line, but in effect, each captain serves one queen, unless that queen somehow endangers the line. His father paused, then added, softly, "We don't discuss that particular charge with our queens, either."

"So . . . there may be times when we act contrary to the interests of our sovereign queen in order to serve the line?"

"Aye," his father said, without apology. "Even if Marianna knew, I doubt she'd take it all that seriously. You know how she is about the temples and the faith. For her, it's rather like believing in garden pixies."

"So," Amon said, looking for the point in this bit of history. "You'll choose your successor when the time comes."

"The next captain in line would serve Raisa. I've chosen you."

Amon sat stunned, his thoughts swirling, a kaleidoscope of images and memories.

How had he ended up here, in this place, poised to assume the role that fate had handed him?

His father had tutored him in swordplay and horsemanship, but no more so than any other father. He'd spent long hours around the Guard barracks and stables at the castle, because his father was posted there, and he was interested in horses, and he loved to hear the talk of tactics and weaponry.

No one had ever said to him, *Go to Oden's Ford and learn to be a soldier.* But he had. And no one had ever said to him, *Join the Queen's Guard.* But he had. Serving in the Guard was a family tradition, though he had many aunts and uncles who had not.

But always, of course, at least one per generation had.

Since he'd been named to the Guard, he'd considered the possibility he might end up captain if he performed well and stayed with it. After all, he'd come in as a corporal, based on his performance at school and the recommendations of his father's friends. He was a skilled swordsman, the best in his class, and excelled in his coursework and received high marks in field operations. Everyone said he took after his father. And he was proud of that.

He'd always assumed, however, that he'd chosen his own way from a range of possibilities. That if he'd wanted to be a trader, or a blacksmith, or an artist like his sister, he could have done it. And now it turned out he'd been treading a narrow path, committed from birth, walled in by magic and a bargain made a thousand years ago.

"You do have a choice," his father said, as if he'd read his thoughts.

Amon looked up at his father. "*How* do I have a choice? Lydia becomes captain?"

"She is a Byrne," his father said.

Amon thought of his dreamer of a sister sitting on the riverbank, skirts spread about her, head bent over a charcoal drawing. He shook his head wordlessly.

"And if she says no, there's Ira," his father said, naming

Amon's ten-year-old brother. "Though he's still young, and we need to choose a captain now." He paused. "You have cousins, of course."

"Why now?" Amon asked. "There can be only one captain of the Guard, and that's you." Perhaps by the time a decision needed to be made, he'd have time to get used to the idea.

"I'm worried about the Princess Raisa. Right now we have no direct connection with her, and my connection with Queen Marianna seems to be failing. If you're willing, bonding with Hanalea's line through Raisa will give you something of a sixth sense. You'll be able to anticipate trouble, to know when she's in danger, to predict what she might do. It's also supposed to give us some influence over them, where their safety is concerned." He smiled wryly.

That won't do any good, Amon thought. They'll do whatever they want anyway.

"This is . . . permanent, I take it?" Amon asked. "What if I change my mind?"

"It is permanent," his father said, toying with the ring on his left hand, the heavy gold wolf ring he was never without. "You won't change your mind once it's done." He paused, smiled faintly. "Don't worry. It's not as if you're going into orders. You can marry, have children, all of that."

To continue the line of Byrnes, of course.

"And if it comes down to a choice between family and queen?"

His father looked into Amon's eyes, his hazel gaze clear and direct. "The queen, of course."

Of course. Amon already knew the answer when he

asked the question. In his heart of hearts he'd known his father's priorities all along.

"What about Oden's Ford? Would I go back, or . . . ?"

"We'll see how things stand when the time comes. It may be you'll go back. Whatever serves the line." His father sighed. "I'd wanted you to complete your training before your naming. But I don't think we can risk waiting."

But—there was this other thing Amon had avoided thinking about. His feelings for Raisa. Even now his heart beat faster when he thought of her. Images rolled through his mind—Raisa, dressed as a boy, in that ridiculous cap, striding unarmed into Southbridge Guardhouse to save gang members who were being tortured. Raisa delivering name day gifts to Speaker Jemson to feed the poor. Raisa demanding that he help her become a better queen.

Raisa in the garden by torchlight—her hair hanging in long strands around her face, chin propped on her fist, green eyes deep enough to drown in. Raisa floating in his arms around the dance floor, her head against his shoulder, her small perfect body pressed against his while he tried to control the hammering of his heart. He remembered those two kisses that she'd probably given without a thought.

Two kisses that still woke him up at night.

Everything about her seduced him—her looks, her speech, the way she moved, the person she was and was meant to be.

"Da," he said, staring down at the table, unable to meet his father's eyes, "the thing is, I'm . . . I have feelings for Raisa—for the princess heir—that I shouldn't have. I'm worried that

I might—that we might—do something that would . . . harm the line."

Amon swallowed hard and looked up into his father's face and saw something that he never expected to see—understanding layered over sorrow.

"Amon," he said. "We love the Gray Wolf queens. But it's like I told you. Once named, we will not harm the line. It is our great strength, and also our burden."

Amon stared at his father. He thought of his mother, dead in childbirth with Ira, and wondered if she had known. By the standards of the day, Edon Byrne had been a good husband and an attentive father, faithful to duty and queen. Now he seemed like a tragic figure, a holder of secrets.

What about my own choice? Amon thought. Raisa would never be his; he knew that. But if he took himself off to Oden's Ford, and after that to a posting at Chalk Cliffs, chances were the pain would fade in a decade or so. He was only seventeen.

What would it be like to be with Raisa constantly for the rest of his life, as her captain and counselor, to see her married, always within reach, knowing he could never have her?

Like his father and Queen Marianna.

But what if he said no, and something happened to Raisa? How could he forgive himself?

His father said he had a choice, and he did. The right thing and the wrong thing.

Amon reached across the table and gripped his father's callused hands. "I'll do it," Amon said.

His father looked down at their joined hands. "You're sure?"

Amon nodded. "I'm sure."

"Then let's go to temple," Edon Byrne said, rising from his chair.

Although it was now four in the morning, Speaker Jemson was waiting for them in his study, dressed for ceremony.

His father had told the speaker they were coming. His father had known what his decision would be.

So much for choices.

"Captain Byrne," the speaker said gravely. "And Corporal Byrne. This is most unusual, to preside over the binding of both father and son. Usually one captain passes on before the next is named."

"These are dangerous times," Edon Byrne said. "Still, the line must be protected."

"Yes, it must," Jemson said. He looked at Amon. "You have agreed to be bound to Hanalea's line?"

"Yes." Amon nodded. He found himself wishing he'd been able to bathe before coming here. He felt filthy and unworthy in his stained uniform, after a night patrolling Ragmarket.

As if Jemson had heard his thoughts, he extended a bundle of cloth toward Amon. "Remove your clothing and put these on. Then join us in the Lady Chapel." Jemson and his father left him alone in the study.

Remove all of his clothing? Or just his uniform? Amon didn't want to get it wrong. He debated, then stripped completely. The robes were rough-spun cotton, undyed, of the sort acolytes wore. He felt rather strange and airy under the voluminous tent of fabric—as if he were still naked.

Amon padded barefoot across the cavernous sanctuary to

the intimate Lady Chapel to the right of the altar. It was dedicated to Althea, Patroness of the Poor. Unlike the private chapels in the temple at Fellsmarch Castle, with their gold statuary and gilt and marble fittings, Althea's chapel was stark in its simplicity, yet obviously well loved. The simple wood altar shown with hand polishing, and there were fresh flowers in vases to either side of the image of the lady. Cool moonlight washed through the clear glass windows, echoing their design on the floor.

Jemson and his father stood to either side of a long table. Several objects were laid out in readiness: a large stone basin, a glittering knife, a stone jar, a small crystal bottle, a silver goblet. Amon studied the display, questions crowding his mind.

Jemson smiled at him. "Your part is quite simple, really, for so important a rite. We mingle your blood with Hanalea's, and you drink the result. The rest we pour into the soil of the Fells, to bind you to the land and the Maker. A sacrifice, of sorts."

I'm dreaming, Amon thought. Byrnes don't do these sorts of things. He thought of his triple sleeping in the barracks. Thought of Raisa back at Fellsmarch Castle, unaware of the link being forged between them. Was it fair to do this without her permission? What if she didn't want to be linked with him?

He licked his lips. "Will she . . . will she know?"

"She may feel something," the speaker said. "Or she may sleep through. If she does wake up she won't know what to make of it."

"Do you really have blood of Hanalea here?" After a thousand years?

"It is taken from her descendants, the queens of the Fells."
The speaker rested his hand on the stoppered bottle. "This is
the blood of the princess heir. I will speak words over it."

Jemson paused as if to see if Amon had any more questions. Then said, "Bare your arm, Corporal Byrne."

Amon did. He scarcely felt the sting of the blade, and
watched, a little amazed, as his blood dripped into the basin,
forming a small pool at the bottom.

Jemson lifted the crystal bottle and spoke some words in
clan speech. Amon made out the words *Raisa ana'Marianna*
and *Hanalea*. The speaker unstoppered the bottle and tipped
a few drops into the basin. Then lifted it high, swirling the
contents, reciting a long incantation.

Amon's thoughts slopped around in his head, mirroring
the mixture in the basin. He pressed his arm against his side to
staunch the flow of blood and felt the wet seep through to his
skin.

The speaker set the basin down, dipped the cup into it, and
lifted it, dripping.

Jemson broke into Valespeech. "Amon Byrne, of the line
of Byrnes, guardians of the line of Hanalea, we ask of you
this thing: that you be bound to the line of queens, and specifically to the blood and issue of Raisa *ana'*Marianna, princess
heir of the Fells. You will swear that her blood is your blood,
that you will protect her and her line until death takes you.
Will you?"

"I will," Amon said, his voice sounding loud in the silence
of the chapel.

"Then drink to signify."

Amon accepted the cup and raised it to his lips, preparing himself for the salty taste of blood. But it was sweet, like summer wine. His surprise was so great, he almost choked. Thankfully he didn't. He drank the full cup down and handed it back to Jemson.

The effect was immediate and dramatic, like being hit over the head with the broad side of a sword. Amon sank to his knees to keep from falling. Sensation flooded into him, overwhelming him, coming from wherever in the realm someone was thinking on the princess heir, or where something was happening that might touch on her future.

It was four in the morning, but Micah Bayar was awake, staring out his window in the castle on Gray Lady, his thoughts fixed on Raisa. The bakers in the royal kitchens shoved cakes into the ovens, thinking on the name day party for the princess heir, wondering if she would notice their efforts. Averill Demonai prepared to leave the city, worrying about the daughter he was leaving behind. Queen Marianna's mind was muddied, clouded by a healer's draft, but she still slept restlessly, dwelling on her daughter's launch into adulthood.

"Shut it out," his father said. "It's the only way at first. You'll get used to it."

Amon pressed his hands against his head, trying to filter some of it out, focusing on the tower room five miles away, where Raisa dreamed in her bed under the stars. She, too, slept restlessly, and Amon was surprised to find she was thinking about him, and whispering his name in her sleep.

"Come," the speaker said, and Amon's father helped him to

his feet, keeping a tight grip on his arm to prevent his falling. Jemson walked in front, carrying the basin, with Amon and Edon Byrne behind. They walked into the cloister garden, where the white spots of night-blooming flowers drew Amon's eye, and their intoxicating fragrance seduced him.

"Amon Byrne, we bind you to the bones of the queens buried in the soil of the Fells. You are bound to the queendom as you are to the queens of the Gray Wolf line. You will defend it as their dwelling place. You may leave the Fells, but this will always be your home."

Jemson poured the blood into the soil of the garden.

It was as though Amon were putting long roots down, deep into the soil, into the groundwater. He tasted the Dyrnnewater on his tongue and sucked in the breath of Hanalea.

As if in a dream, the speaker lifted his hand and slid the Gray Wolf ring into place on Amon's right ring finger. It fit perfectly.

His father embraced him, and the speaker was smiling and saying, "It's done."

CHAPTER TWENTY-TWO

DESPERATE MEASURES

Although Bird still spent most of her time with the Demonai warriors, she and Han found many opportunities to meet—at the cave, at a shelter on Ghost Lake, or on the banks of Old Woman Creek. They even met at Lucius's cabin a time or two when Han knew the old man would be out fishing.

He couldn't have said why they felt like they should keep their new relationship a secret. It was as if they didn't need to deal with all the conflicts around them, if they kept this part of their lives hidden away. Or maybe the whole thing seemed so fragile that it needed sheltering, a seedling that might get tromped on.

Or maybe, as it turned out, it was an instinct for self-preservation.

Bird made Han feel connected, like less of an outsider because she'd chosen him. He wished she weren't going away. If she weren't leaving, he might have settled into clan life and accepted Willo's offer to teach him a trade.

Still, as the time drew nearer for Bird to leave for Demonai Camp, and Dancer for Oden's Ford, Han felt more and more as if he were sitting on a sandbar in a river of events, and it was rapidly washing away beneath him. Soon he'd be alone, marooned at Marisa Pines, while his friends among the clan moved on to new adventures.

Unless he left Marisa Pines and went to Demonai with Bird. He'd never been to the high country camp in the western Spirits, and he didn't know anyone who lived there except a few of the traders. Still, if he was going to be an exile anyway, he might as well see the small part of the world he had access to.

If he couldn't go with Bird and the Demonai warriors, maybe he could find work with a trader who traveled between the camps, and still see her sometimes.

He knew he'd need to ask Willo for permission, so he sought her out one morning when she was mixing medicines in the hearth room of the Matriarch Lodge.

"Bring me the blue bowl, Hunts Alone," she commanded, gesturing toward her storage shelves. Willo was never one to let a person sit idle when she was working.

He handed it to her, and she emptied what looked like chunks of yellow chalk into her mortar and began grinding them into a brilliant powder.

"Willo, I've been thinking about moving to Demonai," he said, squatting next to her.

She said nothing, but scraped the yellow powder into a cup.

"There's a lot more trade going that way into Tamron because of the war in Arden," he added.

"Fetch me the turtle weed," she said, without looking up.

He lifted down the aromatic branches that hung under the eaves of the lodge and handed them to her. She pulled the leaves free, one by one, and dropped them into the mortar.

"So. I could work with one of the traders over there," he said, unsettled by her lack of response. "Maybe you could introduce me."

"I said I would find you work at Marisa Pines," Willo said.

"I know. Thank you. But I just think Demonai might—"

"You cannot go with Bird." She rammed the pestle into the mortar as if to emphasize her words.

He blinked at her. Willo'd always been good at reading people, but he'd thought he and Bird had been discreet. Was it possible everyone knew they were seeing each other?

"I wouldn't have to travel with her. I could go on my own," he said. "Or travel with one of the pack trains."

"It won't work," she said, finally setting aside her mortar and dropping her hands into her lap. "You and Digging Bird, I mean."

"What do you mean? We aren't . . ." he began, but the look on her face shut off the lie. "Why wouldn't it work?"

"You're not right for each other," she said.

"How can you say that?" he said. "We've been friends forever."

"You were friends as children. Now Bird has been named a Demonai warrior. She must follow that path. You must go another way."

"I don't understand," Han said, and he didn't. "She's not allowed to have friends? Or is it because I'm not clan?"

Willo didn't look as if she was enjoying this conversation any more than he was. "It's a calling, the Demonais. You must accept it. It's not easy for any of us. There's a barrier between Bird and Dancer too, that wasn't there before. Because of who and what they are."

"That's Reid Demonai's fault," Han said. He stood, towering over Willo, and that should have made him feel powerful, but it didn't. "I think the real war with wizards was over a thousand years ago," he said. "Since then, the Demonai have been living off their reputations. They're all saber-rattling and stories."

"It is not Reid Demonai's fault," Willo said, her voice like silk plied with steel. "It's tradition built on more than a thousand years of conflict between wizards and the clan. It's the role of the Demonai to keep wizards in check—by force, if necessary."

"So they're fighting *Dancer*? They can't find anything better to do? Or is it because he's an easy target?"

It was a long time before Willo answered, and Han found himself shifting from one foot to the other.

"He *is* an easy target," she said finally, looking up at him, her dark eyes swimming with pain. "Why do you think I'm sending him to Oden's Ford? They'll kill him otherwise."

Han quit shifting and settled his weight squarely. "Then you can't let Bird join the Demonai," he said. "Make her stay here."

"It is out of my hands," Willo said, picking up the pestle again. "She is called, you are not. You cannot go with Bird."

She looked up at him, appeal in her eyes. "Why don't you stay here with me and learn about healing? You already know plants, and you'd be closer to your mother and sister."

"I'm no healer," Han growled, thinking he seemed to be better at causing pain than relieving it. "I don't know what I am, but I'm not that." He turned around and stalked out of the lodge.

Bird wasn't any more help. That night they lay side by side on the bank of Old Woman Creek, connected by their clasped hands and recent kisses. The branches overhead leaked moonlight onto their faces. For once the music of water over stone failed to soothe him.

"I want to go with you to Demonai," he said, staring up at the canopy of trees.

"I wish you could," she said.

I want to go, he'd said. Not *I wish I could go.* Maybe he should have said, *I'm going.*

When Han didn't reply, Bird hurried on. "It would be hard. Reid says we'll be traveling the rest of the summer, and I'll be learning way-finding and weapons and . . . and the rest."

"But you'd be based there, right? After all the training?"

"Based there, but I won't be there much. The Demonai warriors spend most of their time on the move." Turning onto her side, she propped up on her elbow and brushed the hair off Han's forehead. He resisted the urge to flinch away. "Maybe . . . maybe after I see how things are, maybe once this summer is over, you could come," she said.

"Maybe," he said noncommittally, wanting to wound her. "We'll see."

With that option closed to him, he turned back to his plan to go with Dancer to Oden's Ford. He wondered how he could make it happen, when everyone around him seemed opposed to it. He tried going around Willo, approaching several of the silversmiths at the Marisa Pines Market, asking if they knew how to remove his cuffs, and if they'd make him an offer for the metal.

They tried their saws and cutters and knives with no effect. When he told them it didn't matter if the cuffs were damaged, they tried their irons, heating the metal, burning and blistering Han's wrists in the process. He needn't have worried about damage to the cuffs. The silversmiths got nowhere. They didn't even scratch the surface of the metal, or damage the runes inscribed there.

The answer was always the same. They were interested in the silver, intrigued with it, in fact, but had no idea how to get the bracelets off. Or how to work the silver if they did.

The only other thing he could think of was to retrieve the amulet that still lay hidden in the stable yard and find a buyer for it. He saw no reason why he couldn't turn the amulet into enough girlies to support Mam and Mari and attend Wien House too.

No reason except Lucius, who'd told him to keep it out of the Bayars' hands.

But he wouldn't need to take it back to the Bayars. He knew lots of dealers from his previous life as a thief. He could sell it in Southbridge Market. What were the chances that the Bayars would ever go to Southbridge? They never had before.

He chose not to listen to the voice in his head that said

that it wasn't his to sell. That said, if he sold it in Fellsmarch it might still make its way back to the previous owners.

Anyway, he'd had nothing but bad luck since he'd picked the amulet up off the ground on the slopes of Hanalea. Maybe this was a chance to change his luck and improve his fortune.

The idea grew in his mind, until he became convinced that he had no choice.

He decided to leave for the city in the late afternoon, reasoning that he could arrive there under cover of darkness when the guard changed. He'd go straight to Ragmarket and fetch the amulet. He could be back in Southbridge when the markets opened and be on his way up Hanalea while the blue-jackets were still wiping sleep from their eyes.

He slid his money pouch under his shirt, next to his skin. He'd made a little money working for Willo and running errands in camp for anyone who'd pay. Not near enough. He wrapped some smoked trout and flat bread in a napkin and tucked it into his carry bag. Finally he pulled a cap over his pale hair, hoping it would make him stand out less and not more, and it was cool in the mountains. In the Vale the weather would be warm, but when people described him, they always said, "The fair-headed one."

There was little traffic on the trail into Fellsmarch at that time of day, mostly hunters and traders on their way home. He made a wide circle around Lucius's place, not wanting to run into the old man. Han hadn't seen Lucius since the day he'd found him mourning Han's tragic death. Han wondered if Lucius had got another boy to take his place. That stung a little.

He passed through the city gate just at dusk with a crowd

of acolytes from the local temple, all about his age. They'd been gathering blackberries on the slopes of Hanalea.

He kept to the back ways until he reached South Bridge. It seemed that things had cooled off after all. Two sleepy blue-jackets manned each end of the bridge, and no one seemed to be looking for Han Alister.

Lucius had told him word was out that he was dead. Han decided that being dead made travel through the city much easier.

Once across the bridge, Han wove through the familiar web of Ragmarket, heading for home. It was still not fully dark, though the sun had descended behind Westgate, and a few stars pricked the pale sky. This far north, the days were long in midsummer. Those enterprises that required the cover of darkness were compressed into a few intense hours.

Han's heart beat faster. He loved summer nights in the city, when music poured from the open doors of taverns and ven-dors grilled sausages and fish on the sidewalks, and the drunks in the alleys never froze to death. Fancy girls joked with the bluejackets, and people played hard, intoxicated by the notion that anything could happen. And probably would. The streets were more dangerous, yet in some ways more forgiving in the summertime.

The last time he'd been home, Ragmarket and Southbridge had been unnaturally quiet, spooked by the series of Southie murders. Now it was more like he remem-bered it, when he was running with the Raggers.

As he neared home, he began seeing yellow flags nailed onto doors or hanging out of windows, signifying the presence of remittent fever. In the summertime, the yellow flags sprouted in certain neighborhoods, like a crop of garish death flowers or the bright yellow brain fungus that sometimes grew on dead trees.

That was the dark side of summer.

Some said the fever was due to bad air. Willo said it was caused by bad water. Whatever it was, it was confined to the Vale. It was never a problem in the upland camps.

When he reached the stable yard, he looked up to the second floor of the stable and saw a yellow rag stuffed between sash and sill.

Han slammed his way into the stable and took the stairs two at a time. When he flung open the door, he was met by the stink of every kind of sick.

Mari lay on her pallet next to the hearth. Although the air in the room was stifling, the fire was lit and Mari was piled high with blankets, shivering uncontrollably. Mam sat on the floor next to her, leaning against the wall. She blinked up at Han, like she'd fallen asleep sitting there.

"She was better this morning," Mam said, "but the fever's coming back." She said this matter-of-factly, as if she was too weary to react to his sudden appearance after a month away. Her hair had crept out of its plait, half of it hanging around her face. Her bodice was soiled and stained, hanging loose on her body as though she were using herself up.

Han crossed the room and knelt next to Mari's bed. He laid his hand on her forehead. She was burning up. "How long has she been sick?"

Mam rubbed her forehead. "This is the tenth day."

The tenth day. She should be recovering by now. If she was going to.

"Is she eating and drinking?" Willo said a high fever dried people out, so you had to keep getting them to drink. Plus, the fever gave you the runs.

Mam shook her head. "She don't want to take anything when the fever is high."

"Are you giving her willow bark?" This was the extent of his knowledge of healing—the botanicals he collected for Willo and others.

"I was." Mam stared down at her hands. "We're out now." She looked up at him, hope kindling in her eyes. "Do you have any money?"

"A little. Why?"

"There's a healer up in Catgut Alley. People say he can work wonders. But he costs money."

Han took his eyes off Mari and focused on the room around them. It was more barren than usual. There were no baskets of laundry, no sign of food, nothing.

Mam put a hand on his arm. "Would you send your washing where they have the fever?" she asked, as if she could read his mind. "Besides, I haven't been able to leave her on her own, to pick up and deliver."

A bucket of water with a dipper sat next to Mari's bed. "Where'd this water come from?" Han asked Mam.

"The well at the end of the street," Mam said. "Like always."

He grabbed up the bucket and poured the contents into their second-best cooking pot and set it over the flames. "Let this boil a while, and when it cools down you can use it for washing."

"I *know* how to do laundry, Hanson Alister," Mam said, with a little of her old spirit.

"I'm going to go fetch some water from another well," he said. And he did that, walking blocks uptown to the pump at Potter's Square and back. He spent his remaining money on a bit of willow bark and some barley soup for Mari, though he had to wake up the apothecary at the market for that. He got sworn at for his trouble, and paid a pretty price for it too.

By the time that was all done and delivered, it was near dawn. Mari took some clean water and willow bark and barley soup, though she complained she wasn't hungry. After that she looked better and slept more peacefully, and he told himself the color in her cheeks wasn't only fever, and the improvement wasn't just the lull before the fever roared back.

So here it was. More bad luck, worse than he'd ever had before. It had to be the bloody amulet. He had to get rid of it before somebody died.

He needed money. Mam and Mari needed money—for a healer and for everything else. He couldn't expect them to keep hanging on by their fingernails while he lived in relative comfort at Marisa Pines, or wherever else he went. The Guard wasn't looking for him now, but that would change once they spotted his formerly drowned corpse all lively and walking the streets.

Leaving Mam and Mari sleeping, he descended the stairs, murmuring to the horses he'd ignored on his way in. Under cover of darkness, he slipped back to the stone forge in the stable yard and wrestled the stone out of its niche. The leather-wrapped bundle still lay where he'd left it. He could feel the heat emanating from it before he lifted it out.

Carefully, he pulled away the wrapping, revealing the serpent amulet. It flared up, excruciatingly bright, illuminating the yard as if it meant to betray the thief who'd stolen it. He hurriedly rewrapped it, glancing around to make sure no one had noticed.

He slid the amulet into his carry bag and slung it over his shoulder, pulled his cap down over his face, and headed for Southbridge Market. When he reached the bridge, he nodded to the sleepy bluejackets, once again passing between the temple and the guardhouse, wondering what Jemson would think of his former student, and who Mac Gillen was beating these days.

The butcher was just cranking open his awning. He had one of the few permanent structures at the market. The mushroom man was setting baskets of morels and chicken-head fungus out in front of his shop. Han walked past them without speaking and without making eye contact. Han's home market was Ragmarket. He didn't know most of the vendors at Southbridge, which was a good thing on this particular day.

Taz Mackney was another prosperous vendor at the market. His shop was larger than most, filled with exotic fabrics, seductive fragrances, rare artwork, and precious stones—loose and set into jewelry. What most people didn't know was that much of Taz's prosperity derived from his side business in magical pieces, many of them stolen or, at least, of questionable provenance. The Naéming might forbid the buying and selling of talismans and amulets made before the Breaking, but for the right price, Taz could find most anything for a discreet client.

Han only knew this because he'd sold goods to Taz in the past. He didn't always get the best price from Taz, but he liked dealing with him because he had a permanent location, unlike many of the fences who worked the streets. Taz knew the Raggers could always find him again if he cheated them. He also had connections with rich clients who could pay big money for a rare piece. Taz had another, more prestigious location in the castle close, frequented by the gentry, including wizards.

The bell over the door jangled as Han entered the shop. Taz was sitting in the back, his bald head bent over his books. Without looking up he growled, "Not open yet. Come back later."

"If you want," Han said. "But it's your loss. I'll see who else is ready to do business."

Taz looked up, startled. "Cuffs? Blood of the demon!" He lurched to his feet with amazing speed for one so bulky. The dealer glanced out the front windows and then jerked his head toward the back. "Let's go in the back room."

Han followed him back, past bins of beads and shelves lined with bottles of potions larded with time-darkened wax. Rolled-up rugs in brilliant colors stood in the corners, and intricate puzzle boxes, sconces, and candles lay everywhere.

Once through the back door, Taz took refuge behind the large desk that Han knew housed at least three knives and an assassin's dagger. The dealer wore a long velvet coat and a froth of lace at his neck. His belly poured over his breeches, poking out through his coat. Here was someone who was eating well.

"I hear you're dead," Taz said bluntly.

Han nodded, assuming a mournful expression. "Got done in by the Southies," he said. "I sort of like being dead."

Taz laughed his great booming laugh that made you think he wasn't as smart as he really was. "Understood, my boy. To what can I attribute this extracorporeal apparition?"

Taz liked to use big words.

"I've an amulet you might be interested in," Han said.

"Thought you were out of the game," Taz said, his eyes narrowing.

Han shrugged. "I am. Special case. I'm vamping it for a friend."

"Ah. A friend. Of course." Taz's eyes lighted with interest. He'd bought some rare pieces from Han in the past.

"It'll be pricy," Han warned. "I won't let it go for a smile and a promise. If you're short on iron, just say so."

"Have no worries on that account," Taz said, trying to look disinterested. "However, you should know that, given the idiosyncrasies of the current market, I may not be in a position to make a very generous offer. Unfortunately, I've seen less demand for magical objects in recent months."

Han reached into his carry bag and pulled out the amulet. He took his time, all part of the game. He set the parcel on the desk, carefully pulled away the leather.

The light from the stone turned Taz's face a sickly green.

The dealer stared at it for a long moment, then looked up into Han's face. "Where'd you get this?" he whispered.

"I said. From a friend. He's going out of the magic business," Han said.

Taz impulsively reached for it, but Han gripped his wrist. "Don't touch it," he said. "It's dangerous."

Taz swallowed hard. "Right," he said, his supply of big words seemingly dried up. "Well. It's a shame it's so unstable. That will make it hard to sell." He thought a moment. "Ten girlies," he said. "Take it or leave it."

Han could have used ten girlies just then, but he knew he was being lowballed. He shook his head and began rewrapping the amulet.

Taz watched this for a few seconds, then said, "Twenty-five."

Han stuffed the amulet into his carry bag. "Thank you for your time, Taz," he said, turning away.

"Wait!" Taz said quickly.

Han turned and waited.

Taz licked his lips. Beads of sweat stood out on his broad forehead. Evidence that he wanted the piece and wanted it bad.

"I could turn you over to the bluejackets, you know. It's in your best interest to come to terms."

Han shrugged and ran his hand over the interior wall. "This place could burn down, you know. Maybe even with you inside. That'd be a shame."

Taz cleared his throat. "I thought you were out of the business," he repeated.

Han lifted his hands, palms up. "Can you ever really leave the business?"

Taz nodded grudgingly. "Cuffs, you've always had an astute head for commerce. Very rare in one so young."

Han grinned. "Well, thank you, Taz. That and three coppers gets me a pork bun."

"What do you want for it?"

"A hundred girlies, minimum. But I'll be showing it around the market and taking the best offer I get, so you'd best aim high." Han kept his voice casual, glancing around the shop and fingering a silver chalice as if he might be in the market. A hundred girlies hadn't passed through his hands in his lifetime.

"Look, I'm not in a position to buy it outright for the money you want, but I may have clients who would be willing to make an offer. Leave it with me, on consignment, and we'll see what the response is."

Han shook his head. "Can't do. I only have the one, and I have several other dealers to show it to. I an't giving it up until there's money in hand."

Taz clearly didn't want to see the amulet walk out the door. "Where can I reach you?"

"You can't." Han said. "Better work fast. I won't be in town for long. I'll check back day after tomorrow."

CHAPTER TWENTY-THREE

NAME DAY 2

Raisa awoke the next morning, unrefreshed. She'd had the strangest dreams. They seemed to involve Amon, but they slipped away each time she reached for them. She snuggled down under the covers, hoping to enmesh herself again, but her mind raced and sleep eluded her.

Her name day. The day she was officially proclaimed eligible to marry. The day she was officially named heir to the throne and began training for her role as queen.

Tonight, finally, the formal dance of suitors would begin.

Her dress hung on its form, a silhouette against the window, the shape of the person she was supposed to be. She'd issued no proclamations about dress for her party. She hoped for a riotous garden of color, but expected that most would wear virginal white.

Raisa looked awful in white—this was another bone of contention between her and her mother. She would have chosen black, but she'd have settled for crimson or even emerald green, to set off her eyes. She'd ended with a champagne-color satin and lace that exposed her shoulders. There was nothing girlish about it, at least.

Yawning, she climbed out of bed in her nightgown and padded into her sitting room. Magret had breakfast under way.

"I thought you'd sleep later, so as to be fresh for tonight," Magret said. "I could have brought you breakfast in bed."

Raisa stared at Magret. Her nurse was encouraging her to sleep in so she could stay out late. It was an entire season of firsts. "Well, I just couldn't sleep anymore," she said, sorting through the piles of cards, notes, and letters in the basket by the door. "Any word from my father?"

"No, Your Highness," Magret said. "But don't worry. If he's not here already, he's on his way. He wouldn't miss it."

"I know." Raisa couldn't shake a feeling of unease. "Could you . . . could you send to Kendall House and tell them to let me know as soon as he's arrived?" Her father had remained at Kendall House, since he was still out of favor with the queen.

Magret enfolded Raisa in her arms, patting her back. "Don't worry," she said. "It's just name day jitters. Tonight will be a night you'll always remember."

There are different reasons for remembering things, Raisa thought. Some good, some bad.

The rest of the day passed in a blur of bathing, buffing, combing, and coloring. "It probably takes less time to fit out a ship to go to sea," Raisa complained when the nail-painters left and the hairdressers filed in.

Still, no word came from Kendall House.

At six p.m., Raisa was laced into her dress. It fell in long silken folds from a high waist, and had wide romantic sleeves with insets of lace. In truth, she liked it very much.

There was the problem of Elena's ring again. Raisa was determined to wear it, yet her mother had given her a smoky quartz, citrine, and topaz necklace for her name day, a perfect match for her dress. Raisa slid the ring off its chain and tried it on every finger. It had seemed large before, but now she was surprised to find that it fit her middle finger perfectly. Her long trailing sleeves hid it from view.

At six thirty her mother swept in for a final inspection prior to the name day party. Queen Marianna's dress was a deep hunter green that perfectly set off her golden hair and luminous skin. Her necklace and tiara were set with emeralds.

Even in her name day finery, Raisa felt unimpressive in comparison. What would it be like to reign after such a queen? Would she be known as the short, dark, snappish queen that followed the golden one?

Queen Marianna gripped Raisa's elbows and held her out at arm's length.

"Oh, sweetheart," she said, eyes brimming with tears. "You *are* beautiful." It would have meant more if she hadn't sounded so surprised. "I cannot believe that this day has finally come. Please know that I only want what's best for you, always. Do you believe that, Raisa?"

Raisa nodded, that prickle of unease returning. "Have you seen Father since his return?" she asked. "He's to escort me into the hall, but I've not heard from him."

Queen Marianna frowned. "Really? You've not heard from him? I was sure he would be here."

"Of course he'll be here," Raisa said. "It's my name day."

Marianna hesitated. "That's true, yes, but remember, you've already celebrated the occasion at Demonai Camp. Perhaps he thought he'd already met his obligation."

Raisa blinked at her, confused a moment before she remembered. Supposedly her father had taken her to Demonai when she went missing in Southbridge.

"It's not an obligation," Raisa said. "He said he'd be here. He'd want to be." She paused, then rushed on. "Why did you have to send him to Chalk Cliffs now?"

Her mother sighed, sounding exasperated. "It's not that far, sweetheart. It should be no trouble to ride there and back over four days. Your crowning is important, but affairs of the realm cannot come to a halt for a week because of it." The queen smiled, her tawny eyes searching Raisa's face. "Don't worry. I'll send for him at Kendall House and tell him to come to you immediately, just to ease your mind." She kissed Raisa on the forehead. "All will be well, Raisa, you'll see."

She turned and left the room in a rustle of silk.

But time passed, and soon they would have to leave for the temple, and still her father did not come. Raisa peeked out into the corridor, and a stocky young guardsman snapped to attention outside the door.

"Your Highness?" the soldier said. "How may I assist?"

"Oh. I was just looking."

They stood there awkwardly for a moment. Then Raisa said, "Well, carry on," and pulled the door closed.

Unable to sit still, Raisa threw open the doors to the terrace and walked out into the sultry evening.

Thunder grumbled over Hanalea, Rissa, and Althea. Great pillars of clouds tumbled over the peaks, underlit with green-and-yellow lightning. The air was thick with the scent of rain, almost too thick to breathe, and the hair on Raisa's arms and the back of her neck prickled.

The wind picked up, setting the clouds in motion like gray wolves prowling over the distant hills. Raisa hunched her shoulders. Jitters, she said to herself. Just jitters.

Magret was as jumpy as Raisa. She picked through the messages on the front table as if she might find an undiscovered note from Averill. She fussed with Raisa's hair, her hemline, her makeup, and tugged at her laces until Raisa had to struggle not to scream at her.

Every time Magret opened her mouth, words spilled out in a nervous cascade. "Did you hear? Prince Gerard Montaigne of Arden is here. Right in the middle of the war, he's come up here, probably meaning to go home with a marriage contract in hand. He's the youngest of five brothers, so I don't know why he thinks the princess heir of the Fells would give him the time of day. That Prince Liam, now, he's a handsome boy, and such good manners. He's the heir to the throne of Tamron, you know."

Finally there was a knock at the door. Raisa jumped to answer it, but Magret, of course, beat her to it.

It was not her father. It was Gavan Bayar, High Wizard of the Fells, resplendent in silver and black to match his mane of silver hair and thick black brows.

"My Lord Bayar," Magret stammered. "I thought . . . We were expecting . . ."

Lord Bayar stepped past Magret and bowed low to Raisa. "Your Highness, you are a vision. I wish I were a younger man." He paused, his eyes traveling over her from head to toe. "Unfortunately, your father still has not returned from Chalk Cliffs. The queen has asked me to escort you to the temple." He offered his arm. "It would be my honor."

Raisa backed away, shaking her head. "Perhaps . . . he'll still come."

"Everyone is assembled," Lord Bayar said. "It is time. The queen requires your attendance."

Raisa bumped into her dressing table and leaned back against it, suddenly dizzy. There was something wrong about all of this. Every instinct screamed at her. The lamp on the table guttered in the breeze from the open door, and wolf shadows loped along the walls.

The stocky guardsman stood in the doorway, gripping the hilt of his sword. "Your Highness?" he said.

Magret stepped between Raisa and Lord Bayar, her face crinkled with dismay. "Her Highness doesn't feel well," she said. "Perhaps, if you gave her a few minutes . . ."

Anger kindled in Lord Bayar's blue eyes. "Step aside," he said. "We don't have a few minutes. The princess must come with me by order of the queen."

"It's all right, Magret," Raisa said, even though it most certainly wasn't all right. She straightened, shook her head to clear it, and nodded to the guardsman. "Be at ease. I'll go with Lord Bayar. It's kind of him to come and fetch me.

I'm sure Papa will be here in time for the dance."

Still ignoring Lord Bayar's arm, Raisa gripped her skirts on either side, lifted her chin, and walked ahead of him into the corridor. The guardsman followed along behind.

It was difficult to stay ahead of Lord Bayar's long legs, with her more limited stride and fancy shoes. Eventually she allowed him to take her elbow, feeling the sting of power through the wizard's fingers.

Use your trader face, she said to herself.

They followed the covered walkway from castle to church, crossing the courtyard that represented the separation between church and state, between holy and profane. The weather was growing worse, and the wind lashed strands of her carefully coiffed hair around her face. At any moment, it appeared the skies would open. She wondered if her father was out in the storm somewhere, trying to get home. She said a prayer to the Maker, and to Maia, the weather-maker, for his safe return.

The nave of the temple cathedral was candlelit and solemn, her path a long red-carpeted corridor between crowds of the glittering nobility, all craning their necks to catch their first glimpse of the princess heir. Raisa felt like a bride walking into temple on her father's arm. Except this wasn't her father, and this wasn't her wedding.

She could tell that the last-minute substitution of Lord Bayar for her father had not been announced. She heard a whisper roll through the crowd, saw a ripple of heads turning, driven by the usual gossips. Where was Averill Demonai, and why wasn't he here, and what did it all mean?

She wanted to stamp her foot and say, "This wasn't my idea."

Ahead of her, she saw her mother sitting in the queen's chair, her skirts spread around her, the heavier ceremonial crown on her head. And standing next to her, Raisa was surprised to see Speaker Jemson from Southbridge Temple, resplendent in gold and white. Even at that distance she could see the surprise on the speaker's face as Raisa entered with the High Wizard.

Then Raisa understood. Her father would have been in charge of the elements of faith. He would have been the one who invited Speaker Jemson to officiate.

Raisa walked the length of the temple, doing her best to ignore the wizard beside her, doing her best to keep her face a mask of solemnity while her heart pounded within her chest. Despite this distraction, a few images crystallized in her peripheral vision—for instance, the smile frozen on her cousin Missy Hakkam's face. Missy stood next to her brother, the handsome and equally vapid Jon. Kip and Keith Klemath were nudging each other, probably laying bets on who would win the game of courtship at the dance.

Her grandmother Elena stood with a handful of clan elders in Marisa Pines and Demonai ceremonial robes. With the elders were several Demonai warriors, including Reid Nightwalker, Raisa's rumored highland suitor.

As Raisa passed with the High Wizard, Elena leaned over to whisper something to Reid. Elena's face was impassive, but Reid was scowling.

Miphis and Arkeda Mander stood toward the front with Micah Bayar, a triple of wizards. Micah's banishment was over, it seemed. He was impeccably dressed, as usual, breathtakingly handsome, as usual, but he had a pale, rather feverish look, as if something didn't agree with him. His dark eyes followed her to the front of the temple.

A small honor guard stood to either side of the dais. Raisa looked for Captain Edon Byrne, who'd accompanied her father to Chalk Cliffs. He was missing also, but Amon was there in his dress uniform, standing ramrod straight, his hand on the hilt of his sword. He stared straight ahead, cheeks flushed, but she knew he saw her.

I dreamed about you, she thought.

And finally she was before Speaker Jemson and her mother. Lord Bayar released her elbow and stood to the side, next to her sister, the Princess Mellony.

Raisa looked into Speaker Jemson's eyes and saw compassion there. The speaker smiled. That buoyed her somehow, and she smiled back. Her pulse quieted and her fears ebbed. She would be queen, and queens ruled over wizards in the Fells.

"Friends, this is the season for name day ceremonies, and I have presided at many already," Jemson said. "It is always a privilege to launch a child into adulthood and to welcome a new citizen of the realm. But today we are assembled for a very special naming—one that builds on a tradition that has lasted for a thousand years. Today we name Raisa *ana*'Marianna, heir to Hanalea and the Gray Wolf throne."

Jemson looked out over the assembly. "The princess has already proved herself to be compassionate beyond her years. Her Briar Rose Ministry at Southbridge Temple serves hundreds of people every week. Families are fed and clothed, and children are educated because of her generosity. She is a fitting heir to Hanalea's legacy."

The queen looked up at Raisa, a startled expression on her face. Comment rustled through the crowd like wind through winter branches.

Speaker Jemson's voice flowed over Raisa, prompting her as she rededicated herself to the Maker, the Fells, and the line of queens. Her mother asked her the Three Questions, and she gave the Three Answers in a loud clear voice so she could be heard to the far end of the hall.

Raisa mounted the stairs onto the dais and knelt before her mother. Queen Marianna set the glittering Gray Wolf tiara on her head and said, "Rise, Princess Raisa, heir to the Gray Wolf throne."

Outside the temple, the storm broke, and hail clattered against the leaded windows. Her ancestors proclaiming their approval. Or were they shouting a warning?

Applause rolled from one end of the hall to the other, probably because it was time to go to dinner.

The main ballroom had been transformed into a fairy forest, its borders softened by groves of bare-branched trees sparkling with tiny wizard lights. The dining tables were set up at one end, in a woodland bower. The trees were hung with silver cages filled with songbirds.

At dinner, she sat next to the queen at the head of the table. Raisa insisted that Speaker Jemson take the chair on her other side, which should have been her father's (mostly to prevent Lord Bayar's occupying it). She was surprised when the queen readily agreed. Marianna seemed eager to please her often difficult daughter, anxious to fill the hole left by Averill's absence in any way she could.

While protocol would dictate that the southern princes be seated next in line after the royal family, Raisa noticed that her mother had seated them rather far down the table. Not only that, the Tomlins were seated across from a stranger, which, from his elaborate dress, must be the ambitious Gerard Montaigne, the youngest prince of Arden. He was slender, with hair the color of wet sand, and pale, almost colorless, blue eyes.

Elena Demonai and the other clan representatives were also seated at the far end of Raisa's table.

Raisa ate very little, feeling the weight of the tiara and her new title and the sting of her father's absence. She said very little too, but Speaker Jemson and Queen Marianna and Lord Bayar made up for her lack of conversation. Their voices splattered against her skin like rain on canvas, scarcely penetrating.

The queen seemed nervous, her smile forced, and she glanced anxiously in Raisa's direction as if unsure what the new princess heir might do. Speaker Jemson pretended to be relaxed and chatty, but Raisa thought the speaker missed nothing.

"The Princess Raisa has been a wonderful ambassador for the Gray Wolf throne in the city," he said.

"Has she now?" the queen said, fussing with her napkin.

"Oh yes. The street musicians sing her praises. The children at Southbridge Temple school leave flower garlands beneath her portrait in the sanctuary, and the temple dedicates have opened a new healing hall in her name."

"I had no idea," the queen said, poking at her roast quail, a faint frown on her face.

"Everyone praises you, Your Majesty, for raising a daughter with such a compassionate nature," he added, and the queen smiled.

Amon Byrne caught Raisa's eye several times from his post against the wall. He raised an eyebrow as if to say, *What's going on?*

Raisa began to relax a little when dinner was cleared away and they decended to the dance floor. Her dance card was already full, according to protocol, once they got past the awkwardness of the traditional father-daughter dance. (They skipped it.) The evening passed quickly, a kaleidoscope of male faces and brilliant plumage, a cacophony of flattery, the sting of wizard hands, the Klemaths resurfacing repeatedly like a bad dream.

She danced with Prince Gerard Montaigne and found him cold, intense, and condescending, a remarkable combination in a boy so close to her own age. He made no effort to woo or even flatter her, but cut right to politics.

"Does it concern you, Princess," he asked, in his harsh flatlander accent, "that though I'm the son of a king, I'm the youngest of five sons? Four of whom are living?"

"That depends," Raisa said, unable to resist. "Do you have older sisters as well?"

He stared at her a moment with eyes as pale and hard as glacier ice. "I have one older sister," he said. "But in Arden, the crown passes through the line of sons only."

"I see. Do you hope to marry a queen, then, so that your daughters will have an inheritance?" Raisa asked.

"Well . . . ah . . . I had not thought it," the prince

stammered. "I thought that it would make sense to . . . ah . . . marry our kingdoms—and our resources—together."

"I see. Our *king*doms. Well, then. I believe I did not answer your question. You asked whether I'm concerned that you're the youngest son?"

"Yes," Gerard Montaigne said. "I wanted to assure you that, given the situation in Arden, these are not insurmountable obstacles. If you can be patient, Your Highness, I fully expect to wear the crown in the end."

"I am not at all worried about your four brothers," Raisa said. "Although I think they have reason to be worried about themselves. I would, however, be very concerned about the succession in Arden if it seemed at all likely that we would marry."

Fortunately, at that point, the song ended. Raisa stepped back from Prince Gerard, pulling her hands free, though he didn't seem to want to let go of them. "Thank you for the dance, Your Highness," she said. "Have a safe journey home."

She could feel his eyes boring into her back as she walked away, head high. There's one southerner to cross off my list, she thought. He gives me the jittery shudders.

She was apprehensive when Micah's name came up on her dance card. She didn't know what to expect—some sort of proposition, a protestation of love, conspiratorial whispers— something. But she needn't have worried, it seemed. This time he was a perfect gentleman. He seemed so distracted, in fact, so distant, that Raisa asked him, a little sharply, what in the world he was thinking of, just as the music stopped.

"I'm thinking of nothing, Your Highness," he said, bowing

stiffly. "Nothing at all. It's a good skill to have. I recommend it." And he walked away, back straight.

Amon was a different matter. He gripped her hands so hard, she squeaked in pain, and he relaxed his hold. "Sorry," he said. "What is going on? Where is your father?"

"I was hoping you could tell me," Raisa replied. "Have you heard anything at all?"

"A bird came from Chalk Cliffs yesterday, saying that they had left for Fellsmarch yesterday morning," Amon said. "I expected them to arrive last night. I've heard nothing since." He paused. "They've probably stayed over somewhere for the night. What with this storm and all."

Rain clattered against the tiled roof of the temple, and the wind howled around the towers. And yet . . . they should have been here long before the storm began," she said. "I just . . . I have a bad feeling about this. An intuition. Something's happened, or it's going to happen, or both." She rested her head against Amon's shoulder, shivering a little.

"What could happen?" Amon murmured, his warm breath tickling her ear, his firm hand at her back, guiding her around the dance floor. "You're here, in Fellsmarch Castle, in the middle of a party, with your guardsmen around you." He sounded as if he were trying to convince himself. "This . . . intuition—how reliable is it? And, is there any way of knowing *what* or *when*?" Typical, practical Amon.

"I don't know," Raisa said, trying to sort through her feelings. She felt oddly safe there, enclosed within the circle of Amon's arms. Connected to him in a way she hadn't been before. It was as if a channel had opened between them, power and emotion rippling through, and she wished they could just circle forever.

Raisa cleared her throat, trying to concentrate on that other, more nebulous danger. "Magret says it's just name day jitters, and maybe she's right, but I would feel so much better if our fathers were here. I worry that something has happened to them."

"We can't do anything about them," Amon said. "So let's focus on you right now. If you're in danger, what's it likely to be?"

Raisa looked up at his face, afraid he was making fun of her, but he looked completely serious.

"Let's think, now. When would you be most vulnerable to—I don't know—assassins or kidnappers," he went on. "After the party, you'll be going back to your room. Maybe then."

Raisa gripped his elbows. "Stay in my room tonight, Amon," she said impulsively. "I'd feel safer if you did."

"Raisa, I can't do that," Amon said, his expression a mixture of what looked like regret and propriety.

"I don't really care what anyone thinks," Raisa persisted. "Besides, Magret will be there. She can chaperone."

"Right," he said. "Isn't she the one who fell asleep in the garden?" He chewed his lower lip. "I'll get the Wolfpack involved. We've been assigned to your personal guard. Beginning tomorrow."

Raisa stared at him. "Really? I thought your father wanted you to stay away from me."

"He changed his mind," Amon said. He took a breath as if he had something to add, but then shut his mouth and said nothing for an entire circuit of the dance floor.

"Anyway, I'm still worried about the tunnel that you haven't boarded up," he said finally. "When the dancing's done, I'll send some of the Wolfpack to watch the corridor to your room. You'll have your usual guard outside your door. I'll go up in the garden and watch the tunnel entrance. That's one night taken care of. And maybe by tomorrow, our fathers will be back."

That settled, they circled silently a moment. Amon still looked troubled, though.

"What's wrong?" Raisa asked.

"What if they don't come back? I'm supposed to leave for Oden's Ford in another week."

"Already?" Raisa felt a flicker of panic. "But the summer's not even over yet. It's only the end of July. You have all of August, and—"

"I'm taking the long way back to Oden's Ford. We're doing a little scouting for Da. But if he's not back, I can't leave you here on your own."

"He'll come, Amon; they both will, you'll see."

The music had stopped, signaling the end of the dance, and they coasted reluctantly to a standstill. Amon was leaning down, and their faces were inches apart. Gripping both his hands, Raisa whispered, "Thank you." She went up on her toes, sliding her arms around his neck, meaning to finish the dance with a chaste kiss, but just then they were interrupted.

"Your Highness?" The accented voice came from behind. "I believe I have reserved this dance."

Raisa whirled around and saw that it was Prince Liam

Tomlin, of Tamron. The prince offered a graceful bow. "Of course, if it's no longer convenient . . . ?"

"Your Highness," she said, and curtsied, her face burning with embarrassment. She really needed to pay better attention. Especially since Prince Liam was a possible match. "Of course it's convenient. I'm sorry. I was just . . ."

"Distracted," he said. "It happens." His smile was dazzling against his coppery skin.

Raisa looked over her shoulder, but Amon had disappeared.

The prince took her hand, and the orchestra launched into a waltz, a safe dance for southerners, in deference to the royal pair. The musicians needn't have worried. The prince danced with the unconscious grace of someone who'd grown up at court.

He was not especially tall, compared to Micah or Amon, but he was exceedingly well-dressed, in a blue coat and white breeches that displayed his lean, aristocratic build. Tamron was known for being the arbiter of style in the Seven Realms. Next to glittering Tamron Court, Fellsmarch was a backwater.

"It's not often that I must reserve a place on someone's dance card," Prince Liam said. "And wrench my partner from the arms of another. See how far the fortunes of the Tomlins have fallen."

Startled, Raisa studied the prince for evidence of arrogance, but found only a kind of self-deprecating good humor. She liked him at once.

"Right. Well, I'm trying to get used to the idea of being put on display like a fresh side of beef," Raisa said.

Prince Liam laughed out loud, a surprising full-bodied laugh. "Perhaps you subscribe to the notion that princes actually have control over their own lives. I beg to differ. We strut the boards, improvising like mad, only to learn that the script is already written, and we've got it wrong."

"Not always," Raisa countered. "I have to believe that sometimes we can write our own."

"You love your soldier, then?" The question was like a bold blade between the ribs, but Raisa deflected it.

"I am not talking about love," Raisa said, amending silently, Well, not *only* about love.

"I have a chance, then," he said, turning his head and displaying his handsome profile, framed by his tumble of black curls. He peered sideways at her to see if she'd noticed.

She laughed. "You are quite the poseur," she said.

"That is what I was going for," he replied cheerfully. "Everyone else in the room—they're all imposters."

"I'm not playing a role," Raisa said. "I want people to know who I am."

"You are young, Your Highness," Prince Liam said, sounding like one of her cynical elders.

"Why? How old are you?" Raisa demanded.

"I'm seventeen," he said.

I'm almost as old as you, she thought of saying, but didn't, since it sounded like something a child would say. "How goes the hunt for a wife?" she asked. "Any prospects?"

He laughed again. "They said you were blunt."

"They did? What else did they say?"

"They said you were willful, and stubborn, and smart." He

looked into her eyes. "And the most beautiful princess in the Seven Realms."

It was flattery, but it was still pleasant to hear.

"Indeed? I have no way of knowing, since I've never been out of the Fells," Raisa said. "One day I'll visit Tamron and the other southern realms. How have you been affected by the war in Arden?"

"We choose to ignore the war," Liam said, leaning close to speak into her ear, as if confiding a secret. "We distract ourselves with parties and entertainments and other vices, as if that will make it go away."

"And yet you're here, seeking an alliance against the Montaignes," Raisa said, grateful for her tutelage from her father and Amon Byrne.

Liam waved a heavily ringed hand. "I'm looking for a rich wife to pay my gambling debts," he said. "We hear the queens of the Fells are very frugal, that they still have the first coins ever minted with their images."

The music stopped, and he led her from the dance floor to a table in one of her mother's temporary groves. Raisa signaled a server to bring them drinks, and then kicked off her shoes. Her dance card was finished—Prince Liam had been the last on the list. Although the orchestra still played (and would until the princess heir officially departed), Raisa was surprised to find that the room had nearly emptied. She hadn't realized it was so late. Somehow she'd got through her name day party without really noticing. It was kind of a letdown, after the months of buildup.

She refocused. Prince Liam was raising his glass to her.

"You *are* the most beautiful princess in the Seven Realms." He raised his other hand to stop her protest. "I'm a very good judge, Your Highness. I've seen more than my share."

Raisa laughed. Prince Liam's agenda might not entirely coincide with hers, but he was charming.

"You should come visit us," the prince went on. "Tamron lacks the physical beauty of the Fells, but I think you would find the city of Tamron Court very . . . interesting." He made a wry face. "Though summer is not our best season."

"So I hear. Your father, King Markus, invited me to visit his cottage on Leewater."

"The cottage *is* lovely in summer," Liam said. "Though it can seem crowded when all three wives are in residence."

Raisa couldn't help wondering if he'd mentioned them on purpose.

"I prefer summers in the city, where we sleep during the heat of the day and stay up all night. Soon it will be autumn, when the nights grow cool and lovely, and the rains revive the flowers. We call it the *wooing* season." He closed his hand over hers.

Tread carefully, Raisa said to herself. This is the princeling Missy Hakkam fell head over petticoats for. Raisa tended to use Missy Hakkam as a kind of trail marker to warn herself away from foolish behavior.

"Are you here on your father's behalf, or do you represent yourself?" Raisa asked.

Liam laughed, but there was a bitter edge to it. "My father does not need my help in matchmaking," he said. "I am here on my own."

"Well, then, what's your position on multiple wives? If you have two or three, can your wife have multiple husbands?"

Liam was taking a drink of wine as she asked that, and he very nearly splattered it all over the table. "P-Princess Raisa," he spluttered. "I think any man who marries you will find he has more than enough to handle without complicating things."

Raisa laughed also, but noted that he'd not really answered her question. He was looking at her, though, as if he found her absolutely fascinating. His gaze traveled from her mouth to her eyes and back again.

He leaned closer, resting his hands on her bare shoulders, raising gooseflesh there. "At this point, I would usually suggest a walk in the garden, but it's still raining buckets, from the sound of it. Perhaps . . . there's somewhere else we could go to talk, away from the ears of the court."

It occurred to Raisa that maybe Liam was the danger she'd anticipated. But an interesting kind of danger, after all.

Just then Raisa heard a step behind her, and Liam looked up over her shoulder and frowned.

"Your Highness." Raisa knew before she turned around who it was.

"Your Highness, the queen requests your attendance in her privy chamber," Micah Bayar said. "She asked me to fetch you."

Raisa eyed him with distrust. Why would her mother send Micah to fetch her, after all that had happened already? She looked around for Amon, but didn't see him, nor any others of her guardsmen. She wondered if he'd already gone up to the garden.

Micah turned to Liam. "Sorry, Your Highness, but you will have to excuse Princess Raisa. It *is* growing late."

"Yes. It is," Liam said, without rancor. He smiled at Raisa. "Princess Raisa, I will be here for a few more days before I return to Tamron," he said. "I'm staying in Kendall House. I hope to see you again before I leave." He bowed and turned away.

Micah looked after him for a long moment, then took hold of Raisa's arm to lead her from the ballroom.

She pulled free. "I know the way," she said, and walked away, leaving him to follow. She would have liked to have spent more time with Liam Tomlin, and was tired of being dragged around by the Bayars.

"What does my mother want?" Raisa asked as they threaded their way between groups of people still talking in the corridor. "I haven't seen her for hours. I thought by now she'd likely gone to bed."

"Not yet," Micah said, not answering her question. He seemed tense, and Raisa suspected he'd been drinking again.

Raisa herself had been careful not to drink anything but water and oversweet punch. It was her custom to try to learn from experience.

As they neared the queen's apartments, the corridors emptied out. Automatically, Raisa turned off the public corridors into the narrower, private ones used by the royal family. As they passed the small library established by her father, Micah said, "Raisa, before we go in, give me a minute. Please."

She turned to face him. He nodded toward the library.

"Just hear me out. I promise it won't take long." He fussed with his sleeves, seeming uncharacteristically awkward.

Against all common sense, she believed him. After a long moment, she preceded him into the library, putting a table between them.

"I've been trying to get in to see you, ever since the party," he said. "I wanted to tell you that I did not know about the ring and the necklace. I didn't realize they were enchanted."

He was admitting they were jinxpieces, then, that Lord Bayar had lied to the queen. Raisa folded her arms. "Why should I believe you?"

He shrugged. "Because, as you'll see, I have no reason to lie to you."

She tilted her head. "What do you mean, 'as you'll see'?"

He ignored the question. "And because I'd like to think that I'm able to attract a girl on my own."

"Depends on the girl," Raisa said acerbically. "I hear you have had some success in the past."

He half smiled, shrugging his shoulders, reminding her of why she'd always found him so attractive.

"When you . . . when you seemed receptive, I assumed you'd finally succumbed to my personal charm," Micah said. "Imagine my disappointment when I learned that you had been bewitched, not by me, but by an amulet."

"And several glasses of wine," Raisa couldn't resist saying.

Micah dismissed that with a wave of his hand. "No. Wine doesn't work on you. I tried that already."

Well! Raisa thought. You *are* being uncommonly frank.

"Why can't you be satisfied with having every other girl at court falling at your feet?" she asked. "Why do you always want what you can't have?"

"Why aren't you asking me who was responsible for the seduction amulet, if not me?" he countered.

"Because I don't have to," she said. "Tell me this—why would your father want you to seduce me? Was he trying to cause a scandal, to prevent my marrying a southerner?"

"Well," Micah said, rolling his eyes. "That *would* be a side benefit. The last thing we need is to have you marrying a southerner."

"I don't understand this. Your father is magically bound to the Line of Queens. Why is he able to act contrary to their interests?"

"How do you know he is? Acting contrary to their interests, I mean," Micah said. He scanned the volumes on the nearest bookshelf. Running his hand along the dusty spines, he examined his palm, then wiped it on his trousers. Somehow it made him seem very young.

"Blood of the demon, Micah. Spelling the princess heir against her will? That is treason. What did he hope to accomplish?"

"My father expects we will be at war before long," Micah said. "As soon as the civil war in Arden has ended."

That was just what Amon had said. "So? What does that have to do with me?"

"We have to win against the southerners at all costs. That might mean discarding some of the archaic rules that have made us weak."

426

"Me, I like some of the old rules," Raisa said. "Such as rules against treason."

"You know the Church of Malthus sees wizardry as heresy, right?" Micah said. "They burn wizards in the south."

The Church of Malthus had the reputation of being humorless, stern, and conservative. Raisa knew that much. But she'd not known their position on wizardry.

"We'll need all of our weapons if Arden attacks us," Micah said. "We have to win. The clan must be made to see reason. We need unfettered access to the tools of magic."

"You had that," Raisa said, weariness trumping diplomacy. "And you made a mess of things."

Why did they have to talk about this now? She felt tired and irritable, confused by this conversation, under siege by everyone. "Look, can we just go see what my mother wants so we can all go to bed?"

Micah raked back his dark hair. "I just wanted you to know that none of this is my idea. I'm hoping that you can . . . that you'll keep that in mind."

Her intuition pricked her again. Why was Micah Bayar giving this speech, taking her to see the queen in the middle of the night? What if she didn't want to go?

In fact, she wouldn't go. She'd go back to her room, where Amon was waiting. Sort of.

She circled around the table, meaning to slip past Micah and into the hallway. He must have seen something in her face, because he moved to block her path. "Come on, now," he said. "We'd better hurry; we're expected."

She shook her head. "Actually, I'm exhausted, and I'm not

feeling well," she said. "Please give my apologies to the queen, but I think I'd better go on to bed."

Micah sighed. "Raisa, I'm sorry, but I have to bring you. If it makes you feel any better, neither one of us has a choice, all right?"

Raisa looked into his face and saw that he meant it, so she walked past him and turned toward the privy chamber. All the while, her mind raced, struggling to make sense of it.

Neither one of us has a choice.

Who was giving the orders, then? Her mother or Gavan Bayar?

CHAPTER TWENTY-FOUR

UNHOLY CEREMONY

Four guardsmen flanked the doors of the queen's apartments. Holding her head high, Raisa swept past them, with Micah following behind. Raisa heard voices within, but as soon as she pushed the door open, the conversation stopped and several people turned toward them.

Queen Marianna smiled, her cheeks flushed with excitement and wine, still wearing the stunning green dress she'd had on at dinner. Beside her, Gavan Bayar, also in his formal garb, and Micah's sister, Fiona, her pale face alight with—what? Triumph? Satisfaction?

And there, like a plump, giddy turkey among the foxes, was Speaker Horas Redfern, chief cleric of the cathedral temple. Raisa had never cared for Redfern, who, in her opinion, spent too little time tending to his flock and too much time cozying up to the aristocracy.

Redfern, too, looked as if he'd had a little too much

to drink. He seemed rather frenetically cheerful.

"And here they are now," Queen Marianna said. She swept forward and kissed Raisa and Micah in turn.

Raisa scanned the room. It had been transformed from the last time she'd seen it. There were flowers everywhere—two extravagant arrangements of lilies and roses on either side of an altar, bowls of blooms on all the tables, tucked in with thousands of flickering candles. An altar cloth was embroidered with entwined roses and falcons. A peculiar design. To one side was a serving table with wine buckets and glasses. Why, it looked almost like a . . .

"How do you like it, sweetheart?" Queen Marianna took Raisa's hands and gazed into her face as if eager for her approval. "We had very little time to put it together, but I think you can appreciate the importance of discretion. I know it may not be exactly what you pictured, but . . ."

Raisa's mouth was so dry she could scarcely spit out any words. "What . . . what *is* this?" she whispered. "Isn't it late to be having a party?"

"Your Majesty," Lord Bayar said, his blue eyes glittering in the candlelight. "Perhaps you should explain."

"Raisa," Queen Marianna said. "You know we've been talking—well, strategizing—about the best match for you now that you are eligible for marriage."

Raisa glanced at her mother, then at Gavan Bayar. "Who's been talking—you and I, or you and *them*?"

"All of us, of course. Remember, we agreed that a southerner is not the best choice just now with all the upheaval in Arden and Tamron."

"We never agreed on that," Raisa said. "The war has to be over before long, and then we'll have more options," she said, thinking of Prince Liam. "An alliance between Tamron and the Fells might be enough to prevent invasion from Arden, if we time it right."

Marianna stared at Raisa as if her daughter had grown another head with an inconveniently talkative mouth.

"It's not necessarily in our interest to prevent a war between Arden and Tamron, Your Highness," Lord Bayar said, verbally patting her on the head. "Such a war would deplete Arden's resources and distract them from consideration of an attack on us."

"If Arden wins, it will be more of a threat than ever," Raisa said, recalling her conversation with Prince Gerard.

"And there's no one among the clan royalty who would be a suitable match," Marianna rushed on. "Averill is your father, and the Matriarch of Marisa Pines is unmarried with a bastard son."

"There are cousins at Demonai Camp who might be suitable," Raisa said, thinking of Reid. "When Father returns, we can see what he says."

"Your father's opinion might be . . . interesting, but not especially important," Queen Marianna said, looking put out that Raisa was being so uncooperative. "We also need to think about the role wizards may play in any upcoming conflict, and what we might need to do to cement our interests more closely together."

"The High Wizard is magically bound to the queen of the Fells," Raisa said. "Therefore, our interests already coincide. Besides, what does our relationship with wizards have to do with my marriage?"

If she hadn't been so tired, she would have seen it coming. Looking back, she concluded that she was being extraordinarily thick.

Queen Marianna drew herself up the way she always did when she expected Raisa to be obstinate. "Raisa, we have chosen a match for you for the good of the realm and the Line of Queens. You will marry Micah *sul'*Bayar."

For a moment, Raisa was convinced she'd misheard. That her mother was joking, somehow, despite the scowl on her face. That it was some kind of test of her knowledge of the covenant known as the Naéming.

That it couldn't possibly be true.

Then she looked over at Micah and saw the truth in his face. This was what he'd meant in the library when he'd said, *Neither one of us has a choice.*

"But . . . but that's impossible," Raisa whispered. "I cannot marry a wizard. It's forbidden."

"Forbidden by whom?" the queen said. "I am the queen of the Fells. I am sovereign over this realm."

"Forbidden by the Naéming for a thousand years," Raisa said. "You know that. No wizard has married a queen of the Fells since Hanalea. And you know what happened then."

"My dear girl, think of the lost opportunities, the richness of possibility," Lord Bayar said. "The union of royal blood and wizardry will make us once again the most powerful kingdom in the Seven Realms. Why should the actions of one rogue wizard close that door forever?"

Kingdom, she thought. Over my dead body.

"I am not your dear girl," Raisa said, breathing hard and

fast. "I am the princess heir to the *queendom* of the Fells, and I'll thank you to remember it. And it wasn't the actions of one madman that resulted in the Naéming. It was the abuse of power by a dynasty of wizards who invaded and conquered the Fells and enslaved its blooded rulers."

"That's one perspective," Lord Bayar said, smooth as any serpent. "Others call it a golden age, when all of the Seven Realms paid tribute to the Fells. When riches flowed to us from all seven. When the fertile fields of Arden filled our granaries and supplied the funds to build this legendary city."

"The city was built before wizards ever came here," Raisa said.

"Who's been feeding you this misinformation?" Lord Bayar asked. "Your father? Elena Demonai? The days of the clans are over."

Raisa turned away from Lord Bayar and faced the queen. "Mother, you know this isn't right. You know you can't marry me to a wizard. The clan will go to war over it, you know they will. Do you want a civil war here as well as in Arden? How vulnerable will that make us?"

"Bows and arrows cannot protect us against the war machines of Arden," Marianna said. "We need sorcery on our side."

"We already have it, or we should have," Raisa said, glaring at Lord Bayar. "The High Wizard is supposed to be bound to you, and subject to your will. What's happened? Is the link damaged, or broken, or . . . ?"

"Micah," Lord Bayar said pointedly, "please calm your bride so we can get on with this. It's growing late, wedding jitters or not, and we need to ride back to Gray Lady before morning."

Micah moved toward Raisa, hands extended, as one might approach a cornered fellscat. "Come on, Raisa," he coaxed, almost pleading. "Let's just get this over with."

I almost feel sorry for Micah, Raisa thought. She looked around the room for a way out. Her gaze lit on Redfern, who seemed woefully out of place, and it all finally registered. "Hold on. You're planning to marry us *tonight*?"

"Yes," Bayar said impatiently. "We'll send the southerners home with the news. That will stifle any talk of alliances."

"Mother," Raisa said, her heart pounding beneath the creamy silk. A wedding dress. Of course. "Don't do this. I don't want to marry anyone right now."

"We upland queens marry for the good of the realm," Queen Marianna said softly. "As Hanalea did. As I did."

"But this isn't good for us," Raisa persisted, circling a serving table with Micah in pursuit.

"Don't tell me what's good for us!" Queen Marianna turned in a swish of satin and snatched up a wineglass. "I lie awake every night wondering what's to become of us, with war in the south and conflict in the queendom and pirates on the ocean and southern spies and assassins in every back hallway." She shuddered, and droplets of wine spattered on the stone floor, red as blood. "I worry about you, Raisa, with no one to protect you."

"We *have* protection," Raisa protested, bewildered. What had come over her mother? She seemed panicked, desperate. "Captain Byrne and the Queen's Guard."

"Captain Byrne cannot be everywhere," the queen said.

"Right," Raisa said. "For instance, where is he now? And where is my father? When I get married, he needs to be there."

She was watching Gavan Bayar as she said this, and saw something flicker across his face. Maybe it was her imagination, but it was almost as if he knew something about her father's absence.

Both he and Captain Byrne had been sent away just before her name day, when she would be formally named heir to the throne, when she would be eligible for marriage for the first time. Like a cold stone under her breastbone, the realization settled in: if both the queen and Lord Bayar wanted it to happen, she would be married before the night was over.

"Speaker Redfern!" she said, though she had little hope of rescue from that quarter. "You're the representative of the temple, of the old ways. You know I cannot marry a wizard. Tell them."

She strode toward the speaker, and he retreated, holding his wineglass out like a shield. "Not at all, not at all. This should not prove an impediment to your marriage, Your Highness," the speaker said. "I have issued a dish . . . a dispensation."

While Raisa was thus distracted, Micah struck, launching himself over a small settee and wrapping his arms around her. Holding her fast in the circle of one arm, he reached into his neckline and gripped an amulet at his neck while Raisa did her best to struggle free.

Where did you get that? Raisa wanted to ask. You're too young. You've never been to Oden's Ford. You're not allowed to have an amulet.

That was her mistake, thinking wizards would play by the rules.

Micah muttered a few words in the northern speech, bending his head down close to her ear. She felt the sizzle of magic through his hands. It passed through her body and down her left arm, leaving nothing behind but tingling nerves and a vague desire to please.

And then she remembered: she wore Elena's ring on her left hand. *It is what we call a talisman*, Elena had said. *It offers some protection against high magic.*

Here was a chance, if she could somehow take advantage of it. She couldn't let them know about the ring, or they'd have it off her in a trice. She had to play along, make them think he'd charmed her.

What spell would Micah have used on her? *Calm your bride*, Lord Bayar had said.

She looked up at Micah. He was studying her face, obviously trying to determine if his jinx had taken.

She widened her eyes, conjuring an expression of vacancy. "I'm sorry," she said. "I know I'm being silly. It's just that it's all so sudden." She looked down at the floor, fearing Micah would spot the fury in her eyes. "I always dreamed we could be together, but I assumed it was impossible."

She heard an audible release of breath around her, the sound of relief.

"Me too," Micah said cautiously, as if he didn't quite believe it. He released his death grip a fraction. "I can't tell you . . . how frustrating it's been, to yearn for what I could never have." He leaned down and brushed his lips across hers, and she felt the sting of magic again. She resisted the urge to flinch away.

What argument would speak to her mother? Assuming she was reachable at all?

"The thing is, I've always dreamed of a big wedding, Mama," Raisa said, looking directly at the queen. "I wanted everyone to be there—my grandmother Elena, my father, the clan in their colors, heads of state from all over the Seven Realms. I'd have four bridesmaids to carry my train, and I'd walk up the aisle over a carpet of rose petals."

"Of course, sweetheart," the queen said, blinking at her in surprise. "It's what every girl dreams of." Except, until now, her daughter Raisa.

"You *had* that, Mama," Raisa said reproachfully. "You had five hundred people in the temple, and it took the dressmakers a year to stitch the seed pearls onto your dress. Bonfires blazed on every hill to commemorate it. The feasting lasted for six days, and they filled three storehouses with the wedding gifts."

The queen's cheeks flushed with embarrassment. "I know, dear. It's something I'll never forget, but . . ."

"But I'm to wed in a back room before a single priest, as if I'm a serving girl with a growing belly. People will talk about me, Mama. You know they will. They'll question whether I'm married at all."

"They won't dare," the queen said, smoothing down her skirts nervously. "I will forbid it."

"It could affect the succession," Raisa said, very conscious of Micah Bayar right next to her. "If we have children, their legitimacy may be questioned." She turned and gripped Micah's hands. "I couldn't bear that."

"Your Majesty," Lord Bayar said. "Let's proceed. She's just overwhelmed is all." He glared at his son as if to say, *Try something stronger.*

"I know I must serve the realm, Mama," Raisa said. "But why should it be at the expense of my dreams?"

"I had no idea you felt this way," the queen said, flustered, as always, by conflict.

Raisa pressed her advantage. "You are the queen. Proclaim that Micah and I will marry in the fall. That will give us time to plan." She wrapped her arms around Micah's waist and rested her head against his chest. "I want everything to be perfect."

"Your Majesty, we can't risk waiting," Lord Bayar said. He crossed to the queen and took hold of her hands. "Anything could happen before then. We could be invaded. The princess heir could be kidnapped. The clans could rebel. She needs a gifted husband to watch over her."

Raisa watched the two of them out of the corner of her eye. No doubt Bayar was pouring magic into her as Micah had done. She already knew that the wizard held an inappropriate influence over the queen. She just didn't know if her mother could resist it.

She remembered the conversation with Elena in the garden, months ago. The warning her grandmother had given her.

Queen Marianna turned toward Raisa, swiping tears from her eyes. "Oh, sweetheart, we can't risk waiting. I'll make it up to you somehow. We'll throw a reception like the world has never seen. We'll invite everyone. You'll see."

Then Raisa was crying too, tears of fury and disappointment, knowing she was truly on her own.

What would Hanalea do?

"It's all right, Raisa," Micah whispered, patting her back awkwardly. It was all she could do not to swing around and punch him in his perfect nose.

"Where . . . where would we go after?" Raisa asked, thinking there still might be a way out, a way to prevent this thing from being consummated. "Might we go back to my apartments, and . . ."

"We'll host you at Aerie House," Lord Bayar said. "We have an apartment prepared for you. We'll send someone after your things. That way the two of you can have some privacy." He smiled his tiger smile.

"All right," Raisa said, swallowing hard. "If you think it's best. Only . . ." She sniffled and blotted her face on her sleeve, wiping away tears of rage. "If Father can't be here, I would feel so much better if I could wear the rose necklace he gave me. It would . . . it would be more like he was here. I'll fetch it. It will just take a moment."

"Oh, come on!" Lord Bayar exploded, his impatience getting the best of him. "Speaker Redfern has been here for two hours waiting. Let's do it, and if anyone asks, we'll say you had it on. You have the rest of your life to wear the thing."

"No," Queen Marianna said, belatedly developing a backbone. "The princess heir shall wear her father's necklace, if it helps to cheer her. It's the least we can do. She's sacrificed enough for duty in this." And she said it in a way that brooked no argument.

Bayar mastered himself with difficulty. The wizard was definitely forgetting his place. Whatever that place was these days. "Of course, Your Majesty. We'll send one of the guardsmen after it."

"Thank you, Lord Bayar," Raisa said. "But it will be quicker if I go. I'm not sure just where I've left it, and I don't want soldiers pawing through my jewelry. I'll be right back." She tried to pull free from Micah's grip.

"Micah, you go with the princess heir and bring her back safely to us," Lord Bayar said. "I know you won't let her get away." He smiled as he said it, but his blue eyes were bright and hard as sapphires.

And then they were hurrying down the hallway, Micah holding tightly to her wrist. He trickled more magic into her, as if to reinforce his previous efforts.

This time she decided to acknowledge it. "I had no idea you could do magic, Micah," she said. "Where did you learn how? And where did you get an amulet?"

He flinched, as if she'd broken the secret code. "Well, I don't know much. My family has some . . . magical heirlooms."

"No wonder Mama wants us to marry," Raisa said. "That gives you an advantage over other wizard houses, right? Because you don't have to beg your amulets from the clan?"

Micah nodded. "These days, the only amulets you can get are temporary. They lose their effectiveness over time. So you have to keep going back to the clan to restore them, or get new ones. The clan uses that to control the gifted."

"And these don't wear out?" Raisa asked.

"I didn't say that," Micah muttered, glancing around as if they might be overheard. Unfortunately, the corridors were deserted. It was too late even for the late-nighters and too early for the early risers.

"Do you really want to marry me, Micah?" She was genuinely curious. He'd told her they didn't have a choice. Maybe if he saw a way out of it . . .

He seemed to be choosing his words carefully. "Who wouldn't want to marry the princess heir of the Fells?" he said.

"Is that all I am to you? A title?"

He thought a moment, and when he spoke, she thought he told the truth. "You've always fascinated me, Raisa. I could always have any girl but you. And you'd never let me get away with anything. You always say what you think." He almost smiled. "I'd rather kiss you than bed any other girl at court."

Strange praise, she thought.

"I think we could be good together," he went on, "once we get through this."

We could be good together. Not exactly a protestation of love. Nor a promise to give up his wanton ways.

The irony was, she might have given the proposal serious thought, at least, if it were not being forced on her.

They climbed the wide stairs, startling a cat sleeping on the top step, and turned right, past the sleeping Mellony's room, to Raisa's suite.

The stocky guardsman Raisa had met earlier leaned against the wall next to the door. When he saw them coming, he straightened and rested his hand on the hilt of his sword, looking from Micah to Raisa in confusion.

"You wait here," Raisa said to Micah. "I'll just be a few minutes." She pushed open the door.

After a moment's hesitation, Micah made as if to follow her in, and the guardsman stepped in front of him. "You heard Her Highness," the soldier said. "Wait here." And, blessedly, he pulled the door shut.

Micah must have groped for his amulet, because Raisa heard a sword slide free. "Let go of that thing," she heard the guardsman say.

She could hear them arguing back and forth, their voices rising. She figured she had a little time. Micah wouldn't be too alarmed. As far as he knew, there was only one way in and out of her room. She couldn't very well leap from her window, which was high above the river below. Besides, she'd said nothing to make him think she'd rather leap to her death than marry him. So far.

"Your Highness?" Magret blinked sleepily at her from her chair by the fire. She'd fallen asleep waiting up for her. "What time is it getting to be? I know it's your name day and all, but . . ."

"Magret, do you love me?" Raisa asked breathlessly.

"What kind of question is that, my lady?" Magret sputtered. "'Course I—"

"Then pack me some riding clothes," Raisa said. "Clan style, in saddle bags, for several days. Nothing dressy. Hurry!" As she spoke, she shed the creamy silk that was to have been her wedding dress—and wouldn't be, if she could help it. Wadding it up, she tossed it into the corner, then stripped off her slippers and stockings and yanked on a pair of trousers laid out on a side chair.

"What is going on?" Magret asked, now wide awake, throwing open drawers and thrusting clothing into two saddlebags. She paused and straightened, midthrust. "You're not eloping, are you?"

"The opposite. The Bayars mean to force me into a marriage with Micah Bayar," she said, omitting the fact that the queen was in on the scheme.

"That's crazy talk," Magret said, continuing her frenetic preparations. "You can't marry a wizard. They know that."

"They may know that, but they're doing it anyway. They've got a speaker and everything, and afterward they mean to carry me off to Aerie House."

"What?" Magret's voice rose, and Raisa shushed her frantically.

"Micah's just outside the door. He's waiting for me."

Magret glared at the door. The argument was still going on in the corridor. "I don't like wizards, I never have." Magret carried clan blood and, with it, an inborn suspicion of wizards. "You don't mean to go with him, do you?"

"No, I don't. I'm leaving. I need you to keep him out as long as possible so I have a head start."

"Your Highness, I don't like the notion of you climbing down off the balcony, I really don't. You'll break your neck."

"There's another way. Through the closet. You'll see." Raisa went into the closet, dug out her boots, sat on the floor, and yanked them on.

"Through here?" Magret peered into the closet. "A tunnel,

then?" Raisa nodded, and Magret said, "I'd always heard there was one, somewhere in this part of the castle."

"It lets out in the glass house," Raisa said.

Magret's eyes kindled with pride. "You're just like she was," she breathed.

"Like who was?"

"Like Queen Hanalea herself." Shyly, Magret drew back her sleeve, exposing her inner arm. On it was a tattoo of a howling wolf against a rising moon.

"You're a *Maiden*?" Raisa spoke louder than she intended, and now Magret was the one shushing her. The howling wolf was the emblem of Hanalea's Maidens, a mysterious organization of women dedicated to the warrior queen's memory.

"I am," Magret said. "They meant to force her into marriage with a wizard, and she wouldn't stand for it. Said 'twas better to be a maid than married to a demon."

Well, Raisa thought. There's more to Magret than meets the eye.

"Where will you go, Your Highness? The queen must be informed," Magret said.

"She will be, don't worry," Raisa said. She hesitated a moment. "Lord Bayar has my mother spelled, I'm afraid. She's agreed to the marriage."

"Blood and bones of the queens," Magret swore. "The scoundrel. I haven't liked this business going on, no I haven't. I always said your da should spend more time at home."

Tears came to Raisa's eyes. She was touched that her nurse believed her, that she was on her side. She'd begun to think she was losing her mind.

"Will you be needin' any money?" Magret asked. "I have a little put by, you know."

Raisa kissed her formidable nurse on the cheek. "I'll be fine." She lifted her mattress and pulled a small velvet pouch from underneath. "My emergency fund," she said. It was the money she'd made working the markets during the summer. Princesses weren't supposed to make money. She'd put it away to avoid any arguments. She tucked her dagger into her belt and slung the saddlebags over her shoulders.

Someone pounded on the door. "Hurry up, Rai—Your Highness," Micah shouted. "Everyone's waiting."

"You be quiet, Young Bayar," Magret shouted back. "Don't be shouting in the hallways like a besotted sailor! The princess will be ready when she's ready."

Before long, everyone will be awake, Raisa thought.

"Thank you, Magret. I'm off. Tell Micah we're still looking for my necklace if he knocks again. When he forces his way in, tell him I went off the balcony."

Magret yanked down the curtains surrounding Raisa's bed and began ripping them into strips. "I'll make you a ladder, throw him off the scent," she said grimly.

Grabbing a torch from the sconce on the wall, Raisa pushed her way into the closet, sliding between silks, satins, and velvets. She shoved aside the panel and entered the damp stone corridor, sliding the panel closed behind her. She prayed that Amon was waiting in the garden for her. With her luck, he'd given it up and gone home.

She ran as fast as she could, banging her elbows into the stone walls at the turnings, alert for the sounds of pursuit behind. How long could Magret hope to hold Micah off? Would he fall for the balcony ruse? She shuddered at the notion of being chased through the narrow twisting corridor.

The climb up the narrow ladder to the garden house was scary, as it always was, with the added burden of the saddlebags bumping against her sides. Finally she reached the top and pushed at the stone cover.

To her vast relief, someone gripped it from above and wrestled it away. Then Amon's face appeared in the opening, taut and grim. "Where have you been?" he said. "I was beginning to think you'd come back and gone to bed without telling me."

But still you stayed, Raisa thought with a rush of gratitude. Thank the Maker for Amon Byrne.

Amon gripped her hands and hauled her up through the opening, setting her down next to him on the garden house floor. "I've been crazy with worry up here. I had a feeling that . . ." He swallowed hard. "Well, anyway. What's going on?"

Raisa opened her mouth and words poured out, in seemingly random order. "Lord Bayar has put a spell on the queen. I don't know how. It's as if the binding isn't working. They've got a stash of magical pieces that predate the Breaking."

"A spell?" Amon said. "What does he . . . ?"

"He means to marry me off to Micah and name him king," Raisa said. "They've got a priest and everything. Mama's going along with it. I'd be married already, but I insisted on coming back to my room first. It won't be long before they know I'm gone." She grabbed his hand as if she could drag him away. "We've got to leave. Now."

"But . . . ?"

"I know. I'm not allowed to marry a wizard. But the Bayars don't like the old rules. Seems they're too confining. I'm going to have to leave the city until we can sort this out."

Not just the city, Raisa thought. The queendom. She couldn't take refuge with the clan. That would start a war between her parents and make the Fells vulnerable to invasion from the south.

Amon took her saddlebags and slung them over his own shoulders. "Let's go. We've got to clear the drawbridge before they sound the general alarm."

They clattered down staircase after staircase, incredibly loud in the early morning stillness, encountering the occasional sleepy-eyed upstairs servant. Each time, Raisa turned her face away, hoping to go unrecognized. It would cause talk at any time—the princess heir sneaking through back hallways with a soldier the morning after her name day party. They would be remembered, and it wouldn't be long before the Bayars would know she hadn't gone over the balcony, that she'd been seen with Amon Byrne. She didn't wish it on Amon, to have the Bayars for enemies, but she was glad to have him at her side.

She needn't have worried. Just like before, no one recognized the princess heir in breeches and tunic.

Down on the ground floor, the corridors were broader and there was even more traffic about. They forced themselves to walk, so as to be less conspicuous, though Raisa's every nerve was firing. They passed through the Great Hall, where petitioners were already gathering in hopes of an interview with the queen.

They walked through the huge arch that led onto the drawbridge, passing under the portcullis. Raisa put a little space between her and Amon so they wouldn't look like they were together. She might be a clanswoman, on her way back from a delivery to the castle. Amon might be a soldier on the way to his post.

They were midway across the river when she heard a clamor of bells and duty officers calling to one another. With a harsh metallic squeal, the portcullis descended until it slammed into the dirt.

They know I'm gone, Raisa thought.

The guardsmen loitering at the far end of the bridge looked up in curiosity.

"Corporal Byrne!" one of them called to Amon. "What's going on?"

"Maybe some poor crofter stole a loaf of bread from the princess's party," Amon said, rolling his eyes.

The soldier laughed. "They sure seem tizzied up about something," he said, peering toward the castle.

"Showing off for the southern royalty, no doubt," Amon said, without pausing. "I'm leaving so that I don't have to polish any brass."

Once clear of the bridge, Amon pulled Raisa aside, toward the guard barracks and stables that crouched at the far end of the bridge. "Let's go to the stables," he said. "We'll want horses."

They were crossing the stable yard when Raisa heard a rattle of hooves on cobblestones, someone riding into the compound excessively fast. Amon pushed Raisa behind him and drew his sword.

Two riders thundered in, wrenching their mounts to a halt just in front of the stable doors.

"Raisa?" One of the horsemen swung down to the ground. He was sweaty and blood-stained, one arm wrapped in linen, his face stubbled. He pulled Raisa into his arms. "Raisa, thank the Maker."

It was her father.

Joy mingled with surprise and worry, crowding her heart so she thought it might burst. "Father! You're hurt! What happened? Where have you been?"

"It's thanks to Captain Byrne it's not worse," Averill said, nodding at the other rider. "We were ambushed just west of Chalk Cliffs. Ten armed men. They did their best to kill us, but Captain Byrne seems to have a third eye. He spotted the ambush before they closed on us."

Byrne handed off his horse to the stable boy. The captain too was much the worse for wear. Dried blood trickled down his face from a wound over his eye, and he favored his right leg.

"They were masked, but they rode military mounts, Your Highness," Byrne said grimly. "Same as we use in the Guard. I'm thinking they were Guard-trained."

"So the Guard has been compromised," Raisa said bluntly.

Captain Byrne hesitated, then nodded. "Aye."

"I'm sorry, Raisa," her father said. "I meant to be there for your ceremony. It seems someone had other ideas."

"Gavan Bayar," Raisa said with conviction. "It must have been."

Byrne and Averill stared at her, questions in their eyes, but before they could speak, the rattle of chains drew Raisa's attention back to the castle. "Bloody bones!" she said. "They're raising the drawbridge. We've got to go on before they finish searching the castle and realize I'm gone."

"What is going on?" Captain Byrne demanded. "What's happened?"

In a few terse sentences, Amon explained the situation.

Byrne shouted for the stable boy, who reemerged from the tack room, blinking away sleep and confusion.

"Ready four fresh mounts," Byrne said. "Two saddled, two on lead lines. Pack bedrolls and provisions. Not next week! Now!" he roared when the boy didn't move immediately. The boy scurried away.

"Will you go to Marisa Pines?" Averill asked. "That's closest."

Raisa shrugged. "We could go there tonight. But we can't stay there long. It's still within the realm. If the queen demands my return, the clan will refuse, but she won't let that stand. She cannot. I'll have to leave the Fells until things settle."

"I don't like it," Captain Byrne growled. "There's no place safe. Arden's in chaos, Bruinswallow and We'enhaven are likely to be drawn in, even if you could get there. And Tamron's no fit place for the princess, even if it wasn't three days' hard march from Arden. There's pirates on the Indio who would hold you to ransom if you went that way, and—"

"Sir? What about Oden's Ford?" Amon broke in. "No one would dare bother her there. Especially if no one knows who she is."

The two men stared at Amon for a long moment.

"The boy makes sense," Averill said finally, nodding.

"How would she get there?" Captain Byrne said, looking less enthusiastic. "They'll be waiting to intercept her at Marisa Pines Pass."

Amon nodded. "That's what they'd expect because it's closest. She could go west to Demonai and pick up provisions, clothing, and fresh horses." He looked at Averill, who nodded assent. "Then she'd cross at Westgate and travel down through the Shivering Fens to Tamron and east to Oden's Ford."

"The *Fens*?" Captain Byrne frowned. "That'd be rough traveling. They're nearly impassable this time of year. And I've been hearing rumors of trouble with the Waterwalkers."

"There's a way," Amon said. "The road's not bad now, if you know where you're going."

Averill nodded agreement. "It's better that Raisa stays out of Arden—there's too much bloodshed there at present. Too much chance she'll be captured or killed. At least the Waterwalkers respect Hanalea's line. In Arden, they refer to our queens as witches."

Who are the Waterwalkers? Raisa thought, looking from Averill to Byrne. I *am* Hanalea's line, and I'm still the last to know anything.

"Lord Demonai, with all due respect, I cannot send the princess heir into the Fens unprotected," Captain Byrne said. "The queen would be right to demand my head."

Amon cleared his throat. "Da. Sir. We could escort Raisa to Oden's Ford," Amon said. "The Gray Wolves, I mean. It's nearly time for us to return to Wien House anyway. All of the fourth-year cadets will be expected to travel together—that won't draw any attention. I know the Fens; you know Lord Cadri's family, and I've stayed with them before. The princess can travel with my triple as a first-year plebe."

"You're just fourth-years," Byrne said, shaking his head. "Hardly more than boys. It's too dangerous for everyone involved."

Averill put his hand on Captain Byrne's arm. "Edon, I think maybe the boy's idea is a good one—for two reasons. First, my daughter's best protection is to go unnoticed. I've traveled in the south as a trader, remember. We could send a whole salvo of guards with her, but they could still be over-whelmed by a larger force. There are armies of mercenaries, hundreds strong, roaming the countryside.

"Secondly, the queen can't know we've had a hand in this, especially you. If you send any of the Queen's Guard with the princess, Marianna will know you were involved. That's trea-son, in her eyes. You can't offer much protection to Marianna if you're in jail. And she needs your protection more than ever."

Byrne turned to Raisa as if she might be an ally. "What happens to your marriage prospects, Your Highness, if you're discovered traveling with a triple of soldiers?" he said bluntly.

"If I stay here, I'll end up married to a wizard," Raisa said, equally bluntly. "What happens to my prospects then?"

Captain Byrne turned back to Averill, seeming to prefer to debate him than the princess heir. "Where would she stay at Oden's Ford? She can't live in the barracks. She needs some-place safe to lodge until we can get this sorted out."

"Why couldn't I stay in the barracks?" Raisa interjected. "Why couldn't I lodge there as a new cadet?"

Captain Byrne made a pained face. "Your Highness, that's impossible! The princess heir living with pack of soldiers?"

"Hanalea was a warrior queen," Raisa said. "She killed the Demon King and led an army against the usurper when she wasn't much older than me."

"That was a long time ago," Byrne said. "Queens these days are less . . . warlike," he said. He looked at Amon. "Do you really think nine cadets could keep a secret like this, all the way to Oden's Ford?"

"They can't give it away if they don't know about it," Amon said. "We'll pretend she's the daughter of some Chalk Cliff noble. They already know her as Rebecca Morley. We'll say her father asked if she could travel with us to study at the Healer's Hall at Oden's Ford. She'll travel in the guise of a plebe, for her own protection."

"There's a temple at Oden's Ford," Averill said. "The princess could lodge there as a new dedicate. You know, this could be a blessing in disguise. Oden's Ford is a crossroads of ideas. She could learn a lot while in residence there."

"She'll be vulnerable to kidnappers, fortune hunters, and younger sons," Byrne countered.

"Not if they don't know who she is," Averill said. "Besides, the Peace of Oden's Ford will protect her. Even with the wars going on all around, it's held for more than a thousand years."

"She can't stay away for too long," Byrne said. "There's always the risk that Bayar will convince Marianna to name Mellony heir."

"We can debate all this later," Raisa said, glancing back toward the castle, still buttoned up tight as a flatland corset. "Once they've searched the castle, they'll be crossing the bridge. Captain Byrne, please tell the other cadets to meet their corporal at Demonai Camp. Corporal Byrne and I will ride on ahead."

Byrne stared at her a moment, then inclined his head. "Understood, Your Highness," he said, a faint smile over-laying his worry lines. "Corporal Byrne, a moment, please." Byrne drew his son aside, and the two joined in a brief intense conversation that ended in an embrace.

While they'd been talking, the stable boy had led the horses out. Byrne sent the boy off to bed.

Raisa chose the smallest horse, a mare, and untied her reins from the rail. She turned to Amon. "Give me a leg up, if you please?"

Amon boosted her into the saddle and adjusted the stir-rups to her small stature.

Byrne gripped Amon's hand in a soldier's double grip. "Keep her safe," he said, looking his son in the eyes. "And bring her back to us."

Amon nodded, then mounted up himself.

"Travel safely, daughter," Averill said, tears pooling in his eyes, then streaming unmoated down his face.

Byrne clapped him on the back. "Let's go on to the castle, Lord Demonai," Byrne said, grinning. "I want to see Gavan Bayar's face when we arrive alive."

The two men turned away. Raisa dug her heels into the mare's sides, and they clattered out of the stable yard and onto the Way, leading their two spare horses. When they passed out of the city gates, Raisa turned and looked back at Fellsmarch Castle glittering in the morning sun. She was leaving it behind again, sooner than she'd thought possible.

CHAPTER TWENTY-FIVE

THE END
OF DAYS

When Han returned to the stable after visiting the markets, Mari's fever was high again. It seemed to burn the flesh off her—her face had grown noticeably drawn and thin just since he'd been home, and her skin had turned a sickly yellow. He'd seen it before. It was never a good sign.

So he went to see the healer in Catgut Alley and made him come, promising to pay him double his price in a day or two. The man came, all sweaty and shifty-eyed, no doubt aware of Cuffs's bloodthirsty reputation and worried about the cost of failure. The healer fed Mari foul-smelling brews and burned an unidentified incense that released stinky yellow fumes into the room. After an hour in his presence, Han concluded he was a grifter, but Mam insisted Mari looked better afterward, and breathed easier.

The next morning, in desperation, Han left the city and walked all the way up Marisa Pines Trail, meaning to bring

Willo back with him to tend Mari. When he arrived in camp, he learned she'd gone up Althea Mountain to midwife a birth. Bird was out with the Demonais, and Dancer had gone with Willo, so overall it was a wasted trip. Han slept a few hours in the Matriarch Lodge, then returned to Fellsmarch, leaving word for Willo to come as soon as possible.

Back in the city, he went straight to Southbridge Market, to Taz's shop. Though it was late in the day, Han knew the dealer slept in the back so as not to leave his valuable inventory unguarded. Han needed money fast, and it wouldn't be long before the Guard was onto him again and he'd have to leave town for good.

When Han peered through the shop windows, he saw the dealer standing behind his desk, furiously stuffing papers into a leather satchel. Almost like he was packing to leave.

Taz upset his cup of tea when the bell over the door announced Han's entry into the shop. When the dealer looked up and saw Han, he cracked an uneasy smile.

"Cuffs! There you are!" The big man madly blotted at the papers on his desk with a rag. "Where have you been? I found a buyer for the carving you showed me. He's most anxious to see it." Taz always called them "carvings" or "art pieces." He never acknowledged the fact that they were both magical and illegal.

"Really?" Han said. Was it his imagination, or did the dealer seem unusually nervous? "He's met my minimum price, then?"

"Yes, yes. He's good for it, though he wants to see the piece himself, of course. Do you have it on you?" Taz squinted at Han as if he might see it glowing through his clothes.

Han shook his head. "No, but I can go get it." He turned toward the door.

"No, no," Taz said hastily. "As a matter of fact, the buyer is on his way here now. Serendipitous, isn't it? That you're here, and he's coming?" He wet his lips.

Han was confused. "But it does no good if I don't have the amulet," he said.

"My client is most anxious to meet you," Taz said. "He has some questions about the piece. I'll collect my commission, and you can take him to get it."

"I'd rather do business here." Han knew well the risks of selling swag in back alleys. "I can be home and back in no time."

"It was at home all along, then?"

Something in Taz's voice set off alarm bells in Han's head. He hadn't lived so long by ignoring his instincts.

"What do you mean?" he demanded. "Why do you ask?"

"Nothing, nothing," the dealer said, mopping sweat from his brow with the rag he'd used to wipe off the desk. "I just wondered where you'd hidden it is all."

Before Taz could move or say another word, Han had him pressed against the wall with a knife at his throat. "What did you tell the buyer, Taz?" Han asked softly.

"N-nothing. I . . . just described the piece, and he said it sounded like something he'd want to buy. That's all. I swear by the blood and bones of our sainted queens."

"Did you tell him where I live?" Han demanded.

"I never did, I swear it," Taz babbled. "He found out some other way."

"Who's the buyer?" Han whispered, fear pricking him all over. "Who is it?"

"A rich man. A wizard," Taz squeaked. "You wouldn't know him."

"Who?" Han pressed the tip of his knife into Taz's skin.

Just then the bell over the door sounded again. Startled, Han turned his head just as the door opened.

A man stood in the doorway. His expensive clothes and arrogant carriage said he was a rich man. His long stoles and the amulet that hung from a chain around his neck said he was a wizard. His mane of silver hair was streaked with wizard color.

Taz saw his chance, and took it. The dealer flung himself sideways, away from Han's knife, and scrambled on hands and knees across the floor toward the back door. The wizard in the doorway extended a hand lazily, touched the amulet at his neck, and spoke a word.

Flame exploded from his fingertips and engulfed Taz Mackney. The dealer's body twitched and shuddered for a moment, then lay still, smoking. The stench of burning flesh stung Han's nose, and he fought back the urge to vomit.

"You must be Cuffs Alister," the wizard said, spitting his name out like it tasted bad. "I've been looking for you for some time. You are amazingly evasive."

Han swallowed hard and tried to keep from looking at Taz. "I don't even know you." And I don't want to either, he thought. Though there was something familiar about the wizard's finely planed face and the falcons on his stole.

"True," the wizard said. "We've not met. But you have

something I want. Something that was stolen from me."

"You're mixing me up with someone else," Han said. "I got nothing of yours."

"There was some confusion at first. I'd been told that a boy named Shiv stole the amulet. Imagine my distress when, after considerable persuasive effort on my part, and pain on his, I learned that Shiv, in fact, knew nothing. That I'd been misled."

Han's heart stuttered. "You sent the demons," he whispered. "The ones that killed the Southies."

The wizard examined his hands, shimmering with power. "Wizard assassins, actually, cloaked and glamoured up. Hysteria can be a useful tool in forcing a community to give up its own."

Why had this wizard gone after Shiv? What could he have done to draw the attention of this monster?

And then the memory surfaced, like gas bubbling up through a mud pot—that day on Hanalea, the encounter with Micah Bayar when he'd taken the amulet. Bayar had asked Han who he was, and Han had told him, "They call me Shiv, streetlord of Southbridge."

It had been a thoughtless throwaway lie. Though some would see it as payback for years of bitter competition for a few nasty city blocks.

He hadn't meant it that way, had he?

Horrified, Han recalled that last meeting with Shiv, the streetlord on his knees offering his allegiance, begging, *Call them off.*

Han had walked away from him. And Shiv's bloody, beaten, tortured body had been found two days later. Now

Han knew that it was, after all, his fault—the dead Southies were dead because of his lie.

Han judged the distance to the back door. There was no way to get there without being fried, same as Taz.

"Who are you, anyway?" he asked, fighting off a growing suspicion.

"I'm Gavan Bayar," the stranger said. "Lord Bayar to you."

Bones, Han thought, struggling to keep his face a blank. Not just a wizard, but the High Wizard, the most powerful in the Fells. Father of Micah Bayar.

"Well," Han said, swallowing dry spit, "there you go. I'd be a fool to steal something of yours."

The wizard nodded. "Exactly. And so I've been curious about you, thinking there may be more to you than meets the eye." Bayar ran his eyes over Han, obviously unimpressed. "The late Mr. Mackney tells me you are—how did he say it— *streetlord* of the Ragger gang. You're not a wizard, yet you are apparently able to handle an extremely powerful amulet without harm." He sighed. "It's unfortunate that my son chose to experiment with that particular piece."

He's going to kill me, Han thought. Otherwise he wouldn't be telling me all this.

"Look," Han said. "I'm just a street rat. I don't know anything about magic. I tossed the thing into an alley right after I showed Taz. It kept sparking and I was afraid it would blow me to bits." Han took two steps toward the door. "I can show you about where it was, if you want." Once out in the street, he'd have a chance to break away.

Bayar raised his hand to put a stop to the string of lies. "I've already sent the Guard after the amulet. In the meantime, I'll take you back to the dungeons at Aerie House. I'll want to know about your connection with the clans, and how much they know about the amulet. Soon it won't matter, but right now, I'd prefer they know as little as possible about the magical items we have at our disposal. Once I'm satisfied I've wrung you out completely, I'll kill you." The wizard said it matter-of-factly. "You've caused me considerable trouble. I mean to take my time."

But Han had fastened on something Bayar had said earlier. "What do you mean, you sent the Guard after the amulet? You sent them where?"

"Why, to your home. You live over a stable, I believe?" Bayar's voice dripped contempt.

Han's insides turned to water. "It's not there," he said. "Call them off. I hid it somewhere else. I can show you."

"If you did, I'm sure you'll tell me all about it," Bayar said. "Now, my carriage is outside. It would be much more civilized if you came quietly, but I'll use force if necessary." Bayar smiled, his face as cold and hard as marble, and Han got the message—Han was nobody, a nothing, and he'd been a fool to go up against someone like Bayar, to steal an amulet from his son. Now he'd pay for it with his family and his life. He'd be whispered about throughout Southbridge and Ragmarket, an example to anyone who might think of crossing the Bayars in the future.

He's like every other rich, powerful person, Han thought. He does whatever he likes, makes his own rules, breaks the law whenever it suits him, and never spends a day in gaol. Shiv was dead because of him, and the eight Southies, and no doubt countless others. Shiv had been Han's enemy, but still. He should count for more than that.

And now, danger was heading straight for Mam and Mari. He had to get away.

His knife was still in his hand. He shuffled forward, head down, the picture of surrender. As he passed by Bayar, he turned and plunged the blade into the wizard's side just beneath the rib cage, ripping up and forward, metal scraping along bone.

Warm blood welled over his knuckles. Bayar screamed and spun away, wrenching the knife from Han's hand.

Han threw himself toward the door. Behind him, Bayar gasped out a charm. Flame coalesced around Han's shoulders, flowing down both arms, heating the cuffs on his wrists to scorching before dissipating. Once again, the cuffs had seemingly sucked up wizard magic.

Outside, Han practically collided with a black carriage emblazoned with the emblem of a stooping falcon. Matched black horses snorted and tossed their heads, rolling their eyes.

Han pounded his way through the market, twisting and turning around stalls and tents, leaping over smaller obstacles, pushing through crowds of people, running for the bridge.

Southbridge and Ragmarket had never seemed farther apart. It was like one of those dreams when your feet are stuck in mud and you're trying to run from a monster. Only in this case, there were monsters ahead and behind.

When he crossed the bridge, he had to dodge around clots of soldiers. Some sort of search seemed to be going on, but they weren't looking for him, because he was obviously on the run and no one stopped him.

He was still a mile from Cobble Street when he saw the glow through the darkness ahead, the smudge of orange painting the lowering clouds. He sniffed the air. Something was burning, something big, shooting flames into the air.

When he reached the end of Cobble Street he saw it—the stable was ablaze, completely engulfed by now. An inferno. The heat had driven the residents to the end of the street, where they stood in unhappy clumps, staring helplessly at the burning building.

A ring of bluejackets surrounded the stable, keeping potential heroes away. Not that they could have got near it anyway. The heat from the flames scorched Han's face from where he stood.

Some of the bystanders had assembled a bucket brigade, pumping water from the Cobble Street well, a remarkable show of organization for that neighborhood. But all they could do was wet down the surrounding buildings to keep the flames from spreading.

Han grabbed the arm of a gawker. "What happened?"

" 'Twas them—the bloody bluejackets." He jerked his head at the soldiers guarding the burning stable. "Someone said they be searching for Cuffs Alister, though he an't been seen around here for weeks. I heard he was dead. Anyways, they said he lived there, and buried his treasure there. They went into the building, searched the place from top to bottom, tossed the other buildings on the square, even dug up the ground. Then set fire to the place. It went up like tinder."

Han gripped his arm tighter. "Did the Guard take anyone away? Did anyone get out?"

The man pulled free, shaking his head. "Didn't see no one, but I wasn't here when it started. Don't know if they was any people in there. You could hear the horses screaming something awful, kicking at the stalls. But even then it was too hot to get to 'em."

Han circled around and tried to come at the stable from the rear, but the bluejackets were thick, and he was again driven back by heat and flame. He wet his shirt at the pump and wrapped it around his head, determined to get past them or die trying.

He was passing the mouth of Butcher's Alley when someone stepped out in front of him.

It was Cat, her face smudged in soot, a scorched Ragger scarf knotted around her neck. "It's no good, Cuffs. They're gone. You can't help them. You'll just get caught or burned to death yourself."

"I don't care." Han tried to dodge around her, but somebody grabbed him from behind, pinning his arms and relieving him of his knife.

"Leave it, mate," Flinn said over his shoulder.

His own Raggers turning on him. "Let go of me, Flinn," he said, struggling to free himself. "If it was your mam and sis, you'd go after them."

"I already tried," Cat said, her voice breaking. She looked frantic, not like herself. "We all did. We even went over the roofs before the fire got too big. I'm so sorry, mate," she whispered. "So sorry."

"I know where they'll be," Han said. "I can get to them. I know I can." Mari would be lying on her pallet next to the hearth. Mam would be with her. Mam was smart. She'd have wrapped wet blankets around them both. They'd be scared, but . . .

"I an't going to let you kill yourself," Cat said. "Been enough killing tonight."

Cat jerked her head toward the back of the alley, and the Raggers hauled him, kicking and protesting, swearing and throwing punches, away from the fire. They dragged him most of the way to the warehouse they used as headquarters before he finally quit struggling. Once there, they stuck him in a corner with Flinn and Jonas watching over him, while Cat and Sarie whispered in the other corner.

Where's Velvet? Han wondered distractedly.

Han shivered and shuddered through the rest of the night, alternately freezing and sweating. He thought it was shock, or rage, or maybe an aftermath of what Gavan Bayar had done to him with his magic; but by morning he realized he'd caught Mari's fever.

Let me die, he thought gratefully, giving himself up to it. He was out of his head for a while, hours or days, he wasn't sure. When he woke, he saw Willo's face looking down at him with an expression of such sorrow that he found he wanted to make *her* feel better. She cradled him in her arms and rocked him and fed him willow bark and matriarch's tea, which was apparently good for summer fever, because it broke soon after.

Somehow he'd ended up back at Southbridge Temple, in one of the little sleeping rooms that let out onto the courtyard.

A week passed before he was able to get up, and by then Flinn reported that the bluejackets had lost interest in the remains of the stable and had moved on to whatever other murders they meant to commit.

Cat and the Raggers had guarded the site, keeping nearby residents from claiming any spoils. Afraid of what he might find, but no longer worried about who might be watching, Han poked through the rubble of his former home until he found them—two bodies huddled close together amid the ruins of the chimney, one big, one small, too charred to recognize or to tell what had been done to them before they died.

"The smoke would have put them to sleep, Hunts Alone," Willo said. She'd scarcely left him alone for a minute these past seven days. "They probably didn't feel much pain."

Probably. *Probably.* It wasn't good enough.

Han found Mam's locket that was her mother's, half melted from the heat, and Mari's charred little book of stories, the one she'd wanted to read to him when he'd been in too big a hurry to listen. He tucked those into his carry bag. In midmorning, Willo walked to the market to buy food for the road. Han took that opportunity to pull the wrapped amulet from its hiding place in the blacksmith's furnace and drop it into his bag as well. He'd sacrificed too much for the thing to leave it behind.

Without a second glance at Cobble Street, he walked to Cat's crib in the warehouse, where he knew she'd be during the day. Sarie and Flinn were playing nicks-and-bones. Sweets and Jonas were teasing a couple of stripey cats with bits of string. Cat's mandolin leaned against the wall, but no Cat and no Velvet.

Sarie scrambled to her feet when Han entered, an expectant, guarded look on her face. "Hey," she said.

Han didn't waste time on pleasantries. "Where's Cat?" he asked.

"Dunno." she shrugged. "An't seen her for days. Velvet neither. Thought she was with you maybe," she said hopefully.

Han shook his head. "I've been sick. Anyway, when Cat comes back, tell her she can have the place in Pilfer Alley."

Sarie blinked at him, then took his arm and led him away from the others. "Why? An't you staying?" she demanded.

He shrugged. "I'm going away for a while."

She searched his face. "But. You'll need it later, right?"

He shook his head. "No. I won't."

Her grip on his arm tightened. "You not going to do nothin' crazy, are you?"

"Nah."

Sarie cleared her throat and stared at the brick wall. "We thought maybe you was going to come back, be streetlord again. With your family gone and all." She looked at him, then away. "We'd all swear to you, Cuffs."

"You have a streetlord. Cat'll come back." But Han had an uneasy feeling. Streetlords didn't live long in Ragmarket. Could the Southies have found her on her own? If there were any Southies left.

Once again he felt the knife of guilt in his gut. It was like he was the sole survivor of a terrible plague. Why did he deserve to live when everyone around him died?

He looked up at Sarie, who was still waiting, as if hoping for a different answer. "Cat doesn't come back, maybe you can be streetlord," he said. "You want to stay away from me. There's still wizards hunting for me. I don't want anybody else to get hurt."

Sarie chewed on her lower lip. Han knew she had something to say, but she'd never been very good with words. "Look, Cuffs, I'm real sorry about what happened to your mam and sister," Sarie said. She untied the rag around her neck and tied it around Han's. "Anyways. Once a Ragger . . . you know."

There wasn't much to add to that, so he left.

Later, Willo found him standing in the rain on South Bridge, looking past Fellsmarch Castle to where Gray Lady brooded, shrouded in mist.

Willo loaded him onto a horse, and they rode back to Marisa Pines. He climbed onto a sleeping bench in the Matriarch Lodge and slept for three more days.

CHAPTER TWENTY-SIX
SECRETS REVEALED

Dancer came and sat with him most days, not saying much, just being there. They were brothers in grief, each mourning multiple losses, each an exile of sorts. Dancer, at least, had some grip on the future, even if he wasn't happy about it. He didn't have to feel responsible for the death of his family, for ruining his own life.

Han wanted to blame Bird for discouraging him from following her to Demonai. Maybe if she'd allowed him to come, he wouldn't have been desperate enough to try to sell the amulet. He wanted to be mad at her, but his heart wasn't in it, and when she pulled him into her arms, it was a welcome distraction, at least.

The Demonai would stay until Dancer left, but that time was fast approaching. Then Bird would leave for Demonai. After that, Han saw nothing ahead, nothing to look forward to.

Willo, who was usually so serene, seemed edgy, almost

distraught. Han attributed it to the way Dancer was acting and the prospect of his forced departure for the south. And maybe it was a little about Han's situation, because she treated him differently than before, almost as if he were fragile—or as if he might explode if she looked at him the wrong way.

Some days it seemed just possible he might—that the alchemy of pain and rage and guilt and frustration would combust inside him. Mam and Mari had been no threat to Gavan Bayar, or Micah Bayar, or the bloody queen of the Fells.

Han might fancy himself a powerful streetlord, but in truth, the bit of swag he'd managed to take off the rich was mere crumbs from their table—so little as to be scarcely noticed. For that he'd been beaten in the streets, pitched into gaol, hunted all his life.

He'd thought Shiv was his enemy. Shiv was just another victim of the queen and the Wizard Council and all the rest. The streetlords spent their time battling each other when they should have been fighting those who had the real power.

It would serve them right if he gathered his quiver and bow and blades and climbed Gray Lady to the Bayar compound and showed them what it was like to be hunted.

He was likely to fail at that, as well. There was no chance he'd get anywhere near his real enemies, the ones that pulled the strings. At most, a few bodyguards and servants would die.

Willo held long meetings with the elders in the Visitors' Lodge late at night, which was surprising, because such meetings were usually held in the Matriarch Lodge. Maybe, he thought, they didn't want him and Dancer to be privy to their deliberations.

He could stay with Willo and study healing, make a little money as an apprentice, and see Bird now and then when she traveled to Marisa Pines. If, after a year, he wanted to leave, he'd put the money he'd saved toward the warrior school at Oden's Ford. It was that or back to the streets. Either way he was unlikely to have to worry about growing old.

Finally, one sultry night when Dancer was within a week of leaving, Willo called a meeting at the Matriarch Lodge.

Han and Bird came from their hideout by the river, where they'd spent the afternoon before sluicing off the hot stickiness of the day. He'd pulled on clan leggings Willo had made for him and a summer shirt of cotton. Bird had left off her warrior garb for once. She wore an embroidered deerskin vest with no shirt underneath and full trader skirts. She'd laced a beaded anklet Han had given her around her right ankle, and Han couldn't help staring at her tanned and muscled legs as they flashed beneath her brightly colored skirts. He looked down at himself, wondering if she noticed him the way he noticed her.

When Han and Bird entered the lodge, he was surprised to see it was packed full of people, many of them unfamiliar. The clans were great for holding councils. He and Bird found a seat on a bench by the door and sat, hands clasped, hips squeezed tightly together. Han was pleased she chose to sit with him rather than huddle next to the fire with the other Demonai warriors.

Willo opened the meeting. "Thank you for coming, to our Marisa Pines brethren as well as those who've journeyed from Demonai, Rissa, and Escarpment camps."

Han and Bird had been whispering together, but Han looked up, startled, at Willo's words. This must be an important meeting for the Rissa and Escarpment camps to have sent representatives.

"Please share our fire and all we have," Willo said. There was a murmur of greeting from the visitors from other camps.

Han spotted Lord Averill and Elena Demonai standing behind Willo. Once again, Han wondered if Averill would remember him from the incident at Southbridge Temple. And, indeed, Averill's eyes lingered on Han for a long moment of appraisal.

But this night Averill had other things on his mind.

"Lord Demonai has brought news from the Vale," Willo said.

Lord Demonai looked around the circle, and the buzz of conversation died away. The patriarch looked older and wearier than when Han had last seen him. He also looked as if he'd been in a fight, which seemed so out of character, Han couldn't help paying attention.

"I bring troubling news, as Willo has said," Lord Demonai said. "The power of the High Wizard grows stronger by the day. Lord Bayar exerts tremendous influence over the queen. So much so, in fact, that Queen Marianna means to marry our daughter, Raisa, the princess heir, to Bayar's son, the wizardling Micah Bayar."

This was greeted by a clamor of protest and cries of alarm and disbelief.

Beside Han, Bird stiffened and leaned forward, the light from the torches gilding the hard planes of her face. "That cannot happen," she whispered.

They deserve each other, Han thought.

"I accept the blame for this," Lord Demonai went on. "I must confess, I did not see it coming. In fact, Captain Byrne and I were attacked and nearly murdered on our way back from Chalk Cliffs on Raisa *ana*'Marianna's name day."

This was met by another storm of disapproval. Han glanced over at the Demonai warriors. They did not shout and demonstrate with the others, but stood silent and alert and looked more dangerous because of it.

"I cannot believe Her Majesty approved our murders," Lord Demonai said wryly. "Yet we must not underestimate Lord Bayar's potential for treachery. They intended to marry the princess heir and young Bayar on her name day, while Captain Byrne and I were—ah—otherwise occupied." He paused, then added, "Fortunately, Princess Raisa has escaped into exile."

Han heard shouts of "Thank the Maker!" and "Where is she?" and "Our daughter Raisa should take refuge here, with her family, within the highland camps."

At this point Elena Demonai stepped forward, her aged face etched with new lines of worry. "My granddaughter is safe for now. We believe it best if she does not stay here with us, but in some more neutral place outside the realm. To hold the princess here, against the queen's wishes, would be too great a provocation. We hope that there is still a chance to save Marianna. I do not wish to go to war against her."

The Demonai warriors, Bird included, looked to be more than willing to go to war with the queen. One thing they could agree on. Han despised them all—the queen, the wizards, and the Princess Heir. It was the Queen's Guard that had burned the stable down, and Mam and Mari with it—likely on orders from the High Wizard. They could all go to the Breaker as far as he was concerned.

"We must, however, be realistic and prepare for what we would rather avoid," Elena said. "If they've found a way to break the magical binding between the High Wizard and the queen, it's likely that the Bayars hold some magical weapons that were made before the Breaking. We don't know if they have held them all along or if they recently acquired them."

Feeling a prickle of unease, Han leaned aside to Bird and asked, "Why is that important?"

"The clan still makes the amulets that are necessary to channel magic," she said. "But these days they have a limited life span. They must be renewed or replaced by a clan master or matriarch. That gives us some control over the Wizard Council. The amulets made before the Breaking were extremely powerful. Once given, they cannot be taken back. It was a condition of the Naéming that all such pieces be returned to the clan."

Han thought of the amulet hidden beneath his sleeping bench. Could that be one of those special amulets? Was that why the Bayars were so anxious to get it back?

He should have thrown it into the ravine, as Dancer had suggested the day they'd found it.

"For now," Averill said, "we are asking all clan traders to observe a moratorium on trade in amulets, talismans, and other magical pieces. We cannot allow the Wizard Council to collect a greater armory than they have already." He massaged his forehead with the heel of his hand. "I know that this will be a hardship on many of us who rely on that trade."

"The Wizard Council will see this as a provocation," Bird whispered to Han. "Especially with the war in the south going on. They'll say that they need a steady supply of amulets to train their young and defend the Fells against the southerners. If wizards convince the queen this is true, what will happen to clansfolk working or trading in the city?"

There was more discussion of safeguards against possible violence in the Vale and alternatives to the markets for those who relied on trade for their income.

"I will continue to work from the inside, at court, to exert whatever influence I can to turn them from this path," Averill said.

"I'm worried about you, Averill," Willo said. "There's already been one attempt on your life."

The trader shrugged. "Life is as long or short as it is," he said. "The Maker will call me when he is ready."

"If we could just persuade Marianna to come to Marisa Pines, we might be able to cleanse her of whatever magical charm has been laid on her," Willo said.

"She's unlikely to be persuaded with Bayar whispering in her ear," Elena said sourly.

Reid Demonai spoke for the first time. "We could seize the queen," he said, "and bring her here ourselves." His gang of warriors murmured approval.

Reid looked around the lodge as if assessing the backbone of his audience, then added, "Should anything happen to Marianna, we could crown the princess heir."

"No, Reid," Elena said. "We are not queenmakers. Marianna *ana*'Rissa is the blooded queen of the Fells and the descendant of Hanalea. Any attack on her will bring nothing but misfortune to us."

Reid shrugged, but Han could tell he hadn't let go of the idea.

The council came to an end, and the attendees drifted out, talking in twos and threes. Han knew all the guesthouses and fire circles would be crowded with people talking long into the night. Conscious of their dwindling hours together, Han leaned close to Bird and whispered, "Let's go back down by the river."

But Willo put a hand on his shoulder, startling him. He hadn't heard her approach. "Stay a while, Hunts Alone. We need to speak with you."

"All right," he said, wondering, Who's "we"?

Bird stood, and Han said, "Can Bird stay?" Willo shook her head.

Perplexed and a little annoyed, Han said to Bird, "Wait outside, will you? This shouldn't take too long."

"I won't wait forever, Hunts Bird," Bird said, grinning at him. She swept out in a swish of skirts.

After everyone exited, Averill, Elena, Dancer, and Willo remained, all sitting around the hearth. Dancer looked as bewildered as Han.

Han began to feel apprehensive. Willo's expression had bad news all over it. He didn't know Averill and Elena very well, and he'd always been a little afraid of them. Maybe Willo was going to withdraw her offer to train him in healing. Or the elders were going to banish him because he'd continued to see Bird in defiance of Willo's warning. Maybe Averill wanted to ask questions about the girlie he'd kidnapped at Southbridge Temple a lifetime ago. Or they could have found out about the amulet hidden under his sleeping bench.

Too many possibilities, all of them bad.

Just then the door to the lodge opened and Lucius Frowsley came in, which was possibly the most surprising thing that could have happened. Lucius traded with the clan, but Han had never seen him in any of their camps before.

The old man looked less derelict than usual. Although his breeches and shirt were worn, they were clean and finely made, and he'd made some attempt to put his hair and beard into order. His filmy eyes were clearer than usual, and he leaned on an elaborately carved walking stick. Han could have sworn he was sober.

That was frightening in itself.

Han rose from his bench. "Lucius? What are you doing here?"

"You'll see soon enough, boy," Lucius said. The old man seemed almost smug. Han took his arm and led him to one of the benches. Lucius sat down with the others.

Willo rose and stood at the center of the half-circle. She was obviously in charge of this rough assembly.

"Hunts Alone, I want to begin by asking your forgiveness," Willo said.

Han stared at her for a long moment, temporarily speechless. "Why? What for? If you're talking about Mam and Mari, that wasn't your fault."

"In a way it was," Willo said, looking away from him and

lacing her fingers together nervously. That was unlike her, because usually she was very straightforward. She just seemed to be having trouble spitting this story out.

"No," he said. "It was my fault. I was the one who brought the Guard down on them. I should've just stayed away." He didn't mention the amulet. Dancer knew about it, and Lucius did, but neither of them knew what had happened after, or that he still had it.

Han was ashamed he'd kept it, ashamed he'd tried to sell it. That was the story *he* had trouble telling.

"We've kept a secret from you all this time," Willo said. "For many reasons. Partly to protect you. Mostly to protect everyone else. But now, for many reasons, we've decided to tell you the truth."

Han said nothing, but sat and waited, his heart flapping in his chest like a trout stranded on the riverbank.

Willo rose and handed Han a jug of tea and a cup. He gazed at them stupidly, then looked up at Willo.

"Have some," she said. "It will calm you."

So he needed calming, did he, before he heard this news? He poured, then cautiously sipped the muddy brew. The fragrance was familiar, though he'd never tasted it before.

Rowan. Protection against magic and hexes. Did they think he'd been hexed by somebody? Were they worried about the jinx Lord Bayar had used on him? He looked up at Willo in surprise, but again, she avoided his gaze.

Han swallowed down more tea. Perhaps rowan had soothing properties he'd never heard of. Plants were like that. They had multiple uses.

To Han's surprise, it was Lucius who spoke. "Boy, you remember that story I told you down by the creek? About Hanalea and Alger Waterlow? The one you didn't like?"

Han nodded, then remembering Lucius couldn't see him, said, "Yes."

"Well, it was true. Every bit of it. What I didn't tell you was that when Waterlow died, Hanalea was with child. Twins, in fact."

"What?" This was utterly contrary to all of the old stories. Hanalea was practically a saint. The savior of her people. Somehow all the legends skipped over what might have happened between Hanalea and the demon after he'd stolen her away. "I never heard that," he said.

"Not many knew. After Waterlow was killed, everyone was caught up in the Breaking, trying to save the world, and like that. After Hanalea negotiated the Naéming, she went into seclusion. Wasn't nobody going to bother her after all she'd been through. She married, then, quietly, and had the babies—a boy and a girl. Everyone assumed they were issue of the marriage."

Lucius's face slumped into a fleshy puddle of pain. "They were her only children. It was as if she refused to have any but Waterlow's. Their daughter, Alyssa, established the new line of queens. Fortunately, she displayed no sign of wizardry, though it is said the gift of prophecy that runs in Hanalea's line may come from Waterlow."

"You're saying the line of queens descends from the blood of the Demon King?" Han whispered.

"It does," Elena said, almost defensively. "His blood may be tainted, but the pure blood of Hanalea is much stronger." She paused, biting her lower lip. "We had no choice. Alyssa was her only issue. Since then, the demon's blood has been diluted many times."

Well. No wonder that story was kept quiet. If it was true. The dynasty of queens was founded on a lie.

"What about the boy?" Han asked.

Lucius laughed softly. "The boy was a problem, because there was no doubt he was gifted. Word went out to the few who knew about it that the baby died shortly after birth and was buried in an unmarked grave. But I happen to know that the baby lived."

"Why would they let it live?" Han asked. After everything the demon had done, weren't they worried that the son would go bad too?

"The Demonai warriors meant to kill him. They handed him to a clan matriarch and told her to drop him off a high cliff. It was seen as a great honor for the matriarch, at the time."

Instinctively, Han glanced at Elena. She was leaning forward, her face set in hard, defiant lines.

Lucius turned back toward Han as if he could sense his location in the room. "But Hanalea intervened. Dressed as a trader, she came to the matriarch and offered a trade. She offered to give up her child forever in exchange for sparing his life."

An image suddenly came to Han—of a marble statue in the Southbridge Temple garden. It was an old piece, worn down by weather. Jemson said it was made around the time of the Breaking, and had been carried there from somewhere else. It was an image of Hanalea in trader garb—an unusual presentation. The warrior queen cradled a baby in one arm and wielded a sword in the other, fending off an unseen attacker. It was called, *Hanalea Defending the Children*. It never occurred to Han that the scene was more than symbolic, that it might depict a real event.

Lucius continued his story. "The clan couldn't say no to Hanalea, especially after all she'd done, all she'd been through. Yet the matriarch did not wish to turn the boy loose in the world, to grow up unsupervised. So a very small, very secret council was convened to determine what to do."

Thoughts swirled through Han's head. Here it was, another story that contradicted everything he'd heard before. Who knew what to believe anymore? He looked at Dancer to assess his reaction. His friend sat, transfixed, absently toying with the fringes on his leggings. Dancer had never heard Lucius tell a story, had never seen how he could draw a person in.

"How do you know all this?" Han asked, meaning, Where'd you get this story? Did you find it at the bottom of a bottle of product?

"I was the one that married Hanalea after Alger died," Lucius said.

"You?" Han said it louder than he intended. He looked around the circle and saw the truth in every face, as if he and Dancer were the only ones not in on this particular secret.

This old man who bathed once a month at best had been married to a queen? And not just *a* queen, *the* queen who'd saved the world. A legendary beauty preserved in countless statues, etchings, and paintings.

"That's impossible," Han said flatly. "No offense, Lucius, but, I mean, come on—you'd be a thousand years old."

"Aye, I am over a thousant, though I quit counting a long time ago," Lucius said, smiling, revealing his intermittent teeth. "Look at me close, and you'll see the mark of every one of those years. I was a wizard once. Alger Waterlow's best friend. I was blinded in the Breaking, and my gift was burned right out of me."

His voice changed, and he sounded like a blueblood. "The council that wrote the Naéming chose me to carry the memory of those times, to remind Hanalea of it, in case her memory faded. I was cursed with the truth and the compulsion to tell it. That's what keeps me alive. This way, no matter how much everyone wants to forget, there's someone who remembers everything, clear as if it were yesterday."

Han couldn't help thinking that he wouldn't choose a scruffy old drunk for the job, if it was that important. Well spoken or not, who'd listen to him?

Then it struck him: maybe it was the burden of carrying a truth that no one wanted to hear that had made Lucius a scruffy old drunk.

A memory came back from that afternoon on the banks of Old Woman Creek—Lucius telling the story of Hanalea and Alger Waterlow.

She bent her knee for the greater good and married somebody she didn't love. Meaning himself. Han shivered, feeling sorry for Lucius. But sorry went only so far.

"What's all this got to do with me and Dancer?" Han asked, thinking of Bird, who'd be waiting impatiently outside, unless she'd already given up. The world was full of secrets, apparently, but maybe he didn't need to know them all.

"You'll see," Elena said. There was no rushing a clan story. "As you can imagine, there was bitter disagreement about what to do with the demon's gifted child, who might grow to be an extremely powerful wizard.

"The Demonai warriors still argued that the child should be killed, whatever Hanalea said. But the boy inherited something of Alger's charm. There was something about the Waterlows—they had a way about them."

Here it was again—people talking about the Demon King as if he were handsome, attractive, someone a queen could fall in love with. Instead of a heartless monster.

"In addition to Hanalea, it was Hanalea's consort, Lucius Frowsley, who argued most persuasively for the boy's life," Elena said, looking at Lucius.

There's no love between those two, Han thought.

"Because this child was brother to the princess heir, and a wizard, there was concern that he might align himself with the Wizard Council. He might even try to establish a line of blooded wizard kings, and prove a threat to the sitting queens," Averill said.

"In the end, the elder council chose mercy. The decision was made to allow the boy to live, but to remove him from Hanalea's care, to bind and control his magical gift so it wasn't apparent. The boy's ancestry was hidden from himself and everyone else in order to prevent them from using his line for their own ends. We've been watching over the boy's descendants ever since, ensuring that they pose no threat to the queen."

Averill shrugged. "Was that a good decision? It's been a

thousand years, but we still don't know. But recent events have forced us to reconsider it. Given the threat from Arden, a protracted war between wizards and the clan might be the end of the realm."

"For generations, our council of elders has tracked the descendants of the Demon King," Elena said. "The magical trait has remained virulent when it manifests, but has appeared less and less often, perhaps moderated by those who married in. Right now, we know of only one living gifted descendant. A male child."

"So . . . what? You're going to hunt him down and kill him? Because of who his ancestor was?" Han asked. "Because he might join with the Wizard Council and somehow threaten the queen?"

Was that why they were here? Did they expect him and Dancer to help with that?

The question seemed to startle Averill. "Ah, no." He looked over at Elena, who always seemed to take the tough questions.

"It occurred to the original council that there might be an advantage to a line of wizards, relations to the queen, who might support the throne in times of conflict. Particularly in a conflict with wizards," Elena added delicately. "We've learned through bitter experience that green magic has its limitations."

I'll bet the Demonai warriors love that idea, Han thought.

"Therefore, we have required that each gifted descendant of the Demon King be fostered in the camps," Elena said, "so that we can teach them about clan ways and, we hope, bind their fortunes and hearts to our own. For generations we have done this. The secret passes through clan elders. We have never had to reveal it until now. That is why we have convened this council." She gestured at the others in the lodge.

And then Han finally understood: a truth that should have been apparent all along, despite the circuitous ways of clan stories.

The mysterious gifted descendant was Dancer; it had to be. Fire Dancer. It was an apt name for the get of a wizard. Dancer was gifted, and now the magic that had lain hidden so long was pouring out.

Han glanced sideways at his friend, who seemed to be deep in his own thoughts, oblivious to Han's epiphany. Had Dancer known? Had he ever suspected? Was he really Willo's child, or had they only pretended so he could be housed with the matriarch, the wisest woman at Marisa Pines?

Well, if they meant to target Dancer, Han would have his back, though he couldn't say what help he could provide to a wizard.

Han was so involved in his own thoughts that he didn't quite follow when Elena began speaking again in the rich cadence of the matriarch.

"This council calls forward Hunts Alone, whose flatland name is Hanson Alister."

There was a long moment of silence while Han waited for someone else to answer. "What?" he said stupidly. "What did you say?"

"It's you, Hunts Alone," Willo said, taking his hands in hers. "You are Waterlow's only living gifted descendant."

CHAPTER TWENTY-SEVEN
GIFTED

"No!" Han said, pulling his hands free. "What are you talking about? I'm not gifted. You want Dancer." He looked at Dancer for support, but his friend had the same look on his face as everyone else—mingled wariness and hope.

"But you *are* gifted," Willo said. "Even at birth, you manifested so strongly that your mother nearly died in childbirth. I tended you both. I called in Elena *Cennestre*."

Han shook his head, backing away until he came up against the sleeping bench. Elena came and stood in front of him. He felt cornered even though he towered over her.

"I made your bracelets," she said, touching his silver cuffs. "They absorb magic—your own as well as any used against you. They protect you and also prevent you from using magic yourself, accidentally or on purpose. They keep you from giving off the aura of magic or storing it in an amulet. All of the gifted descendants of Waterlow have worn them, from that first child of Alger's." She paused, then added, "His name was Alister."

Han lifted his arms and stared at his cuffs as if he'd never seen them before. He remembered when Gavan Bayar had jinxed him, and the flames seemed to flow into his cuffs and disappear. He recalled how the demon assassins in Southbridge had attacked him with magic, and it had seemed to roll off him. How despite Micah Bayar's warning, he'd picked up the serpent amulet, feeling its sting but remaining otherwise unharmed. That same amulet had thrown the Southies against the wall.

Han Alister—streetlord of the Raggers, a wayward hustler with blood on his hands and a grudge in his heart and too many enemies to count—Han Alister was also a wizard who could shoot flame out of his fingers and fling jinxes and bend others to his will.

Han Alister was the descendant of a madman who had ravished a queen and broke the world. Or he was the final representative of a love that had defied convention, and those who paid the price for it.

Shiv's words came back to him. *What is it about you? People can't stop talking about you. Telling stories. It's all I hear about. Cuffs Alister this, Cuffs Alister that. It's like you're golden.*

But Han didn't come from royal blood. He was the son of a laundress and a soldier.

"Your grandfather wore the bracelets also," Elena said, as if she'd read his mind. "He was fostered at Escarpment Camp." She paused, and a flicker in her eyes said she was covering over a secret. "The gift did not manifest in your father. He died never knowing about his lineage."

"What did you tell my mother?" Han found himself asking. "Did she know what the cuffs were for?"

Elena shook her head. "We told her you had been possessed by a demon while still in the womb. That the cuffs would protect you. That she couldn't tell you the truth because it would make you vulnerable to evil." The matriarch said this with no trace of apology.

Han stared at her, horrified. It was no wonder Mam had always seemed convinced that he would fall prey to the siren call of the streets. Even when he left the life, she always questioned it, never believed he'd reformed. That lie had been a barrier between them. He recalled one of their last conversations. "You're cursed, Han Alister," she'd said, "and you'll come to no good."

"We arranged to foster you each summer at Marisa Pines," Elena went on. "We paid your mother a small stipend."

"So . . . you paid my mother to let you take me?" Han said, his voice cracking. "She didn't . . . ask any questions?"

Wouldn't Mam have wondered why the clan was interested in him?

Not if it brought in a little money. People with nothing don't have the luxury of asking questions.

"Your mother hoped it would be good for you to get out of the city," Willo said. "She hoped it would keep you out of the street life, that you might learn a fresh-air trade. That it might protect you from that early . . . damage."

Han felt under siege as he never had in the camps before. They had always been a place of safety, of refuge. And here it had all been just another game of slide-hand. Willo and Elena and the others were nothing more than grifters in clan garb.

He'd been made a fool of—stung like a loaded mark on the streets of Ragmarket.

"And so . . . you took me because you thought I might go insane and break the world like Alger Waterlow?" Han wanted to sound cold, matter-of-fact, indifferent, but he was having trouble keeping the tremor out of his voice.

"Alger Waterlow was not insane," Lucius growled, startling Han, who'd forgotten he was there. He glared sightlessly around the lodge. "I don't care what you all say."

Ah, Han thought bitterly. I should be reassured because crazy Lucius Frowsley says my ancestor *wasn't* crazy?

"Hunts Alone, you've been like a son to me," Willo said. "Maybe it began as an obligation, but now . . ."

"You're not my mother," Han said, indulging a cold, mean place inside of him. "I had a mother, and she's dead."

Averill, at least, had the grace to look embarrassed. "I'm sorry. We know this is too much to take in all at once."

"So what's this all about?" Han said, anxious to get it over with, to get out of their presence so he could deal with it on his own. He was beginning to worry that his street face would fail him. "Why are you telling me this now, after all this time?"

"We believe that these are the most dangerous times since the Breaking," Willo said. "Gavan Bayar represents a grave threat to the queen and the royal line. The power of the Wizard Council is growing, and they very nearly married one of their own to the princess heir."

"What does that have to do with me?" Han asked.

"We have told you this because you have a choice," Elena said. "We will leave the cuffs on, and you can continue much as you have been. If you would like to stay at Marisa Pines, Willo will teach you the art of healing."

"What about Demonai Camp? Could I go there?" Han demanded, knowing he was testing Elena's patience.

"That depends," Elena said, looking over at Dancer, "on how well this secret can be kept. If you are known to be a wizard, your life will be in danger at Demonai, even if you wear the cuffs. Above all, no one must know whose blood you carry."

Han looked into her hard warrior face and wondered, *Does she mean the Demon King's, or Hanalea's?*

"So the Demonai warriors don't know about me?" Han asked, thinking of Bird. And Reid Demonai.

Elena shook her head. "None except Lord Demonai and me. If you decided to keep the cuffs on, it's best if they don't."

Han massaged his forehead. His cup of tea had gone cold. "You said I had a choice."

Elena looked him in the eyes. "We will remove the cuffs, Hunts Alone, on the condition that you go to Mystwerk House at Oden's Ford with Fire Dancer and learn to control and use this gift the Maker has given you. We will sponsor you, provide your amulet, and pay your master's fees and board. When you complete the courses, you will come back here and use your skills on behalf of the clan and the true line of blooded queens."

Han stared at her. "So wizards are all right as long as they're working for you?"

Apparently so, he thought, since they all shrugged and looked away.

"Why me?" Han said. "Why not Dancer? He's a wizard, and he's not likely to go mad on you." Just then he was rather taken with the notion of going mad, of breaking things. It seemed like a good out.

"If Gavan Bayar has been able to break the binding placed on him when he was elevated to High Wizard, he must have used old magic," Averill said. "We're worried about what else the Bayars have hidden away. If they have access to old amulets, they can use them to win other wizards to their side. We'll need someone very powerful to oppose them. More powerful than Dancer."

"What makes you think I'm so powerful?" Han asked. "I've never done anything magical."

"I put the cuffs on you when you were just a baby," Elena said. Her expression said it was an experience she wouldn't care to repeat. "I know what you're capable of."

Lucius broke into a high wheezing laugh. "The thing is, ever'body knows what young Alger Waterlow could do, boy," he said. "They're hoping you take after your many-greats-grandpa. Except for the destroying the world part. They're hoping to keep you on a tighter leash."

"So," Han said, "you're looking for a magical sell-sword? A mercenary."

Elena Demonai shook her head. "We are looking for a champion. Someone who will support the camps against the

Wizard Council, should the need arise. We cannot wait to see what the Bayars have planned. You need training, and that takes time."

"And if I refuse, you'll send Dancer against the Wizard Council on his own."

Elena nodded. "We'll have no choice."

The clan elders were focused on Han, intent on persuasion. They kept talking about Dancer like he wasn't even there. Which irritated Han.

What if they removed the cuffs, and it turned out Han's powers were a flash in the pan, a spark that burned out almost immediately? He would have all his same problems and lose the protection the cuffs provided. The next time Gavan Bayar flamed him, he'd go down.

Besides, he knew better than to make a deal when he didn't know all the details.

"What if you take the cuffs off and I refuse to carry out my end of the bargain?" Han asked. "How do you know I'll go to Oden's Ford? How do you know I'll side with you against the wizards, if it comes to that?"

"Hunts Alone," Willo said in a rush, "of course you'll keep your word."

Lord Averill raised his hand. "No. The boy needs to know." The patriarch faced Han. "If we remove the restraints and you fail to do what you promised, we will hunt you down and kill you."

I bet Reid Demonai gets that assignment, Han thought, his neck prickling with unease. Even though he'd been hunted his whole life, he'd always been able to take refuge in the camps when things got hot. This time that sanctuary would be closed to him.

The Demonai matriarch stepped in close to Han, her deep-set eyes fixed on his face as if she thought he might be wavering. "Willo tells us you have lost your family at Lord Bayar's hands," she said. "This could be your chance to take your revenge."

"Elena *Cennestre*," Willo said. "Revenge never satisfies the way we think it will. You know that."

Han stayed fixed on Elena. "What if I change my mind? Can you put the cuffs back on?"

Elena shook her head. "It was hard enough the first time. You'll be much more powerful now than you were then. I won't be able to bind the magic again."

"Take a few days to decide," Willo urged. "You can come to any of us for counsel."

Like any of them but Willo would talk him out of it. Han had to admit, the clan reputation for being skilled traders was well earned.

He knew what Mam would say. *Keep the cuffs, stay with Willo, learn a trade, make an honest living. Stay out of the Bayars' way. Play it safe.* That's what he should do.

But what was he risking, really? Mam and Mari had already paid the price for his stupid mistakes. He'd made a mess of things. That couldn't be undone.

But he wasn't the only one to blame. The High Wizard and the queen and her Guard had played a role. The only way he might make them regret what they'd done, might make them think differently about the price of a life—the only way he might make a mark on the world big enough to catch their attention, was to take a chance himself.

At that particular moment he didn't really care what happened to him. Which was a good thing, because when he looked ahead, he couldn't really see how he could win this thing.

He extended his hands toward Elena. "I've already decided. Take them off." He glanced over at Dancer as he said it, and saw the relief mingled with pain and regret on his friend's face.

"Hunts Alone, wait!" Willo said. She turned to the others. "This boy has lost his mother and sister within the month. He is in mourning and he needs time to heal. We should not force him to decide this now."

"We haven't much time," Elena said. "Dancer leaves for Oden's Ford day after tomorrow, and it would be safer if they traveled together. The term begins in a month, and it will take time to travel there, even if they don't encounter trouble along the way."

"I just don't want him to make a decision he'll regret later," Willo said.

"It's all right. I've decided," Han said again, louder. "Who's going to do it?" He looked from Elena to Lord Averill.

"Sit down," Elena said abruptly, not looking at Willo. Han sat on one of the sleeping benches. She brought her carry bag and sat beside him. "Bring the torches closer," she said, and Dancer and Averill obliged. The acrid smoke stung Han's nose.

Digging deep into her deerskin pouch, Elena produced a small parcel. She unfolded the leather covering, revealing a set of delicate silver-working tools. Choosing a hammer and chisel, she pressed Han's arm down across her bony knees and motioned to Willo. Willo knelt next to them and gripped his right hand hard, holding his wrist steady and looking into his eyes. He looked back, struggling to keep his face blank.

Using the jeweler's hammer and chisel, muttering under her breath, Elena tapped along a line of runes engraved in the silver. Fine cracks appeared all along the line, widening as she continued to work.

Han's hand began to tingle, and he wasn't sure if it was the vibration from the multiple blows or magic leaking through. Willo's eyes widened, so maybe she felt it too.

Elena stopped abruptly, seized his other hand, and began working on that cuff.

"It's important that they break together," she said. "Otherwise the imbalance might kill you."

Han thought of the times he'd asked clan silversmiths at the market to try removing them, and shuddered.

"Hold still," Elena said grimly. Before long, the right cuff resembled the left one.

"Now," Elena said, taking a deep breath, "we will break the cuffs. Are you ready, Hunts Alone?"

So it was as simple as that, removing the silver he'd worn all his life. Han nodded, suddenly apprehensive, his mouth dry, his palms sweating. What if it killed him? His heart accelerated, as if it were trying to get in as many beats as possible before it stopped.

"Wait." Willo brought him the cup of rowan tea. "Here. Drink more of this. Just in case."

Han drained the cup and set it aside. Willo refilled it,

seeming determined to drown him in it, until Elena impatiently motioned her away.

Elena slid her thumbs under the two cuffs. With a quick twisting motion she ripped them away and dropped them on the ground. Han stared down at his arms. The skin on his wrists was fish-belly pale where the cuffs had blocked the sun.

Then heat ripped through him, welling up from within and penetrating all the way to his fingers and toes. If he'd had any doubts about the story he'd been told, it was blasted away in a heartbeat.

It reminded Han of the time he'd drunk a cup of Lucius's product on a dare. Lurid images rolled through his brain, colliding behind his eyes. His hair stood on end and flame rippled over his skin. Sparks dripped from him, burned holes in his shirt, scorched his leggings. He stretched out his arms, thinking he must look like one of the flaming straw men the clan erected at the harvest. What if he set the lodge on fire? It was built of wood, after all.

Panicking, he pushed himself up onto his feet and blindly staggered to the door, out into the cool night air.

Han heard Elena shout, "Fire Dancer, go after him, help him."

Han felt incandescent, illuminated, lighter than he'd ever felt before. He was a flame in a lamp of a body that threatened to dissolve at any moment. He extended his hands, and they glowed in the darkness, bone shining through flesh.

Then Dancer gripped his hands, power flowed between them, and that somehow stabilized him.

"Blood and bones," Dancer said. "You can't just turn it

loose like that. Settle yourself, or you'll burn down the whole camp." He thrust something hard and cold into Han's hands. "Here. Try this. Release it slowly, and this will take it up."

It was the amulet Dancer had been given at his naming ceremony, the clan dancer surrounded by flames.

Han took a deep breath, let it out, and focused on the amulet. Magic seemed to flow into the carving through his hands, and the rivulets of flame under his skin died to a trickle. In a matter of minutes he felt drained and less incendiary.

"Thank you," Han whispered, handing the amulet back to Dancer.

"I've learned a few things by trial and error," Dancer said. "You can store magic in these things and save it for later."

"Will that cause a problem?" Han asked. "My magic— your amulet?"

Dancer shrugged. "I have no idea. I've been working on controlling this for more than a year, but I haven't had any real training." Dancer's mouth quirked into a smile, the first Han had seen on him since the naming ceremony. "I think the elders are right—you're much more powerful than me. Either that or it's been building up since you were a baby."

Han was selfishly glad Dancer shared his predicament, glad he had someone to travel with to Oden's Ford, glad he didn't have to figure this out on his own.

"You'll need to speak with Elena about your amulet," Dancer said. "She'll make something special for you."

What would she make for him, Han wondered. Would he have any choice in the matter? He extended his hands, watching in fascination as tiny flames flickered over his skin.

Then some tiny sound, an intake of breath, made him look up into the shadows, under the trees. Bird stood there, frozen, a horrified look on her face. And beyond her, Reid Demonai, his handsome face hard and wary, as if he'd discovered a viper in the woodpile and was trying to decide how to kill it.

And then Han remembered: he'd told Bird to wait for him, that they'd go down to the river after the meeting. She must have seen him dripping flame, must have overheard the exchange between him and Dancer.

"Bird!" Han called, as she turned away. He took a step toward her. "Wait!"

But Bird faded silently into the trees. Reid stood staring at him a moment longer, then followed.

Later that night, Han lay on his sleeping bench in the Matriarch Lodge, unable to sleep. Elena had given him a small amulet, a carving of a badger, to use until she could make him one of his own. It rested on his chest, underneath his shirt, but Han paid it little attention.

He was acutely conscious of the Demon King's amulet that lay hidden beneath him. It was like someone had built a fire underneath his bed, and it scorched his skin no matter what position he lay in. Finally he slid his hand underneath the ticking and closed it on the jinxpiece. Magic flowed out of him and into the carving, a blessed release. Was this how it was going to be? Was he going to constantly seep magic and have to find a place to put it?

Unfamiliar images rolled through his mind: flames illuminating a battlefield, the clash of soldiers, blood pooling on the ground. A beautiful woman, hands outstretched, weeping, calling, "Alger." And pain, blinding pain.

Han released his hold on the amulet and sat up. Those kinds of dreams he could do without.

Willo was still out, no doubt planning his future with Averill and Elena. Dancer was asleep—Han could hear his steady breathing from the far side of the lodge.

When he heard someone outside the lodge, he thought at first it was Willo returning. But the intruder moved furtively, in stops and starts, and by the time he saw a silhouette in the doorway, Han had his knife in his hand but hope in his heart.

"Bird?" he whispered. Maybe she'd come back. Maybe they could talk it over. Maybe . . .

"That you, boy?" a muffled voice came back. It was Lucius.

"It's me," Han said, slumping back and sliding his knife under his pillow.

"I thought you might still be awake." Lucius shuffled forward, poking in front of him with his staff until he encountered the sleeping bench. He sat down on the edge of it next to Han.

"What do you want?" Han muttered. "It's late."

"Guess you got a lot to think about."

"Guess so."

There was a long pause. Then Lucius whispered, "You're powerful, boy. I can feel it. You remind me of Alger." He extended a hand cautiously, like he might get burned, and touched Han's arm.

"I'm not Alger," Han said, twisting away from Lucius's hand. He'd thought Lucius was his friend. But everyone around him, including Lucius, had withheld the truth.

"You still got that amulet you took off the Bayar boy?"

Lucius asked. The old man tried to act casual, but his hands rattled around in his lap like they did when he was vexed. "You didn't lose it in the fire, did you?"

"I still have it," Han said. "What about it?"

"You should learn to use it, is all."

"I should pitch it into a mud pot," Han said. "I've had nothing but trouble since I picked the thing up."

"Trouble's gonna come your way regardless," Lucius said. "Might as well have some firepower to deal with it."

"Elena's going to make me an amulet," Han said. "What's wrong with that?"

"Elena wants to control you, just like ever'body else. Any amulet she gives you's gonna put you on a leash. That amulet you took is yours by rights."

"Right. And maybe it'll turn me into a demon just like it did Alger Waterlow. Give me delusions." Han was baiting Lucius on purpose. He just didn't know why.

Lucius spat on the ground in answer.

"What's your dog in this fight, anyway?" Han demanded. "I may not like Lord Demonai's deal, but at least I get it. What's in this for you?"

"Alger Waterlow was my friend," Lucius said. "You're his blood. The clans won't tell nobody who you really are. You keep your mouth shut too, for now. I don't want to see you betrayed and murdered like he was."

With that, the old man rose and shuffled out.

A week later, Raisa *ana'*Marianna, Princess Heir of the Fells, rode out of Demonai Camp on her new mare, renamed

Switcher to match the old. Raisa wore the drab brown-and-green scout colors of the Queen's Guard, and her hair was gathered into a sober braid. With her rode Amon Byrne, his officer's scarf knotted around his neck, and the other fourth-year cadets who called themselves the Gray Wolves. Altogether, they were a triple of nine. Plus one.

The Wolfpack swarmed about her like self-important bees, hands on their weapons, glaring into the underbrush as if that alone would ward off an ambush. They'd been told she was the daughter of a Fellsian duke traveling under their protection. They took their role quite seriously. Raisa hoped it would wear off before they reached the flatlands.

The palace was in a quiet uproar, if such a thing is possible. Once again, the news of Raisa's disappearance was kept close, this time by the queen, her Guard, and her cabinet. Presumably, Queen Marianna was loath to announce that she'd tried to marry the princess heir off to a wizard, and the princess had left him at the altar.

The Guard came out in force, searching city and countryside for any trace of the wayward princess. In meeting with her small cabinet, Queen Marianna expressed concern that the same vicious brigands who had attacked Averill and Edon Byrne might have spirited away her daughter. Per reports from Averill, the queen was distraught and Mellony was inconsolable. Raisa was pricked by guilt, but the thought that she could already be married to Micah Bayar dampened it down considerably. She was pleased to hear that Gavan Bayar looked like he wanted to incinerate someone; he just didn't have the right target.

Autumn came early in the Spirits. A snap in the air said winter wasn't far off. The leaves on the aspens quivered in the northern breeze, glittering gold, raising her spirits. Since her arrival back in court, she'd felt like a sheep in a chute, relentlessly driven along a narrowing path to a place she'd never wanted to go.

Now she was leaving the Fells for the very first time, descending into the strange flatlands beyond the border. She was well aware of the gravity of the situation; she knew she was taking a risk, yet she couldn't help looking forward to escaping the confines of court life. She might learn more at Oden's Ford than she ever would in the shelter of home. She was adventuring with Amon again, only it was a new Amon, more intriguing than the old, representing risks of a different kind.

Anything could happen, she thought. It pleased her to think so.

Amon had been oddly standoffish and formal during their time at Demonai Camp. They'd spent endless time in meetings with Elena and Averill. When they weren't in meetings, he was drilling her in swordplay, since those weapons weren't used in the upland camps. He'd pull back her shoulders and press in at her waist to improve her stance; he'd slide arms around her and grip her at elbow and wrist to correct her swing, but he might have been attending a horse in dressage.

Some days he seemed as dour—as restrained—as tightly controlled as his father.

Raisa sweated through grueling practice matches with the Wolfpack, while Amon stood by, barking at her, "Bring it up! Bring the tip up! Don't let him get inside! Move! Move your feet!" She couldn't help it that everyone's reach was longer than hers. She'd work out until she could no longer lift her arms, then fall exhausted into bed.

Exhaustion wasn't the only barrier to romance. It almost seemed that Amon avoided being alone with her. Still, Raisa was a naturally hopeful person. There'd been no more kisses, but that didn't mean there wouldn't be in the future.

As if called by her thoughts, Amon guided his horse up beside hers, the breeze ruffling his dark hair. "I mean to keep moving so we can be well on our way to North Branch Camp by dark. We'll be eating our midday in the saddle. I don't want to call attention to ourselves by arriving in the middle of the night."

"Yes, sir," Raisa said, trying to get used to addressing him as her commanding officer. For his part, Amon seemed to take a certain perverse pleasure in ordering her around.

Westgate would be the first test of her disguise. They'd be looking for her at the border of the Fens. The notion was thrilling and frightening at the same time.

Bending low over her horse's neck, she kneed Switcher into a canter.

At almost the same moment, hundreds of miles to the east, Han Alister and Fire Dancer rode out of Marisa Pines Camp on the sturdy mountain ponies the clan favored. They left unannounced, almost furtively, at a time known only to Han's handlers among the clan. They could go west into the Shivering Fens, and south through Tamron, but that would take them past Demonai Camp and the warriors who strenuously disapproved of their mission.

So they'd decided to go due south, preferring to take their chances with the roving bandits and festering war in Arden than with the Demonai warriors on their home ground. It was the prudent thing to do.

Still, Han felt a dull ache of regret, the burden of words unspoken. Bird had left for Demonai Camp the night of the intercamp meeting. There was no telling when he'd see her again.

The clan had been generous to their new champion—the pony was a gift, as were the saddle and fittings and a clan-made dagger and sword and longbow. Han wore a fine new cloak to turn the rain, and money jingled in the pouch he wore at his waist.

Dancer was similarly well-arrayed. He was in rare good humor, laughing and joking, making up new names for Han that reflected his exalted status. Names like Wizard Hunter and Wizard's Bane and Sir Hanson Jinxflinger, Savior of the Clan.

Dancer, for one, seemed glad to be leaving Marisa Pines and its whispers behind. Maybe, away from familiar ground, it would be easier to pretend that nothing had changed.

Elena's amulet hung from a silver chain around Han's neck—a bow hunter cunningly carved from jasper and jade. He prominently displayed it for everyone to see. But underneath his tunic, the ruby-eyed amulet sizzled against his skin, constantly drinking in magic and storing it away.

The pain of his losses was a blade in his heart, but it had dulled with time and use so that he scarcely noticed it. His guilt was another thing, but he'd learn to live with that too.

Behind him lay Fellsmarch—a city that had chewed him

up and spit him out like a peach pit. He was also leaving behind the upland camps where he'd spent nearly every summer of his boyhood, and the betrayal of the clan who'd withheld the secret of his birthright.

Ahead lay the strange flatlands of the south, Oden's Ford, and the teachers who held the keys to the power that had lain dormant inside him for so long.

One thing he knew: he was tired of being powerless, helpless to defend himself and those he cared about from the wizards and bluebloods who ruled the Vale. He meant to change that. That was his agenda, and for now it coincided with the clan's.

For the first time in a long time, he had a goal, a way forward, and a focus for his restless energy.

"Come on, Dancer," he said, feeling optimistic for the first time in days. "Let's see if these ponies can get us to Wayfarer's Camp by nightfall."

THE SEVEN
THE QUEENDOM of the FELLS
Shivering Fens
Hallowmere
Rivertown
Eastgate
Dyrnnewater R.
Westgate
Demonai Camp
LEEWATER
Delphi Rd.
Swansea
THE KINGDOM of TAMRON
Fetters Ford
TAMRON FOREST
Malthus Shrine
Tamron R. (West branch)
Tamron R.
Tamron Court
Tamron Rd.
West Rd.
Harbor Rd.
Oden's Ford
South Rd.
Sand Harbor
South Gate
SOUTHERN ISLANDS
Bruinsport
BRUINSWALLOW